Dramatists Sourcebook

1997–98 EDITION

Dramatists Sourcebook

1997–98 Edition

Complete opportunities for playwrights, translators, composers, lyricists and librettists

**EDITED BY
Kathy Sova
Wendy Weiner**

Theatre Communications Group • New York

Copyright © 1997 by Theatre Communications Group, Inc.

Published by Theatre Communications Group, Inc.
355 Lexington Ave., New York, NY 10017-0217

All rights reserved. No part of this book may be reproduced in any manner whatsoever without written permission from the publisher, except in the case of brief quotations embodied in critical articles and reviews.

Manufactured in the United States of America

ISSN 0733-1606
ISBN 1-55936-141-7

Contents

Preface — vii

Prologue — ix
A Simple Working Guide for Playwrights
by Tony Kushner

1: Script Opportunities — 1

Production — 3

Prizes — 101

Publication — 144

Development — 160

2: Career Opportunities — 187

Agents — 189

Fellowships and Grants — 194

Emergency Funds — 213

State Arts Agencies — 215

Colonies and Residencies — 223

Membership and Service Organizations — 237

Epilogue — 273

Useful Publications — 275

Submission Calendar — 281

Special Interests — 291

Index — 308

Preface

You are now thumbing through the 17th annual edition of the *Dramatists Sourcebook*.

Every year we work with crossed fingers as we try to expand the *Sourcebook*, offering more listings to our many playwrights and artists. This year we can happily say that we have managed to add more than 75 new entries. Sadly, some theatres and producing organizations have closed their doors, and others have lost their ability to facilitate new work and to fund new artists, and so we have had to delete others. But despite the losses, we are listing more entries than ever (more than 950), and this is very good indeed. Amazingly, each year there are many new opportunities for playwrights and artists. And it is very gratifying to bring them to your attention.

What's new this year? Well, we've added founding dates for the theatres in our Production section. We thought establishing the longevity of our included theatres would be helpful to you. In the past, this information has been included only in our Membership and Service Organizations section. We also continue to add E-mail and Web site addresses as they become available to us.

Each listing is updated annually, so it is important that you work with the most current *Sourcebook* (in addition to the inclusion and deletion of listings, most addresses and contact information, not to mention deadlines and guidelines, are modified in some way every year).

Each listing in this book has been contacted by us. If an organization doesn't respond on behalf of their listing (and we try countless times and by countless means to get a response), their listing is not included. If we can't reach an organization, it makes sense that you will have difficulty as well. And with each *Sourcebook* we try to minimize your frustration, not exacerbate it.

viii / PREFACE

Advice on using the *Sourcebook*. Select those listings your work is best suited for and follow the guidelines meticulously. The Special Interests Index is helpful in finding those listings that may be suited to your type of work. When instructed to write for guidelines, do so. This is a good idea in general as sometimes dates and guidelines change after the *Sourcebook* publishes. Most important is to ALWAYS enclose an SASE with every mailed script if you'd like it returned (unless the entry specifies that scripts will not be returned). If a listing says it accepts scripts, it is always assumed that an SASE must be sent along for return; we do not restate this for every listing. Also, always assume the deadline dates in this book refer to the day materials should arrive, not the postmark date.

Study—and restudy—Tony Kushner's "A Simple Working Guide for Playwrights" (page ix, the Prologue). It's filled with great advice on everything from preparing the physical manuscript to what to do while waiting, while waiting, while waiting...

You should know that throughout this book, "full-length play" means just that—a full-length, original work for adult audiences, without a score or libretto. One-acts, musicals, adaptations, translations, plays for young audiences, solo pieces and screenplays are listed separately. "Young audiences" refers to audiences age 18 or younger, "young playwrights" refers to playwrights age 18 or younger, "students" refers to college students or students in an affiliated writing program.

Entries are alphabetized by first word (excluding "the") even if they start with a proper name. So, for example, the Mark Taper Forum is listed under M. In the index, you will also find this theatre cross-listed under T. Regardless of the way "theatre" is spelled in an organization's name, we still alphabetize it as if it were spelled "re," not "er."

As always, we try to improve the *Sourcebook* each year. We'd love to hear any suggestions from you. A few of you wrote during the past year and because of your comments we were able to weed out some listings that weren't serving you properly, and correct the listings of others to reflect their policies more accurately. We thank all you E-mailers and letter writers. So, is the book helping you? Are there any ways we can improve? Write or E-mail: Sova@tcg.org or Kathy Sova, *Dramatists Sourcebook* Editor, TCG, 355 Lexington Ave, New York, NY 10017.

So until next time, keep writing! The work is the thing. We wish you much success and happiness in the noblest of professions.

Insurmountable appreciation goes to Wendy Weiner, expert editor/person and computer wiz. She helps a seven-month project sail along (almost) effortlessly. And many thanks to Tim Cusick, a meticulous and funny editor, and Jeremy Antunes, our persistent intern.

Kathy Sova
July 1997

Prologue

A Simple Working Guide for Playwrights
by Tony Kushner

A) *Format:* Most playwrights use a format in which character headings are placed centered above the line and capitalized:

<u>LIONEL</u>

I don't possess a mansion, a car, or a string of polo ponies...

Lines should be one-and-a-half spaced. Stage directions should be indented and single-spaced. If a character's line is interrupted at the end of the page, its continuance on the following page should be marked as such:

<u>LIONEL</u> (cont'd)

or a string of polo ponies...

There are denser, and thus more economical, formats; since Xeroxing is expensive, and heavy scripts cost more to ship, you may be tempted to use these, but a generously spaced format is much easier to read, and in these matters it doesn't pay to be parsimonious.

B) *Typing and reproducing:* Scripts should be typed neatly and reproduced clearly. Remember that everyone who reads your script will be reading many others additionally, and it will work to your serious disadvantage if the copy's sloppy, faded, or otherwise unappealing. If you use a computer printer, eschew old-fashioned dot-matrix and other robotic kinds of print. Also, I think it's best to avoid using incredibly fancy word-processing printing programs with eight different typefaces and decorative borders. Simple typescript, carefully done, is best. Check for typos. A playwright's punctuation may be idiosyncratic for purposes of expressiveness, but not too idiosyncratic, and spelling should be correct.

C) *Sending the script:*

1) The script should have a title page with the title, your name, address and phone number, or that of your agent or representative. Scripts are now automatically copyrighted at the moment of creation, but simply writing © and the date on the title page can serve as a kind of scarecrow for thievish magpies.

2) Never, never send an unbound script. Loose pages held together by a rubber band don't qualify as bound, nor do pages clamped together with a mega-paperclip. A heavy paper cover will protect the script as it passes from hand to hand.

3) Always, always enclose a self-addressed stamped envelope (SASE) or you will never see your script again. You may enclose a note telling the theatre to dispose of the copy instead of returning it; but you must have the ultimate fate of the script planned for in the eventuality of its not being selected for production. Don't leave this up to the theatre! If you want receipt of the script acknowledged, include a self-addressed, stamped postcard (SASP).

D) *Letter of inquiry and synopsis:* If a theatre states, in its entry in the *Sourcebook*, that it does not accept unsolicited scripts, believe it. Don't call and ask if there are exceptions; there aren't. A well-written and concise letter of inquiry, however, accompanied by a synopsis possessed of similar virtues *can* get you an invitation to submit your play. It's prudent, then, to spend time on both letter and synopsis. It is, admittedly, very hard for a writer to sum up his or her work in less than a page, but this kind of boiling-down can be of value beyond its necessity as a tool for marketing; use it to help clarify for yourself what's central and essential about your play. A good synopsis should *briefly* summarize the basic features of the plot without going into excessive detail; it should evoke both the style and the thematic substance of the play without recourse to clichéd description ("This play is about what happens when people lose their dreams..."); and it should convey essential information, such as cast size, gender breakdown, period, location, or anything else a literary manager deciding whether to send for the play might want to know. Make reference to other productions in your letter, but don't send thick packets of reviews and photos. And don't offer your opinion of the play's worth, which will be inferred as being positive from the fact that you are its parent.

E) *Waiting:* Theatres almost always take a long time to respond to playwrights about a specific play, frequently far in excess of the time given in their listings in the *Sourcebook*. This is due neither to spite nor indolence. Literary departments are usually understaffed and their workload is fearsome. Then, too, the process of selection invariably involves a host of people and considerations of all kinds. In my opinion you do yourself no good by repeatedly calling after the status of your script; you will become identified as a pest. It's terribly expensive to copy and mail scripts, but you must be prepared to shoulder the expense and keep making copies if they don't get returned. If, after a certain length of time past the deadline, you haven't heard from a theatre, send a letter inquiring politely about the play, reminding the appropriate people that you'd sent an SASE with the script; and then forget about it. In most cases, you will get a response and the script returned eventually.

One way to cut down on the expenses involved is to be selective about venues for submission. Reading *Sourcebook* entries and scrutinizing a copy of *Theatre Profiles* (see Useful Publications) will help you select the theatres most compatible with your work. If you've written a musical celebration of the life of Phyllis Schlafly, for example, you won't want to send it to theatres with an interest in radical feminist dramas. Or you won't necessarily want to send your play about the history of Western imperialism to a theatre that produces an annual season of musical comedy.

F) *Produce yourself!* In *Endgame*, Clov asks Hamm, "Do you believe in the life to come?" and Hamm responds, "Mine was always that." The condition of endless deferment is one that modern American playwrights share with Beckett's characters and other denizens of the postmodern world. Don't spend your life waiting. You may not be an actor, but that doesn't mean that action is forbidden you. Playwrights can, with very little expense, mount readings of their work; they can band together with other playwrights for readings and discussions; and they can, if they want to, produce their work themselves. Growth as a writer for the stage depends on seeing your work on stage, and if no one else will put it there, the job is up to you. At the very least, and above all else, while waiting, waiting, waiting for responses and offers, keep reading, thinking and writing.

Tony Kushner's plays include *Angels in America, A Gay Fantasia on National Themes, Part One: Millennium Approaches* and *Part Two: Perestroika*; *A Bright Room Called Day*; *The Illusion*, freely adapted from Corneille's *L'Illusion Comique*; *Slavs! (Thinking About the Longstanding Problems of Virtue and Happiness)*; and adaptations of Goethe's *Stella*, Brecht's *The Good Person of Setzuan* and Ansky's *The Dybbuk* (to be published by TCG in December 1997). His work has been produced by theatres throughout the United States, including Mark Taper Forum, Public Theater/New York Shakespeare Festival, New York Theatre Workshop, Hartford Stage Company, Berkeley Repertory Theatre and Los Angeles Theatre Center, as well as other theatres around the country and abroad. *Angels in America* has been produced in over 30 countries. Mr. Kushner is the recipient of numerous awards, including the 1993 Pulitzer Prize for Drama.

Script Opportunities

- Production
- Prizes
- Publication
- Development

Production

What theatres are included in this section?

The overwhelming majority of the nonprofit professional theatres throughout the United States are represented here. In order to be included, a theatre must have been operating for at least two years and must meet professional standards of staffing, programming and budget. *Commercial and amateur producers are not included.*

How should I go about deciding where to submit my play?

Don't send it out indiscriminately. Take time to study the listings and select those theatres most likely to be receptive to your material. Find out all you can about each of the theatres you select. Look to TCG's *Theatre Profiles 12* for information on most of these theatres, including seasonal lists of plays each performed from 1993–95. Read *American Theatre* to see what plays the theatres are currently presenting and what their other activities are. (See Useful Publications for more information.) Whenever possible, go to see the theatre's work.

PRODUCTION

When I submit my play, what can I do to maximize its chances?

First, read carefully the Simple Working Guide for Playwrights in the Prologue of this *Sourcebook* for good advice on script submission. Then follow each theatre's guidelines meticulously. Pay particular attention to the Special Interests section: If a theatre specifies "gay and lesbian themes only," do not send them your heterosexual romantic comedy, however witty and well-written it is. Also, bear in mind the following points about the various submission procedures:

1) "Accepts unsolicited scripts": Don't waste the theatre's time and yours by writing to ask permission to submit your play—just send it. If you want an acknowledgment of receipt, say so and enclose a self-addressed stamped postcard (SASP) for this purpose. *Always* enclose a self-addressed stamped envelope (SASE) for the return of the script. Note that you may not receive any response to your work if you don't include this SASE. Many theatres enclose their response letter with the script when returning it.

2) "Synopsis and letter of inquiry": An increasing number of theatres require a synopsis rather than the script itself. Never send an unsolicited script to these theatres. Prepare a clear, cogent and *brief* synopsis of your play and send it along with any other materials requested in the listing. The letter of inquiry is a cover note asking for permission to submit the script; if there is something about your play or about yourself as a writer that you think may spark the theatre's interest, by all means mention it, but keep the letter brief. Unless the theatre specifies that it only responds if it wants to see the script, always enclose an SASP for the theatre's response.

3) "Professional recommendation": Send a script (not a letter of inquiry) accompanied by a letter of recommendation from a theatre professional. Wait until you can obtain such a letter before approaching these theatres.

4) "Agent submission": If you do not have an agent yet, do not submit to these theatres. Wait until you have had a production or two and have acquired a representative who can submit your script for you.

5) "Direct solicitation to playwright or agent": Do not submit to these theatres. If they are interested in your work you will hear from them!

Note that we've persuaded theatres requiring letters and synopses to give us two response times—one for letters and one for scripts they ask to see. All response times are average and approximate. Even if it takes the theatres longer to respond than they say it will, don't pester them; practice patience, and get on with your life and your art.

A CONTEMPORARY THEATRE
(Founded 1965)
The Eagles Building, 700 Union St; Seattle, WA 98101-2330; (206) 292-7660, FAX 292-7670
Leslie Swackhamer, *Acting Artistic Director*

Submission procedure: no unsolicited scripts; direct solicitation to playwright or agent; will accept synopsis, 10 pages of dialogue and letter of inquiry from Northwest playwrights only. **Types of material:** full-length plays, one-acts, translations, adaptations, musicals, solo pieces. **Special interests:** current social, political and psychological issues; plays theatrical in imagination and execution; multicultural themes; not keen on "kitchen-sink" realism or "message" plays. **Facilities:** 390 seats, thrust stage; 390 seats, arena stage; 150 seats, cabaret. **Best submission time:** Sep–Apr. **Response time:** 1 month letter; 4–6 months script. **Special programs:** new play development workshops. FirstACT: play commissions and workshops. Young ACT Company: tours WA schools annually. Theatre As a Learning Tool: artist-led classroom workshops use drama to educate children in such issues as literacy and self-esteem.

A. D. PLAYERS
(Founded 1967)
2710 West Alabama St; Houston, TX 77098; (713) 526-2721, FAX 439-0905
Literary Manager

Submission procedure: no unsolicited scripts; synopsis, resume and letter of inquiry. **Types of material:** full-length plays, one-acts, adaptations, plays for young audiences, musicals. **Special interests:** works that "state or affirm the centrality of God's love and power in the issue of life." **Facilities:** Grace Theater, 212 seats, proscenium stage. **Production considerations:** cast limit of 12, prefers less than 10; no more than 2 sets, maximum height 11' 6"; no fly space, minimal lighting. **Best submission time:** year-round. **Response time:** 2 months letter; 12 months script. **Special programs:** staged reading series. Theater Arts Academy: includes playwriting classes; contact theatre for information.

ACADEMY THEATRE
(Founded 1956)
501 Means St NW; Atlanta, GA 30318; (404) 525-4111, FAX 688-8009;
E-mail academytheatre@mindspring.com;
Web http://www.mindspring.com/~academytheatre
Frank Wittow, *Artistic Director*

Submission procedure: accepts unsolicited scripts with bio and letter of inquiry with SASE for response; $20 fee or $10 fee for plays less than 20 minutes in length. **Types of material:** full-length plays, one-acts, solo pieces. **Special interests:** plays completed within last 2 years or plays-in-process; shorter works with current political themes; primarily metro-Atlanta or Southeast-region playwrights. **Facilities:** Studio, 60 seats, black box. **Best submission time:** year-round. **Response**

6 / PRODUCTION

time: 3 months letter. **Special programs:** New Play Reading: most promising play-in-process receives rehearsed reading followed by audience discussion. New Play Workshop Production: most promising new play receives workshop production followed by audience discussion. New PlayShorts Revue: a touring series of short plays presented at various venues. Actors Ensemble. Theatre for Youth Touring Company. Community Outreach Training Program. Academy Theatre New Play Development Program (see Development).

THE ACTING COMPANY
(Founded 1972)
Box 898, Times Square Station; New York, NY 10108; (212) 564-3510,
  FAX 714-2643
Margot Harley, *Producing Director*
James Bundy, *Associate Producing Director*

Submission procedure: no unsolicited scripts; professional recommendation. **Types of material:** full-length plays, one-acts, translations, adaptations, musicals. **Special interests:** mainly classical repertory but occasionally produces new works suited to acting ensemble of approximately 8 men, 3 women, age range 24–45; prefers works with poetic dimension and heightened language. **Facilities:** no permanent facility; touring company which plays in New York City for 1 or 2 weeks a year. **Production considerations:** productions tour in repertory; simple, transportable proscenium-stage set. **Best submission time:** Nov–Jan. **Response time:** 12 months.

ACTORS ALLEY
(Founded 1971)
5269 Lankershim Blvd; North Hollywood, CA 91601; (818) 508-4200,
  FAX 508-5113
Jeremiah Morris, *Artistic Director*

Submission procedure: accepts unsolicited scripts. **Types of material:** full-length plays, one-acts, translations, adaptations, plays for young audiences. **Special interests:** works by southern CA-based writers. **Facilities:** Pavilion, 350 seats, proscenium/thrust stage; Circle Forum, 99 seats, flexible stage; Store Front Theatre, 42 seats, proscenium stage. **Production considerations:** small cast for Store Front. **Best submission time:** Nov. **Response time:** 12 months. **Special programs:** year-round reading series.

ACTORS ALLIANCE THEATRE COMPANY
(Founded 1982)
Box 1579; Royal Oak, MI 48068-1579; (810) 559-4100, FAX 552-1225
Jeff Nahan, *Artistic Director*

Submission procedure: no unsolicited scripts; synopsis and letter of inquiry. **Types of material:** full-length plays, adaptations, plays for young audiences. **Facilities:** Millennium Theatre Center, 499 seats, thrust stage; Studio Space, 49 seats, flexible stage. **Production considerations:** simple set; no fly or wing space. **Best submission time:** Oct–Feb. **Response time:** 1–2 months letter; 3 months script.

ACTORS & PLAYWRIGHTS' INITIATIVE
(Founded 1989)
Box 50051; Kalamazoo, MI 49005-0051; (616) 343-8310, FAX 343-8310
Robert C. Walker, *Artistic Director*

Submission procedure: no unsolicited scripts; synopsis, resume and letter of inquiry with SASE for response. **Types of material:** full-length plays, one-acts, translations, adaptations, plays for young audiences, musicals, solo pieces. **Special interests:** aggressive and provocative social-political plays; plays that explore heterosexual, gay and bisexual relationships. **Facilities:** API Theatre, 60 seats, thrust stage. **Production considerations:** cast limit of 10; minimal set, costumes, props; no fly space. **Best submission time:** Oct–Feb. **Response time:** 2 months letter; 6 months script. **Special programs:** Firstage Script Development Reader's Theatre: developmental year-round reading series.

ACTOR'S COMPANY OF PENNSYLVANIA
(Formerly Fulton Theatre Company)
(Founded 1963)
Box 1865; Lancaster, PA 17603-1865; (717) 394-7133, FAX 397-3780
Kathleen A. Collins, *Artistic Director*

Submission procedure: no unsolicited scripts; accepts synopsis and letter of inquiry; prefers professional recommendation. **Types of material:** full-length plays, musicals. **Special interests:** contemporary themes. **Facilities:** Fulton Opera House, 684 seats, proscenium stage. **Production considerations:** cast limit of 10, unit set. **Best submission time:** year-round. **Response time:** 3 weeks letter; 4 months script.

THE ACTOR'S EXPRESS
(Founded 1988)
King Plow Arts Center, J-107; 887 West Marietta St NW; Atlanta, GA 30318;
    (404) 875-1606
Literary Manager

Founded: 1988. **Submission procedure:** no unsolicited scripts; synopsis and letter of inquiry, accompanied by professional recommendation if possible. **Types of material:** full-length plays, translations, adaptations, musicals. **Special interests:** socially relevant material; minority and gay themes; works with poetic dimension. **Facilities:** Actor's Express, 200 seats, black box. **Production considerations:** small cast; no fly space. **Best submission time:** Nov–Jan. **Response time:** 1 month letter; 4–6 months script.

8 / PRODUCTION

ACTORS' GANG THEATER
(Founded 1981)
6201 Santa Monica Blvd; Hollywood, CA 90038; (213) 465-0566,
   FAX 465-0566; E-mail actorsgng@aol.com
Clare Wren, *Submissions Coordinator*

Submission procedure: no unsolicited scripts; direct solicitation to agent. **Types of material:** full-length plays, plays for young audiences. **Special interests:** highly theatrical political or avant-garde works. **Facilities:** Actors' Gang Theater, 99 seats, flexible stage; Actors' Gang Workshop Space, 30 seats, flexible stage. **Response time:** 2 months.

THE ACTORS THEATER
(Founded 1995)
Box 5858; Providence, RI 02903
David Tulli, *Associate Artistic Director*

Submission procedure: accepts unsolicited scripts. **Types of material:** full-length plays, one-acts, solo pieces, performance art (short pieces only). **Special interests:** works that "provide hopeful, innovative solutions to social and cultural problems." **Facilities:** no permanent facility. **Production considerations:** minimal production demands. **Best submission time:** year-round. **Response time:** 1–2 months. **Special programs:** Men's Stories Short Play Festival: festival of plays 10–30 min in length that depict "nonstereotypical men" exploring feelings about relationships, sex, self-image and violence; possible theme for 1998 festival is "Fathers and Sons"; selected plays are given full production in annual fall festival; *deadline:* 1 Feb 1998; *dates:* fall 1998.

ACTORS THEATRE OF LOUISVILLE
(Founded 1964)
316 West Main St; Louisville, KY 40202-4218; (502) 584-1265, FAX 561-3300
Michael Bigelow Dixon, *Literary Manager*
Liz Engelman, *Assistant Literary Manager*

Submission procedure: accepts unsolicited 10-page one-acts for contest (see below); accepts unsolicited videotapes/scripts for festival (see below); professional recommendation for all other plays. **Types of material** full-length plays, one-acts, translations, adaptations, solo pieces. **Special interests:** plays of ideas; language-oriented plays; passion, humor and experimentation. **Facilities:** Pamela Brown Auditorium, 637 seats, thrust stage; Bingham Theatre, 340 seats, arena stage; Victor Jory Theatre, 159 seats, 3/4-arena stage. **Best submission time:** year-round. **Response time:** 6–9 months (most scripts returned in fall). **Special programs:** National Ten-Minute Play Contest (see Prizes); Flying Solo and Friends Festival: presentation of new solo and small ensemble performances; *deadline:* 31 Dec 1997; *notification:* Jan 1998; *dates:* Sep 1998.

ADOBE THEATRE COMPANY
(Founded 1991)
21 East 22nd St, #2F; New York, NY 10010; (212) 477-3661, FAX 477-3661;
   Web http://www.adobe.org
Jeremy Dobriol, *Artistic Director*

Submission procedure: no unsolicited scripts; synopsis, dialogue sample and letter of inquiry. **Types of material:** full-length plays, one-acts, translations, adaptations. **Special interests:** mysteries, comedies. **Facilities:** Soho Rep, 75 seats, black box; Ohio Theatre, 75 seats, flexible. **Production considerations:** prefers large cast and characters in their thirties. **Best submission time:** year-round. **Response time:** 1 month letter; 2 months script.

ALABAMA SHAKESPEARE FESTIVAL
(Founded 1972)
1 Festival Dr; Montgomery, AL 36117-4605; (334) 271-5300
Kent Thompson, *Artistic Director*
Eric Schmiedl, *Literary Associate*

Submission procedure: accepts unsolicited scripts with letter of inquiry for Southern Writers' Project only (see below); agent submission for all other plays. **Types of material:** full-length plays, adaptations, plays for young audiences. **Special interests:** new plays with southern or African-American themes; plays for young audiences. **Facilities:** Festival Stage, 750 seats, modified thrust stage; Octagon, 225 seats, flexible space. **Best submission time:** year-round. **Response time:** 2 months letter; 12 months script. **Special programs:** Southern Writers' Project: project to commission and develop plays based on southern and/or African-American issues; address submissions to Southern Writers' Project.

ALLEY THEATRE
(Founded 1947)
615 Texas Ave; Houston, TX 77002; (713) 228-9341
Gregory Boyd, *Artistic Director*

Submission procedure: no unsolicited scripts; professional recommendation. **Types of material:** full-length plays, translations, adaptations, musicals. **Facilities:** Main Stage, 800 seats, thrust stage; Arena Stage, 300 seats, arena stage. **Best submission time:** year-round. **Response time:** 2–6 months.

ALLIANCE THEATRE COMPANY
(Founded 1968)
1280 Peachtree St NE; Atlanta, GA 30309; (404) 733-4650,
   FAX 733-4625
Literary Department

Submission procedure: no unsolicited scripts; synopsis, dialogue sample if possible, and letter of inquiry. **Types of material:** full-length plays, musicals. **Special interests:** new musicals; works that deal with moral and/or spiritual questions of life in multicultural America. **Facilities:** Alliance Theatre, 800 seats, proscenium stage; Studio Theatre, 200 seats, flexible stage. **Best submission time:** Mar–Sep. **Response time:** 1–2 months letter; 6 months script.

AMAS MUSICAL THEATRE, INC.
(Founded 1968)
450 West 42nd St, Suite 2J; New York, NY 10036; (212) 563-2565,
    FAX 268-5501,
Donna Trinkoff, *Producing Director*

Submission procedure: accepts unsolicited scripts. **Types of material:** musicals, cabaret/revues. **Special interests:** multicultural casts and themes. **Facilities:** no permanent facility; company performs in various proscenium or black box venues with 74–99 seats. **Production considerations:** cast limit of 15. **Best submission time:** summer, winter. **Response time:** 3–6 months. **Special programs:** The AMAS Six O'Clock Musical Theatre Lab: a reading series for new musicals open to composers, lyricists and librettists; writer must supply cast and musical director; AMAS provides theatre and publicity.

AMERICAN CABARET THEATRE
(Founded 1989)
401 East Michigan St; Indianapolis, IN 46204; (317) 631-0334, FAX 686-5443
Mary Lou Szczesiul, *Associate Director*

Submission procedure: no unsolicited scripts; synopsis and letter of inquiry; prefers professional recommendation. **Types of material:** cabaret/revues. **Special interests:** cabaret/revues dealing with original American themes. **Facilities:** Mainstage, 400 seats, proscenium stage; Second Stage, 150 seats, proscenium stage. **Production considerations:** cast size of 6–12; limited fly, wing and storage space. **Best submission time:** Jul–Sep. **Response time:** 1–2 months letter; 2–3 months script.

AMERICAN CONSERVATORY THEATER
(Founded 1965)
30 Grant Ave, 6th Floor; San Francisco, CA 94108-5800; (415) 439-2445,
    FAX 834-3360
Literary Manager

Submission procedure: no unsolicited scripts; agents and theatre professionals only may send synopsis, maximum 10 pages of dialogue and letter of inquiry. **Types of material:** full-length plays, translations, adaptations. **Special interests:** theatre plans to work with selected playwrights on company projects and adaptations. **Facilities:** Geary Theater, 1,000 seats, proscenium stage. **Best submission time:** year-round. **Response time:** 1–2 months letter; 3 months script.

PRODUCTION / 11

AMERICAN JEWISH THEATRE
(Founded 1974)
307 West 26th St; New York, NY 10001; (212) 633-9797
Ned Levinson, *Literary Manager*

Submission procedure: accepts unsolicited scripts. **Types of material:** full-length plays, musicals. **Special interests:** works with Jewish themes. **Facilities:** American Jewish Theatre, 150 seats, flexible stage. **Production considerations:** cast limit of 8. **Best submission time:** year-round. **Response time:** 3 months.

AMERICAN MUSIC THEATER FESTIVAL
(Founded 1984)
123 South Broad St, 18th Floor; Philadelphia, PA 19109; (215) 893-1570,
    FAX 893-1233
David McCane, *Artistic Administrator*

Submission procedure: no unsolicited scripts; direct solicitation to playwright or agent. **Types of material:** music-theatre works including musical comedy, music drama, opera, experimental works, solo pieces. **Facilities:** Plays and Players Theatre, 300 seats, proscenium stage.

THE AMERICAN PLACE THEATRE
(Founded 1964)
111 West 46th St; New York, NY 10036; (212) 840-2960
Literary Department

Submission procedure: no unsolicited scripts; synopsis, first 20 pages of script and letter of inquiry with SASE for response. **Types of material:** full-length plays, adaptations, performance art. **Special interests:** works by American playwrights only; works innovative in form and perspective; multicultural themes. **Facilities:** Main Stage, 180–299 seats, flexible stage; Cabaret Space, 75 seats, flexible stage; First Floor Theatre, 75 seats, flexible stage. **Best submission time:** Sep–Jun. **Response time:** 2 months letter; 3–4 months script. **Special programs:** The Humor Hatchery: developmental program of humorous plays by American playwrights. American Humorist Series: development of works by or about American humorists. First Floor Theatre: program of new experimental works and performance pieces.

AMERICAN RENEGADE THEATRE COMPANY
(Founded 1991)
5303 Lankershim Blvd; North Hollywood, CA 91601; (818) 763-4430
Barry Thompson, *Literary Manager*

Submission procedure: accepts unsolicited scripts. **Types of material:** full-length plays. **Special interests:** contemporary American plays. **Facilities:** 99 seats, black box; 45 seats, black box. **Best submission time:** year-round. **Response time:** 3–6 months.

AMERICAN REPERTORY THEATRE
(Founded 1979)
64 Brattle St; Cambridge, MA 02138; (617) 495-2668;
  Web http://www.amrep.org
Scott Zigler, *Artistic Associate*

Submission procedure: no unsolicited scripts; agent submission. **Types of material:** full-length plays, translations, adaptations, musicals, cabaret/revues. **Special interests:** prefers plays "which lend themselves to poetic use of the stage." **Facilities:** Loeb Drama Center, 556 seats, flexible stage; 12 Holyoke Street, 350 seats, proscenium stage; 0 Church Street, 200 seats, black box. **Production considerations:** cast limit of 15.

AMERICAN STAGE
(Founded 1977)
Box 1560; St. Petersburg, Fl 33731; (813) 823-1600, FAX 823-7529
Lisa Powers, *Artistic Director*

Submission procedure: no unsolicited scripts; professional recommendation. **Types of material:** full-length plays, adaptations, plays for young audiences. **Facilities:** American Stage, 130 seats, thrust stage. **Production considerations:** cast limit of 6; 1 set. **Best submission time:** year-round. **Response time:** 12 months. **Special programs:** New Visions: new play festival.

AMERICAN STAGE COMPANY
(Founded 1986)
Box 336; Teaneck, NJ 07666
James Vagias, *Executive Producer*

Submission procedure: no unsolicited scripts. **Types of material:** full-length plays, musicals. **Facilities:** American Stage in Residence at Fairleigh Dickinson University, 270 seats, proscenium stage. **Production considerations:** cast limit of 6–8.

AMERICAN STAGE FESTIVAL
(Founded 1974)
14 Court St; Nashua, NH 03060; (603) 889-2336
Attn: New Scripts, EARLY STAGES

Submission procedure: no unsolicited scripts; synopsis, 10 pages of dialogue and letter of inquiry with SASE for response; include cassette of 2–3 songs for musicals. **Types of material:** full-length plays, musicals. **Special interests:** material with strong emotional content that tells a compelling story; material that encourages new theatrical techniques and a new sense of theatrical reality. **Facilities:** American Stage Festival, 497 seats, proscenium stage. **Production considerations:** cast limit of 10 for plays, 15 plus 5 musicians for musicals. **Best submission time:** Sep–Dec. **Response time:** 2–3 months letter; 4–6 months script.

AMERICAN THEATRE OF ACTORS, INC.
(Founded 1976)
314 West 54th St; New York, NY 10019; (212) 581-3044
James Jennings, *Artistic Director*

Submission procedure: accepts unsolicited scripts. **Types of material:** full-length plays, one-acts. **Facilities:** Chernuchin Theatre, 140 seats, proscenium stage; Sargent Theatre, 65 seats, proscenium stage; Beckmann Theatre, 35 seats, arena stage. **Production considerations:** cast limit of 8; minimal sets. **Best submission time:** year-round. **Response time:** 2 weeks.

APPLE TREE THEATRE
(Founded 1983)
595 Elm Pl, Suite 210; Highland Park, IL 60035; (847) 432-8223,
    FAX 432-5214
Beth Larson, *Literary Manager*

Submission procedure: no unsolicited scripts; will accept synopsis and letter of inquiry; include cassette for musicals. **Types of material:** full-length plays, adaptations, plays for young audiences, musicals. **Facilities:** Apple Tree Theatre, 171 seats, modified thrust stage. **Production considerations:** cast limit of 9, unit set. **Best submission time:** year-round. **Response time:** 1 month letter; 4 months script. **Special programs:** staged readings.

ARDEN THEATRE COMPANY
(Founded 1988)
40 North 2nd St; Philadelphia, PA 19106; (215) 922-8900;
    Web http://www.libertynet.org/~arden
Terrence J. Nolen, *Producing Artistic Director*
Aaron Posner, *Artistic Director*

Submission procedure: no unsolicited scripts; synopsis and letter of inquiry. **Types of material:** full-length plays, translations, adaptations, musicals. **Special interests:** new adaptations of literary works. **Facilities:** Mainstage, 400 seats, flexible stage; Arcadia Stage/Studio Theatre, 175 seats, flexible stage. **Best submission time:** year-round. **Response time:** 3 months letter; 6 months script.

ARENA STAGE
(Founded 1950)
6th and Maine Ave SW; Washington, DC 20024; (202) 554-9066, FAX 488-4056
Cathy Madison, *Literary Manager*

Submission procedure: no unsolicited scripts; synopsis, bio and letter of inquiry; submissions will be considered for PlayQuest developmental program (see Development). **Types of material:** full-length plays, translations, adaptations. **Special interests:** unproduced works; plays for a multicultural company; plays by women, writers of color, physically disabled writers and other "nonmainstream" artists. **Facilities:** Fichandler Stage, 827 seats, arena stage; The Kreeger Theater,

514 seats, modified thrust stage; The Old Vat Room, 110 seats, cabaret stage. **Best submission time:** spring–early fall. **Response time:** 1 day letter; 6–12 months script. **Special programs:** PlayQuest (see Development).

ARIZONA THEATRE COMPANY
(Founded 1966)
Box 1631; Tucson, AZ 85702-1631; (520) 884-8210
Literary Manager

Submission procedure: accepts unsolicited scripts from Southwest playwrights only. **Types of material:** full-length plays, translations, adaptations, musicals. **Facilities:** Herberger Theater Center (in Phoenix), 800 seats, proscenium stage; Temple of Music and Art (in Tucson), 600 seats, proscenium stage. **Best submission time:** spring–summer. **Response time:** 6–12 months. **Special programs:** New Play Reading Series: rehearsed readings followed by discussion with audience. National Hispanic Playwriting Contest (see Prizes).

ARKANSAS REPERTORY THEATRE
(Founded 1976)
Box 110; Little Rock, AR 72203-0110; (501) 378-0445, FAX 378-0012
Brad Mooy, *Literary Manager*

Submission procedure: no unsolicited scripts; synopsis and letter of inquiry. **Types of material:** full-length plays, musicals, cabaret/revues, solo pieces. **Facilities:** Arkansas Repertory Theatre, 354 seats, proscenium stage; Second Stage, 99 seats, black box. **Production considerations:** prefers small cast. **Best submission time:** year-round. **Response time:** 3 months letter; 3 months script. **Special programs:** New Playreading Series.

ARROW ROCK LYCEUM THEATRE
(Founded 1961)
High St; Arrow Rock, MO 65320; (816) 837-3311, FAX (573) 815-7564
Michael Bollinger, *Artistic Producing Director*

Submission procedure: no unsolicited scripts; direct solicitation to playwright or agent. **Types of material:** full-length plays, translations, adaptations, musicals. **Facilities:** Arrow Rock Lyceum Theatre, 410 seats, semithrust stage.

ART STATION
(Founded 1986)
Box 1998; Stone Mountain, GA 30086; (770) 469-1105, FAX 469-0355
Jon Goldstein, *Literary Manager*

Submission procedure: accepts unsolicited scripts. **Types of material:** full-length plays, adaptations, musicals, solo pieces. **Special interests:** work not previously professionally produced; new works by southern playwrights. **Facilities:** ART Station Theatre, 100 seats, proscenium/thrust stage. **Production considerations:** cast limit of 6; single set; no fly space. **Best submission time:** Jun–Dec. **Response**

time: 2 months. **Special programs:** I.T.C. Playwrights Project: year-round playwrights group meets bimonthly to critique and develop new works; presents monthly staged readings.

ARTISTS REPERTORY THEATRE
(Founded 1981)
1111 Southwest 10th Ave; Portland, OR 97205; (503) 294-7373, FAX 294-7370; E-mail allen@artistsrep.org; Web http://www.europa.com/artistrep
Allen Nause, *Artistic Director*

Submission procedure: no unsolicited scripts; synopsis and letter of inquiry. **Types of material:** full-length plays, adaptations. **Facilities:** Winningstadt Theatre, 275 seats, flexible stage; Alder Street Theatre, 150–170 seats, flexible black box. **Production considerations:** cast limit of 10, 1 set or unit set. **Best submission time:** year-round. **Response time:** 6 months. **Special programs:** Play Lab: staged reading series.

ArtReach Touring Theatre
(Founded 1975)
3567 Edwards Rd, Suite 5; Cincinnati, OH 45208; (513) 871-2300, FAX 533-1295
Kelly German, *Artistic Director*

Submission procedure: accepts unsolicited scripts. **Types of material:** plays for young audiences. **Special interests:** intelligent, well-plotted plays; subjects not usually explored in children's theatre, e.g., Vietnam, Hiroshima. **Facilities:** touring company. **Production considerations:** cast limit of 3–5; plays must be 50–60 minutes in length and easy to tour. **Best submission time:** Jan–Mar. **Response time:** 3 months.

ARTS AT ST. ANN'S
(Founded 1979)
157 Montague St; Brooklyn, NY 11201; (718) 834-8794, FAX 522-2470
Susan Feldman, *Artistic Director*

Submission procedure: no unsolicited scripts; synopsis and letter of inquiry. **Types of material:** full-length plays, musicals. **Special interests:** musical theatre works. **Facilities:** Church of St. Ann and Holy Trinity, 652 seats, flexible stage; Parish Hall, 100 seats, flexible stage. **Best submission time:** year-round. **Response time:** 2 months letter; 3 months script.

ASIAN AMERICAN THEATER COMPANY
(Founded 1973)
1840 Sutter St, Suite 207; San Francisco, CA 94115; FAX (415) 440-5597
Karen Amano, *Artistic Director*

Submission procedure: accepts unsolicited scripts with synopsis, character breakdown, resume and letter of inquiry. **Types of material:** full-length plays, adaptations, plays for young audiences. **Special interests:** plays that explore diversity of the Asian-Pacific–American experience. **Facilities:** no permanent facility. **Best submission time:** year-round. **Response time:** 3–6 months.

ASOLO THEATRE COMPANY
(Founded 1960)
Asolo Center for the Performing Arts; 5555 North Tamiami Trail;
 Sarasota, FL 34243; (941) 351-9010, FAX 351-5796;
 E-mail brodge@netline.net
Bruce E. Rodgers, *Associate Artistic Director*

Submission procedure: no unsolicited scripts; 1-page synopsis and letter of inquiry with SASE for response. **Types of material:** full-length plays, translations, adaptations, solo pieces. **Special interests:** adaptations of great literature. **Facilities:** The Mertz Theatre, 499 seats, proscenium stage; The Conservatory Theatre, 161 seats, proscenium stage. **Best submission time:** Jun–Aug. **Response time:** 2 months letter; 6 months script.

ATLANTIC THEATER COMPANY
(Founded 1984)
336 West 20th St; New York, NY 10011; (212) 645-8015, FAX 645-8755
Toni Amicarella, *Literary Manager*

Submission procedure: no unsolicited scripts; agent submission. **Types of material:** full-length plays, one-acts, adaptations. **Facilities:** Atlantic Theater, 150 seats, proscenium stage. **Special programs:** FastForward: year-round play readings; scripts selected through theatre's normal submission procedure.

ATTIC THEATRE CENTRE
(Founded 1987)
6562½ Santa Monica Blvd; Hollywood, CA 90038; (213) 469-3786,
 FAX 463-9571
James Carey, *Producing Artistic Director*

Submission procedure: no unsolicited scripts; synopsis, dialogue sample and letter of inquiry with SASE for response. **Types of material:** full-length plays, one-acts, solo pieces. **Facilities:** Mainstage, 53 seats, black box; Attic 2, 43 seats, black box. **Production considerations:** simple sets; no fly or wing space. **Best submission time:** year-round. **Response time:** 1 month letter; 3–6 months script. **Special programs:** play reading series; developmental workshops; Attic Theatre Ensemble's One-Act Marathon (see Prizes).

THE B STREET THEATRE
(Founded 1992)
2711 B St; Sacramento, CA 95816; (916) 443-5391
Buck Busfield, *Producing Director*

Submission procedure: no unsolicited scripts; synopsis, sample pages and letter of inquiry with SASP for response. **Types of material:** full-length plays. **Special interests:** contemporary comedies and dramas with an edge; no "TV writing." **Facilities:** The B Street Theatre, 150 seats, black box. **Production considerations:** cast limit of 6; no fly space; modest production demands. **Best submission time:** year-round. **Response time:** 1 month letter; 3–6 months script.

BAILIWICK REPERTORY
(Founded 1982)
1229 West Belmont; Chicago, IL 60657-3205; (773) 883-1090
Literary Department

Submission procedure: send SASE for manuscript submission guidelines. **Types of material:** full-length plays, translations, adaptations, musicals, solo pieces. **Special interests:** translations and adaptations; theatrically inventive and/or politically intriguing works; plays by women for Women's Work series. **Facilities:** Bailiwick Arts Center: mainstage, 160 seats, flexible/thrust stage; cabaret/studio, 100 seats, flexible stage. **Best submission time:** year-round. **Response time:** 8–12 months. **Special programs:** note: all playwrights submitting to these programs must first send SASE for submission guidelines. Pride Performance Series: year-round exploration of works of interest to the lesbian and gay communities, culminating in summer festival. New Directions Series: fully staged performances of works that experiment boldly with form and content. Director's Festival: annual directors' showcase of 48 plays, 10–50 minutes long, staged in black-box setting. Studio series to include workshops and readings of plays, performance pieces and musicals to be instituted during 1997–98.

BARKSDALE THEATRE
(Founded 1953)
1601 Willow Lawn Dr, Suite 301E; Richmond, VA 23230; (804) 282-9440
John Glenn, *Artistic Director*

Submission procedure: no unsolicited scripts; synopsis and letter of inquiry. **Types of material:** full-length plays, one-acts, translations, adaptations, plays for young audiences, musicals, cabaret/revues, solo pieces. **Facilities:** Mainstage, 214 seats, arena stage. **Production considerations:** small cast, minimal production demands; no fly or wing space. **Best submission time:** summer. **Response time:** 2 months letter; 6 months script.

THE BARROW GROUP
(Founded 1986)
Box 5112; New York, NY 10185; (212) 522-1421, FAX 522-1402
Seth Barrish, *Artistic Director*

Submission procedure: no unsolicited scripts; professional recommendation. **Types of material:** full-length plays, translations, adaptations. **Facilities:** no permanent facility. **Production considerations:** cast limit of 12; minimal sets. **Best submission time:** year-round. **Response time:** 1 month letter; 6 months script.

18 / PRODUCTION

BARTER THEATRE
(Founded 1933)
Box 867; Abingdon, VA 24212-0867; (540) 628-2281, FAX 628-4551;
 E-mail barter@naxs.com
Richard Rose, *Producing Artistic Director*

Submission procedure: no unsolicited scripts; synopsis, dialogue sample and letter of inquiry; send sample cassette for musicals. **Types of material:** full-length plays, translations, adaptations, musicals, plays for young audiences. **Special interests:** social issues and current events; works that expand theatrical form; nonurban-oriented material. **Facilities:** Barter Theatre, 508 seats, proscenium stage; Barter's Stage II, 150 seats, flexible stage. **Production considerations:** cast of 4–12. **Best submission time:** Mar, Sep. **Response time:** 6 months letter; 9 months script. **Special programs:** Barter's Early Stages: script development program.

BAY STREET THEATRE
(Founded 1991)
Box 810; Sag Harbor, NY 11963; (516) 725-0818, FAX 725-0906;
 Web http://www.baystreet.org
Mia Emlen Grosjean, *Literary Manager*

Submission procedure: no unsolicited scripts; agent submission. **Types of material:** full-length plays, musicals, solo pieces. **Special interests:** plays that challenge as well as entertain; plays that "address the heart of our community and champion the human spirit." **Facilities:** Mainstage, 299 seats, thrust stage. **Production considerations:** cast limit of 8–9; prefers unit set; no fly or wing space; small-scale musicals only. **Best submission time:** year-round. **Response time:** 3–6 months. **Special programs:** Reading series: readings of 2 new plays each fall and spring; playwright receives $50 honorarium and travel from New York City; scripts for special programs selected through theatre's normal submission procedure.

BERKELEY REPERTORY THEATRE
(Founded 1968)
2025 Addison St; Berkeley, CA 94704; (510) 204-8901, FAX 841-7711;
 E-mail litman@berkeleyrep.org
Tony Kelly, *Literary Manager*

Submission procedure: no unsolicited scripts; agent submission. **Types of material:** full-length plays, translations, adaptations. **Facilities:** Mark Taper Mainstage, 400 seats, thrust stage. **Best submission time:** Sep–May. **Response time:** 2–3 months. **Special programs:** Parallel Season: productions of 2–3 new plays each season. Commissioning program. In-house readings.

BERKSHIRE THEATRE FESTIVAL
(Founded 1908)
Box 797; Stockbridge, MA 01262; (413) 298-5536, FAX 298-3368;
 E-mail info@berkshiretheatre.org; Web http://www.berkshiretheatre.org
Arthur Storch, *Artistic Director*

Submission procedure: no unsolicited scripts; agent submission. **Types of material:** full-length plays, one-acts, musicals, solo pieces. **Special interests:** thought-provoking vacation entertainment; theatre on the "cutting edge." **Facilities:** Playhouse, 413 seats, proscenium stage; Unicorn Theatre, 99 seats, thrust stage. **Production considerations:** cast limit of 8 for plays; small orchestra for musicals; prefers simple set. **Best submission time:** Nov–Dec. **Response time:** 3 months. **Special programs:** staged reading series.

BILINGUAL FOUNDATION OF THE ARTS
(Founded 1973)
421 North Ave 19; Los Angeles, CA 90031; (213) 225-4044, FAX 225-1250
Agustin Coppola, *Dramaturg*

Submission procedure: accepts unsolicited scripts. **Types of material:** full-length plays, translations, adaptations, plays for young audiences. **Special interests:** plays with Hispanic themes or by Hispanic playwrights only. **Facilities:** BFA's Little Theatre, 99 seats, thrust stage; uses theatres at Los Angeles Center for the Arts for some mainstage productions. **Production considerations:** cast limit of 10, simple set. **Best submission time:** year-round. **Response time:** 3–6 months.

BIRMINGHAM CHILDREN'S THEATRE
(Founded 1947)
Box 1362; Birmingham, AL 35201; (205) 458-8181, FAX 458-8895;
 Web http://www.bham.net/bct
Charlotte Lane Dominick, *Executive Director*

Submission procedure: accepts scripts; prefers synopsis and letter of inquiry. **Types of material:** plays for young audiences. **Special interests:** interactive plays for preschool–grade 2; presentational plays for K–6. **Facilities:** Birmingham-Jefferson Civic Center Theatre, 1073 seats, thrust stage; Studio Theatre, up to 250 seats, lab space. **Production considerations:** prefers cast of 4–6. **Best submission time:** Sep–Dec. **Response time:** 2 weeks letter; several months script.

BLOOMSBURG THEATRE ENSEMBLE
(Founded 1978)
Box 66; Bloomsburg, PA 17815; (717) 784-5530, FAX 784-4912
Tom Byrn, *Play Selection Chair*

Submission procedure: no unsolicited scripts; synopsis, dialogue sample, letter of recommendation from theatre professional and letter of inquiry. **Types of material:** full-length plays, translations, adaptations. **Special interests:** new translations of classics; plays suitable for 9-member acting ensemble. **Facilities:**

Alvina Krause Theatre, 369 seats, proscenium stage. **Production considerations:** small to mid-sized cast, 1 set or unit set. **Best submission time:** year-round. **Response time:** 3 months letter; 6 months script.

BOARSHEAD: MICHIGAN PUBLIC THEATER
(Founded 1966)
425 South Grand Ave; Lansing, MI 48933; (517) 484-7800
John Peakes, *Artistic Director*

Submission procedure: no unsolicited scripts; synopsis, character breakdown, 10 pages of dialogue and letter of inquiry with SASP for response. **Types of material:** full-length plays, plays for young audiences. **Special interests:** plays that make use of theatrical conventions or create new ones; social issues; comedies; no musicals. **Facilities:** Center for the Arts, 249 seats, thrust stage. **Best submission time:** year-round. **Response time:** 1 month letter; 3–6 months script. **Special programs:** staged readings of 5 new plays a year.

BORDERLANDS THEATER
(Founded 1986)
Box 2791; Tucson, AZ 85702; (520) 882-8607, FAX 882-7406 (call first)

Submission procedure: no unsolicited scripts; synopsis and letter of iquiry. **Types of material:** full-length plays, translations, adaptations. **Special interests:** cultural diversity; race relations; "border" issues, including concerns of the geographical border region as well as the metaphorical borders of gender, class and race. **Facilities:** Pima Community College Center for the Arts: 1st theatre, 400 seats, proscenium stage; 2nd theatre, 160 seats, black box. **Production considerations:** cast limit of 12, minimal set. **Best submission time:** year-round. **Response time:** 1 month letter; 3–6 months script.

BRISTOL RIVERSIDE THEATRE
(Founded 1986)
Box 1250; Bristol, PA 19007; (215) 785-6664, FAX 785-2762
David J. Abers, *Assistant to Artistic Director*

Submission procedure: accepts unsolicited scripts. **Types of material:** full-length plays, one-acts, translations, adaptations, musicals, solo pieces, performance art. **Special interests:** cutting-edge works; plays that experiment with form; translations; musicals. **Facilities:** Bristol Riverside Theatre, 302 seats, flexible stage. **Production considerations:** cast limit of 10 for plays, 18 for musicals, 9 for orchestra; minimal production demands. **Best submission time:** spring. **Response time:** 4–6 months letter; 6–8 months script. **Special programs:** year-round reading series.

CALIFORNIA REPERTORY COMPANY
(Founded 1989)
1250 Bellflower Blvd; Long Beach, CA 90840-2701; (310) 985-5357, FAX 985-2263
Ron Lindblom, *Associate Artistic Producing Director*

Submission procedure: direct solicitation to playwright or agent. **Types of material:** full-length plays, translations, adaptations. **Special interests:** international works. **Facilities:** UT Theatre, 400 seats, proscenium stage; Studio Theatre, 225 seats, flexible stage; Cal Rep Theatre, 90 seats, proscenium stage. **Production considerations:** cast of 8–18. **Best submission time:** Sep, Mar. **Response time:** 3 weeks letter; 2 months script.

CALIFORNIA THEATRE CENTER
(Founded 1976)
Box 2007; Sunnyvale, CA 94087; (408) 245-2979, FAX 245-0235
Will Huddleston, *Resident Director*

Submission procedure: accepts unsolicited scripts; prefers synopsis and letter of inquiry. **Types of material:** plays for young audiences. **Special interests:** classics adapted for young audiences; comedies; historical material. **Facilities:** company primarily tours to large proscenium-stage theatres; home base: Sunnyvale Performing Arts Center, 200 seats, proscenium stage. **Production considerations:** cast limit of 8 for professional touring productions; minimum cast of 15 for conservatory productions; modest production demands. **Best submission time:** year-round. **Response time:** 4–6 months.

CAPITAL REPERTORY COMPANY
(Founded 1981)
111 North Pearl St; Albany, NY 12207; (518) 462-4531, FAX 462-4531

Submission procedure: no unsolicited scripts; agent submission. **Types of material:** full-length plays, translations, adaptations, music-theatre works. **Facilities:** Capital Rep Theatre, 299 seats, thrust stage. **Production considerations:** simple set. **Best submission time:** late spring. **Response time:** 4–6 months.

CARMEL PERFORMING ARTS FESTIVAL
(Founded 1996)
Box 221473; Carmel, CA 93922; (408) 644-8383, FAX 647-0758;
    E-mail dpgw83f@prodigy.com; Web http://www.carmelfest.org
Robin McKee, *Producing Artistic Director*

Submission procedure: no unsolicited scripts; professional recommendation. **Types of material:** full-length plays, one-acts, translations, adaptations, plays for young audiences, solo pieces, performance art. **Facilities:** Golden Bough, 305 seats, proscenium; Circle Theatre, 99 seats, 3/4 arena; Cherry Center for the Arts, 48 seats, proscenium. **Production considerations:** prefers cast limit of 10. **Best submission time:** Mar–Apr. **Response time:** 4–5 months. **Special programs:** CPAF

Reading Series: annual staged readings and workshops; playwright receives modest honorarium, travel, housing; submit synopsis and letter of inquiry to Barbara Bishop; *deadline:* 15 April 1998; *notification:* 15 May 1998; *dates:* Oct 1998.

THE CAST THEATRE
(Founded 1976)
804 North El Centro Ave; Hollywood, CA 90038; (213) 462-0265
Literary Manager

Submission procedure: accepts unsolicited scripts. **Types of material:** full-length plays. **Special interests:** previously unproduced works. **Facilities:** Cast of the Circle, 99 seats, proscenium stage; Cast, 65 seats, proscenium stage. **Best submission time:** year-round. **Response time:** 6 months

CASTILLO THEATRE
(Founded 1983)
500 Greenwich St, Suite 201; New York, NY 10013; (212) 941-5800,
    FAX 941-8340; E-mail chstreet@pipeline.com; Web http://www.castillo.org
Fred Newman, *Artistic Director*

Submission procedure: no unsolicited scripts; synopsis, 5–10 page dialogue sample and letter of inquiry; prefers playwright see theatre production before submitting. **Types of material:** full-length plays, one-acts. **Special interests:** plays that address social, cultural and political concerns and challenge theatrical and social convention; multiracial/multicultural issues. **Facilities:** Castillo Theatre, 71 seats, 3/4-arena stage. **Best submission time:** year-round. **Response time:** 2 months letter; 6 months script. **Special programs:** weekly playwriting workshop in spring; contact Dan Friedman, dramaturg, for information.

CENTER STAGE
(Founded 1963)
700 North Calvert St; Baltimore, MD 21202-3686; (410) 685-3200,
    FAX 539-3912
James Magruder, *Resident Dramaturg*

Submission procedure: no unsolicited scripts; synopsis, sample pages and letter of inquiry. **Types of material:** full-length plays, translations, adaptations, music-theatre works, solo pieces. **Special interests:** plays with no previous mainstage production. **Facilities:** Pearlstone Theater, 541 seats, modified thrust stage; Head Theater, 100–400 seats, flexible space. **Best submission time:** year-round. **Response time:** 5–7 weeks letter; 4–6 months script.

CENTER THEATER ENSEMBLE
(Founded 1985)
1346 West Devon Ave; Chicago, IL 60660; (773) 508-0200
Dale Calandra, *Literary Manager*

Submission procedure: no unsolicited scripts; synopsis, resume and letter of inquiry with SASE for response. **Types of material:** full-length plays, translations, adaptations, musicals, solo pieces. **Special interests:** comedies; plays creating a heightened reality; language-oriented plays; dramas of substance; original musicals only. **Facilities:** Mainstage, 75 seats, modified thrust stage; Studio, 35 seats, black box. **Production considerations:** cast limit of approximately 12; limited wing space, no fly loft. **Best submission time:** year-round. **Response time:** 3 months letter; 3 months script. **Special programs:** Playwrights Workshop Series: participation by invitation only. Actor/Director/Playwright Unit: participants meet monthly to work on scripts; some scripts given staged reading, possibly leading to 2-week developmental workshop and performances and/or full production; participants selected through personal interview; Chicago-area playwrights contact Dale Calandra, Workshop Coordinator, for appointment. Center Theater International Playwriting Contest (see Prizes).

CENTRE STAGE–SOUTH CAROLINA!
(Founded 1983)
Box 8451; Greenville, SC 29604-8451; (864) 233-6733, FAX 233-6733;
 E-mail cblakely@infoave.net
Claude W. Blakely, *Administrative Director*

Submission procedure: accepts unsolicited scripts. **Types of material:** full-length plays, one-acts, plays for young audiences, musicals, cabaret/revues. **Special interests:** plays for young audiences; issues of interest to senior citizens and minorities; musical revues. **Facilities:** Mainstage, 300 seats, thrust; Youth Theatre, 175 seats, thrust. **Production considerations:** 2 sets; no fly space; limited wing space. **Best submission time:** year-round. **Response time:** 2 months. **Special programs:** Sunday Evenings Readers Theatre: regularly scheduled rehearsed readings presented for public followed by audience discussion.

THE CHANGING SCENE
(Founded 1968)
1527½ Champa St; Denver, CO 80202; (303) 893-5775
Maxine Munt, *Literary Manager*

Submission procedure: accepts unsolicited scripts. **Types of material:** full-length plays, performance art. **Special interests:** previously unproduced work only; nonrealistic plays. **Facilities:** The Changing Scene, 76 seats, black box. **Production considerations:** cast limit of 10; prefers single adjustable set. **Best submission time:** year-round. **Response time:** 4–6 months.

CHARLOTTE REPERTORY THEATRE
(Founded 1976)
201 South College St, Suite 2040; Charlotte, NC 28244; (704) 333-8587,
 FAX 333-0224
Claudia Carter Covington, *Literary Manager*

Submission procedure: accepts unsolicited scripts. **Types of material:** full-length plays. **Special interests:** work not previously professionally produced; no children's

24 / PRODUCTION

works. **Facilities:** Booth Theatre at North Carolina Blumenthal Performing Arts Center, 450 seats, flexible stage. **Best submission time:** year-round. **Response time:** 3–6 months. **Special programs:** Festival of New American Plays: annual festival of staged readings; stipend, transportation and housing provided.

CHELTENHAM CENTER FOR THE ARTS
(Founded 1991)
439 Ashbourne Rd; Cheltenham, PA 19012; (215) 379-4660

Submission procedure: no unsolicited scripts; direct solicitation to playwright or agent. **Types of material:** full-length plays, translations, adaptations. **Facilities:** Bernard H. Berger Theater, 140 seats, proscenium stage. **Production considerations:** cast limit of 10. **Best submission time:** Jul–Feb. **Response time:** 1 month letter; 6 months script.

CHICAGO DRAMATISTS WORKSHOP

See Membership and Service Organizations.

THE CHILDREN'S THEATRE COMPANY
(Founded 1965)
2400 Third Ave S; Minneapolis, MN 55404-3597; (612) 874-0500,
    FAX 874-8119
Jon Cranney, *Artistic Director*

Submission procedure: no unsolicited scripts; synopsis, resume and letter of inquiry. **Types of material:** full-length plays, one-acts, translations, adaptations, plays for young audiences, musicals. **Special interests:** adaptations or original plays for young audiences. **Facilities:** Children's Theatre Company, 745 seats, proscenium stage; Studio Theatre, 80–100 seats, black box. **Best submission time:** Oct–Apr. **Response time:** 2 weeks letter; 5 months script.

CHILDSPLAY
(Founded 1977)
Box 517; Tempe, AZ 85280; (602) 350-8101, FAX 350-8584
David Saar, *Artistic Director*

Submission procedure: no unsolicited scripts; synopsis and letter of inquiry. **Types of material:** plays for young audiences, including full-length plays, adaptations, musicals, performance pieces. **Special interests:** nontraditional plays; material that entertains and challenges both performers and audiences; new work; 2nd and 3rd productions prior to publication. **Facilities:** Herberger Theater Center: Center Stage, 800 seats, proscenium stage; Scottsdale Center for the Arts, 800 seats, proscenium stage; Stage West, 350 seats, proscenium stage; Tempe Performing Arts Center, 175 seats, black box; also performs in Tucson (no permanent space). **Production considerations:** some van-sized touring productions. **Best submission time:** Jun–Oct. **Response time:** 1 month letter; 3 months script. **Special programs:**

1–3 works commissioned each season; each receives minimum 2 years of development.

CINCINNATI PLAYHOUSE IN THE PARK
(Founded 1960)
Box 6537; Cincinnati, OH 45206-0537; (513) 345-2242
Edward Stern, *Producing Artistic Director*

Submission procedure: no unsolicited scripts; maximum 2-page abstract including synopsis, character breakdown and playwright's bio, 5 pages of dialogue and letter of inquiry, submitted by playwright or agent. **Types of material:** full-length plays, translations, adaptations, musicals. **Facilities:** Robert S. Marx Theatre, 629 seats, thrust stage; Thompson Shelterhouse, 220 seats, thrust stage. **Best submission time:** year-round. **Response time:** 2 months letter; 8 months script. **Special programs:** Lois and Richard Rosenthal New Play Prize (see Prizes).

CIRCLE IN THE SQUARE
(Founded 1951)
1633 Broadway; New York, NY 10019-6795; (212) 307-2700, FAX 581-6371

Submission procedure: no unsolicited scripts; direct solicitation to playwright or agent. **Types of material:** full-length plays, translations, adaptations. **Facilities:** Circle in the Square, 625 seats, thrust stage.

CITY THEATRE COMPANY
(Founded 1974)
57 South 13th St; Pittsburgh, PA 15203; (412) 431-4400, FAX 431-5535
Marc Masterson, *Producing Director*

Submission procedure: no unsolicited scripts; synopsis, dialogue sample and letter of inquiry. **Types of material:** full-length plays, translations, adaptations, chamber musicals, solo pieces. **Special interests:** comedies of substance; plays with strong storyline; American themes. **Facilities:** mainstage, 250 seats, proscenium-thrust stage; laboratory theatre, 99 seats, black box. **Best submission time:** year-round. **Re-sponse time:** 2 months letter; 4 months script.

CLARENCE BROWN THEATRE COMPANY
(Founded 1974)
206 McClung Tower; Knoxville, TN 37996; (423) 974-6011, FAX 974-4867
Thomas P. Cooke, *Producing Artistic Director*

Submission procedure: no unsolicited scripts; synopsis, character breakdown, 1–2 pages of dialogue and letter of inquiry. **Types of material:** full-length plays. **Special interests:** contemporary American plays. **Facilities:** Clarence Brown Theatre, 600 seats, proscenium stage; Carousel Theatre, 250 seats, arena stage.

26 / PRODUCTION

Classic Stage Company (CSC)
(Founded 1969)
136 East 13th St; New York, NY 10003; (212) 677-4210, FAX 477-7504
Lenora Champagne, *Artistic Associate*

Submission procedure: no unsolicited scripts; synopsis, dialogue sample and letter of inquiry. **Types of material:** translations and adaptations of "classic literature and themes only." **Special interests:** translations and adaptations of classic plays; adaptations of major nondramatic classics; prefers highly theatrical work. **Facilities:** CSC, 180 seats, flexible stage. **Production considerations:** cast limit of 8. **Best submission time:** year-round. **Response time:** 1 month letter; 3 months script. **Special programs:** developmental program of rehearsed readings.

The Cleveland Play House
(Founded 1916)
8500 Euclid Ave; Cleveland, OH 44106-0189; (216) 795-7010, FAX 795-7010
Scott Kanoff, *Literary Manager/Dramaturg*

Submission procedure: no unsolicited scripts; resume and letter of inquiry. **Types of material:** full-length plays, adaptations, musicals. **Facilities:** Kenyon C. Bolton Theatre, 612 seats, proscenium stage; Francis E. Drury Theatre, 501 seats, proscenium stage. **Best submission time:** Sep–Dec. **Response time:** 2–4 weeks letter; 1–3 months script. **Special programs:** The Next Stage (see Development).

Cleveland Public Theatre
(Founded 1981)
6415 Detroit Ave; Cleveland, OH 44102-3011; (216) 631-2727, FAX 631-2575;
    E-mail cpt@en.com
James A. Levin, *Artistic Director*

Submission procedure: no unsolicited scripts except for New Plays Festival (see below); synopsis and letter of inquiry; 5–10 sample pages optional. **Types of material:** full-length plays, one-acts, solo pieces. **Special interests:** experimental, alternative, poetic, political works; voices not heard in the mainstream (people of color, women, gays and lesbians); "no sitcoms or made-for-TV movies." **Facilities:** Cleveland Public Theatre, 150–175 seats, adaptable stage (arena/proscenium). **Production considerations:** simple set; cast limit of 10. **Best submission time:** 1 Feb–31 Oct; New Plays Festival, 1 Mar–1 Sep. **Response time:** 6 weeks letter; 9 months script. **Special programs:** Katherine and Lee Chilcote Award (see Prizes). New Plays Festival: staged readings of 10–13 full-length and one-act plays; submit script and $10 reading fee to Terence Cranendonk, Director, New Plays Festival; *deadline:* 1 Sep 1997; *notification:* Dec 1997; *dates:* Jan 1998.

COCONUT GROVE PLAYHOUSE
(Founded 1954)
3500 Main Highway; Miami, FL 33133; (305) 442-2662, FAX 444-6437
Arnold Mittelman, *Producing Artistic Director*

Submission procedure: no unsolicited scripts; synopsis and letter of inquiry. **Types of material:** full-length plays, translations, musicals, cabaret/revues. **Special interests:** dramas, musicals. **Facilities:** Mainstage, 1100 seats, proscenium stage; Encore Room, 150 seats, cabaret. **Best submission time:** year-round. **Response time:** 1 week letter; 2 months script.

THE COLONY STUDIO THEATRE
(Founded 1975)
1944 Riverside Dr; Los Angeles, CA 90039
Judith Goldstein, *New Play Selection Committee*

Submission procedure: no unsolicited scripts; send SASE for submission guidelines. **Types of material:** full-length plays, adaptations. **Facilities:** Studio Theatre, 99 seats, thrust stage. **Production considerations:** cast of 4–12; plays cast from resident company. **Best submission time:** year-round. **Response time:** 12 months.

COMMONWEAL THEATRE COMPANY
(Founded 1989)
Box 15; Lanesboro, MN 55949; (507) 467-2525, FAX 467-2468;
    E-mail cmmnweal@polaristel.net
Hal Cropp, *Core Artist*

Submission procedure: no unsolicited scripts; professional recommendation. **Types of material:** full-length plays, translations, adaptations. **Facilities:** St. Mane Theatre, 126 seats, proscenium. **Production considerations:** prefers cast limit of 9; 1 set; no wing space. **Best submission time:** Oct–Dec. **Response time:** 4 weeks. **Special programs:** Commonweal New Play Workshop: annual 2-week developmental workshop for 1 script chosen from regular submissions; play receives rehearsals culminating in staged reading for invited audience; playwright receives housing during workshop.

CONEY ISLAND, USA
(Founded 1980)
1208 Surf Ave; Coney Island, NY 11224; (718) 372-5159
Dick D. Zigun, *Artistic Director*

Submission procedure: no unsolicited scripts; synopsis, resume, reviews of prior work and letter of inquiry. **Types of material:** company books in already existing productions of plays and performance art. **Special interests:** new and old vaudeville; pop music; pop culture; Americana bizarro. **Facilities:** Sideshows by the Seashore, 150 seats, arena stage; also open-air performances on streets, boardwalk, beach. **Best submission time:** year-round. **Response time:** 1 month letter; 6 months script.

28 / PRODUCTION

CONTEMPORARY AMERICAN THEATER FESTIVAL
(Founded 1991)
Box 429; Shepherdstown, WV 25443; (304) 876-3473, FAX 876-0955
Ed Herendeen, *Producing Director*

Submission procedure: no unsolicited scripts; synopsis and letter of inquiry. **Types of material:** full-length plays. **Special interests:** new American plays; contemporary issues. **Facilities:** Main Stage, 350 seats, proscenium stage; Studio Theater, 99 seats, black box. **Best submission time:** fall. **Response time:** 1 month letter; 2 months script. **Special programs:** staged readings each Tuesday night during summer season.

CORNERSTONE THEATER COMPANY
(Founded 1986)
1653 18th St, #6; Santa Monica, CA 90404; (310) 449-1700, FAX 453-4347;
    E-mail cornerstn@aol.com
Daniel Forcey, *Administrative Associate*

Submission procedure: no unsolicited scripts; letter of inquiry only. **Types of material:** full-length plays, adaptations, musicals. **Special interests:** company primarily interested in collaborating with playwrights to develop new works or contemporary adaptations of classics, focusing on specific communities. **Facilities:** no permanent facility. **Best submission time:** year-round. **Response time:** 2 months.

THE COTERIE THEATRE
(Founded 1979)
2450 Grand Ave; Kansas City, MO 64108-2520; (816) 474-6785, FAX 474-7112
Jeff Church, *Producing Artistic Director*

Submission procedure: accepts unsolicited scripts from established playwrights in youth-theatre field; others send brief synopsis, dialogue sample, resume and letter of inquiry. **Types of material:** works for young and family audiences, including adaptations, musicals and solo pieces. **Special interests:** ground-breaking works only; plays with culturally diverse casts or themes; social issues; adaptations of classic or contemporary literature; musicals. **Facilities:** The Coterie Theatre, 240 seats, flexible stage. **Production considerations:** cast limit of 12, prefers 5–7; no fly or wing space. **Best submission time:** year-round. **Response time:** 4 months letter; 10 months script.

COURT THEATRE
(Founded 1955)
5535 South Ellis Ave; Chicago, IL 60637; (773) 702-7005, FAX 702-6417;
    E-mail ghwitt@midway.uchicago.edu
Gavin Witt, *Dramaturg*

Submission procedure: accepts unsolicited scripts; prefers synopsis and letter of inquiry. **Types of material:** full-length plays, translations, adaptations. **Special**

interests: translations or adaptations of classic, literary or dramatic sources. **Facilities:** Abelson Auditorium, 253 seats, thrust stage. **Production considerations:** cast of 6–8; 1–2 sets; limited fly space. **Best submission time:** year-round; prefers fall. **Response time:** 3 weeks letter; 1–6 months script.

CROSSROADS THEATRE COMPANY
(Founded 1978)
7 Livingston Ave; New Brunswick, NJ 08901; (908) 249-5581, FAX 249-1861
Faedra N. Chatard, *Literary Manager*
Sydné Mahone, *Director of Play Development*

Submission procedure: no unsolicited scripts; synopsis, 10-page dialogue sample, bio and/or resume and letter of inquiry. **Types of material:** full-length plays, one-acts, translations, adaptations, musicals, cabaret/revues, performance art. **Special interests:** African-American, African and West Indian issue-oriented, experimental plays that examine the complexity of the human experience. **Facilities:** Crossroads Theatre, 264 seats, thrust stage. **Best submission time:** year-round. **Response time:** 3 months letter; 12 months script. **Special programs:** The Genesis Festival: A Celebration of New Voices in African American Theatre: spring series of public readings and special events for the purpose of developing new plays; scripts selected through theatre's normal submission procedure.

CUMBERLAND COUNTY PLAYHOUSE
(Founded 1965)
Box 830; Crossville, TN 38557; (615) 484-4324, FAX 484-6299
Jim Crabtree, *Producing Director*

Submission procedure: no unsolicited scripts; synopsis and letter of inquiry. **Types of material:** full-length plays, adaptations, plays for young audiences, musicals. **Special interests:** works for family audiences; works with southern or rural background; works about Tennessee history or culture. **Facilities:** Cumberland County Playhouse, 490 seats, proscenium stage; Theater-in-the-Woods, 200 seats, outdoor arena; Adventure Theater, 180–220 seats, flexible black box. **Best submission time:** Aug–Dec. **Response time:** 2 weeks letter (if interested); 6–12 months script.

DALLAS CHILDREN'S THEATER
(Founded 1984)
2215 Cedar Springs; Dallas, TX 75201; (214) 978-0110, FAX 978-0118
Artie Olaisen, *Administrative Artist*

Submission procedure: accepts unsolicited scripts with synopsis, character breakdown and letter of inquiry; include production history and professional recommendation if available. **Types of material:** full-length plays, adaptations, plays for young audiences. **Special interests:** works for family audiences; adaptations of classics; historical plays; socially relevant works. **Facilities:** El Centro Theater, 500 seats, proscenium stage; Crescent Theater, 180 seats, flexible stage. **Best submission time:** year-round. **Response time:** 3–6 months.

Dallas Theater Center
(Founded 1959)
3636 Turtle Creek Blvd; Dallas, TX 75219-5598; (214) 526-8210, FAX 521-7666
Stefan Novinski, *Artistic Administrator*

Submission procedure: no unsolicited scripts; professional recommendation. **Types of material:** full-length plays, adaptations, translations, solo pieces. **Special interests:** plays that explore language or form; African-American or Hispanic material. **Facilities:** Kalita Humphreys Theater, 466 seats, thrust stage; Arts District Theater, 530 seats, flexible stage. **Best submission time:** year-round. **Response time:** 6–9 months.

Delaware Theatre Company
(Founded 1978)
200 Water St; Wilmington, DE 19801-5030; (302) 594-1104, FAX 594-1107
Cleveland Morris, *Artistic Director*

Submission procedure: accepts unsolicited scripts. **Types of material:** full-length plays, translations, adaptations. **Facilities:** Delaware Theatre Company, 390 seats, thrust stage. **Production considerations:** cast limit of 10. **Best submission time:** Feb–May. **Response time:** 6 months. **Special programs:** Connections (see Prizes).

Dell'Arte Players Company
(Founded 1971)
Box 816; Blue Lake, CA 95525; (707) 668-5663, FAX 668-5665;
    E-mail dellarte@aol.com
Michael Fields, *Managing Artistic Director*

Submission procedure: no unsolicited scripts; synopsis and letter of inquiry (company customarily creates its own original works but may from time to time produce plays by or collaborate with other writers). **Types of material:** full-length plays, translations, adaptations, plays for young audiences, solo pieces. **Special interests:** comedies; issue-oriented works in commedia dell'arte style; Christmas plays for young audiences. **Facilities:** Dell'Arte Players, 100 seats, flexible stage. **Production considerations:** company of 3–4 actors; production demands adaptable to touring. **Best submission time:** Jan–Mar. **Response time:** 3 weeks letter; 6 weeks script.

Denver Center Theatre Company
(Founded 1979)
1050 13th St; Denver, CO 80204; (303) 893-4000
Bruce K. Sevy, *Associate Artistic Director/New Play Development*

Submission procedure: accepts unsolicited scripts from Rocky Mountain region playwrights only; others send synopsis, 10 pages of dialogue, resume of writing experience and letter of inquiry. **Types of material:** full-length plays. **Special interests:** work not previously professionally produced. **Facilities:** The Stage, 642 seats, thrust stage; The Space, 450 seats, arena stage; The Ricketson, 196 seats, proscenium stage; The Source, 155 seats, thrust stage. **Best submission time:** year-round. **Response time:** 4–6 weeks letter; 4–6 months script. **Special programs:** Denver Center Theatre Company U S WEST Theatre Fest (see Development).

DETROIT REPERTORY THEATRE
(Founded 1957)
13103 Woodrow Wilson Ave; Detroit, MI 48238; (313) 868-1347, FAX 868-1705
Barbara Busby, *Literary Manager*

Submission procedure: accepts unsolicited scripts. **Types of material:** full-length plays. **Special interests:** issue-oriented plays. **Facilities:** Detroit Repertory Theatre, 194 seats, proscenium stage. **Production considerations:** prefers cast limit of 8. **Best submission time:** Sep–Feb. **Response time:** 3–6 months.

DIAMOND HEAD THEATRE
See Diamond Head Theatre Originals in Development.

DIXON PLACE
(Founded 1986)
258 Bowery; New York, NY 10012; (212) 219-3088, FAX 274-9114
Bru Dye, *Curator of New Play Reading Series*

Submission procedure: accepts unsolicited scripts; prefers 10-page writing sample and letter of inquiry. **Types of material:** full-length plays, one-acts. **Special interests:** works by New York City–based writers only; works by women; writers of color; "adventurous settings"; no "kitchen-sink soap operas." **Facilities:** Dixon Place, 50 seats, 3/4-stage. **Production considerations:** readings only; small stage; no sets; minimal lighting. **Best submission time:** year-round. **Response time:** 6 months.

DO GOODER PRODUCTIONS, INC.
(Founded 1994)
359 West 54th St, Suite 4FS; New York, NY 10019; (212) 581-8852,
    FAX 541-7928
Mark Robert Gordon, *Founding Artistic Director*

Submission procedure: accepts unsolicited scripts for Award only (see below); agent submission. **Types of material:** full-length plays, one-acts, solo pieces. **Facilities:** no permanent facility; performs in various 99–150-seat venues. **Best submission time:** year-round. **Response time:** 4 months. **Special programs:** DGP New Playwright Award: annual competition for playwrights who have never had professional New York City production under paid Equity contract; winner receives Off-Broadway production in following season; submit script of full-length play or evening-length collection of one-acts, bio and SASE to Joseph C. Koenenn, Award Chair; *deadline:* 1 Dec 1997 (no submissions before 1 Sep 1997); *notification:* Apr 1998.

DOBAMA THEATRE
(Founded 1960)
1846 Coventry Rd; Cleveland Heights, OH 44118; (216) 932-6838, FAX 932-3259
Sue Ott Rowlands, *Literary Manager*

Submission procedure: accepts unsolicited scripts from OH playwrights only; others send synopsis, sample pages and letter of inquiry. **Types of material:** full-length plays, solo pieces. **Special interests:** plays with opportunities for ethnically diverse casting; plays that make a statement about contemporary life. **Facilities:** Dobama Theatre, 200 seats, thrust stage. **Production considerations:** prefers cast limit of 9; limited production demands; no fly space. **Best submission time:** year-round. **Response time:** 9 months. **Special programs:** One World Premiere: production of 1 new play included in mainstage season each year; *deadline:* 1 Feb 1998; *notification:* 15 May 1998 for 1998–99 season. Owen Kelly Adopt-a-Playwright Program: 2 full-length plays by OH residents each given 2 weeks of developmental work with director, dramaturg and cast, culminating in workshop production; playwright must be available to participate; to apply, submit script to the attention of the program; *deadline:* 1 Feb 1998; *notification:* 15 May 1998; *dates:* Jul 1998. Marilyn Bianchi Kids' Playwriting Festival: annual short-play competition open to students attending Cuyahoga County schools, grades 1–12; several winners may receive savings bonds, publication and/or full production; write for application in Sep 1997; *deadline:* Feb 1998; exact date TBA.

DORSET THEATRE FESTIVAL
(Founded 1976)
Box 510; Dorset, VT 05251; (802) 867-2223, FAX 867-0144;
   E-mail theatre@sover.net; Web http://www.genghis.com/theatre.htm
Jill Charles, *Artistic Director*

Submission procedure: no unsolicited scripts; synopsis, 10 pages of dialogue, character/set breakdown and letter of inquiry with SASP for response; include production history of readings in New York City–New England area if available. **Types of material:** full-length plays. **Special interests:** plays with broad commercial appeal. **Facilities:** Dorset Playhouse, 218 seats, proscenium stage. **Production considerations:** cast limit of 8; prefers 1 set or unit set. **Best submission time:** Sep–Dec. **Response time:** 1–2 months letter; 3 months script. **Special programs:** Dorset Colony for Writers (see Colonies).

DUDLEY RIGGS INSTANT THEATRE COMPANY
(Formerly Brave New Workshop & Instant Theatre Company)
(Founded 1954)
1586 Burton St; St. Paul, MN 55108; (612) 644-3024,
   FAX 647-5637
Dudley Riggs, *Producing Director*
Linda Jacobs, *Associate Producer*

Submission procedure: accepts unsolicited scripts with synopsis and letter of inquiry; include cassette for musicals. **Types of material:** capsule musicals/songs, cabaret/revues, solo pieces. **Special interests:** prefers work with no previous main stage productions; issues of aging and retirement. **Facilities:** Dudley Riggs Theatre, 260 seats, modified thrust stage. **Best submission time:** year-round. **Response time:** 8 months.

EAST WEST PLAYERS
(Founded 1965)
4424 Santa Monica Blvd; Los Angeles, CA 90029; (213) 660-0366, FAX 666-0896
Ken Narasaki, *Literary Manager*

Submission procedure: accepts unsolicited scripts with SASE for response. **Types of material:** full-length plays, translations, adaptations, plays for young audiences, musicals. **Special interests:** plays by or about Asian-Pacific–Americans. **Facilities:** East West Players, 99 seats, thrust stage. **Production considerations:** minimal production demands. **Best submission time:** year-round. **Response time:** 3–8 months.

EL TEATRO CAMPESINO
(Founded 1965)
Box 1240; San Juan Bautista, CA 95045; (408) 623-2444, FAX 623-4127
Managing Director

Submission procedure: no unsolicited scripts; synopsis, character breakdown, resume and letter of inquiry. **Types of material:** full-length plays, one-acts, translations, adaptations, plays for young audiences, musicals, cabaret/revues, solo pieces. **Special interests:** socially relevant works; works that reflect a multiethnic world; contemporary adaptations of classics. **Facilities:** El Teatro Campesino Playhouse, 150 seats, flexible stage. **Best submission time:** Jan–Apr. **Response time:** 6 months letter; 12 months script.

THE EMELIN THEATRE FOR THE PERFORMING ARTS
(Founded 1973)
Library Lane; Mamaroneck, NY 10543; (914) 698-3045
David G. Watson, *Executive Director*

Submission procedure: accepts unsolicited scripts with professional recommendation only; include video for solo pieces. **Types of material:** full-length plays, chamber musicals, cabaret/revues, solo pieces. **Facilities:** The Emelin Theatre, 280 seats, proscenium stage. **Production considerations:** small cast; no fly space. **Best submission time:** year-round. **Response time:** 2 months.

The Empty Space Theatre
(Founded 1970)
3509 Fremont Ave N; Seattle, WA 98103-8813; (206) 547-7633, FAX 547-7635;
Web http://emptyspace.com
Eddie Levi Lee, *Artistic Director*

Submission procedure: no unsolicited scripts; synopsis and letter of inquiry. **Types of material:** full-length plays, one-acts, translations, adaptations, musicals, solo pieces. **Facilities:** The Empty Space Theatre at the Fremont Palace, 150 seats, endstage. **Production considerations:** prefers small casts. **Best submission time:** year-round. **Response time:** 3 months letter; 4–6 months script.

En Garde Arts
(Founded 1986)
509 Greenwich St; New York, NY 10013; (212) 941-9793, FAX 343-1137;
E-mail engardeart@aol.com
Carol Bixler, *Managing Director/Associate Producer*

Submission procedure: professional recommendation. **Types of material:** full-length plays, translations, adaptations, musicals, solo pieces, performance art. **Special interests:** prefers site-specific works. **Facilities:** no permanent facility; various sites in and outside of New York City, e.g., Central Park Lake, Chelsea Hotel, Victory Theatre, meatpacking district. **Best submission time:** Aug. **Response time:** 6–8 months.

Ensemble Studio Theatre
(Founded 1972)
549 West 52nd St; New York, NY 10019; (212) 247-4982, FAX 664-0041
Jamie Richards, *Executive Producer*

Submission procedure: accepts unsolicited scripts. **Types of material:** full-length plays, one-acts. **Facilities:** Mainstage, 99 seats, black box; Studio, 60 seats, proscenium stage. **Best submission time:** year-round. **Response time:** 6 months. **Special programs:** summer reading series and playwriting workshops. First Look: reading series of full-length plays. Annual Marathon of One-Act Plays: one-act play festival; *deadline:* 1 Dec 1997.

The Ensemble Theatre
(Founded 1977)
3535 Main St; Houston, TX 77002-9529; (713) 520-0055, FAX 520-1269
Eileen J. Morris, *Artistic Director*

Submission procedure: accepts unsolicited scripts. **Types of material:** full-length plays, adaptations, plays for young audiences, musicals, solo pieces. **Special interests:** works reflecting the African-American experience. **Facilities:** Hawkins Stage, 199 seats, proscenium stage; Arena Stage, 80 seats, black box. **Production considerations:** cast limit of 10, maximum 2 sets. **Best submission time:** Aug. **Response time:** 5 months.

Ensemble Theatre of Cincinnati
(Founded 1986)
1127 Vine St; Cincinnati, OH 45210; (513) 421-3555, FAX 421-8002
D. Lynn Meyers, *Producing Artistic Director*

Submission procedure: no unsolicited scripts; synopsis, dialogue sample, resume and letter of inquiry. **Types of material:** full-length plays, adaptations, plays for young audiences. **Special interests:** contemporary and social issues. **Facilities:** Ensemble Theatre of Cincinnati, 202 seats, 3/4-arena stage. **Production considerations:** cast limit of 6, simple set. **Best submission time:** Sep. **Response time:** 1 month letter; 4 months script.

Eureka Theatre Company
(Founded 1972)
330 Townsend St, Suite 210; San Francisco, CA 94107; (415) 243-9899, FAX 243-0789
Bill Schwartz, *Producing Executive Director*

Submission procedure: no unsolicited scripts; synopsis, 15 pages of dialogue, resume and letter of inquiry. **Types of material:** full-length plays, one-acts, translations, adaptations, solo pieces. **Special interests:** dynamic contemporary plays "strongly theatrical with an eye toward the millennium." **Facilities:** no permanent facility. **Best submission time:** year-round. **Response time:** 2 months letter; 6 months script. **Special programs:** Discovery Series: regularly scheduled rehearsed readings of new plays presented for public and followed by audience discussion.

Falstaff Presents
(Founded 1993)
49 Downing St, #3B; New York, NY 10014; (212) 888-0080
Michael Winter, *Producer*

Submission procedure: no unsolicited scripts; synopsis, resume and letter of inquiry. **Types of material:** full-length plays, translations, adaptations. **Special interests:** plays with strong female characters. **Facilities:** no permanent facility. **Best submission time:** year-round. **Response time:** 1 month letter; 3–6 months script.

First Stage Milwaukee
(Founded 1987)
929 North Water St; Milwaukee, WI 53202; (414) 273-7121, FAX 273-5595
Rob Goodman, *Producer/Artistic Director*

Submission procedure: no unsolicited scripts; synopsis, resume and letter of inquiry. **Types of material:** works for young audiences, including translations, adaptations and musicals. **Facilities:** Marcus Center for the Performing Arts's Todd Wehr Theater, 500 seats, thrust stage. **Best submission time:** spring–summer. **Response time:** 1 month letter; 3 months script.

36 / PRODUCTION

FLEETWOOD STAGE
(Founded 1993)
701 North MacQuesten Pkwy; Mt Vernon, NY 10552; (914) 699-6449, FAX 699-1536
Bruce Post, Literary Manager

Submission procedure: accepts unsolicited scripts; prefers professional recommendation. **Types of material:** full-length plays. **Facilities:** Playhouse at the Wartburg, 120 seats, thrust stage. **Production considerations:** cast limit of 8; prefers unit set. **Best submission time:** year-round. **Response time:** 3–5 months.

FLORIDA STUDIO THEATRE
(Founded 1973)
1241 North Palm Ave; Sarasota, FL 34236; (941) 366-9017
Chris Angermann, Associate Director

Submission procedure: no unsolicited scripts; synopsis and letter of inquiry. **Types of material:** full-length plays, one-acts, translations, adaptations, musicals, cabaret/revues, solo pieces. **Facilities:** Florida Studio Theatre, 173 seats, semi-thrust stage; FST Cabaret Club, 100 seats, cabaret space. **Best submission time:** Apr–Nov. **Response time:** 1–2 weeks letter; 6 months script. **Special programs:** Sarasota Festival of New Plays: 4-tier festival includes Young Playwrights Festival (May): workshop productions of plays by playwrights grades 2–12; *deadline:* 1 Apr 1998. Florida Playwrights Festival (Jul–Aug): workshops, seminars, staged readings and cabaret performances in conjunction with workshop productions of 3 plays by FL playwrights; scripts selected through theatre's normal submission procedure. National Playwrights Festival (May): workshop productions of 3 new plays; playwright receives stipend, travel, housing; scripts selected through theatre's normal submission procedure. Vanguard Festival: workshop productions of 3 new plays; "cutting-edge" material; scripts selected through theatre's normal submission procedure. Fall reading series. American Shorts Contest (see Prizes).

THE FOOTHILL THEATRE COMPANY
(Founded 1977)
Box 1812; Nevada City, CA 95959; (916) 265-9320
Philip Charles Sneed, Artistic Director

Submission procedure: accepts unsolicited scripts. **Types of material:** full-length plays, one-acts, translations, adaptations, plays for young audiences, solo pieces. **Special interests:** plays dealing with history of northern CA and/or the western U.S. **Facilities:** The Nevada Theatre, 246 seats, proscenium stage; also rents small spaces with 50–100 seats. **Production considerations:** very limited fly and wing space. **Best submission time:** year-round. **Response time:** 3–6 months.

FORD'S THEATRE
(Founded 1968)
511 Tenth Ave NW; Washington, DC 20004; (202) 638-2941, FAX 347-6269
Ellen Hause, *Literary Associate*

Submission procedure: no unsolicited scripts; synopsis, sample pages and letter of inquiry. **Types of material:** full-length plays, musicals. **Special interests:** small-scale musicals and works celebrating the African-American experience. **Facilities:** Ford's Theatre, 699 seats, proscenium/thrust stage. **Production considerations:** cast limit of 15. **Best submission time:** spring–summer. **Response time:** 3 weeks letter; 6 months script.

THE FOUNTAIN THEATRE
(Founded 1990)
5060 Fountain Ave; Los Angeles, CA 90029; (213) 663-2235, FAX 663-1629
Simon Levy, *Producing Director/Dramaturg*

Submission procedure: no unsolicited scripts; synopsis, and letter of inquiry. **Types of material:** full-length plays, translations, adaptations, musicals. **Special interests:** lyrical dramas; contemporary comedies; works with dance; adaptations of American literature. **Facilities:** Fountain Theatre Mainstage, 78 seats, thrust stage; The Lab, 22 seats, black box. **Production considerations:** cast limit of 12; 1 set; no fly space; low ceiling. **Best submission time:** year-round. **Response time:** 3 months letter; 6 months script.

FREE STREET PROGRAMS
(Founded 1969)
1419 West Blackhawk St; Chicago, IL 60622; (773) 772-7248, FAX 772-7248
Ron Bieganski, *Artistic Director*
David Schein, *Executive Director*

Submission procedure: no unsolicited scripts; letter from writer with "a concept for a show or a brilliant idea for a new theatre program for inner-city kids/teens." **Types of material:** plays and performance pieces, including shows to be performed in public places or out of doors. **Special interests:** inner-city kids/teenagers; "cultural empowerment of new populations"; developing works with communities; enhancing literacy through the arts; new work by Chicago-area artists. **Facilities:** national/international touring company (teens). **Production considerations:** no expensive production demands. **Response time:** 2 months letter; two months script.

FREEDOM THEATRE
(Formerly Freedom Repertory Theatre)
(Founded 1966)
1346 North Broad St; Philadelphia, PA 19121; (215) 765-2793, FAX 765-4191
Walter Dallas, *Artistic Director*

Submission procedure: no unsolicited scripts; synopsis, resume and letter of inquiry. **Types of material:** full-length plays, musicals, cabaret/revues. **Special interests:** contemporary plays with African-American themes. **Facilities:** John E. Allen Theatre, 298 seats, proscenium stage; Freedom Cabaret Theatre, 120 seats, flexible stage. **Best submission time:** year-round. **Response time:** 6–12 weeks. **Special programs:** Freedom Fest: play reading series; resident playwright program; commissioning program; all programs are by invitation only.

FRONTERA @ HYDE PARK THEATRE
(Founded 1992)
511 West 43rd St; Austin, TX 78751; (512) 419-7408, FAX 419-7408
Megan Monaghan, *Literary Manager*

Submission procedure: accepts unsolicited scripts. **Types of material:** full-length plays, one-acts, translations, adaptations, musicals, solo pieces. **Special interests:** nonnaturalistic plays; work involving ethnic, gender, generational and/or cultural "border issues," literal or metaphorical. **Facilities:** Hyde Park Theatre, 90 seats, flexible. **Best submission time:** year-round. **Response time:** 3–6 months.

GALA HISPANIC THEATRE
(Founded 1976)
Box 43209; Washington, DC 20010; (202) 234-7174, FAX 332-1247
Hugo J. Medrano, *Producing/Artistic Director*

Submission procedure: accepts unsolicited scripts; prefers synopsis/description of play and letter of inquiry. **Types of material:** full-length plays, solo pieces. **Special interests:** plays by Spanish, Latino or Hispanic-American writers in Spanish or English only; prefers Spanish-language works with accompanying English translation; works that reflect sociocultural realities of Hispanics in Latin America, the Caribbean or Spain, as well as the Hispanic-American experience. **Facilities:** GALA Hispanic Theatre, 200 seats, proscenium stage. **Production considerations:** cast of 6–8. **Best submission time:** Apr–May. **Response time:** 1 month letter; 12 months script. **Special programs:** poetry onstage.

GEORGE STREET PLAYHOUSE
(Founded 1974)
9 Livingston Ave; New Brunswick, NJ 08901; (908) 846-2895, FAX 247-9151;
E-mail trishroche@aol.com
Tricia Roche, *Literary Manager*

Submission procedure: no unsolicited scripts; professional recommendation. **Types of material:** full-length plays, one-acts for young audiences, musicals. **Special interests:** social-issue one-acts suitable for touring to schools (not seeking any other type of one-act for young audiences); comedies and dramas that present a fresh perspective on our society; "work that tells a compelling, personal human story while entertaining, challenging and stretching the imagination." **Facilities:** Mainstage, 367 seats, proscenium-thrust stage. **Production considerations:** prefers cast limit of 7 for plays, 10 for musicals. **Best submission time:** year-round. **Response time:** 8–10 months. **Special programs:** staged reading series.

GEORGIA REPERTORY THEATRE
(Founded 1990)
Department of Drama, University of Georgia; Athens, GA 30602-3154;
(706) 542-2836, FAX 542-2080; E-mail longman@uga.cc.uga.edu
Stanley V. Longman, *Dramaturg*

Submission procedure: accepts unsolicited scripts. **Types of material:** full-length plays. **Special interests:** plays not previously professionally produced. **Facilities:** Fine Arts Theatre, 750 seats, proscenium stage; Cellar Theatre, 100 seats, proscenium stage. **Production considerations:** cast limit of 8; minimal set. **Best submission time:** late spring. **Response time:** 3–6 months.

GERMINAL STAGE DENVER
(Founded 1974)
2450 West 44th Ave; Denver, CO 80211; (303) 455-7108;
E-mail gsden@privatei.com; Web http://www2.privatei.com/~gsden
Edward Baierlein, *Director/Manager*

Submission procedure: no unsolicited scripts; synopsis, 5 pages of dialogue and letter of inquiry with SASP for response. **Types of material:** full-length plays, translations, adaptations. **Special interests:** adaptations that use both dialogue and narration. **Facilities:** Germinal Stage Denver, 100 seats, thrust stage. **Production considerations:** cast limit of 10, minimal production requirements. **Best submission time:** year-round. **Response time:** 2 weeks letter; 6 months script.

GEVA THEATRE
(Founded 1972)
75 Woodbury Blvd; Rochester, NY 14607-1717; (716) 232-1366
Jean Ryon, *New Plays Coordinator*

Submission procedure: no unsolicited scripts; synopsis, dialogue sample, production history, resume and letter of inquiry. **Types of material:** full-length plays, translations, adaptations. **Facilities:** GeVa Theatre, 552 seats, modified thrust stage; The Second Stage, 175 seats, flexible stage. **Best submission time:** year-round. **Response time:** 1 week letter; 6 months script. **Special programs:** American Voices Reading Series; American Voices Winter Festival of New Works: 10–day workshops of 3 plays, followed by 2 staged readings of each; scripts selected through theatre's normal submission procedure.

THE GLINES
(Founded 1976)
240 West 44th St; New York, NY 10036; (212) 354-8899

Submission procedure: accepts unsolicited scripts. **Types of material:** full-length plays. **Special interests:** plays dealing with gay experience only; plays not previously produced in New York City. **Facilities:** no permanent facility. **Best submission time:** year-round. **Response time:** 2 months.

GOODMAN THEATRE
(Founded 1925)
200 South Columbus Dr; Chicago, IL 60603-6491; (312) 443-3811,
FAX 263-6004; E-mail staff@goodman-theatre.org
Susan V. Booth, *Director of New Play Development*

Submission procedure: no unsolicited scripts; synopsis, professional recommendation and letter of inquiry. **Types of material:** full-length plays, translations, musicals, solo pieces. **Special interests:** social or political themes. **Facilities:** Goodman Mainstage, 683 seats, proscenium stage; Goodman Studio, 135 seats, proscenium stage. **Best submission time:** year-round. **Response time:** 2–3 months letter; 6–8 months script.

GOODSPEED OPERA HOUSE
(Founded 1963)
Box A; East Haddam, CT 06423; (860) 873-8664, FAX 873-2329
Sue Frost, *Associate Producer*

Submission procedure: no unsolicited scripts; synopsis and letter of inquiry. **Types of material:** original musicals only. **Facilities:** Goodspeed Opera House, 400 seats, proscenium stage; Goodspeed-at-Chester, 200 seats, adaptable proscenium stage. **Best submission time:** Jan–Mar. **Response time:** 3 months letter; 12 months script.

GREAT AMERICAN HISTORY THEATRE
(Founded 1978)
30 East Tenth St; St. Paul, MN 55101; (612) 292-4323, FAX 292-4322
Ron Peluso, *Artistic Director*

Submission procedure: no unsolicited scripts; synopsis and letter of inquiry. **Types of material:** full-length plays, adaptations, musicals, solo pieces. **Special interests:** works involving historical American events, issues, ideas and places; no pageants. **Facilities:** Crawford Livingston Theatre, 597 seats, thrust stage. **Production considerations:** cast limit of 10; moderate production demands; small musicals only. **Best submission time:** spring. **Response time:** 2 months letter; 2–6 months script.

GRETNA THEATRE
(Founded 1977)
Box 578; Mt. Gretna, PA 17064; (717) 964-3322, FAX 964-2189

Submission procedure: no unsolicited scripts; synopsis, 5 pages of dialogue, character list with descriptions, production history and letter of inquiry; include cassette for musicals. **Types of material:** full-length plays, musicals. **Special interests:** plays suitable for summer audiences; prefers comedies; musicals. **Facilities:** Mt. Gretna Playhouse, 700 seats, proscenium stage. **Production considerations:** open-air facility; 14′ ceiling over stage. **Best submission time:** Aug–Apr. **Response time:** 1 month letter; 3 months script.

THE GROUP: SEATTLE'S MULTICULTURAL THEATRE
(Founded 1978)
305 Harrison St; Seattle, WA 98109; (206) 441-9480, FAX 441-9839
Literary Department

Submission procedure: no unsolicited scripts; synopsis, 10–15 pages of dialogue, resume and letter of inquiry with SASE for response. **Types of material:** full-length plays, translations, adaptations, plays for young audiences, musicals, solo pieces. **Special interests:** plays suitable for multiethnic casts; serious plays on social/cultural issues; satires, musicals or comedies with bite. **Facilities:** Seattle Center's Carlton Playhouse, 200 seats, modified thrust stage. **Production considerations:** cast limit of 10; prefers unit set or simple sets. **Best submission time:** year-round. **Response time:** 4–6 months.

THE GUTHRIE THEATER
(Founded 1963)
725 Vineland Pl; Minneapolis, MN 55403; (612) 347-1100, FAX 347-1188
Literary Department

Submission procedure: no unsolicited scripts; synopsis, resume and letter of inquiry with professional recommendation and SASE for response. **Types of material:** full-length plays, translations, adaptations. **Special interests:** contemporary full-length plays not previously professionally produced; translations/adaptations from classic literature; adaptations of folktales from diverse cultures exploring themes of universal scope; no sitcoms. **Facilities:** Guthrie Theater, 1309 seats, thrust stage; Guthrie Lab, 350 seats, flexible stage. **Best submission time:** Jan–Apr. **Response time:** 3 months letter; scripts vary.

HARTFORD STAGE COMPANY
(Founded 1964)
50 Church St; Hartford, CT 06103; (860) 525-5601, FAX 525-4420
Kim Euell, *Director of New Play Development*

Submission procedure: no unsolicited scripts; synopsis, 10 pages of dialogue, resume and letter of inquiry. **Types of material:** full-length plays, translations, adaptations. **Facilities:** John W. Huntington Theatre, 489 seats, thrust stage. **Best submission time:** year-round. **Response time:** 1 month letter; 6–9 months script.

HEDGEROW THEATRE
(Founded 1923)
146 West Rose Valley Rd; Rose Valley, PA 19065; (610) 565-4211
Margaret Royal, *Literary Director*

Submission procedure: no unsolicited scripts; synopsis and letter of inquiry. **Types of material:** full-length plays, plays for young audiences. **Special interests:** new plays by DE, NJ and PA playwrights; mysteries; comedies. **Facilities:** Mainstage, 144 seats, proscenium stage. **Production considerations:** small stage; minimal production demands. **Best submission time:** year-round. **Response time:** 2 months letter; 4 months script.

HIP POCKET THEATRE
(Founded 1977)
7344 Love Circle; Fort Worth, TX 76135; (817) 237-5977,
	FAX 272-2697
Johnny Simons, *Artistic Director*

Submission procedure: accepts unsolicited scripts; include cassette for musicals. **Types of material:** full-length plays, translations, adaptations, plays for young audiences, musicals, solo pieces, multimedia works. **Special interests:** well-crafted stories with poetic, mythic slant that incorporate ritual and ensemble; works utilizing masks, puppetry, music, dance, mime and strong visual elements. **Facilities:** Oak Acres Amphitheatre, 175 seats, outdoor amphitheatre. **Production considerations:** prefers cast size of 10–15; simple sets. **Best submission time:** Oct–Feb. **Response time:** 6 weeks.

THE HIPPODROME STATE THEATRE
(Founded 1973)
25 Southeast Second Pl; Gainesville, FL 32601-6596; (352) 373-5968,
	FAX 371-9130; Web http://hipp.gator.net
Tamerin Corn, *Dramaturg*

Submission procedure: no unsolicited scripts; synopsis and letter of inquiry. **Types of material:** full-length plays, translations, adaptations. **Facilities:** Mainstage Theatre, 266 seats, thrust stage; Second Stage, 87 seats, flexible stage. **Production considerations:** prefers small cast, unit set. **Best submission time:** summer–fall. **Response time:** 3–5 months letter; 5–7 months script

HONOLULU THEATRE FOR YOUTH
(Founded 1955)
2846 Ualena St; Honolulu, HI 96819-1910; (808) 839-9885, FAX 839-7018
Peter C. Brosius, *Artistic Director*

Submission procedure: no unsolicited scripts; synopsis, resume and letter of inquiry. **Types of material:** one-acts, plays for young audiences. **Special interests:** plays for audiences up to high school age, with contemporary themes; adaptations of literary classics; new works based on Pacific Rim cultures; plays with compelling language that are imaginative and socially relevant. **Facilities:** Leeward Community College Theatre, 650 seats, proscenium stage; McCoy Pavilion, 300 seats, flexible stage. **Production considerations:** cast limit of 10. **Best submission time:** year-round. **Response time:** 1 month letter; 4–5 months script.

Horizon Theatre Company
(Founded 1993)
Box 5376, Station E; Atlanta, GA 30307; (404) 523-1477,
    FAX 523-1477 (call first);
    Web http://www.mindspring.com/~horizoncol
Lisa Adler, *Co-Artistic Director*

Submission procedure: accepts unsolicited scripts from GA playwrights only; others send synopsis, resume and letter of inquiry. **Types of material:** full-length plays, translations, adaptations, musicals. **Special interests:** contemporary issues; plays by women; southern urban themes; comedies. **Facilities:** Horizon Theatre, 170–200 seats, flexible stage. **Production considerations:** plays cast from ensemble of up to 12 actors. **Best submission time:** May–Jun. **Response time:** 6 months letter; 12 months script. **Special programs:** Teen Ensemble: one-acts about teen issues to be performed by teens. Senior Citizens Ensemble: one-acts about senior-citizen issues to be performed by senior citizens.

Horse Cave Theatre
(Founded 1977)
Box 215; Horse Cave, KY 42749; (502) 786-1200, FAX 786-5298
Warren Hammack, *Artistic Director*

Submission procedure: no unsolicited scripts; professional recommendation. **Types of material:** full-length plays. **Special interests:** KY-based plays by KY playwrights. **Facilities:** Horse Cave Theatre, 345 seats, thrust stage. **Production considerations:** cast limit of 10, 1 set. **Best submission time:** Oct–Apr. **Response time:** varies.

The Human Race Theatre Company
(Founded 1986)
126 North Main St, Suite 300; Dayton, OH 45402-1710; (513) 461-3823,
    FAX 461-7223
Tony Dallas, *Playwright in Residence*

Submission procedure: no unsolicited scripts; professional recommendation. **Types of material:** full-length plays, one-acts, plays for young audiences. **Special interests:** OH playwrights; works for junior and senior high school audiences; contemporary issues. **Facilities:** The Loft, 219 seats, thrust stage. **Production considerations:** small casts; no fly space; plays for young audiences tour to schools. **Best submission time:** year-round. **Response time:** 6 months.

Huntington Theatre Company
(Founded 1981)
264 Huntington Ave; Boston MA 02115-4606; (617) 266-7900, FAX 353-8300
Scott Edmiston, *Literary Associate*

Submission procedure: no unsolicited scripts; synopsis and letter of inquiry. **Types of material:** full-length plays, translations, adaptations. **Special interests:** New

England playwrights; plays based on literary sources. **Facilities:** Huntington Theatre, 850 seats, proscenium stage. **Best submission time:** May–Sep. **Response time:** 3 months letter; 6 months script.

ILLINOIS THEATRE CENTER
(Founded 1976)
400A Lakewood Blvd; Park Forest, IL 60466; (708) 481-3510;
    E-mail itcbillig@juno.com
Etel Billig, *Producing Director*

Submission procedure: no unsolicited scripts; synopsis and letter of inquiry with SASE for response. **Types of material:** full-length plays, musicals. **Facilities:** Illinois Theatre Center, 200 seats, proscenium-thrust stage. **Production considerations:** cast limit of 9 for plays, 14 for musicals. **Best submission time:** year-round. **Response time:** 1 month letter; 2 months script.

ILLUSION THEATER
(Founded 1974)
528 Hennepin Ave, Suite 704; Minneapolis, MN 55403; (612) 339-4944,
    FAX 337-8042
Michael Robins, *Executive Producing Director*

Submission procedure: no unsolicited scripts; professional recommendation. **Types of material:** full-length plays, one-acts, translations, adaptations, musicals, solo pieces. **Special interests:** writers to collaborate on new works with company. **Facilities:** Illusion Theater, 250 seats, semi-thrust stage. **Best submission time:** Jul–Nov. **Response time:** 6–12 months. **Special programs:** Fresh Ink Series: 5–6 plays each presented with minimal set and costumes for 1 weekend; post-performance discussion with audience, who are seated onstage; scripts selected through theatre's normal submission procedure.

INDIANA REPERTORY THEATRE
(Founded 1972)
140 West Washington St; Indianapolis, IN 46204-3465; (317) 635-5277,
    FAX 236-0767
Richard J. Roberts, *Literary Manager*

Submission procedure: no unsolicited scripts; synopsis and letter of inquiry from playwright with SASE for response; inquiries only from agents (no scripts). **Types of material:** full-length plays, translations, adaptations, solo pieces. **Special interests:** adaptations of classic literature; plays that explore cultural/ethnic issues "with a Midwestern voice." **Facilities:** Mainstage, 600 seats, modified proscenium stage; Upperstage, 300 seats, modified thrust stage. **Production considerations:** cast limit of 6–8. **Best submission time:** year-round (season chosen by Jan each year). **Response time:** 3–4 months letter; 6 months script. **Special programs:** Discovery Series: presentation of plays for family audiences with a focus on youth and culturally/ethnically diverse plays with an emphasis on history and literature; follow theatre's normal submission procedure above.

INTAR Hispanic American Arts Center
(Founded 1979)
Box 788; New York, NY 10108; (212) 695-6134, -6135, FAX 268-0102
Lorenzo Mans, *Literary Manager*

Submission procedure: accepts unsolicited scripts. **Types of material:** full-length plays, one-acts, translations, adaptations, musicals, solo pieces. **Special interests:** new plays by Hispanic-American writers and translations and adaptations of Hispanic works only. **Facilities:** INTAR on Theatre Row, 99 seats, proscenium stage; INTAR Stage Two, 75 seats, proscenium stage. **Production considerations:** prefers cast limit of 8; no wing space. **Best submission time:** year-round (season chosen late summer–early fall). **Response time:** 3–6 months. **Special programs:** New Works Lab: workshop productions. Reading series.

InterAct Theatre Company
(Founded 1988)
Box 42138; Philadelphia, PA 19101; (215) 568-8077, FAX 568-8095
Seth Rozin, *Artistic Director*
Tom Gibbons, *Literary Manager*

Submission procedure: no unsolicited scripts; synopsis, resume and letter of inquiry. **Types of material:** full-length plays. **Special interests:** plays that theatrically explore issues of cultural conflict only (political, social, historical, etc.). **Facilities:** Sansom Space, 104 seats, proscenium stage. **Production considerations:** cast limit of 10. **Best submission time:** year-round. **Response time:** 2 months letter; 4 months script. **Special programs:** script-in-hand reading series.

Intiman Theatre
(Founded 1972)
Box 19760; Seattle, WA 98109; (206) 269-1901, FAX 269-1928;
    E-mail intiman@scn.org; Web http://www.seattlesquare.com/intiman
Robert Menna, *Dramaturg/Literary Manager*

Submission procedure: no unsolicited scripts; professional recommendation. **Types of material:** full-length plays, translations, adaptations. **Special interests:** well-crafted plays that fully utilize the power of language and character relationships to explore enduring themes. **Facilities:** Intiman Playhouse, 424 seats, thrust stage. **Production considerations:** prefers cast limit of 12. **Best submission time:** Dec–Mar. **Response time:** 6 months. **Special programs:** New Voices at Intiman: developmental readings of unproduced new plays.

Invisible Theatre
(Founded 1976)
1400 North 1st Ave; Tucson, AZ 85719; (520) 882-9721, FAX 884-0672
Deborah Dickey, *Literary Manager*

Submission procedure: no unsolicited scripts; professional recommendation. **Types of material:** full-length plays, one-acts, musicals, solo pieces. **Special interests:** mainly but not exclusively works with contemporary settings; works with strong female roles; social and political issues. **Facilities:** Invisible Theatre, 78 seats, black box. **Production considerations:** cast limit of 10; simple set; minimal props; small-cast musicals only. **Best submission time:** after 1 Sep 1997 only. **Response time:** 6–12 months.

IRONDALE ENSEMBLE PROJECT
(Founded 1983)
Box 1314, Old Chelsea Station; New York, NY 10011-1314; (212) 633-1292, FAX 633-2078; E-mail irondalert@aol.com
Jim Niesen, *Artistic Director*

Submission procedure: no unsolicited scripts; letter of inquiry from playwright interested in developing work with ensemble through ongoing workshop process. **Types of material:** full-length plays, adaptations, plays with music. **Special interests:** works with political or social relevance. **Facilities:** no permanent facility. **Production considerations:** cast limit of 8–9. **Best submission time:** Sep–Jun. **Response time:** 10 weeks.

JEWISH ENSEMBLE THEATRE
(Founded 1989)
6600 West Maple Rd; West Bloomfield, MI 48322-3002; (810) 788-2900, FAX 661-3680
Evelyn Orbach, *Artistic Director*

Submission procedure: accepts unsolicited scripts. **Types of material:** full-length plays, one-acts, plays for young audiences. **Special interests:** works on Jewish themes and/or by Jewish writers; work not previously professionally produced. **Facilities:** Aaron DeRoy Theatre, 194 seats, thrust stage. **Production considerations:** no fly space. **Best submission time:** late spring–early fall. **Response time:** 6 months. **Special programs:** Festival of New Plays in Staged Readings: 4 plays given readings, possibly leading to mainstage production; scripts selected through theatre's normal submission procedure.

JEWISH REPERTORY THEATRE
(Founded 1974)
92nd Street Y; 1395 Lexington Ave; New York, NY 10128; (212) 415-5550
Ran Avni, *Artistic Director*

Submission procedure: accepts unsolicited scripts. **Types of material:** full-length plays, musicals. **Special interests:** works that address some aspect of Jewish life; no plays that have been reviewed in New York during the past 5 years. **Facilities:** Playhouse 91, 299 seats, thrust stage. **Production considerations:** small cast. **Best submission time:** Sep–May. **Response time:** 1 month. **Special programs:** Lee Guber Playwrights' Lab: readings of new plays.

John Drew Theater
(Founded 1931)
158 Main St; East Hampton, NY 11937; (516) 324-4051, FAX 324-2722
Brigitte Blachere, *General Manager*

Submission procedure: no unsolicited scripts; 1-page synopsis, character and set breakdown and letter of inquiry. **Types of material:** full-length plays, solo pieces. **Special interests:** comedies; plays with contemporary setting. **Facilities:** John Drew Theater, 387 seats, proscenium. **Production considerations:** cast limit of 4; unit set; no fly space. **Best submission time:** year-round. **Response time:** 3 months letter; 3 months script.

Jomandi Productions
(Founded 1978)
1444 Mayson St NE; Atlanta, GA 30324; (404) 876-6346, FAX 872-5764
Literary Manager

Submission procedure: no unsolicited scripts; synopsis, dialogue sample, resume and letter of inquiry. **Types of material:** full-length plays, adaptations, plays for young audiences, musicals, solo pieces. **Special interests:** historical or contemporary portrayals of the African-American experience; adaptations of African-American literature. **Facilities:** 14th Street Playhouse main stage, 370 seats, proscenium/thrust stage. **Production considerations:** produces some large-cast plays but prefers average cast of 7; prefers unit set. **Best submission time:** spring–summer. **Response time:** 1 month letter; 4–6 months script.

Jungle Theater
(Founded 1990)
709 West Lake St; Minneapolis, MN 55408; (612) 822-7063, FAX 822-9408
Bain Boehlke, *Artistic Director*

Submission procedure: no unsolicited scripts; synopsis, sample pages, resume and letter of inquiry. **Types of material:** full-length plays. **Facilities:** Jungle Theater, 95 seats, proscenium stage. **Best submission time:** year-round. **Response time:** 1 month letter; 3 months script.

L. A. Theatre Works
(Founded 1974)
681 Venice Blvd; Venice, CA 90291; (310) 827-0808, FAX 827-4949;
    E-mail latworks@aol.com
Kirsten Dahl, *Literary Manager*

Submission procedure: no unsolicited scripts; agent submission. **Types of material:** full-length plays, one-acts, adaptations. **Special interests:** highly theatrical, nonrealistic new plays; contemporary adaptations of classic themes. **Facilities:** no permanent facility. **Best submission time:** year-round. **Response time:** 4–6 months. **Special programs:** Radio Theatre Series for New Plays: bimonthly performances; scripts selected from among those received through theatre's normal submission procedure. Writers Dialogue: series of advanced playwriting workshops; $300 fee for 10-week session; contact theatre for information.

LA JOLLA PLAYHOUSE
(Founded 1947)
Box 12039; La Jolla, CA 92039; (619) 550-1070, FAX 550-1075
Gregory Gunter, *Dramaturg*

Submission procedure: no unsolicited scripts; professional recommendation. **Types of material:** full-length plays, translations, musicals. **Special interests:** material pertinent to the lives we are leading at the end of this century; innovative form and language. **Facilities:** Mandell Weiss Center for the Performing Arts, 500 seats, proscenium stage; Weiss Forum, 400 seats, thrust stage. **Best submission time:** Feb–Sep. **Response time:** 6 months.

LA MAMA EXPERIMENTAL THEATER CLUB
(Founded 1961)
74A East 4th St; New York, NY 10003; (212) 254-6468, FAX 254-7908
Ellen Stewart, *Artistic Director*
Meryl Vladimer, *Associate Director*

Submission procedure: no unsolicited scripts; accepts unsolicited videotapes of projects with synopsis; prefers professional recommendation. **Types of material:** full-length plays, one-acts, musicals, solo pieces, performance art. **Special interests:** culturally diverse works with music, movement and media. **Facilities:** Annex Theater, 299 seats, flexible stage; Club, 125 seats, black box; 1st Floor Theater, 99 seats, black box. **Best submission time:** year-round. **Response time:** 2–6 months. **Special programs:** New Voices/New Plays: weekly series of readings followed by informal audience-response sessions. One Night Stand Series: weekly performance series for emerging multidisciplinary performance artists, including writers, who perform own work; theatre provides lighting, sound and stage management. Cross Cultural Institute of Theater Art Studies: promotes intercultural understanding and artistic exchange developed or created through theatrical workshops, artistic explorations and premiere productions involving collaboration among artists of varying geographic and ethnic origins.

LAGUNA PLAYHOUSE
(Founded 1920)
606 Laguna Canyon Rd; Laguna Beach, CA 92651; (714) 494-8022,
    FAX 497-6948
Andrew Barnicle, *Artistic Director*

Submission procedure: no unsolicited scripts; direct solicitation to playwright or agent. **Types of material:** full-length plays, plays for young audiences, musicals. **Facilities:** Moulton Theater, 418 seats, proscenium stage.

Lamb's Players Theatre
(Founded 1971)
Box 182229; Coronado, CA 92178; (619) 437-6050, FAX 437-6053
Jeffrey S. Miller, *Director of Outreach*

Submission procedure: no unsolicited scripts; synopsis, maximum 10-page dialogue sample and letter of inquiry; include cassette for musicals. **Types of material:** full-length plays, one-acts, plays for young audiences, musicals, cabaret/revues. **Facilities:** Harder Stage, 350 seats, thrust stage; Hahn, 250 seats, proscenium stage; Lyceum, 200 seats, flexible. **Best submission time:** year-round. **Response time:** 4–6 weeks letter; 4–6 months script.

Lincoln Center Theater
(Founded 1966)
150 West 65th St; New York, NY 10023; (212) 362-7600
Anne Cattaneo, *Dramaturg*

Submission procedure: no unsolicited scripts; agent submission. **Types of material:** full-length plays, one-acts, translations, adaptations, musicals. **Facilities:** Vivian Beaumont, 1000 seats, thrust stage; Mitzi E. Newhouse, 300 seats, thrust stage. **Best submission time:** year-round. **Response time:** 2–4 months.

Live Bait Theatrical Company
(Founded 1987)
3914 North Clark; Chicago, IL 60613; (773) 871-1212, FAX 871-3191;
   E-mail lbtheater@aol.com
Tina Lilly, *Managing Director*

Submission procedure: no unsolicited scripts; synopsis and letter of inquiry from Chicago-area playwrights only; no other submissions accepted. **Types of material:** full-length plays, translations, adaptations, solo pieces, performance art. **Special interests:** nonrealistic plays; performance poetry; performance art; multimedia works; works that emphasize visual aspects of staging. **Facilities:** Live Bait Theater, 70 seats, black box. **Production considerations:** prefers cast limit of 9; 1 set; no fly or wing space. **Best submission time:** year-round. **Response time:** 6 weeks letter; 6 months script.

Live Oak Theatre
(Founded 1982)
719 Congress Ave; Austin, TX 78701; (512) 472-5143, FAX 472-7199;
   E-mail liveoak@eden.com;
   Web http://www.austinlink.com/arts/liveoak.html
Michael Hankin, *Associate Director*

Submission procedure: accepts unsolicited scripts or synopsis, dialogue sample and letter of inquiry; include cassette for musicals. **Types of material:** full-length plays, adaptations, solo pieces. **Special interests:** work not previously professionally produced only; Texas plays; comedies. **Facilities:** Live Oak Theatre, 400 seats, proscenium stage. **Production considerations:** limited wing space; small stage. **Best submission time:** year-round. **Response time:** scripts chosen in summer of year after submission. **Special programs:** Live Oak Theatre's Harvest Festival of New American Plays (see Prizes).

THE LIVING THEATRE
(Founded 1947)
800 West End Ave, #5A; New York, NY 10025; (212) 865-3957, FAX 865-3234
Craig Peritz, *Administrative Assistant*

Submission procedure: no unsolicited scripts; synopsis and letter of inquiry. **Types of material:** full-length plays, translations, adaptations. **Special interests:** plays that creatively incorporate audience participation; experimental works; new theatre forms; nonfictional plays dealing with current issues performed by actors who play themselves. **Facilities:** no permanent facility; touring company; street and various outdoor venues. **Production considerations:** plays must accommodate ensemble of 12. **Best submission time:** year-round. **Response time:** 2 months letter; 6 months script.

THE LOFT PRODUCTION COMPANY
(Founded 1987)
Box 173405; Tampa, FL 33672; (813) 275-9400, FAX 222-1057
(Mr.) Kelly Smith, *Artistic Director*

Submission procedure: accepts unsolicited scripts with maximum 1-page synopsis, scene/set breakdown and $5 fee; playwright's name, address and phone number must appear on title page; submissions not returned. **Types of material:** unproduced and unpublished full-length plays, adaptations, musicals, performance art. **Special interests:** work with no previous main stage productions only; gay and lesbian works; women's works. **Facilities:** Resident Theatre Company of the Off-Center Theater at Tampa Bay Performing Arts Center, 130 seats, black box. **Production considerations:** cast limit 8; cast age of 20–40; simple set; minimal production demands. **Best submission time:** year-round. **Response time:** 3 months. **Special programs:** The Loft Fest '98—Festival of Shorts (see Development).

LONG WHARF THEATRE
(Founded 1965)
222 Sargent Dr; New Haven, CT 06511; (203) 787-4284, FAX 776-2287
John Tillinger, *Literary Consultant*

Submission procedure: no unsolicited scripts; professional recommendation. **Types of material:** full-length plays, translations, adaptations. **Special interests:** plays about human relationships, social concerns, ethical and moral dilemmas; will also consider farces and comedies of manners. **Facilities:** Long Wharf Theatre, 484 seats, thrust stage; Stage II, 199 seats, flexible stage. **Best submission time:** year-round. **Response time:** 6 months. **Special programs:** in-house readings of new plays. Long Wharf Theatre Stage II Workshops (see Development).

MABOU MINES
(Founded 1970)
150 First Ave; New York, NY 10009; (212) 473-0559, FAX 473-2410
Sharon Fogarty, *Company Manager*

Submission procedure: no unsolicited scripts; professional recommendation. **Types of material:** full-length plays, one-acts, translations, adaptations. **Special interests:** contemporary works on contemporary issues. **Facilities:** The TOny, ROn, NAncy & DAvid–TORO-NADA: NO BULL Theater at the 122 Community Center, 60 seats, flexible stage. **Best submission time:** year-round. **Response time:** 6 months.

MAD RIVER THEATER WORKS
(Founded 1978)
Box 248; West Liberty, OH 43357; (937) 465-6751
Jeff Hooper, *Producing Director*

Submission procedure: no unsolicited scripts; direct solicitation to playwright or agent. **Types of material:** full-length plays, one-acts, adaptations. **Special interests:** company-developed works; Midwestern or rural subject matter. **Facilities:** Center Stage, 150 seats, flexible stage. **Production considerations:** cast limit of 6, simple set and costumes. **Best submission time:** year-round. **Response time:** 3–4 months.

MADISON REPERTORY THEATRE
(Founded 1969)
122 State St, Suite 201; Madison, WI 53703-2500; (608) 256-0029,
    FAX 256-7433; E-mail madisonrep@aol.com
D. Scott Glasser, *Artistic Director*

Submission procedure: no unsolicited scripts; synopsis and letter of inquiry. **Types of material:** full-length plays, one-acts, translations, adaptations, musicals. **Special interests:** works with midwestern themes. **Facilities:** Isthmus Playhouse, 335 seats, thrust stage. **Production considerations:** cast limit of 15; no fly space. **Best submission time:** year-round. **Response time:** 3–4 months letter; 3–4 months script. **Special programs:** reading series for plays in development.

MAGIC THEATRE
(Founded 1967)
Fort Mason Center, Bldg D; San Francisco, CA 94123; (415) 441-8001,
    FAX 771-5505
Kent Nicholson, *Literary Manager*

Submission procedure: no unsolicited scripts; synopsis, first 10 pages of play, resume and letter of inquiry. **Types of material:** full-length plays, solo pieces. **Special interests:** new plays that are innovative and/or nonlinear in form and content; political themes. **Facilities:** Magic Theatre Southside, 170 seats, proscenium stage; Magic Theatre Northside, 155 seats, thrust stage. **Production**

considerations: prefers cast limit of 6. **Best submission time:** Sep–May. **Response time:** 6 weeks letter; 6–8 months script.

MANHATTAN THEATRE CLUB
(Founded 1972)
453 West 16th St; New York, NY 10011; (212) 645-5590, FAX 691-9106;
E-mail 76735.3316@compuserve.com
Kate Loewald, *Director of Play Development*
Clifford Lee Johnson III, *Director of Musical Theatre Program*

Submission procedure: no unsolicited scripts; agent submission. **Types of material:** full-length plays, musicals. **Facilities:** Stage I at City Center, 299 seats, proscenium stage; Stage II, 150 seats, thrust stage. **Production considerations:** cast of 6–8; 1 set or unit set. **Best submission time:** year-round. **Response time:** 6 months. **Special programs:** readings and workshop productions of new musicals. "First-hearing" readings: in-house readings of new plays or first drafts. Manhattan Theatre Club Playwriting Fellowships (see Fellowships and Grants).

MARIN THEATRE COMPANY
(Founded 1967)
397 Miller Ave; Mill Valley, CA 94941; (415) 388-5200, FAX 388-0768
Lee Sankowich, *Artistic Director*

Submission procedure: no unsolicited scripts; agent submission. **Types of material:** full-length plays, translations, adaptations, plays for young audiences. **Facilities:** Marin Theatre, 250 seats, proscenium stage; 2nd theatre, 109 seats, black box. **Best submission time:** Jun–Aug. **Response time:** 6 months.

MARK TAPER FORUM
(Founded 1967)
135 North Grand Ave; Los Angeles, CA 90012; (213) 972-7574
Pier Carlo Talenti, *Associate Literary Manager*

Submission procedure: no unsolicited scripts; description of work, 5–10 sample pages and letter of inquiry. **Types of material:** full-length plays, one-acts, translations, adaptations, plays for young audiences, musicals, literary cabaret, solo pieces, performance art. **Facilities:** Mark Taper Forum, 742 seats, thrust stage; Taper, Too, 80–90 seats, flexible stage. **Best submission time:** year-round. **Response time:** 4–6 weeks letter; 8–10 weeks script. **Special programs:** Performing for Los Angeles Youth: 55-minute plays that tour Southern CA schools; maximum 6 actors and suitable for grades K–8; send script and resume to Delores Chavez; Mark Taper Forum Developmental Programs (see Development).

MCC Theater
(Founded 1986)
120 West 28th St; New York, NY 10001; (212) 727-7722, FAX 727-7780
Stephen Willems, *Literary Manager*

Submission procedure: no unsolicited scripts; synopsis and letter of inquiry with SASE or SASP for response. **Types of material:** full-length plays, one-acts, translations, adaptations, musicals. **Facilities:** 99 seats, black box. **Production considerations:** cast limit of 10. **Best submission time:** year-round. **Response time:** 2 weeks letter; 2 months script.

McCarter Theatre Center for the Performing Arts
(Founded 1972)
91 University Pl; Princeton, NJ 08540; (609) 683-9100, FAX 497-0369
Janice Paran, *Literary Manager/Dramaturg*

Submission procedure: no unsolicited scripts; synopsis, 10-page dialogue sample and letter of inquiry. **Types of material:** full-length plays, musicals. **Facilities:** McCarter Theatre, 1077 seats, proscenium stage. **Best submission time:** Sep–May. **Response time:** 1 month letter; 3 months script.

Meadow Brook Theatre
(Founded 1967)
Oakland University; Rochester, MI 48309-4401; (248) 370-3310, FAX 370-3108;
    E-mail mbrkthea@oakland.edu
Literary Manager

Submission procedure: no unsolicited scripts; synopsis, sample pages and letter of inquiry. **Types of material:** full-length plays, one-acts, translations, adaptations, plays for young audiences, musicals. **Special interests:** one-act plays suitable for young audiences. **Facilities:** Meadow Brook Theatre, 608 seats, proscenium stage. **Best submission time:** year-round. **Response time:** 1–2 months letter; 3–5 months script.

Merrimack Repertory Theatre
(Founded 1979)
50 East Merrimack St; Lowell, MA 01852; (508) 454-6324, FAX 934-0166;
    Web http://www.mrtlowell.com
David G. Kent, *Producing Artistic Director*

Submission procedure: no unsolicited scripts; synopsis and letter of inquiry. **Types of material:** full-length plays, translations, adaptations, plays for young audiences, musicals. **Special interests:** well-crafted stories with a poetic and human focus; varied ethnic tapestries of American life and love. **Facilities:** Liberty Hall, 372 seats, thrust stage. **Production considerations:** moderate cast size, simple set. **Best submission time:** spring–summer. **Response time:** 1 month letter (if interested); 6 months script.

MERRY-GO-ROUND PLAYHOUSE
(Founded 1958)
Box 506; Auburn, NY 13021; (315) 255-1305, FAX 252-3815
Emily Mattina, *Literary Manager*

Submission procedure: accepts unsolicited scripts. **Types of material:** full-length plays, translations, adaptations, plays for young audiences, musicals. **Special interests:** participatory plays for young audiences with cast limit of 3–4; plays for grades K–12. **Facilities:** Merry-Go-Round Playhouse (adaptable), 325 seats, proscenium stage or 100 seats, thrust stage. **Production considerations:** cast limit of 5. **Best submission time:** Jan–Feb. **Response time:** 2 months.

METRO THEATER COMPANY
(Founded 1973)
8308 Olive Blvd; St. Louis, MO 63132-2814; (314) 997-6777, FAX 997-1811;
    E-mail bravomtc@aol.com
Carol North, *Producing Director*

Submission procedure: no unsolicited scripts; professional recommendation. **Types of material:** plays and musicals for young audiences. **Special interests:** no works longer than 60 minutes; plays with music and musicals that are not dramatically limited by traditional concepts of "children's theatre." **Facilities:** touring company. **Production considerations:** works cast from ensemble of 5; sets suitable for touring. **Best submission time:** year-round. **Response time:** 2–3 months. **Special programs:** new plays readings; commissioning program; interested writers send letter of inquiry with recommendations from theatres who have produced writer's work.

METROSTAGE
(Founded 1984)
Box 329; Alexandria, VA 22313; (703) 548-9044, FAX 548-9089
Carolyn Griffin, *Producing Director*

Submission procedure: no unsolicited scripts; synopsis, first 10 pages of dialogue, list of productions and readings, and letter of inquiry. **Types of material:** full-length plays. **Facilities:** MetroStage, 100 seats, thrust stage. **Production considerations:** cast limit of 8, prefers 4; prefers 1 set. **Best submission time:** year-round. **Response time:** 1 month letter; 1 month script. **Special programs:** First Stage: staged reading series Oct–May.

MILL MOUNTAIN THEATRE
(Founded 1964)
1 Market Square SE; Roanoke, VA 24011-1437; (703) 342-5730,
    FAX (540) 342-5749
Jo Weinstein, *Literary Manager*

Submission procedure: accepts unsolicited one-acts only; synopsis, 10 pages of dialogue and letter of inquiry for all other submissions; include cassette for musicals. **Types of material:** full-length plays, one-acts, musicals, solo pieces. **Special interests:** plays with racially mixed casts. **Facilities:** Mill Mountain Theatre, 400 seats, flexible proscenium stage; Theatre B, 125 seats, flexible space. **Production considerations:** cast limit of 15 for plays, 24 for musicals; prefers unit set. **Best submission time:** year-round. **Response time:** 6 weeks letter; 6–8 months script. **Special programs:** Centerpieces: monthly lunchtime staged readings of one-acts by emerging playwrights; unpublished one-acts 25–35 minutes long (no 10-minute plays). The Mill Mountain Theatre New Play Competition: The Norfolk Southern Festival of New Works (see Prizes).

MILWAUKEE CHAMBER THEATRE
(Founded 1975)
158 North Broadway; Milwaukee, WI 53202; (414) 276-8842, FAX 277-4477;
    E-mail mct@execpc.com
Montgomery Davis, *Artistic Director*

Submission procedure: no unsolicited scripts; professional recommendation. **Types of material:** full-length plays, one-acts, translations, adaptations. **Special interests:** strong, well-crafted plays; plays about Shaw for annual Shaw Festival. **Facilities:** Broadway Theatre Center: Cabot Theatre, 372 seats, proscenium stage; studio, 99 seats, black box. **Production considerations:** 1 set or unit set. **Best submission time:** summer. **Response time:** 2 months.

MILWAUKEE PUBLIC THEATRE
(Founded 1974)
626 East Kilbourn Ave, #802; Milwaukee, WI 53202-3237; (414) 347-1685,
    FAX 347-1685 (call first); E-mail bleigh@omnifest.uwm.edu
Barbara Leigh, *Co-Artistic/Producing Director*

Submission procedure: no unsolicited scripts; synopsis and letter of inquiry with SASE for response. **Types of material:** full-length plays, one-acts, translations, adaptations, plays for young audiences, cabaret/revues, clown/vaudeville shows. **Special interests:** works with cast of 1–3 playing multiple roles; political satire; social-political and regional or local themes; plays dealing with disabilities; interart works; new clown/vaudeville shows; works for young and family audiences. **Facilities:** no permanent facility. **Production considerations:** simple production demands; productions tour. **Best submission time:** year-round for plays dealing with disabilities; Sep only for all other submissions. **Response time:** 6 months letter; 12 months script. **Special programs:** outdoor park performances.

MILWAUKEE REPERTORY THEATER
(Founded 1954)
108 East Wells St; Milwaukee, WI 53202; (414) 224-1761
Joseph Hanreddy, *Artistic Director*

Submission procedure: no unsolicited scripts; agent submission. **Types of material:** full-length plays, translations, adaptations, cabaret/revues. **Facilities:** Powerhouse Theatre, 720 seats, thrust stage; Stiemke Theatre, 200 seats, flexible

56 / PRODUCTION

stage; Stackner Cabaret, 100 seats, cabaret stage. **Production considerations:** works for cabaret must not exceed 80 minutes in length. **Best submission time:** year-round. **Response time:** 2–3 months.

MINT THEATER COMPANY
(Founded 1992)
311 West 43rd St, 5th Floor; New York, NY 10036; (212) 315-9434
Jonathan Bank, *Artistic Director*

Submission procedure: synopsis, 10-page dialogue sample and letter of inquiry. **Types of material:** full-length plays, translations, adaptations. **Facilities:** Mint Space, 74 seats, black box. **Best submission time:** year-round. **Response time:** 3 months letter; 9 months script.

MISSOURI REPERTORY THEATRE
(Founded 1964)
4949 Cherry St; Kansas City, MO 64110-2499; (816) 235-2727, FAX 235-5367;
    E-mail kreece@cctr.umkc.edu
George Keathley, *Artistic Director*

Submission procedure: no unsolicited scripts; synopsis and letter of inquiry. **Types of material:** full-length plays, translations, adaptations. **Facilities:** Helen F. Spencer Theatre, 740 seats, modified thrust stage. **Best submission time:** year-round. **Response time:** 1 month letter; script varies. **Special programs:** Playwrights' Stage: scripts developed through series of readings, possibly leading to production.

MIXED BLOOD THEATRE COMPANY
(Founded 1975)
1501 South Fourth St; Minneapolis, MN 55454; (612) 338-0937
David Kunz, *Script Czar*

Submission procedure: no unsolicited scripts; synopsis and letter of inquiry. **Types of material:** full-length plays, musicals, cabaret/revues. **Special interests:** comedies. **Facilities:** Main Stage, 200 seats, flexible stage. **Best submission time:** Aug–Jan. **Response time:** 1 month letter; 2–6 months script. **Special programs:** We Don't Need No Stinkin' Dramas (see Prizes).

THE MONTANA REPERTORY THEATRE
(Founded 1968)
Department of Drama and Dance; The University of Montana;
    Missoula, MT 59812-1582; (406) 243-6809, FAX 243-5726
Greg Johnson, *Artistic Director*

Submission procedure: no unsolicited scripts; synopsis, resume and letter of inquiry. **Types of material:** full-length plays, one-acts, musicals. **Special interests:** plays by and about Native Americans. **Facilities:** touring company. **Best submission time:** summer. **Response time:** 3 months letter; 6 months script.

MOVING ARTS
(Founded 1992)
1822 Hyperion Ave; Los Angeles, CA 90027; (213) 665-8961, FAX 665-1816;
 E-mail movnarts@primenet.com;
 Web http://www.primenet.com/~movnarts
Troy Nichols, *Literary Director*

Submission procedure: no unsolicited scripts; synopsis, dialogue sample, resume and letter of inquiry. **Types of material:** full-length plays, translations, adaptations. **Special interests:** work previously unproduced on West Coast. **Facilities:** Moving Arts Theatre, 36 seats, black box. **Production considerations:** cast limit of 7; modest production demands; no wing or fly space. **Best submission time:** year-round. **Response time:** 1–3 months letter; 6–8 months script.

MUSIC-THEATRE GROUP
(Founded 1971)
30 West 26th St, Suite 1001; New York, NY 10010; (212) 366-5260 ext 22, FAX 366-5265
Lyn Austin, *Producing Director*
Diane Wondisford, *General Director*

Submission procedure: no unsolicited scripts; direct solicitation to playwright or agent. **Types of material:** music-theatre works, operas, cabaret. **Special interests:** work not previously professionally produced only; experimental musical works; collaborations between music-theatre, dance and the visual arts. **Facilities:** no permanent facility.

NATIONAL THEATRE OF THE DEAF
(Founded 1967)
Box 659; Chester, CT 06412; (860) 526-4971 (voice), -4974 (TTY), FAX 526-0066
Camille Jeter and Will Rhys, *Artistic Directors*

Submission procedure: no unsolicited scripts; synopsis, character breakdown, sample pages and letter of inquiry with SASE for response. **Types of material:** full-length plays, adaptations, plays for young audiences. **Special interests:** work not previously professionally produced only; deaf issues; culturally diverse plays. **Facilities:** touring company. **Production considerations:** cast limit of 10; production must tour. **Best submission time:** year-round. **Response time:** 1 month letter; 3–6 months script.

NAUTILUS MUSIC-THEATER
(Formerly New Music-Theater Ensemble)
(Founded 1986)
308 Prince St, #250; St. Paul, MN 55101; (612) 298-9913, FAX 298-9924
Ben Krywosz, *Artistic Director*

Submission procedure: no unsolicited scripts; direct solicitation to playwright or

58 / PRODUCTION

agent. **Types of material:** musicals, music-theatre works, opera. **Facilities:** Southern Theater, 150 seats, proscenium stage; Nautilus Studio, 40 seats, black box. **Special programs:** Composer/Librettist Studio: annual 2-week music-theatre lab for Minnesota composers and writers only; send postcard with name and address for information.

NEBRASKA REPERTORY THEATRE
(Founded 1968)
215 Temple Bldg; 12th and R Sts; Lincoln, NE 68588-0201; (402) 472-2072, FAX 472-9055; E-mail jeh@unlgrad1.unl.edu
Kevin Paul Hofeditz, *Executive Director*

Submission procedure: no unsolicited scripts; synopsis and letter of inquiry with SASE for response. **Types of material:** full-length plays, one-acts, musicals. **Special interests:** unpublished scripts for NEW THEATRE series (see below); plays that contribute to multicultural awareness. **Facilities:** Howell Theatre, 380 seats, proscenium stage; Studio Theatre, 180 seats, black box. **Production considerations:** simple set for Studio Theatre. **Best submission time:** Aug–Feb. **Response time:** 1 month letter; 2–6 months script. **Special programs:** NEW THEATRE: reading and performance series.

NEBRASKA THEATRE CARAVAN
(Founded 1976)
6915 Cass St; Omaha, NE 68132; (402) 553-4890, FAX 553-6288; E-mail necaravan@aol.com
Richard L. Scott, *Managing Director*

Submission procedure: no unsolicited scripts; synopsis and letter of inquiry. **Types of material:** full-length plays, adaptations, plays for young audiences, musicals. **Facilities:** touring company. **Production considerations:** cast limit of 12, 1 set. **Best submission time:** year-round. **Response time:** 1 month letter; 3 months script.

NEW AMERICAN THEATER
(Founded 1972)
118 North Main Street; Rockford, IL 61101; (815) 963-9454, FAX 963-7215
William Gregg, *Producing Artistic Director*

Submission procedure: no unsolicited scripts; agent submission. **Types of material:** full-length plays, adapatations, cabaret/revues. **Facilities:** Mainstage, 282 seats, thrust stage; Second stage, 90 seats, flexible. **Production considerations:** small-to-medium cast size; modest production demands. **Best submission time:** fall. **Response time:** 3 months letter; 3 months script.

NEW DRAMATISTS

See Membership and Service Organizations.

New Federal Theatre
(Founded 1970)
292 Henry St; New York, NY 10002; (212) 353-1176, FAX 353-1088
Woodie King, Jr., *Producing Director*
(Ms.) Pat White, *Company Manager*

Submission procedure: no unsolicited scripts; professional recommendation. **Types of material:** full-length plays. **Special interests:** social and political issues; family and community themes related to minorities. **Facilities:** Henry Street Settlement Abron Arts Center: Harry Dejour Theatre, 350 seats, proscenium stage; Recital Hall, 100 seats, 3/4-arena stage; Experimental Theatre, 100 seats, endstage. **Production considerations:** small cast, no more than 2 sets. **Best submission time:** year-round. **Response time:** 5 months.

The New Group
(Founded 1991)
85 Fifth Ave, New York, NY 10003
Kevin Scott, *Literary Manager*

Submission procedure: accepts unsolicited scripts with resume (only 1 submission per playwright per year). **Types of material:** full-length plays. **Special interests:** work not previously produced in New York City only; "plays which reflect the spirit of our times and tell their stories with immediacy, fearlessness and discipline." **Facilities:** no permanent facility. **Best submission time:** year-round. **Response time:** 6 months. **Special programs:** Playwrights Unit: weekly developmental workshop with playwrights and actors; writers admitted for 3 months based on quality of submitted script.

New Jersey Shakespeare Festival
(Founded 1962)
c/o Drew University; 36 Madison Ave; Madison, NJ 07940; (201) 408-3278, FAX 408-3361
Bonnie J. Monte, *Artistic Director*

Submission procedure: no unsolicited scripts; synopsis and letter of inquiry. **Types of material:** full-length plays, translations, adaptations, solo pieces. **Special interests:** translations and/or adaptations of classic works only. **Facilities:** Festival Theatre, 238 seats, thrust stage. **Production considerations:** modest technical demands; limited wing space. **Best submission time:** no synopses before Sep 1998. **Response time:** 2 months letter; 1 month script.

New Repertory Theatre
(Founded 1985)
Box 418; Newton Highlands, MA 02161; (617) 332-7058, FAX 527-5217
Rick Lombardo, *Artistic Director*

Submission procedure: no unsolicited scripts; synopsis, dialogue sample and letter of inquiry. **Types of material:** full-length plays, translations, adaptations. **Special**

interests: multicultural themes; intimate, interpersonal themes. **Facilities:** New Repertory Theatre, 170 seats, thrust stage. **Production considerations:** cast limit of 7. **Best submission time:** May–Aug. **Response time:** 6 months.

NEW STAGE THEATRE
(Founded 1966)
Box 4792; Jackson, MS 39296-4792; (601) 948-0143, FAX 948-3538
John Maxwell, *Artistic Director*

Submission procedure: no unsolicited scripts; synopsis and letter of inquiry. **Types of material:** full-length plays, solo pieces. **Facilities:** Meyer Crystal Auditorium, 364 seats, proscenium stage. **Production considerations:** cast of 3–8. **Best submission time:** summer–fall. **Response time:** 4 weeks letter; 3 months script. **Special programs:** Eudora Welty New Play Series: public readings of 8 new plays every year; full production of a new play every season.

NEW TUNERS THEATRE
(Founded 1969)
1225 West Belmont; Chicago, IL 60657; (773) 929-7367, FAX 327-1404;
    E-mail judytune@aol.com
Judy Myers, *Music Director*

Submission procedure: no unsolicited scripts; synopsis, 3-song cassette, letter of inquiry with SASE for response. **Types of material:** musicals. **Facilities:** North Theatre, 150 seats, thrust stage; South Theatre, 150 seats, proscenium stage; West Theatre, 150 seats, proscenium stage. **Best submission time:** Jan. **Response time:** 2 months letter; 6 months script. **Special programs:** Annual Festival of Staged Readings in Jul; New Tuners Workshop: new musical developmental workshop; *deadline:* 1 Aug 1998; *dates:* Sep–Jul.

NEW YORK STAGE AND FILM
(Founded 1984)
515 Madison Ave, 28th Floor; New York, NY 10022; (212) 750-6703,
    FAX 750-6784
Peter Manning, *Producer*

Submission procedure: accepts unsolicited scripts with letter of inquiry. **Types of material:** full-length plays. **Facilities:** Powerhouse Theatre, 135 seats, proscenium stage; Coalbin, 110 seats, black box. **Best submission time:** 1 Sep–31 Oct only. **Response time:** 3 months.

NEW YORK STATE THEATRE INSTITUTE
(Founded 1976)
155 River St; Troy, NY 12180; (518) 274-3200, FAX 274-3815
Patricia Di Benedetto Snyder, *Producing Artistic Director*

Submission procedure: no unsolicited scripts; synopsis, cast/scene breakdown and letter of inquiry. **Types of material:** full-length plays, adaptations, musicals.

Special interests: mainly presents works for family audiences. **Facilities:** Schacht Fine Arts Center, 900 seats, proscenium stage. **Best submission time:** Mar–Sep. **Response time:** 2–4 weeks. **Special programs:** new works developmental workshops; playwrights receive staged reading or workshop production, negotiable remuneration, travel and housing.

NEW YORK THEATRE WORKSHOP
(Founded 1979)
79 East 4th St; New York, NY 10003; (212) 780-9037
Mandy Mishell, *Artistic Associate, Literary*

Submission procedure: no unsolicited scripts; synopsis, 10-page sample scene, resume and letter of inquiry. **Types of material:** full-length plays, one-acts, translations, music-theatre works, solo pieces, proposals for performance projects. **Special interests:** socially relevant and/or minority issues; innovative form and language. **Facilities:** 79 East 4th Street Theatre, 150 seats, proscenium stage. **Best submission time:** fall–spring. **Response time:** 4 weeks letter; 5 months script. **Special programs:** Mondays at Three: reading series, developmental workshops and symposiums. Summer writing residency. Van Lier Playwriting Fellowship for emerging writers of color based in New York. (see Fellowships and Grants).

NEXT THEATRE COMPANY
(Founded 1981)
927 Noyes St; Evanston, IL 60201; (847) 475-6763, FAX 475-6767;
　　　E-mail sarah@lightoperaworks.org
Sarah Tucker, *Associate Artistic Director*

Submission procedure: no unsolicited scripts; synopsis, 10–15 pages of dialogue and letter of inquiry. **Types of material:** full-length plays, translations, adaptations. **Facilities:** Mainstage, 175 seats, proscenium stage. **Production considerations:** no fly space; limited wing space. **Best submission time:** year-round. **Response time:** 1 month letter; 1–3 months script.

NONE OF THE ABOVE THEATRE COMPANY
(Founded 1981)
425 East 76th St, Suite 6B; New York, NY 10021; (212) 861-4998
Robert Liebowitz, *Artistic Director*

Submission procedure: no unsolicited scripts; synopsis, first 10 pages of script and letter of inquiry. **Types of material:** full-length plays, one-acts. **Special interests:** plays dealing with "the varied splendor of life in New York City." **Facilities:** Theatre 22, 75 seats, black box. **Production considerations:** cast limit of 10; modest production demands; limited wing space. **Best submission time:** year-round. **Response time:** 2 weeks letter; 6–8 weeks script.

Northlight Theatre
(Founded 1975)
600 Davis St; Evanston, IL 60201; (847) 679-9501, ext 3303, FAX 869-9445
Cecilie Keenan, *Assistant Artistic Director*

Submission procedure: no unsolicited scripts; synopsis and letter of inquiry. **Types of material:** full-length plays, translations, adaptations, musicals, solo pieces. **Special interests:** translations and adaptations of "lost" plays; the public world and public issues; plays of ideas; works that are passionate and/or hilarious; stylistic exploration and complexity; no domestic realism. **Facilities:** Northlight Theatre, 345 seats, thrust stage. **Best submission time:** Sep–Feb. **Response time:** 1 month letter; 2–4 months script.

Novel Stages
(Founded 1989)
Box 58879; Philadelphia, PA 19102-8879; (215) 836-0222, FAX 844-2060
Clista Townsend, *Artistic Associate*

Submission procedure: no unsolicited scripts; synopsis and letter of inquiry with SASP for response. **Types of material:** full-length plays, one-acts, translations, adaptations, plays for young audiences, solo pieces. **Facilities:** Stage III at 1619 Walnut St, 130 seats, endstage. **Production considerations:** simple set; no fly space, very little wing space. **Best submission time:** year-round. **Response time:** 6 months letter; 9–12 months script.

Odyssey Theatre Ensemble
(Founded 1969)
2055 South Sepulveda Blvd; Los Angeles, CA 90025; (310) 477-2055
Jan Lewis, *Director of Literary Programs*

Submission procedure: no unsolicited scripts; synopsis, 8–10 pages of dialogue, play's production history (if any), resume and letter of inquiry with SASE for response; include cassette for musicals. **Types of material:** full-length plays, translations, adaptations, musicals. **Special interests:** culturally diverse works; works with innovative form or provocative subject matter; works exploring the enduring questions of human existence and the possibilities of the live-theatre experience; works with political or sociological impact. **Facilities:** Odyssey 1, 99 seats, flexible stage; Odyssey 2, 99 seats, thrust stage; Odyssey 3, 99 seats, endstage. **Production considerations:** plays must be 90 minutes or longer. **Best submission time:** year-round. **Response time:** 2–4 weeks letter; 6 months script.

Old Globe Theatre
(Founded 1935)
Box 2171; San Diego, CA 92112-2171; (619) 231-1941
Raúl Moncada, *Literary Manager*

Submission procedure: no unsolicited scripts; synopsis and letter of inquiry with SASE for response. **Types of material:** full-length plays, translations, adaptations.

Special interests: well-crafted plays; strongly theatrical material. **Facilities:** Lowell Davies Festival Stage, 620 seats, outdoor stage; Old Globe Theatre, 581 seats, modified thrust stage; Cassius Carter Centre Stage, 225 seats, arena stage. **Production considerations:** prefers cast limit of 8. **Best submission time:** year-round. **Response time:** 2–3 months letter; 6–10 months script.

OLDCASTLE THEATRE COMPANY
(Founded 1972)
Box 1555; Bennington, VT 05201-1555; (802) 447-1267, FAX 442-3704
Eric Peterson, *Producing Artistic Director*

Submission procedure: accepts unsolicited scripts. **Types of material:** full-length plays, musicals. **Facilities:** Bennington Center for the Arts, 300 seats, modified proscenium stage. **Best submission time:** winter. **Response time:** 4–6 months.

OLNEY THEATRE CENTER FOR THE ARTS
(Founded 1937)
2001 Olney-Sandy Spring Rd; Olney, MD 20832; (301) 924-4485, FAX 924-2654
David Jackson, *Literary Manager*

Submission procedure: no unsolicited scripts; professional recommendation. **Types of material:** full-length plays, translations, adaptations, solo pieces. **Facilities:** Mainstage, 500 seats, proscenium stage. **Production considerations:** cast limit of 8. **Best submission time:** year-round. **Response time:** 6 months.

OMAHA THEATER COMPANY FOR YOUNG PEOPLE
(Founded 1949)
2001 Farnam St; Omaha, NE 68102; (402) 345-9718, FAX 345-7255
James Larson, *Artistic Director*

Submission procedure: no unsolicited scripts; professional recommendation. **Types of material:** full-length plays. **Special interests:** plays for family audiences only; plays based on children's literature and contemporary issues; multicultural themes. **Facilities:** Omaha Theater Company, 932 seats, proscenium stage; second stage, 150 seats, black box. **Production considerations:** cast limit of 15; prefers unit set. **Best submission time:** year-round. **Response time:** 6 months.

ONTOLOGICAL-HYSTERIC THEATER
(Founded 1968)
260 West Broadway; New York, NY 10013; (212) 941-8911, FAX 334-5149

Submission procedure: no unsolicited scripts; direct solicitation to playwright or agent. **Types of material:** full-length plays. **Facilities:** Ontological at St. Mark's Theater, 80 seats, black box.

THE OPEN EYE THEATER
(Founded 1972)
Box 959; Margaretville, NY 12455; (914) 586-1660, FAX 586-1689
Amie Brockway, *Producing Artistic Director*

Submission procedure: no unsolicited scripts; synopsis and letter of inquiry with self-addressed, unstamped envelope for possible response. **Types of material:** full-length plays, one-acts, translations, adaptations. **Special interests:** plays for multigenerational audiences only; culturally diverse themes; plays with music; ensemble plays; plays of any length (10 minutes or more) by upstate NY residents, especially Catskill Mountain-area writers, about life in rural upstate NY. **Facilities:** no permanent facility. **Production considerations:** minimal set. **Best submission time:** Oct–Apr. **Response time:** 1 week letter (if interested); 3–6 months script. **Special programs:** New Play Works: new-play developmental program of readings and workshop productions.

OREGON SHAKESPEARE FESTIVAL
(Founded 1935)
Box 158; Ashland, OR 97520; (541) 482-2111, FAX 482-0446
Douglas Langworthy, *Director of Literary Development and Dramaturgy*

Submission procedure: no unsolicited scripts; professional recommendation. **Types of material:** full-length plays, translations, adaptations. **Special interests:** plays of ideas; language-oriented plays; translations; adaptations; submissions by women and minorities encouraged. **Facilities:** Elizabethan Theatre, 1194 seats, outdoor Elizabethan stage; Angus Bowmer Theatre, 600 seats, thrust stage; Black Swan, 140 seats, black box. **Best submission time:** year-round. **Response time:** 3 months. **Special programs:** reading series; commissioning programs; developmental workshops.

ORGANIC TOUCHSTONE COMPANY
(Formerly Organic Theater Company)
(Founded 1969)
3319 North Clark St; Chicago, IL 60657; (773) 477-5779, FAX 477-8993
Ina Marlowe, *Producing Artistic Director*

Submission procedure: no unsolicited scripts; direct solicitation to playwright or agent. **Types of material:** full-length plays, long one-acts. **Facilities:** Mainstage, 250–350 seats, modified thrust stage; Studio Theatre, 70 seats, thrust stage.

PAN ASIAN REPERTORY THEATRE
(Founded 1977)
47 Great Jones St; New York, NY 10012; (212) 505-5655, FAX 505-6014
Tisa Chang, *Artistic/Producing Director*

Submission procedure: accepts unsolicited scripts with resume. **Types of material:** full-length plays, translations, adaptations, musicals. **Special interests:** Asian or Asian-American themes only. **Facilities:** St. Clement's Theatre, 150 seats, 38' x 40' open stage. **Production considerations:** prefers cast limit of 8. **Best submission time:** summer. **Response time:** 9 months. **Special programs:** staged readings and workshops.

THE PASADENA PLAYHOUSE
(Founded 1917)
39 South El Molino Ave; Pasadena, CA 91101; (818) 792-8672

Submission procedure: no unsolicited scripts; synopsis, character breakdown, first 15 pages of text and letter of inquiry. **Types of material:** full-length plays, musicals. **Special interests:** works with broad commercial appeal. **Facilities:** The Pasadena Playhouse, 686 seats, proscenium stage. **Production considerations:** cast size of 2–7; 1 set or unit set; modest musical requirements. **Best submission time:** year-round. **Response time:** 3 months letter; 12 months script.

PEGASUS PLAYERS
(Founded 1978)
1145 West Wilson; Chicago, IL 60640; (773) 878-9761, FAX 271-8057;
Arlene Crewdson, *Executive Director*

Submission procedure: no unsolicited scripts; synopsis and letter of inquiry. **Types of material:** full-length plays, translations, adaptations, musicals, solo pieces. **Facilities:** The O'Rourke Center for the Performing Arts, 250 seats, proscenium stage. **Best submission time:** year-round. **Response time:** 1 month letter; 4–6 months script. **Special programs:** Chicago Young Playwrights Festival: annual Jan festival of plays by Chicago-area high school students; write for information.

PEGASUS THEATRE
(Founded 1985)
3916 Main St; Dallas, TX 75226-1228; (214) 821-6005, FAX 826-1671
Steve Erwin, *Literary Manager*

Submission procedure: no unsolicited scripts; synopsis, 10-page dialogue sample, character breakdown and letter of inquiry. **Types of material:** full-length plays. **Special interests:** contemporary satire. **Facilities:** Mainstage, 141 seats, proscenium stage. **Production considerations:** cast limit of 10, single set, limited fly space. **Best submission time:** Mar–Jun. **Response time:** 1 month letter; 6 months script.

PENDRAGON THEATRE
(Founded 1980)
148 River St; Saranac Lake, NY 12983-2031; (518) 891-1854, FAX 891-7012; E-mail pdragon@northnet.org;
 Web http://www.northnet.org/pendragon
Bob Pettee, *Managing Director*

Submission procedure: no unsolicited scripts; synopsis, dialogue sample and letter of inquiry with SASP for response. **Types of material:** full-length plays, plays for young audiences. **Facilities:** Pendragon Theatre, 132 seats, black box. **Production**

66 / PRODUCTION

considerations: cast limit of 8; simple set. **Best submission time:** year-round. **Response time:** 3–4 weeks letter; 3 months script.

PENGUIN REPERTORY COMPANY
(Founded 1977)
Box 91; Stony Point, NY 10980; (914) 786-2873, FAX 786-5919
Joe Brancato, *Artistic Director*

Submission procedure: accepts unsolicited scripts. **Types of material:** full-length plays, adaptations. **Facilities:** Barn Playhouse, 108 seats, proscenium stage. **Production considerations:** cast limit of 4; simple set. **Best submission time:** Jun–Sep. **Response time:** 3 months.

PENNSYLVANIA SHAKESPEARE FESTIVAL
(Founded 1991)
2755 Station Ave; Center Valley, PA 18034; (610) 282-9455, FAX 282-2240
J. Kline, *Assistant Professor*

Submission procedure: no unsolicited scripts; synopsis and letter of inquiry. **Types of material:** full-length plays. **Facilities:** Mainstage, 473 seats, modified thrust stage; Arena Stage, 215 seats, arena stage. **Best submission time:** year-round. **Response time:** 6 months letter; 6 months script.

PENOBSCOT THEATRE COMPANY
(Founded 1977)
183 Main St; Bangor, ME 04401; (207) 942-3333, FAX 947-6678
Mark Torres, *Producing Artistic Director*

Submission procedure: no unsolicited scripts; synopsis and letter of inquiry. **Types of material:** full-length plays, plays for young audiences. **Special interests:** new American plays. **Facilities:** Penobscot Theatre, 132 seats, proscenium/thrust stage. **Production considerations:** small cast, limited production requirements; small performance space. **Best submission time:** late fall. **Response time:** 1 month letter; 2 months script. **Special programs:** play reading series in late spring; scripts selected through theatre's normal submission procedure.

THE PENUMBRA THEATRE COMPANY
(Founded 1976)
The Martin Luther King Bldg; 270 North Kent St; St. Paul, MN 55102-1794;
    (612) 224-4601, FAX 224-7074
Lou Bellamy, *Artistic Director*

Submission procedure: accepts unsolicited scripts with resume. **Types of material:** full-length plays, one-acts, translations, adaptations, plays for young audiences, musicals. **Special interests:** works that address the African-American experience. **Facilities:** Hallie Q. Brown Theatre, 260 seats, proscenium/thrust stage. **Best submission time:** year-round. **Response time:** 6–9 months. **Special programs:** Cornerstone Dramaturgy and Development Project (see Development).

THE PEOPLE'S LIGHT AND THEATRE COMPANY
(Founded 1974)
39 Conestoga Rd; Malvern, PA 19355-1798; (215) 647-1900
Alda Cortese, *Literary Manager*

Submission procedure: no unsolicited scripts; synopsis, cast list, 10 pages of dialogue and letter of inquiry. **Types of material:** full-length plays, translations, adaptations. **Facilities:** People's Light and Theatre, 350 seats, flexible stage; Steinbright Stage, 99–150 seats, flexible stage. **Production considerations:** prefers cast limit of 12, 1 set or unit set. **Best submission time:** year-round. **Response time:** 2 weeks letter; 8–10 months script.

PERSEVERANCE THEATRE
(Founded 1979)
914 3rd St; Douglas, AK 99824; (907) 364-2421, -2151, FAX 364-2603;
   E-mail persthr@ptialaska.net
Molly Smith, *Artistic Director*

Submission procedure: no unsolicited scripts; synopsis, list of previous productions, resume and letter of inquiry. **Types of material:** full-length plays, one-acts, solo pieces. **Special interests:** new plays by AK playwrights; plays about ethnic experiences, gender, sexual orientation and disabilities. **Facilities:** Mainstage, 150 seats, thrust stage; Phoenix Stage, 50–75 seats, flexible space. **Best submission time:** year-round. **Response time:** 2 months letter; 6 months script.

PHILADELPHIA THEATRE COMPANY
(Founded 1974)
The Belgravia, Suite 300; 1811 Chestnut St; Philadelphia, PA 19103;
   (215) 568-1920, FAX 568-1944
John Rea, *Literary Associate*

Submission procedure: no unsolicited scripts; agent submission. **Types of material:** full-length plays, small-scale musicals, solo pieces. **Special interests:** new American plays; social/humanistic themes; sense of theatricality; no mysteries. **Facilities:** Plays and Players Theater, 324 seats, proscenium stage. **Best submission time:** year-round. **Response time:** 6–8 months. **Special programs:** STAGES: program of staged readings.

PHOENIX THEATRE
(Founded 1920)
100 East McDowell Rd; Phoenix, AZ 85004; (602) 258-1974, FAX 253-3626
Michael Mitchell, *Artistic Director*

Submission procedure: no unsolicited scripts; synopsis and letter of inquiry with SASE for response; send production history if available. **Types of material:** plays for young audiences, musicals, cabaret/revues. **Special interests:** plays suitable for a general audience. **Facilities:** Mainstage, 346 seats, proscenium stage; Cookie

Company, 175 seats, arena stage. **Best submission time:** Jan, Aug. **Response time:** 1 month letter; 3 months script.

THE PHOENIX THEATRE
(Founded 1983)
749 North Park Ave; Indianapolis, IN 46202; (317) 635-7529, FAX 635-7529
Bryan Fonseca, *Producing Director*

Submission procedure: no unsolicited scripts. **Types of material:** full-length plays, one-acts. **Facilities:** Mainstage, 150 seats, proscenium stage; Underground, 75 seats, black box. **Special programs:** The Festival of Emerging American Theatre (FEAT) Competition (see Prizes).

PING CHONG & COMPANY
(Founded 1975)
47 Great Jones St; New York, NY 10012; (212) 529-1557, FAX 529-1703;
E-mail 103034.434@compuserve.com

Submission procedure: no unsolicited scripts; direct solicitation to playwright. **Types of material:** full-length works by company only. **Facilities:** no permanent facility.

PIONEER THEATRE COMPANY
(Founded 1962)
University of Utah; Salt Lake City, UT 84112; (801) 581-6356, FAX 581-5472
Charles Morey, *Artistic Director*

Submission procedure: no unsolicited scripts; synopsis and letter of inquiry. **Types of material:** full-length plays, translations, adaptations, musicals. **Facilities:** Pioneer Memorial Theatre, 1000 seats, proscenium stage. **Best submission time:** fall. **Response time:** 1 month letter; 6 months script.

PIRATE PLAYHOUSE—ISLAND THEATRE
(Founded 1991)
2200 Periwinkle Way; Sanibel Island, FL 33957; (941) 472-4109, FAX 472-0055;
E-mail pirateplay@aol.com
Robert Cacioppo, *Artistic Director*

Submission procedure: no unsolicited scripts; synopsis, 10-page dialogue sample, character breakdown and letter of inquiry with SASP for response. **Types of material:** full-length plays, plays for young audiences, musicals, cabaret/revues, solo pieces. **Facilities:** Pirate Playhouse, 180 seats, thrust/proscenium/arena stage. **Best submission time:** year-round. **Response time:** 1–3 months letter; 3–5 months script.

PITTSBURGH PUBLIC THEATER
(Founded 1975)
Allegheny Square; Pittsburgh, PA 15212-5349; (412) 323-8200, FAX 323-8550
Rob Zellers, *Literary Manager*

Submission procedure: no unsolicited scripts; synopsis, dialogue sample and letter of inquiry with SASE for response. **Types of material:** full-length plays, translations, adaptations, musicals. **Facilities:** Theodore L. Hazlett, Jr. Theater, 457 seats, thrust or arena stage. **Best submission time:** year-round. **Response time:** 1 month letter; 3 months script.

PLAYHOUSE ON THE SQUARE
(Founded 1968)
51 South Cooper St; Memphis, TN 38104; (901) 725-0776, FAX 272-7530
Jackie Nichols, *Executive Producer*

Submission procedure: accepts unsolicited scripts. **Types of material:** full-length plays, musicals. **Facilities:** Playhouse on the Square, 250 seats, proscenium stage; Circuit Playhouse, 136 seats, proscenium stage. **Best submission time:** year-round. **Response time:** 3–5 months. **Special programs:** Playhouse on the Square New Play Competition (see Prizes).

PLAYMAKERS REPERTORY COMPANY
(Founded 1976)
CB# 3235 Graham Memorial Bldg, 052A; Chapel Hill, NC 27599-3235;
(919) 962-1132, FAX 962-4069
Milly S. Barranger, *Producing Director*

Submission procedure: no unsolicited scripts; professional recommendation. **Types of material:** full-length plays, translations, adaptations, solo pieces. **Facilities:** Paul Green Theatre, 498 seats, thrust stage. **Best submission time:** Aug–May. **Response time:** 6 months.

THE PLAYWRIGHTS' CENTER

See Membership and Service Organizations.

PLAYWRIGHTS HORIZONS
(Founded 1971)
416 West 42nd St; New York, NY 10036-6896; (212) 564-1235, FAX 594-0296
Sonya Sobieski, *Literary Manager*

Submission procedure: accepts unsolicited scripts with resume and cover letter; if necessary, will accept synopsis, dialogue sample and letter of inquiry; for musicals, send script and cassette (no synopses). **Types of material:** full-length plays, musicals. **Special interests:** works by American writers only; works with strong sense of language that take theatrical risks. **Facilities:** Mainstage, 145 seats, proscenium stage; Studio Theater, 72 seats, black box. **Best submission time:** year-round. **Response time:** 6 weeks letter; 3–6 months script.

POPE THEATRE COMPANY
(Founded 1987)
262 South Ocean Blvd; Manalapan, FL 33462; (407) 585-3404, FAX 588-4708
Louis Tyrrell, *Producing Director*

Submission procedure: no unsolicited scripts; agent submission. **Types of material:** full-length plays, plays for young audiences. **Special interests:** contemporary issues and ideas. **Facilities:** Lois Pope Theatre, 250 seats, thrust stage. **Production considerations:** cast of 2–6; 1 set. **Best submission time:** year-round. **Response time:** 3–4 months. **Special programs:** reading series.

PORTLAND CENTER STAGE
(Founded 1988)
1111 Southwest Broadway; Portland, OR 97205; (503) 248-6309
Elizabeth Huddle, *Producing Artistic Director*

Submission procedure: no unsolicited scripts; synopsis and letter of inquiry. **Types of material:** full-length plays, translations, adaptations. **Facilities:** Intermediate Theatre, Portland Center for the Performing Arts, 860 seats, proscenium stage. **Production considerations:** prefers cast of 8–12. **Best submission time:** year-round. **Response time:** 1–2 months letter; 2–3 months script.

PORTLAND REPERTORY THEATRE
(Founded 1980)
2 World Trade Center; 25 Southwest Salmon St; Portland, OR 97204-3233;
    (503) 224-4491, FAX 224-1316
Literary Manager/Dramaturg

Submission procedure: no unsolicited scripts; synopsis, first 10–15 pages of script, character breakdown, set description and letter of inquiry with SASE for response. **Types of material:** full-length plays, translations, adaptations. **Facilities:** Portland Repertory Theatre, 230 seats, proscenium stage. **Production considerations:** cast limit of 10; maximum 2 sets. **Best submission time:** May–Aug. **Response time:** 4 months letter; 6–12 months script. **Special programs:** staged reading series.

PORTLAND STAGE COMPANY
(Founded 1970)
Box 1458; Portland, ME 04104; (207) 774-1043
Matthew Arbour, *Literary Manager*

Submission procedure: no unsolicited scripts; synopsis, dialogue sample and letter of inquiry. **Types of material:** full-length plays, translations, adaptations. **Facilities:** Performing Arts Center Theatre, 290 seats, proscenium stage; PSC Rehearsal Hall, 90 seats, flexible space (readings only). **Best submission time:** Sep–May. **Response time:** 3 months letter; 6 months script. **Special programs:** in-house play readings.

PRIMARY STAGES COMPANY
(Founded 1983)
584 9th Ave; New York, NY 10036; (212) 333-7471, FAX 333-2025
Andrew Leynse, *Literary Manager*

Submission procedure: no unsolicited scripts; synopsis, resume and letter of inquiry with SASE for response; include cassette for musicals. **Types of material:** full-length plays, musicals, solo pieces. **Special interests:** new American plays and musicals previously unproduced in New York City. **Facilities:** Primary Stages Theatre, 99 seats, proscenium stage; Phil Bosakowski Theatre, 65 seats, proscenium stage. **Production considerations:** prefers small cast; single set or unit set; no fly or wing space. **Best submission time:** Sep–Jun. **Response time:** 1 month letter; 3–5 months script. **Special programs:** Ten-Minute Play Festival: festival of single-theme 10-minute plays; by invitation only; *dates:* Oct 1997.

THE PUBLIC THEATER/NEW YORK SHAKESPEARE FESTIVAL
(Founded 1954)
Joseph Papp Public Theater; 425 Lafayette St; New York, NY 10003;
(212) 539-8530, FAX 539-8505
Shelby Jiggetts, *Play Development Department*
Wiley Hausam, *Associate Producer, Musicals*

Submission procedure: no unsolicited scripts; synopsis, 10-page sample scene and letter of inquiry; include cassette of 3–5 songs for musicals and operas. **Types of material:** full-length plays, translations, adaptations, musicals, operas, solo pieces. **Facilities:** Newman Theater, 299 seats, proscenium stage; Anspacher Theater, 275 seats, thrust stage; Martinson Hall, 200 seats, proscenium stage; LuEsther Hall, 150 seats, flexible stage; Shiva Theater, 100 seats, flexible stage. **Best submission time:** year-round. **Response time:** 1 month letter; 6 months script.

THE PURPLE ROSE THEATRE COMPANY
(Founded 1991)
137 Park St; Chelsea, MI 48118; (313) 475-5817, FAX 475-0802
Anthony Caselli, *Literary Manager*

Submission procedure: no unsolicited scripts; synopsis, dialogue sample and letter of inquiry. **Types of material:** full-length plays. **Special interests:** plays that speak to a middle-American audience. **Facilities:** Garage Theatre, 119 seats, thrust stage. **Production considerations:** cast limit of 10; no fly or wing space. **Best submission time:** year-round. **Response time:** 6–9 months. **Special programs:** Playwrights Unit: area playwrights meet monthly to discuss works; developmental workshops: members of Playwrights Unit or playwrights found through theatre's normal submission procedure work with company to develop scripts through readings and conferences.

72 / PRODUCTION

RED EYE
(Founded 1983)
15 West 14th St; Minneapolis, MN 55403-2301; (612) 870-7531;
E-mail redeye@mtn.org
Steve Busa, *Artistic Director*

Submission procedure: no unsolicited scripts; synopsis, 10 pages of dialogue and letter of inquiry with SASE for response. **Types of material:** full-length plays, solo pieces, performance art. **Special interests:** multimedia works. **Facilities:** Mainstage, 76–120 seats, proscenium stage. **Best submission time:** year-round. **Response time:** 6 months letter; 6–9 months script. **Special programs:** Isolated Acts: annual multidisciplinary festival held Feb–Apr, by invitation only.

REPERTORIO ESPAÑOL
(Founded 1968)
138 East 27th St; New York, NY 10016; (212) 889-2850
Robert Weber Federico, *Artistic Associate Producer*

Submission procedure: no unsolicited scripts; synopsis and letter of inquiry. **Types of material:** full-length plays, adaptations, plays for young audiences, musicals, operas. **Special interests:** plays dealing with Hispanic themes. **Facilities:** Gramercy Arts Theatre, 135 seats, proscenium stage. **Production considerations:** small cast. **Best submission time:** summer. **Response time:** 1 month letter; 6 months script.

THE REPERTORY THEATRE OF ST. LOUIS
(Founded 1966)
Box 191730; St. Louis, MO 63119; (314) 968-7340
Susan Gregg, *Associate Artistic Director*

Submission procedure: no unsolicited scripts; synopsis, character breakdown, technical requirements and letter of inquiry. **Types of material:** full-length plays. **Special interests:** nonnaturalistic plays; contemporary social and political issues. **Facilities:** Main Stage, 750 seats, thrust stage; Studio Theatre, 130 seats, black box. **Production considerations:** small cast, modest production demands. **Best submission time:** year-round. **Response time:** 1 month letter; 2 years script. **Special programs:** developmental workshop for new plays; scripts selected through theatre's normal submission procedure.

RIVERSIDE THEATRE
(Founded 1985)
Box 3788; Vero Beach, FL 32964; (407) 231-5860
Sherrie Dee Brewer, *Production Manager*

Submission procedure: no unsolicited scripts; synopsis and letter of inquiry. **Types of material:** full-length plays, translations, adaptations, plays for young audiences, musicals. **Facilities:** Riverside Theatre, 615 seats, proscenium stage; Agnes Wahlstrom Youth Playhouse, 150 seats, flexible stage. **Production considerations:** cast limit of 10. **Best submission time:** spring. **Response time:** 1 month letter (if

PRODUCTION / 73

interested); 3–5 months script. **Special programs:** New Century Voices: play reading series focusing on FL playwrights.

RIVERSIDE THEATRE
(Founded 1981)
Box 1651; Iowa City, IA 52244; (319) 338-7672, FAX 338-7672
Ron Clark, *Artistic Director*

Submission procedure: no unsolicited scripts; synopsis and letter of inquiry. **Types of material:** full-length plays, translations, adaptations, cabaret/revues, solo pieces. **Facilities:** Riverside Theatre, 110 seats, flexible stage. **Production considerations:** small cast; simple set. **Best submission time:** year-round. **Response time:** 1 month letter (if interested); 3–5 months script.

THE ROAD COMPANY
(Founded 1972)
Box 5278 EKS; Johnson City, TN 37603-5278; (423) 926-7726,
    FAX 926-7726 (call first); E-mail roadcomp@aol.com
Christine Murdock, *General Manager*

Submission procedure: no unsolicited scripts; synopsis and letter of inquiry. **Types of material:** full-length plays, one-acts, adaptations, cabaret/revues. **Special interests:** plays suitable for elementary–high school actors only. **Facilities:** Beeson Hall, 100–150 seats, flexible space. **Response time:** 2 months letter; 2 months script.

ROADSIDE THEATER
(Founded 1975)
306 Madison St; Whitesburg, KY 41858; (606) 633-0108, FAX 633-1009;
    E-mail roadsideth@aol.com
Dudley Cocke, *Director*

Submission procedure: no unsolicited scripts; synopsis, dialogue sample and letter of inquiry. **Types of material:** full-length plays. **Special interests:** plays about the Appalachian region only. **Facilities:** Appalshop Theater, 150 seats, thrust stage. **Production considerations:** small cast; simple sets suitable for touring. **Best submission time:** year-round. **Response time:** 2 weeks letter; 1 month script. **Special programs:** reading and workshop series. Playwright residencies initiated by theatre; playwright may not apply.

ROADWORKS PRODUCTIONS
(Founded 1992)
1532 Milwaukee Ave; Chicago, IL 60622; (773) 489-7623, FAX 489-7698; E-mail roadworks@aol.com
Shade Murray, *Literary Manager*

Submission procedure: no unsolicited scripts; synopsis, dialogue sample and letter of inquiry. **Types of material:** full-length plays. **Special interests:** scripts suitable for ensemble aged 20–30; "explosive, high-energy" plays. **Facilities:** no permanent facility. **Best submission time:** Sep–Nov. **Response time:** 1 month letter; 3 months script.

ROUND HOUSE THEATRE
(Founded 1978)
12210 Bushey Dr; Silver Spring, MD 20902; (301) 933-9530, FAX 933-2321
Jerry Whiddon, *Producing Artistic Director*

Submission procedure: no unsolicited scripts; synopsis, dialogue sample, cast breakdown, technical requirements and letter of inquiry. **Types of material:** full-length plays, translations, adaptations, plays for young audiences, musicals. **Special interests:** contemporary issues; new translations of lesser-known classics; experimental works; humorous plays. **Facilities:** Round House Theatre, 216 seats, modified thrust stage. **Production considerations:** cast limit of 6; prefers 1 set. **Best submission time:** year-round. **Response time:** 2 months letter (if interested); at least 12 months script.

SACRAMENTO THEATRE COMPANY
(Founded 1942)
1419 H St; Sacramento, CA 95814; (916) 446-7501, FAX 446-4066
Ernest A. Figueroa, *Associate Artistic Director*

Submission procedure: no unsolicited scripts; synopsis, resume and letter of inquiry with SASE for response. **Types of material:** full-length plays, adaptations, cabaret/revues. **Special interests:** contemporary social and political issues; craftsmanship; theatricality; vital language; "characters an audience will care about." **Facilities:** McClatchy Mainstage, 300 seats, proscenium stage; Stage II, 90 seats, black box. **Production considerations:** cast of 3–5. **Best submission time:** Jun–Dec. **Response time:** 1 month letter; 3 months script.

THE SALT LAKE ACTING COMPANY
(Founded 1970)
168 West 500 N; Salt Lake City, UT 84103; (801) 363-0526
David Mong, *Literary Manager*

Submission procedure: no unsolicited scripts; synopsis, 5–10 pages of dialogue, resume and letter of inquiry with SASE for response. **Types of material:** full-length plays, translations, adaptations, musicals. **Special interests:** western American writers "who understand the unique synergistic effect that playwright, actor and audience enjoy when a work is produced for the stage." **Facilities:** Upstairs, 99–130 seats, thrust stage; Chapel Theatre, 90 seats, thrust stage. **Best submission time:** year-round. **Response time:** 4 months letter; 8 months script. **Special programs:** reading series in winter, spring and fall.

SAN DIEGO REPERTORY THEATRE
(Founded 1976)
79 Horton Plaza; San Diego, CA 92101; (619) 231-3586, FAX 235-0939
Nakissa Etemad, *Resident Dramaturg*

Submission procedure: no unsolicited scripts; synopsis and letter of inquiry. **Types of material:** full-length plays, translations, adaptations, musicals, literary cabaret, mixed-media events. **Special interests:** multiethnic work; hard-hitting social and political work; offbeat hip musicals; dramatic work with unusual incorporation of music; women's issues; sharp-edged comedy; poetic visions; Hispanic plays suitable for presentation in both Spanish and English. **Facilities:** Lyceum Stage, 570 seats, modified thrust stage; Lyceum Space, 270 seats, flexible stage. **Production considerations:** no fly loft in Lyceum Space. **Best submission time:** year-round. **Response time:** 3 months letter; 12 months script. **Special programs:** readings and workshop productions.

SAN JOSE REPERTORY THEATRE
(Founded 1980)
Box 2399; San Jose, CA 95109-2399; (408) 291-2266, FAX 995-0737
Kim Euell, *Director of Play Development*

Submission procedure: no unsolicited scripts; agent submission. **Types of material:** full-length plays, translations, adaptations, musicals, solo pieces. **Special interests:** small-cast musicals. **Facilities:** San Jose Repertory Theatre, 525 seats, proscenium stage. **Best submission time:** Sep–Nov. **Response time:** 1–3 months.

SANTA FE STAGES
(Founded 1995)
105 East Marcy St, Suite 107; Santa Fe, NM 87505; (505) 982-6680,
    FAX 982-6682; E-mail rr19@ix.netcom.com
Martin Platt, *Artistic Director*

Submission procedure: no unsolicited scripts; agent submission. **Types of material:** full-length plays, translations, adaptations. **Special interests:** cutting-edge works. **Facilities:** Greer Garson Theatre, 525 seats, proscenium stage; Weckesser Studio Theatre, 100 seats, flexible stage. **Best submission time:** Sep–Apr. **Response time:** 1 week letter; 3 months script.

SANTA MONICA PLAYHOUSE
(Founded 1962)
1211 4th St; Santa Monica, CA 90401-1391; (310) 394-9779, FAX 393-5573
Chris DeCarlo, *Co-Artistic Director*
Evelyn Rudie, *Co-Artistic Director*

Submission procedure: no unsolicited scripts; synopsis and letter of inquiry. **Types of material:** full-length plays, one-acts, translations, adaptations, plays for young audiences, musicals. **Facilities:** The Main Stage, 88 seats, arena/thrust stage; The Other Space, 70 seats, black box. **Production considerations:** cast limit of 8, simple production demands. **Best submission time:** year-round. **Response time:** 3 months letter; 6 months script.

SEACOAST REPERTORY THEATRE
(Founded 1986)
125 Bow St; Portsmouth, NH 03801; (603) 433-4793, FAX 431-7818
Roy M. Rogosin, *Producing Artistic Director*

Submission procedure: no unsolicited scripts; agent submission (1-page synopsis only; include cassette for musicals). **Types of material:** full-length plays, plays for young audiences, musicals. **Special interests:** new American plays; small-scale musicals; plays for young audiences. **Facilities:** Seacoast Repertory Theatre of the Portsmouth Academy of Performing Arts, 175 seats, thrust stage. **Best submission time:** year-round. **Response time:** 3–6 months.

SEASIDE MUSIC THEATER
(Founded 1977)
Box 2835; Daytona Beach, FL 32120; (904) 252-3394, FAX 252-8991;
    E-mail smthead@aol.com
Lester Malizia, *General Manager*

Submission procedure: no unsolicited scripts; synopsis, cassette of music and letter of inquiry. **Types of material:** musicals for young and adult audiences, cabaret/revues. **Facilities:** Winter Theater, 600 seats, proscenium stage; Summer Repertory Theater, 500 seats, proscenium stage; Theater for Children, 150 seats, modified thrust stage. **Production considerations:** cast limit of 8 for Winter Theater, 30 for Summer Repertory Theater, 10 for Theater for Children; small musical combo for Theater for Children and Winter Theater, 25-member orchestra for Summer Repertory Theater; no wing or orchestra space in Winter Theater; no fly space except in Summer Repertory Theater. **Best submission time:** Sep–Nov. **Response time:** 1 month letter; 3 months script.

SEATTLE CHILDREN'S THEATRE
(Founded 1975)
Box 9640; Seattle, WA 98109-0640; (206) 443-0807
Deborah Frockt, *Dramaturg/Literary Manager*

Submission procedure: accepts unsolicited scripts for Drama School Summerstages only; professional recommendation for all other submissions. **Types of material:** full-length plays for young audiences, including translations, adaptations, musicals, solo pieces. **Special interests:** sophisticated works for young audiences that also appeal to adults. **Facilities:** Charlotte Martin Theatre, 485 seats, proscenium stage; Eve Alvord Theatre, 280 seats, black box. **Best submission time:** year-round. **Response time:** 8 months. **Special programs:** Drama School Summerstages: one-act plays, 30–60 minutes long for student performance; must have roles for 12–18 actors, ages 8–19; submit script with SASE for response to Don Fleming, Program Director. *deadline:* 1 Dec 1997.

SEATTLE REPERTORY THEATRE
(Founded 1963)
155 Mercer St; Seattle, WA 98109; (206) 443-2210
Kurt Beattie, *Artistic Associate/Literary Manager*

Submission procedure: no unsolicited scripts; professional recommendation. **Types of material:** full-length plays, translations, adaptations, musicals, solo pieces. **Facilities:** Seattle Repertory Theatre, 856 seats, proscenium stage; second theatre, 284 seats, proscenium stage. **Best submission time:** year-round. **Response time:** 2–3 months. **Special programs:** New Plays in Process Project: program of workshop productions; playwright receives travel and per diem.

SECOND STAGE THEATRE
(Founded 1979)
Box 1807, Ansonia Station; New York, NY 10023; (212) 787-8302,
    FAX 877-9886
Christopher Burney, *Literary Manager/Dramaturg*

Submission procedure: no unsolicited scripts; synopsis, 5–10-page dialogue sample, resume and letter of inquiry. **Types of material:** full-length plays, adaptations, musicals. **Special interests:** new and previously produced American plays (include production history with script); "heightened" realism; sociopolitical issues; plays by women and minority writers. **Facilities:** McGinn/Cazale Theatre, 108 seats, endstage. **Best submission time:** year-round. **Response time:** 1 month letter; 4–6 months script. **Special programs:** annual series of 4–6 readings of new and previously produced plays.

7 STAGES
(Founded 1979)
1105 Euclid Ave NE; Atlanta, GA 30307; (404) 522-0911
Del Hamilton, *Artistic Director*

Submission procedure: no unsolicited scripts; synopsis, dialogue sample, resume and letter of inquiry. **Types of material:** full-length plays, translations, adaptations, performance pieces. **Special interests:** nontraditional plays and performance texts focusing on social, political or spiritual themes. **Facilities:** 7 Stages, 250 seats, thrust stage; Back Door, 100 seats, flexible stage. **Best submission time:** year-round. **Response time:** 4 months letter; 12 months script.

SHAKESPEARE & COMPANY
(Founded 1978)
The Mount; Box 865; Lenox, MA 01240; (413) 637-1199
Artistic Associates

Submission procedure: no unsolicited scripts; synopsis, 4-page dialogue sample and letter of inquiry. **Types of material:** full-length and one-act adaptations. **Special interests:** plays based on or adapted from works by Edith Wharton or Henry James only. **Facilities:** Mainstage Theatre, 500 seats, outdoor amphitheatre;

Oxford Court, 250 seats, outdoor amphitheatre; Stables Theatre, 108 seats, thrust stage; Salon Theatre, 75–90 seats, endstage. **Production considerations:** minimal set pieces only; all theatre spaces part of historic estate (former home of Edith Wharton). **Best submission time:** fall–winter. **Response time:** 6 months letter (if interested); 6 months script.

SHAKESPEARE SANTA CRUZ
(Founded 1981)
Performing Arts Complex; University of California–Santa Cruz;
    Santa Cruz, CA 95064; (408) 459-5109, FAX 459-3552;
    E-mail karin_magaldi-unger@macmail.ucsc.edu
Karin Magaldi-Unger, *Literary Manager*

Submission procedure: no unsolicited scripts; will accept synopsis, resume and letter of inquiry; prefers professional recommendation. **Types of material:** full-length plays, one-acts, plays for young audiences. **Special interests:** Shakespearean spinoffs, i.e., plays that use Shakespeare's characters or plots. **Facilities:** Sinsheimer-Stanley Glen, 500–800 seats, outdoor amphitheatre; Performing Arts Theater, 500 seats, thrust stage. **Production considerations:** small cast; minimal set. **Best submission time:** fall–winter. **Response time:** 1 month letter; 1 month script.

THE SHAKESPEARE THEATRE
(Founded 1986)
301 East Capitol St SE; Washington, DC 20003-3808; (202) 547-3230,
    FAX 546-9447; E-mail shakespearedc.org
Michael Kahn, *Artistic Director*

Submission procedure: no unsolicited scripts; professional recommendation. **Types of material:** translations, adaptations. **Special interests:** translations and adaptations of classics only. **Facilities:** The Shakespeare Theatre, 449 seats, proscenium stage. **Best submission time:** summer. **Response time:** 2 months.

SIGNATURE THEATRE
(Founded 1990)
3806 South Four Mile Run Dr; Arlington, VA 22206; (703) 820-9771
Marcia Gardner, *Literary Manager*

Submission procedure: accepts unsolicited scripts. **Types of material:** full-length plays, adaptations, musicals. **Special interests:** work not previously professionally produced only; social issues; comedies. **Facilities:** Signature Theatre, 126 seats, black box. **Production considerations:** prefers cast limit of 10; no fly space. **Best submission time:** Sep–May. **Response time:** 6 months. **Special programs:** Stages: staged readings of new plays-in-process; scripts selected through theatre's normal submission procedure; On the Edge Series: full production of 1 new play a year.

SIGNATURE THEATRE COMPANY, INC.
(Founded 1991)
424 West 42nd St, 2nd Floor; New York, NY 10036-6809; (212) 967-1913, FAX 967-2957
James Houghton, *Founding Artistic Director*

Submission procedure: no unsolicited scripts; direct solicitation to playwright or agent. **Types of material:** full-length plays, one-acts. **Special interests:** playwrights with substantial body of work to be produced over course of season. **Facilities:** no permanent facility; company performs in various end- or proscenium-stage venues with 99–125 seats.

SINGULAR PRODUCTIONS
(Founded 1989)
10824 Lindblade St; Culver City, CA 90230; (310) 558-1555, FAX 558-0513
Pat Destro, *Literary Manager*

Submission procedure: no unsolicited scripts; synopsis, 10-page dialogue sample and letter of inquiry with SASE for response. **Types of material:** full-length plays, translations, adaptations. **Facilities:** The Ivy Substation, 99 seats, flexible stage. **Production considerations:** cast minimum of 6 to accommodate ensemble. **Best submission time:** year-round. **Response time:** 2 months letter; 6–8 months script.

SOCIETY HILL PLAYHOUSE
(Founded 1959)
507 South 8th St; Philadelphia, PA 19147; (215) 923-0210, FAX 923-1789
Walter Vail, *Literary Manager*

Submission procedure: no unsolicited scripts; synopsis and letter of inquiry with SASE for response. **Types of material:** full-length plays, translations, adaptations, musicals. **Special interests:** musicals and comedies with casts of 5–7. **Facilities:** Society Hill Playhouse, 223 seats, proscenium stage; Second Space, 90 seats, flexible stage. **Production considerations:** prefers small cast. **Best submission time:** year-round. **Response time:** 1 month letter; 6 months script.

SOHO REPERTORY THEATRE
(Founded 1975)
46 Walker St; New York, NY 10013; (212) 941-8632, FAX 941-7148
Renée Lasher, *Business Manager*

Submission procedure: no unsolicited scripts; direct solicitation to playwright or agent. **Types of material:** full-length plays, one-acts, solo pieces. **Facilities:** Soho Rep, 99 seats, black box.

Source Theatre Company
(Founded 1978)
1835 14th St NW; Washington, DC 20009; (202) 462-1073
Keith Parker, *Literary Manager*

Submission procedure: accepts unsolicited scripts that have not been professionally produced with synopsis, resume, letter of inquiry and letter-size SASE for response (scripts not returned); enclose reviews for scripts previously produced once. **Types of material:** full-length plays, one-acts, musicals, solo pieces. **Facilities:** Source Theatre Company, 98 seats, thrust stage. **Best submission time:** before 15 Jan 1998 only. **Response time:** 15 Feb 1998 letter; 15 May 1998 script. **Special programs:** 18th Annual Washington Theatre Festival: new-play workshop productions; scripts selected through competition (see below); *deadline:* 15 Jan 1998; *dates:* 8 Jul–8 Aug 1998. Source Theatre Company 1998 Literary Prize (see Prizes).

South Coast Repertory
(Founded 1964)
Box 2197; Costa Mesa, CA 92628-2197; (714) 957-2602
Jerry Patch, *Dramaturg*
John Glore, *Literary Manager*

Submission procedure: no unsolicited scripts; synopsis and letter of inquiry; dialogue sample is optional. **Types of material:** full-length plays, one-acts, translations, adaptations, musicals. **Facilities:** Mainstage, 507 seats, modified thrust stage; Second Stage, 161 seats, thrust stage. **Best submission time:** year-round. **Response time:** 1–3 weeks letter; 2–4 months script. **Special programs:** COLAB (Collaboration Laboratory) New Play Program: developmental program involving readings, staged readings, workshop and full productions; participation and all commissions offered by David Emmes and Martin Benson, artistic directors; playwright receives grant, commission and/or royalties depending on nature of project. Hispanic Playwrights Project (see Development).

Spokane Interplayers Ensemble
(Founded 1981)
Box 1961; Spokane, WA 99210; (509) 455-7529, FAX 624-5902;
     E-mail interplayers@inteplayers.com; Web http://www.interplayers.com
Robert A. Welch, *Managing Director*

Submission procedure: no unsolicited scripts; synopsis with cast list, set requirements, play's production history and reviews (if any), dialogue sample and letter of inquiry. **Types of material:** full-length plays. **Facilities:** Spokane Interplayers Ensemble, 255 seats, thrust stage. **Production considerations:** prefers cast limit of 8, 1 set. **Best submission time:** year-round. **Response time:** 3 months letter (if interested); 3–6 months script.

St. Louis Black Repertory Company

(Founded 1977)
634 North Grand Blvd, Suite 10-F; St. Louis, MO 63103; (314) 534-3807,
  FAX 533-3345
Ronald J. Himes, *Producing Director*

Submission procedure: no unsolicited scripts; synopsis, 3–5-page dialogue sample, resume and letter of inquiry. **Types of material:** full-length plays, plays for young audiences, musicals. **Special interests:** works by African-American and Third World playwrights. **Facilities:** Grandel Square Theatre, 470 seats, thrust stage. **Best submission time:** Jun–Aug. **Response time:** 2 months letter; 2 months script. **Special programs:** touring company presenting works for young audiences.

Stage One: The Louisville Children's Theatre

(Founded 1946)
5 Riverfront Plaza; Louisville, KY 40202-2957; (502) 589-5946,
  FAX 588-5910; E-mail kystageone@aol.com
Moses Goldberg, *Producing Director*

Submission procedure: accepts unsolicited scripts. **Types of material:** plays for young audiences. **Special interests:** plays about young people in the real world; good, honest treatments of familiar titles. **Facilities:** Moritz von Bomard Theater, 610 seats, thrust stage; Louisville Gardens, 300 seats, arena stage. **Production considerations:** prefers cast limit of 12; some productions tour. **Best submission time:** Oct–Dec. **Response time:** 3 months. **Special programs:** Tomorrow's Playwrights: annual one-act competition open to high school students throughout KY region; 3 finalists receive staged readings and prepare rewrite to determine placement; scholarship check for winner, cash awards for 2 runners-up and 3 sponsoring schools; submit play through school; *deadline:* 1 Mar 1998.

Stage West

(Founded 1979)
Box 2587; Fort Worth, TX 76113; (817) 924-9454, FAX 926-8650
Jerry Russell, *Artistic Director*

Submission procedure: no unsolicited scripts; synopsis and letter of inquiry. **Types of material:** full-length plays, translations, adaptations, solo pieces. **Special interests:** plays with universal themes; contemporary issues. **Facilities:** Stage West, 190 seats, arena stage. **Production considerations:** prefers cast limit of 9. **Best submission time:** Jan–Mar. **Response time:** 1 month letter; 3 months script.

Stages

(Founded 1982)
1540 North McCadden Pl; Hollywood, CA 90028; (213) 463-5356;
  FAX (310) 440-3989
Marcella Meharg, *Dramaturg*

Submission procedure: no unsolicited scripts; synopsis and letter of inquiry. **Types**

of material: full-length plays, one-acts, translations, adaptations. **Special interests:** plays by foreign writers both in original language and in translation; theatre regularly produces plays in Spanish, French and English but can also find actors fluent in other languages; challenging, experimental work. **Facilities:** Amphitheatre, 99 seats, outdoor flexible stage; Mainstage, 49 seats, proscenium stage; Lab, 25 seats, classroom. **Production considerations:** prefers cast limit of 5. **Best submission time:** year-round. **Response time:** 1 month letter; 3 months script.

STAGEWEST
(Founded 1967)
One Columbus Center; Springfield, MA 01103; (413) 781-4470, FAX 781-3741
Albert Ihde, *Producing Director*

Submission procedure: no unsolicited scripts; synopsis and letter of inquiry with SASP for response. **Types of material:** full-length plays, translations, adaptations, solo pieces. **Facilities:** Mainstage, 479 seats, thrust stage; Studio, 99 seats, flexible stage. **Best submission time:** year-round. **Response time:** 6 months letter; 6 months script.

STAMFORD THEATRE WORKS
(Founded 1988)
95 Atlantic St; Stamford, CT 06901; (203) 359-4414, FAX 356-1846
Jane Desy, *Literary Manager*

Submission procedure: no unsolicited scripts; synopsis, dialogue sample and letter of inquiry; include cassette for musicals. **Types of material:** full-length plays, translations, adaptations, musicals. **Special interests:** plays that are contemporary, innovative and thought-provoking; socially and culturally relevant; challenging and entertaining. **Facilities:** Center Stage, 150 seats, modified thrust stage. **Production considerations:** prefers small cast, unit set. **Best submission time:** year-round. **Response time:** 2 months letter; 6 months script. **Special programs:** Windows on the Work: developmental workshop for 3 new plays, each play receives rehearsals, staged readings and audience discussions; scripts selected through theatre's normal submission procedure; do not submit plays that have been professionally produced; *dates:* Feb–Mar.

STEPPENWOLF THEATRE COMPANY
(Founded 1976)
1650 North Halsted; Chicago, IL 60614; (312) 335-1888, FAX 335-0808
Michele Volansky, *Dramaturg/Literary Manager*

Submission procedure: no unsolicited scripts; synopsis, 10 pages of dialogue and letter of inquiry. **Types of material:** full-length plays, one-acts, translations, adaptations. **Special interests:** ensemble pieces with dynamic acting roles. **Facilities:** Mainstage, 510 seats, proscenium stage; Studio, 50–300 seats, flexible stage. **Best submission time:** year-round. **Response time:** 3–6 months letter; 3–6 months script.

STRAWDOG THEATRE COMPANY
(Founded 1988)
3829 North Broadway; Chicago, IL 60613; (773) 528-9889, FAX 528-7238;
 E-mail tcz@synet.net
Stephanie Heller, *Literary Manager*

Submission procedure: no unsolicited scripts; first 10 pages of script and letter of inquiry with SASE for response (include optional SASP for acknowledgment of receipt). **Types of material:** full-length plays, one-acts, translations, adaptations. **Special interests:** scripts suitable for ensemble aged 20–30; "off-the-wall," dark comedies. **Facilities:** Mainstage, 74 seats, black box. **Production considerations:** no fly or wing space. **Best submission time:** year-round. **Response time:** 1–8 weeks letter; 1–8 weeks script.

STUDIO ARENA THEATRE
(Founded 1965)
710 Main St; Buffalo, NY 14202-1990; (716) 856-8025, FAX 856-3415
Gavin Cameron-Webb, *Artistic Director*

Submission procedure: no unsolicited scripts; agent submission. **Types of material:** full-length plays, translations, adaptations. **Special interests:** plays of local interest; plays of a theatrical nature; American history and culture; ethnic cultures, including plays about minorities. **Facilities:** Studio Arena Theatre, 637 seats, thrust stage. **Production considerations:** cast limit of 12 (prefers smaller-cast plays); no fly system, limited wing space. **Best submission time:** year-round. **Response time:** 6 months.

THE STUDIO THEATRE
(Founded 1979)
1333 P St NW; Washington, DC 20005; (202) 232-7267, FAX 588-5262;
 E-mail sseiden580@aol.com
Serge Seiden, *Literary Manager*

Submission procedure: no unsolicited scripts; direct solicitation to playwright or agent. **Types of material:** full-length plays, translations, adaptations, musicals, solo pieces. **Special interests:** American lyric realism; ethnic American themes; translations of new European and Asian plays. **Facilities:** Mead Theatre, 200 seats, thrust stage; Milton Theatre, 200 seats, thrust stage; Secondstage, 50 seats, flexible stage.

SWINE PALACE PRODUCTIONS
(Founded 1991)
217 M&DA Building; Baton Rouge, LA 70803; (504) 388-3533, FAX 388-4135
Lucy Maycock, *Dramaturg*

Submission procedure: accepts unsolicited scripts. **Types of material:** full-length plays, musicals. **Special interests:** works that explore issues pertinent to Louisiana.

84 / PRODUCTION

Facilities: LSU Theatre, 400 seats, proscenium stage. **Best submission time:** summer. **Response time:** 1 month.

SYRACUSE STAGE
(Founded 1973)
820 East Genesee St; Syracuse, NY 13210-1508; (315) 443-4008, FAX 443-9846;
  E-mial syrstage@syr.edu; Web http://web.syr.edu/~syrstage
Robert Moss, *Artistic Director*

Submission procedure: no unsolicited scripts; synopsis, 10-page dialogue sample, resume, character breakdown and letter of inquiry; include cassette for musicals. **Types of material:** full-length plays, translations, adaptations, musicals. **Facilities:** John D. Archbold Theatre, 499 seats, proscenium stage. **Production considerations:** prefers cast limit of 8. **Best submission time:** year-round. **Response time:** 2 months letter; 6–9 months script.

TACOMA ACTORS GUILD
(Founded 1978)
901 Broadway, 6th Floor; Tacoma, WA 98402-4404; (206) 272-3107,
  FAX 272-3358
(Mr.) Pat Patton, *Producing Artistic Director*

Submission procedure: no unsolicited scripts; synopsis and letter of inquiry. **Types of material:** full-length plays, translations, adaptations, musicals. **Facilities:** Theatre on the Square, 302 seats, proscenium stage. **Production considerations:** prefers small cast; 1 set or unit set. **Best submission time:** spring–summer. **Response time:** 1–2 months letter; 8–12 months script.

TADA!
(Founded 1984)
120 West 28th St, 2nd Floor; New York, NY 10001; (212) 627-1732,
  FAX 243-6736
Janine Nina Trevens, *Artistic Director*

Submission procedure: accepts unsolicited scripts. **Types of material:** one-acts, plays for young audiences, musicals. **Special interests:** work to be performed by children and teenagers. **Facilities:** Mainstage, 98 seats, black box. **Production considerations:** modest production demands. **Best submission time:** year-round. **Response time:** 6 months. **Special programs:** Staged Reading Series: readings of one-acts written for age-specific groups (i.e. 5–8, teenager, etc.) with no more than 2–3 adult characters; *deadline:* 1 Jul 1998; *notification:* 15 Sep 1998; *dates:* ongoing throughout 1998/99 season.

Tennessee Repertory Theatre
(Founded 1985)
427 Chestnut St; Nashville, TN 37203-4826; (615) 244-4878, FAX 244-1232;
    E-mail tnrep@isdn.net
Don Jones, *Associate Artistic Director*

Submission procedure: no unsolicited scripts; synopsis, dialogue sample, cassette of music and lyrics, and letter of inquiry. **Types of material:** musicals, musical solo pieces. **Special interests:** new American musicals, preferably in a developmental stage. **Facilities:** Polk Theatre, 1050 seats, proscenium stage. **Best submission time:** Jun–Sep. **Response time:** 4–6 weeks letter; 9–12 months script.

Thalia Spanish Theatre
(Founded 1977)
Box 4368; Sun2nyside, NY 11104; (718) 729-3880, FAX 729-3388
Silvia Brito, *Artistic/Executive Director*

Submission procedure: accepts unsolicited scripts. **Types of material:** full-length plays, translations, adaptations. **Special interests:** plays in Spanish only. **Facilities:** Thalia Spanish Theatre, 74 seats, proscenium stage. **Production considerations:** cast limit of 6; 1 set. **Best submission time:** Dec–Jan. **Response time:** 3 months.

Theater at Lime Kiln
(Founded 1984)
Lime Kiln Arts; Box 663; Lexington, VA 24450; (540) 463-7088, FAX 463-1082;
    E-mail limekiln@cfw.com
Barry Mines, *Artistic Director*

Submission procedure: accepts unsolicited scripts. **Types of material:** full-length plays, adaptations, musicals. **Special interests:** work not previously professionally produced only; issues, language and music indigenous to VA and region; nontraditional staging. **Facilities:** The Kiln, 299 seats, outdoor amphitheatre. **Production considerations:** prefers cast limit of 9. **Best submission time:** fall. **Response time:** 3 months. **Special Programs:** Theater at Lime Kiln Regional Playwriting Contest (see Prizes).

The Theater At Monmouth
(Founded 1970)
Box 385; Monmouth, ME 04259-0385; (207) 933-2952, FAX 933-2952
Michael O'Brien, *Artistic Director*

Submission procedure: no unsolicited scripts; synopsis and letter of inquiry. **Types of material:** plays for young audiences. **Special interests:** small-cast traditional plays for young audiences, particularly work based on fairy tales (no musicals). **Facilities:** Cumston Hall, 275 seats, thrust stage. **Production considerations:** simple set. **Best submission time:** Nov. **Response time:** 4–6 weeks letter; 4–6 months script.

Theater by the Blind
(Founded 1979)
306 West 18th St; New York, NY 10011; (212) 243-4337, FAX 727-2778
Ike Schambelan, *Artistic Director*

Submission procedure: accepts unsolicited scripts. **Types of material:** full-length plays, one-acts, musicals. **Special interests:** work by and about the blind. **Facilities:** no permanent facility; company performs in various 99-seat venues. **Best submission time:** year-round. **Response time:** 2 months.

Theatre de la Jeune Lune
(Founded 1979)
105 First St N; Minneapolis, MN 55401; (612) 332-3968, FAX 332-0048
Barbara Berlovitz Desbois, *Co-Artistic Director*

Submission procedure: no unsolicited scripts; synopsis and letter of inquiry. **Types of material:** full-length plays, translations, adaptations, musicals, cabaret/revues. **Special interests:** large-cast plays dealing with universal themes. **Facilities:** Theatre de la Jeune Lune, 500 seats, flexible stage. **Best submission time:** year-round. **Response time:** 8–10 weeks letter; 4 months script.

Theater Emory
(Founded 1985)
Annex C, Emory University; Atlanta, GA 30322; (404) 727-3465, FAX 727-6253; E-mail vmurphy@emory.edu
Vincent Murphy, *Artistic Producing Director*

Submission procedure: accepts unsolicited scripts through members of Southeast Playwrights Project, Atlanta, GA, only; professional recommendation from artistic director for all others. **Types of material:** full-length plays, one-acts, translations, adaptations. **Special interests:** adaptations and translations of literary and classic works. **Facilities:** MGM-I, 120 seats, flexible stage; MGM-II, 70 seats, flexible stage; Annex Studio, 60 seats, flexible stage. **Production considerations:** cast limit of 20; no fly or wing space. **Best submission time:** year-round. **Response time:** 2 months letter; 4 months script. **Special programs:** Brave New Works: annual staged reading marathon of new plays in conjunction with the Southeast Playwrights Project; scripts chosen through regular submission procedure; *deadline:* fall 1997; *dates:* spring 1998. The Playwriting Center of Theater Emory: biennial 5–13 week residency of major playwright to develop new work and teach playwriting workshop; remuneration: $25,000; residency during 1998–99 academic year.

Theatre for a New Audience
(Founded 1979)
154 Christopher St, Suite 3D; New York, NY 10014-2839; (212) 229-2819

Submission procedure: no unsolicited scripts; direct solicitation to playwright or agent. **Types of material:** full-length plays, one-acts. **Special interests:** plays with compelling use of language. **Facilities:** Theatre at St. Clement's, 175 seats, proscenium stage. **Special programs:** commissioning program; participation by invitation only.

THEATER FOR THE NEW CITY
(Founded 1970)
155-57 First Ave; New York, NY 10003-2906; (212) 254-1109
Crystal Field, *Artistic Director*

Submission procedure: accepts unsolicited scripts with SASE for response. **Types of material:** full-length plays. **Special interests:** plays with no previous main stage production; experimental American works; plays with poetry, music and dance; social issues. **Facilities:** Joyce and Seward Johnson Theater, 200 seats, flexible space; 2nd theatre, 75 seats, flexible space; 3rd theatre, 100 seats, flexible space; also cabaret space. **Best submission time:** summer. **Response time:** 9–12 months.

THEATRE IV
(Founded 1975)
114 West Broad St; Richmond, VA 23220; (804) 783-1688, FAX 775-2325
Bruce Miller, *Artistic Director*

Submission procedure: no unsolicited scripts; synopsis and letter of inquiry. **Types of material:** plays for young audiences only, including full-length plays, translations and adaptations. **Facilities:** Empire Theatre, 604 seats, proscenium stage. **Production considerations:** moderate budget for all productions. **Best submission time:** spring and summer. **Response time:** 6 months letter; 6 months script.

THEATRE GAEL
(Founded 1984)
Box 77156; Atlanta, GA 30357; (404) 876-1138, FAX 733-4756;
E-mail gael@atlanta.com
John Stephens, *Artistic Director*

Submission procedure: no unsolicited scripts; synopsis and letter of inquiry. **Types of material:** full-length plays, translations, adaptations, plays for young audiences, solo pieces. **Special interests:** plays depicting life in Ireland, Scotland, Wales; plays about Americans of Celtic heritage; plays that compare different cultural backgrounds, e.g., the African-American versus Irish-American experiences. **Facilities:** 14th Street Playhouse, 90–180 seats, flexible stage; company tours to 80–330-seat flexible-stage theatres. **Production considerations:** productions tour to local schools, festivals and churches. **Best submission time:** year-round. **Response time:** 1 month letter; 3 months script. **Special programs:** Worldsong Children's Theatre: company tours to local schools, recreational areas and libraries.

THEATRE IN THE SQUARE
(Founded 1982)
11 Whitlock Ave; Marietta, GA 30064; (770) 422-8369, FAX 424-2637
Literary Manager

Submission procedure: no unsolicited scripts; synopsis and letter of inquiry. **Types of material:** full-length plays, one-acts, translations, musicals. **Special interests:** world and southeastern premieres. **Facilities:** Mainstage, 225 seats, proscenium stage; Alley Stage, up to 80 seats, flexible stage. **Production considerations:** cast limit of 9; unit set; no fly space. **Best submission time:** Dec–Feb. **Response time:** 1 month letter (if interested); 6 months script.

THEATER OF THE FIRST AMENDMENT
(Founded 1990)
MS 3E6; George Mason University; Fairfax, VA 22030-4444; (703) 993-2195, FAX 993-2191; E-mail rdavi4@gmu.edu
Rick Davis, *Artistic Director*

Submission procedure: no unsolicited scripts; synopsis, sample pages, resume and letter of inquiry. **Types of material:** full-length plays, one-acts, translations, adaptations, plays for young audiences, solo pieces. **Special interests:** sophisticated plays for younger audiences; "cultural history made dramatic as opposed to history dramatized; large battles joined; hard questions asked; word and image stretched." **Facilities:** TheaterSpace, 150–200 seats, flexible space. **Production considerations:** roles for younger actors welcome as TFA works with training program. **Best submission time:** Aug–Jan. **Response time:** 2 weeks letter; 6 months script. **Special programs:** readings, workshops and other development activities tailored to work under serious consideration for production.

THEATRE ON THE SQUARE
(Founded 1982)
450 Post St; San Francisco, CA 94102; (415) 433-6461, FAX 433-2910; E-mail tot@hooked.net
Jonathan Reinis, *Owner*

Submission procedure: no unsolicited scripts; synopsis and letter of inquiry. **Types of material:** full-length plays, musicals. **Facilities:** Theatre on the Square, 750 seats, proscenium/thrust stage. **Production considerations:** no fly space. **Best submission time:** year-round. **Response time:** 6 months letter; 12 months script.

THE THEATRE OUTLET
(Founded 1988)
146 North 10th St; Allentown, PA 18102; (610) 820-9270, FAX 820-9130; E-mail theaterout@aol.com
George Miller, *Artistic Director*

Submission procedure: no unsolicited scripts; synopsis and letter of inquiry. **Types of material:** full-length plays, one-acts, translations, adaptations, solo pieces.

Special interests: historical material relevant to eastern Pennsylvania; plays dealing with the Irish/Scotch/Welsh experience; topical work; work exploring cultural diversity; **Facilities:** Mainstage, 100 seats, black box. **Production considerations:** limited fly and wing space. **Best submission time:** summer. **Response time:** 1 month letter; 2 months script. **Special programs:** The Counter-Culture Monday Cafe Series: 3 10-week series of readings of new plays and performance pieces.

THEATRE RHINOCEROS
(Founded 1977)
2926 16th St; San Francisco, CA 94103; (415) 552-4100, FAX 558-9044
Doug Holsclaw, *Literary Manager*

Submission procedure: accepts unsolicited scripts. **Types of material:** full-length plays, one-acts, solo pieces. **Special interests:** gay and lesbian works only. **Facilities:** Theatre Rhinoceros, 112 seats, proscenium stage; The Studio at Theatre Rhinoceros, 60 seats, studio. **Best submission time:** year-round. **Response time:** 3–4 months.

THEATRE THREE
(Founded 1969)
Box 512; Port Jefferson, NY 11777-0512; (516) 928-9202, FAX 928-9120
Jeffrey Sanzel, *Artistic Director*

Submission procedure: no unsolicited scripts; synopsis, resume, press clippings (if any) and letter of inquiry. **Types of material:** full-length plays, one-acts. **Facilities:** Main Stage, 400 seats, proscenium; Second Stage, 80–100 seats, black box. **Production considerations:** prefers cast of 2–6; 1 set; minimal production demands; no fly or wing space in Main Stage. **Best submission time:** Jan-Apr. **Response time:** 1 month letter; 2 months script.

THEATRE THREE, INC.
(Founded 1961)
2800 Routh St; Dallas, TX 75201; (214) 871-2933, FAX 871-3139
Jac Alder, *Executive Producer/Director*

Submission procedure: accepts unsolicited scripts; prefers synopsis and letter of inquiry. **Types of material:** full-length plays, musicals. **Special interests:** musicals; sophisticated comedies with socially relevant themes. **Facilities:** Theatre Three, 242 seats, arena stage. **Production considerations:** cast of 6–15; modest production demands. **Best submission time:** year-round; prefers Sep–Dec. **Response time:** 1 week letter; 2 months script.

THEATRE WEST
(Founded 1962)
3333 Cahuenga Blvd W; Los Angeles, CA 90068; (213) 851-4839, FAX 851-5286
Arden Lewis and Doug Haverty, *Workshop Moderators*

Submission procedure: no unsolicited scripts; scripts developed in weekly workshops open to member playwrights only; submit script, resume and letter of inquiry; dues of $40 per month upon acceptance. **Types of material:** full-length plays, one-acts, translations, adaptations, plays for young audiences, musicals. **Facilities:** Theatre West, 180 seats, proscenium stage. **Best submission time:** year-round. **Response time:** 4 months.

THEATRE X
(Founded 1969)
Box 92206; Milwaukee, WI 53202; (414) 278-0555
Michael Ramach, *Producing Director*

Submission procedure: accepts unsolicited scripts with SASE for response. **Types of material:** full-length plays, solo pieces. **Special interests:** work with no previous professional production; contemporary plays. **Facilities:** Black Box, 99 seats, flexible stage. **Best submission time:** year-round. **Response time:** 6 months.

THE THEATRE-STUDIO INC.
(Founded 1980)
750 Eighth Ave, #200; New York, NY 10036; (212) 719-0500
A. M. Raychel, *Artistic Director/Producer*

Submission procedure: accepts unsolicited scripts. **Types of material:** one-acts, plays for young audiences, solo pieces, performance art. **Special interests:** one-acts. **Facilities:** The Theatre-Studio, 60 seats, studio. **Best submission time:** year-round. **Response time:** 3 months. **Special programs:** Playtime Series: year-round developmental program.

THEATREVIRGINIA
(Founded 1955)
2800 Grove Ave; Richmond, VA 23221-2466; (804) 353-6100
George Black, *Producing Artistic Director*

Submission procedure: no unsolicited scripts; agent submission. **Types of material:** full-length plays, musicals. **Facilities:** Main Stage, 500 seats, proscenium stage. **Best submission time:** year-round. **Response time:** 3–8 months. **Special programs:** New Voices for the Theatre: playwriting competition open to VA students grades 5–12; winners grades 9–12 attend 3-week summer residency program and receive dramaturgical assistance and professional staged reading; contact Education and Outreach Department for more information; *deadline:* 1 Feb 1998.

THEATERWORKS
(Founded 1985)
1 Gold St; Hartford, CT 06103; (860) 727-4027, FAX 525-0758
Steve Campo, *Artistic Director*

Submission procedure: accepts unsolicited scripts. **Types of material:** full-length plays, solo pieces. **Facilities:** Hutensky Theater, 200 seats, thrust stage. **Production**

considerations: cast limit of 6; simple set. **Best submission time:** year-round. **Response time:** 3–6 months.

THEATREWORKS

1100 Hamilton Ct, Menlo Park, CA 94025; (415) 463-7126, FAX 463-1963; E-mail jodi@theatreworks.org
Jeannie Barroga, *Literary Manager*

Submission procedure: accepts unsolicited full-length plays and musicals; for translations and adaptations, send only letter of inquiry with SASP for response. **Types of material:** full-length plays, translations, adaptations, musicals. **Special interests:** works offering opportunities for multicultural casting. **Facilities:** Mountain View Center, 625 seats, proscenium stage; Stage II, 117 seats, thrust stage. **Best submission time:** Jul–Nov. **Response time:** 1 month letter; 4 months script.

THEATREWORKS/USA

(Founded 1961)
890 Broadway, 7th Floor; New York, NY 10003; (212) 677-5959, FAX 353-1632
Barbara Pasternack, *Associate Artistic Director*

Submission procedure: accepts unsolicited scripts; prefers synopsis, sample scene(s) and songs (include cassette and lyric sheet) and letter of inquiry. **Types of material:** plays and musicals for young audiences. **Special interests:** literary adaptations; historical/biographical themes; fairy tales; contemporary issues. **Facilities:** Promenade Theatre, 398 seats, proscenium stage; also tours. **Production considerations:** cast limit of 5 (can play multiple roles); sets suitable for touring. **Best submission time:** summer. **Response time:** 1 month letter; 6 months script. **Special programs:** Theatreworks/USA Commissioning Program (see Development).

THEATRICAL OUTFIT

(Founded 1976)
Box 7098; Atlanta, GA 30357; (404) 872-0665, -8077, FAX 872-1164
Kate Warner, *Managing Director*

Submission procedure: no unsolicited scripts; 1-page synopsis and letter of inquiry with SASP for reply. **Types of material:** full-length plays, adaptations, solo pieces. **Facilities:** Theatrical Outfit, 400 seats, proscenium stage. **Best submission time:** summer. **Response time:** 2 months letter; 2 months script.

TOTEM POLE PLAYHOUSE

(Founded 1950)
Box 603; Fayetteville, PA 17222; (717) 352-2164, FAX 352-8870
Carl Schurr, *Producing Artistic Director*

Submission procedure: no unsolicited scripts; synopsis, sample pages and letter of inquiry. **Types of material:** full-length plays, one-acts, musicals. **Special**

interests: light comedies and musicals that appeal to a general audience. **Facilities:** Mainstage, 453 seats, proscenium stage. **Best submission time:** year-round. **Response time:** 1–2 months letter; 6 months script.

TOUCHSTONE THEATRE
(Founded 1981)
321 East 4th St; Bethlehem, PA 18015; (610) 867-1689, FAX 867-0561;
    E-mail ttheatre@aol.com
Mark McKenna, *Artistic Director*

Submission procedure: no unsolicited scripts; letter of inquiry. **Types of material:** proposals for works to be created in collaboration with company's ensemble only. **Facilities:** Touchstone Theatre, 74 seats, black box. **Production considerations:** 18' x 21' playing area. **Best submission time:** year-round. **Response time:** 1 month.

TRINITY REPERTORY COMPANY
(Founded 1964)
201 Washington St; Providence, RI 02903; (401) 521-1100
Oskar Eustis, *Artistic Director*

Submission procedure: no unsolicited scripts; dialogue sample, resume and letter of inquiry. **Types of material:** full-length plays, translations, adaptations, musicals, solo pieces. **Facilities:** Upstairs Theatre, 500 seats, thrust stage; Downstairs Theatre, 297 seats, thrust stage. **Best submission time:** year-round. **Response time:** 4 months letter; 4 months script.

TRUSTUS THEATRE
See South Carolina Playwrights' Festival in Prizes.

TURNIP THEATRE COMPANY
(Founded 1991)
145 West 46th St; New York, NY 10036; (212) 768-4016
Literary Committee

Submission procedure: no unsolicited scripts; professional recommendation. **Types of material:** full-length plays. **Special interests:** New York-area playwrights. **Facilities:** The Studio, 74–90 seats, black box. **Production considerations:** cast size of 4–10; simple set. **Best submission time:** Aug–Nov. **Response time:** 2 months. **Special programs:** 15 Minute Play Festival: annual one-act contest and festival; cash prizes in 4 categories; send SASE for guidelines; *deadline:* 1 Dec 1997; *notification:* Jan 1998; *dates:* spring 1998.

Ubu Repertory Theater
(Founded 1982)
15 West 28th St; New York, NY 10001; (212) 679-7540, FAX 679-2033;
  E mail uburep@spacelab.net
Françoise Kourilsky, *Artistic Director*

Submission procedure: no unsolicited scripts; synopsis and letter of inquiry. **Types of material:** full-length plays, one-acts, translations. **Special interests:** French-language plays or their translations only; contemporary plays from French-speaking countries and regions. **Facilities:** Ubu Repertory Theater, 99 seats, proscenium stage. **Production considerations:** cast limit of 7; 1 set or simple sets. **Best submission time:** year-round. **Response time:** 2 months letter; 6 months script.

Unicorn Theatre
(Founded 1974)
3820 Main St; Kansas City, MO 64111; (816) 531-7529, FAX 531-0421
Herman Wilson, *Literary Assistant*

Submission procedure: accepts unsolicited scripts. **Types of material:** full-length plays. **Special interests:** contemporary social issues. **Facilities:** Unicorn Theatre, 180 seats, thrust stage. **Best submission time:** Jan-Apr. **Response time:** 3 months. **Special programs:** Unicorn Theatre National Playwrights' Award (see Prizes).

Utah Shakespearean Festival
(Founded 1961)
351 West Center St; Cedar City, UT 84720-2498; (801) 586-7880, FAX 865-8003
Douglas N. Cook, *Producing Artistic Director*

Submission procedure: no unsolicited scripts; professional recommendation. **Types of material:** full-length plays for Aug staged reading series. **Special interest:** plays with no previous main stage production only; plays by writers from western intermountain region; plays about minorities or the underserved. **Facilities:** Thorley Recital Hall, 235 seats, modified thrust stage. **Production considerations:** cast limit of 10–12; no sets, minimal props and costumes; 5-rehearsal limit per production. **Best submission time:** Sep–Dec. **Response time:** 3 months.

Vermont Stage Company
(Founded 1994)
Box 874; Burlington, VT 05402; (802) 656-4351, FAX 656-0349
Blake Robison, *Producing Artistic Director*

Submission procedure: no unsolicited scripts; letter of inquiry. **Types of material:** full-length plays. **Facilities:** Royall Tyler Theatre, 300 seats, thrust stage. **Best submission time:** year-round. **Response time:** 1 month letter; script varies. **Special programs:** Vermont Young Playwrights Project: educational program staffed by Vermont-based playwrights serving VT secondary schools.

VICTORY GARDENS THEATER
(Founded 1974)
2257 North Lincoln Ave; Chicago, IL 60614; (773) 549-5788, FAX 549-2779
Sandy Shinner, *Associate Artistic Director*

Submission procedure: accepts unsolicited scripts from Chicago-area writers only; others send synopsis, 10-page dialogue sample and letter of inquiry with SASE for response. **Types of material:** full-length plays, adaptations, musicals. **Special interests:** Chicago and Midwest playwrights; plays by women and writers of color. **Facilities:** Mainstage one, 195 seats, modified thrust stage; Mainstage two, 200 seats, thrust stage; 2 Studio Theaters, 70 seats each, black box. **Production considerations:** prefers cast limit of 10; simple set; small-cast musicals only. **Best submission time:** Mar–Jun. **Response time:** 2 months letter; 9 months script. **Special programs:** Readers Theater: staged readings of works-in-progress by area writers twice a month; Artist Development Workshops: playwriting classes offered throughout the year that bring people with and without disabilities together in a creative environment.

THE VINEYARD PLAYHOUSE
(Founded 1982)
Box 2452, 24 Church St; Vineyard Haven, MA 02568; (508) 693-6450
(Ms.) M. J. Munafo, *Artistic Director*

Submission procedure: no unsolicited scripts; direct solicitation to playwright or agent. **Types of material:** full-length plays, translations, adaptations, plays for young audiences, solo pieces. **Special interests:** contemporary American works; culturally diverse plays; plays that address social issues. **Facilities:** The Vineyard Playhouse, 120 seats, black box. **Production considerations:** prefers cast limit of 10; simple sets.

VINEYARD THEATRE
(Founded 1981)
108 East 15th St; New York, NY 10003-9689; (212) 353-3366, FAX 353-3803
Douglas Aibel, *Artistic Director*

Submission procedure: no unsolicited scripts; synopsis, 10-page dialogue sample and letter of inquiry; include cassette for musicals. **Types of material:** full-length plays, musicals. **Special interests:** plays that incorporate music in a unique way; musicals with strong narrative; "nervy, eccentric theatrical forms." **Facilities:** Vineyard at Union Square, 130 seats, flexible stage; Vineyard Theatre, 70 seats, thrust stage. **Best submission time:** year-round. **Response time:** 6 months letter; 6 months script. **Special programs:** New Works at the Vineyard: play reading series. The Lab Program: developmental workshops for new plays and musicals.

VIRGINIA STAGE COMPANY
(Founded 1979)
Box 3770; Norfolk, VA 23514; (757) 627-6988, FAX 628-5958

Submission procedure: no unsolicited scripts; synopsis and letter of inquiry. **Types**

of material: full-length plays, musicals. Special interests: world premieres; plays by VA writers; poetic drama and comedy; hard-hitting, issue-oriented plays; no "kitchen-sink" drama. Facilities: main stage, 700 seats, proscenium stage; laboratory theatre, 99 seats, flexible space. Best submission time: year-round. Response time: 1 month letter; 6 months script.

VOICE & VISION
(Founded 1990)
220 East 4th St; New York, NY 10009; (212) 502-1151
Marya Mazor and Jean Wagner, *Artistic Directors*

Submission procedure: accepts unsolicited scripts. Types of material: full length plays, one-acts, translations, adaptations, plays for young audiences, musicals, performance art, dance-theatre. Special interests: culturally diverse works written by or about women; multidisciplinary collaborations; plays for young casts. Facilities: The Connelly Theater, 99–250 seats, proscenium stage. Best submission time: year-round. Response time: 12 months. Special programs: Play with Your Food: dinner-and-a-play reading series; Dramatic Action: educational program for young women.

THE WALNUT STREET THEATRE COMPANY
(Founded 1809)
825 Walnut St; Philadelphia, PA 19107-5107; (215) 574-3550, FAX 574-3598
Beverly Elliott, *Literary Manager*

Submission procedure: no unsolicited scripts; synopsis, cast list, 10–20 pages of dialogue and letter of inquiry with SASE for response from Dramatist Guild members only; include professional-quality cassette for musicals. Types of material: full-length plays, musicals. Special interests: original, socially relevant musicals with uplifting themes; commercially viable works for Main Stage; meaningful comedies and dramas with some broad social relevance for Studio 3. Facilities: Main Stage, 1050 seats, proscenium stage; Studio 3, 80 seats, flexible stage. Production considerations: cast limit of 4 for Studio 3. Response time: 3 months letter; 6 months script.

WATERTOWER THEATRE, INC.
(Founded 1976)
15650 Addison Rd; Addison, TX 75248; (972) 450-6220, FAX 458-7529
Gayle Pearson, *Producing Director*

Submission procedure: accepts unsolicited scripts. Types of material: full-length plays, one-acts, plays for young audiences, musicals, solo pieces. Special interests: plays that make creative use of flexible space. Facilities: Addison Conference & Theatre Centre, 100–300 seats, flexible stage. Response time: 2 months.

96 / PRODUCTION

WEISSBERGER THEATER GROUP
(Founded 1992)
909 Third Ave, 27th Floor; New York, NY 10022-9998; (212) 339-5529,
  FAX 486-8996
Jay Harris, *Producer*

Submission procedure: no unsolicited scripts; synopsis and letter of inquiry. **Types of material:** full-length plays. **Special interests:** topical issue-oriented plays. **Facilities:** no permanent facility. **Production considerations:** cast limit of 7. **Best submission time:** year-round. **Response time:** 1 month letter; 2 months script.

WEST COAST ENSEMBLE
(Founded 1982)
Box 38728; Los Angeles, CA 90038; (310) 449-1447, FAX 453-2254
Les Hanson, *Artistic Director*

Submission procedure: accepts unsolicited scripts. **Types of material:** full-length plays, one-acts, translations, adaptations, musicals. **Special interests:** plays not previously produced in Southern CA only; musicals; short plays. **Facilities:** main stage, 85 seats, proscenium stage. **Production considerations:** simple set; no fly space. **Best submission time:** Jun–Dec. **Response time:** 6 months. **Special programs:** staged readings of new plays. West Coast Ensemble Contests (see Prizes).

WESTBETH THEATRE CENTER
(Founded 1977)
151 Bank St; New York, NY 10014; (212) 691-2272, FAX 924-7185
Craig Carlisle, *Director, Playwright Program*

Submission procedure: no unsolicited scripts; synopsis and letter of inquiry with SASE for response. **Types of material:** full-length plays, one-acts, musicals, solo pieces. **Facilities:** Music Hall, 100–200 seats, proscenium; Big Room, 99 seats, black box; Studio Theatre, 85 seats, black box. **Production considerations:** cast limit of 10; modest technical demands. **Best submission time:** year-round. **Response time:** 3 months letter; 4 months script. **Special programs:** Westbeth Playwright Program (see Development).

THE WESTERN STAGE
(Founded 1970)
156 Homestead Ave; Salinas, CA 93901; (408) 755-6990, FAX 755-6954
Joyce Lower, *Associate Artistic Director*

Submission procedure: no unsolicited scripts; synopsis and letter of inquiry; include cassette for musicals; for adaptations of work not in public domain, enclose copy of letter granting rights. **Types of material:** full-length plays, adaptations, plays for young audiences, musicals, cabaret/revues. **Facilities:** Mainstage, 500 seats, proscenium stage; Cabaret, 250 seats, proscenium stage;

Studio, 100 seats, thrust stage. **Best submission time:** year-round. **Response time:** 2 weeks letter; 3 months script.

WILL GEER THEATRICUM BOTANICUM
(Founded 1973)
Box 1222; Topanga, CA 90290; (310) 455-2322; FAX 455-3724
Ellen Geer, *Artistic Director*

Submission procedure: no unsolicited scripts; synopsis, dialogue sample and letter of inquiry; include cassette for musicals. **Types of material:** full-length plays, musicals. **Special interests:** work suitable for large outdoor playing space. **Facilities:** Will Geer Theatricum Botanicum, 300 seats, outdoor amphitheatre. **Production considerations:** cast size of 4–10; simple sets. **Best submission time:** Sep. **Response time:** 3 weeks letter; 6 months script.

WILLIAMSTOWN THEATRE FESTIVAL
(Founded 1955)
Sep–May: 100 East 17th St, 3rd Fl; New York, NY 10003; (212) 228-2286, FAX 228-9091
Jun–Aug: Box 517; Williamstown, MA 01267-0517; (413) 458-3200, FAX 458-3147
Christina Sibul, *Literary Manager*

Submission procedure: no unsolicited scripts; agent submission only. **Types of material:** full-length plays, adaptations, musicals, solo pieces. **Facilities:** Main Stage, 521 seats, proscenium stage; 2nd stage, 96 seats, thrust stage. **Best submission time:** 1 Oct–15 Feb. **Response time:** several months script. **Special programs:** New Play Staged Readings Series.

WILLOWS THEATRE COMPANY
(Founded 1977)
1975 Diamond Blvd, Suite A-20; Concord, CA 94520; (510) 798-1300, FAX 676-5726; E-mail willowsth@aol.com
Richard H. Elliott, *Artistic Director*

Submission procedure: no unsolicited scripts; synopsis, character breakdown and letter of inquiry. **Types of material:** full-length plays, translations, adaptations, musicals. **Special interests:** small-scale plays, musicals and revues with an edge and commercial potential that will appeal to both urban and suburban audiences. **Facilities:** Willows Theatre, 203 seats, proscenium stage. **Production considerations:** cast of 2–15; limit of 8 musicians for musical works; prefers simple set, unit set or environmental staging which uses theatre space as setting. **Best submission time:** 1 Apr–1 Jul. **Response time:** 3 months. **Special programs:** staged readings and workshop productions.

98 / PRODUCTION

THE WILMA THEATER
(Founded 1972)
265 South Broad St; Philadelphia, PA 19107; (215) 893-9456, FAX 893-0895;
E-mail wilma@libertynet.org; Web http://www.libertynet.org/~wilma
Michael Hollinger, *Literary Manager/Dramaturg*

Submission procedure: no unsolicited scripts; synopsis, dialogue sample and letter of inquiry. **Types of material:** full-length plays, translations, adaptations, musicals, full-length solo pieces. **Special interests:** new translations and adaptations from the international repertoire with emphasis on innovative, bold staging; world premieres; ensemble works; works with poetic dimension; plays with music; multimedia works; social issues. **Facilities:** Wilma Theater, 300 seats, flexible/proscenium stage. **Production considerations:** prefers cast limit of 12; stage 44′ x 46′. **Best submission time:** year-round. **Response time:** 2–4 months letter; 9–12 months script.

WOMEN'S PROJECT & PRODUCTIONS
(Founded 1978)
55 West End Ave; New York, NY 10023; (212) 765-1706, FAX 765-2024
Christina Sibul, *Literary Manager*

Submission procedure: no unsolicited scripts; synopsis, 10-page dialogue sample and letter of inquiry with SASE for response. **Types of material:** full-length plays, solo pieces. **Special interests:** plays by women only. **Facilities:** no permanent space. **Best submission time:** year-round. **Response time:** 2–4 weeks letter; 3–6 months script. **Special programs:** developmental program including play readings, work-in-progress presentations, playwright's lab and directors' forum; participation by invitation only. Commissioning program.

WOOLLY MAMMOTH THEATRE COMPANY
(Founded 1981)
1401 Church St NW; Washington, DC 20005; (202) 393-3939, FAX 667-0904
Gary Oiler, *Literary Manager*

Submission procedure: accepts unsolicited scripts. **Types of material:** full-length plays, translations, adaptations, solo pieces. **Special interests:** offbeat topics and styles; nonrealism. **Facilities:** Woolly Mammoth, 132 seats, thrust stage. **Production considerations:** small cast; minimal staging requirements. **Best submission time:** year-round. **Response time:** 4–6 months.

THE WOOSTER GROUP
(Founded 1969)
Box 654, Canal Street Station; New York, NY 10013; (212) 966-9796,
FAX 226-6576; E-mail woostergrp@aol.com;
Web http://www.escape.com/~philbus/wooster.html
Anne Reiss, *Administrative Director*

Submission procedure: no unsolicited scripts (company customarily collaborates on its own original work). **Types of material:** full-length plays. **Special interests:** experimental works. **Facilities:** The Performing Garage, 99 seats, black box.

WORCESTER FOOTHILLS THEATRE COMPANY
(Founded 1974)
100 Front St, Suite 137; Worcester, MA 01608; (508) 754-3314, FAX 767-0676
Marc P. Smith, *Executive Producer/Artistic Director*

Submission procedure: no unsolicited scripts; synopsis and letter of inquiry. **Types of material:** full-length plays, translations, adaptations, musicals. **Special interests:** plays suited to multigenerational audiences. **Facilities:** Worcester Foothills Theatre, 349 seats, proscenium stage. **Production considerations:** prefers cast limit of 10, simple set; small-scale musicals only. **Best submission time:** year-round. **Response time:** 3 months letter; 4 months script.

YALE REPERTORY THEATRE
(Founded 1965)
Box 208244, Yale Station; New Haven, CT 06520-8244; (203) 432-1560,
    FAX 432-1550; E-mail yale.dramaturgy@yale.edu
Resident Dramaturg

Submission procedure: no unsolicited scripts; synopsis and letter of inquiry. **Types of material:** full-length plays, translations, adaptations, solo pieces. **Special interests:** new work; new translations of classics; contemporary foreign plays. **Facilities:** Yale Repertory Theatre, 487 seats, modified thrust stage; University Theatre, 654 seats, proscenium stage. **Best submission time:** year-round. **Response time:** 6 weeks letter; 3 months script.

THE YORK THEATRE COMPANY
(Founded 1968)
The Theatre at St Peter's Church, Citicorp Center, 619 Lexington Ave,
    New York, NY 10022-4610; (212) 935-5820, FAX 832-0037
James Morgan, *Associate Artistic Director*

Submission procedure: no unsolicited scripts; synopsis and letter of inquiry with SASE for response. **Types of material:** musicals, cabaret/revues. **Special interests:** small-cast musicals. **Facilities:** The Theatre at Saint Peter's Church, 147 seats, flexible. **Best submission time:** year-round. **Response time:** 1 week letter; 6 months script.

YOUNG PLAYWRIGHTS INC.
See Young Playwrights Festival in Prizes and Young Playwrights Inc. in Organizations.

Zachary Scott Theatre Center (ZACH)
(Founded 1933)
1510 Toomey Rd; Austin, TX 78704-1078; (512) 476-0594, FAX 476-0314;
    E-mail zach@io.com; Web http://www.zachscott.com
Alice Wilson, *Producing Artistic Director*

Submission procedure: no unsolicited scripts; synopsis, dialogue sample, resume and letter of inquiry. **Types of material:** full-length plays, plays for young audiences. **Facilities:** Mainstage 1, 200 seats, thrust stage; Mainstage 2, 130 seats, arena stage. **Production considerations:** plays for young audiences tour. **Best submission time:** Jul–Aug. **Response time:** 6 weeks letter; 4–6 months script.

Prizes

What competitions are included here?

All the playwriting contests we've heard of that offer prizes of at least $200 or, in the case of awards to playwrights under the age of 19, the equivalent in production or publication. Most awards for which the playwright cannot apply—the Joseph Kesselring Award, the Pulitzer Prize—are not listed. Exceptions are made when, as with the Susan Smith Blackburn Prize, the nominating process allows playwrights to encourage nomination of their work by theatre professionals who are familiar with it.

How can I give myself the best chance of winning?

When a prize entry lists a notification date, make sure you don't mistake it for the deadline for submission. (One prize sponsor asked us to delete their notification date because so many playwrights were confusing the two!) If a listing specifies "write for guidelines," be sure to follow this instruction. It usually means that we don't have space in our brief listing to give you all the information you'll need to enter the contest. Write for the guidelines (and entry form, where applicable) several months ahead. Don't wait till the last minute since contests may occasionally change their rules or their deadlines after this book has been published. Follow the guidelines precisely. Send your script in well before the deadline, when the readers are fresh and enthusiastic rather than buried by an avalanche of submissions. If you can't submit well in advance, assume the deadline is the date your script must be received (not the postmark date). Except in the few cases where sponsors note that scripts won't be returned, always send an SASE with your submission. Many competitions enclose their response letter with the script when returning it.

Should I enter contests that charge entry fees?

It's true that a number of listings in this section (and in other sections as well) require a payment of a fee. You need not conclude from this that the whole world is out to rip off playwrights. It is unfortunately the case that many contest sponsors do not secure sufficient funding to cover their costs, which are considerable. Some playwrights as a matter of principle will not pay fees, and are prepared to protest their imposition. Other writers are willing to add an entry fee to the costs of copying and postage as a part of doing business. It's up to you.

How can I find out about new prizes and updates throughout the year?

Besides writing for guidelines to ensure that you have the most recent rules for applying (changes to prizes guidelines can take place after the *Sourcebook* publishes), you should also refer to the Membership and Service Organizations and Useful Publications sections in this book for those groups that publish newsletters listing current contest news. You may also check the "Opportunities" and "Call Board" columns of *American Theatre* magazine for such announcements and updates.

A couple of *Sourcebook* reminders:

Throughout the *Sourcebook*, "full-length play" means just that—a full-length, original work without a score or libretto. One-acts, musicals, adaptations, translations, plays for young audiences and solo pieces are not called full-length plays for our purposes. If an organization is interested in those dramatic works, we'll list them separately.

Sourcebook entries are alphabetized by first word (excluding "the") even if the title starts with a proper name. So, for instance, you'll find the David James Ellis Memorial Award under D. In the index, you will also find this prize cross-listed under E. This section also includes full listings of biennial prizes whose next deadline falls after the dates of this *Sourcebook* (after August 1998). By providing this added information, we hope to give you as much lead time as possible, but please read the deadlines carefully—don't mistake a March 1999 deadline for 1998!

Alaska Native Plays Contest

Department of Theatre; University of Alaska, Anchorage; 3211 Providence Dr; Anchorage, AK 99508-8120; (907) 786-1794, FAX 786-1799; E-mail afdpe@orion.alaska.edu

David Edgecombe, *Associate Professor*

Types of material: full-length plays, one-acts, adaptations, plays for young audiences. **Frequency:** annual. **Remuneration:** $500 1st prize; $300 2nd prize; $200 3rd prize; possible production, travel to performance for Alaska playwrights only. **Guidelines:** Native North American characters and/or themes. **Submission procedure:** script only. **Deadline:** 20 Mar 1998. **Notification:** 10 May 1998.

American Shorts Contest

Florida Studio Theatre; 1241 North Palm Ave; Sarasota, FL 34236

Types of material: very short plays and solo pieces. **Frequency:** annual. **Remuneration:** $500; production for winning script and up to 12 others as part of evening of short works. **Guidelines:** play of 5 pages or less on specified theme TBA; write for guidelines. **Submission procedure:** script only. **Deadline:** TBA (15 Mar in 1997).

American Translators Association Awards

1800 Diagonal Rd, Suite 220; Alexandria, VA 22134-2840; FAX (703) 683-6122; E-mail 73564.2032@compuserve.com

Eric McMillan, *Chair, ATA Honors and Awards*

German Literary Translation Prize

Types of material: translations of full-length plays and one-acts. **Frequency:** biennial. **Remuneration:** $1000; up to $500 expenses to attend ATA annual conference. **Guidelines:** translation from German published in U.S. by American publisher during 2 years before deadline as single volume or in collection. **Submission procedure:** no submission by translator; publisher nominates translation and submits 2 copies of book plus 10 consecutive pages of German original, extra jacket and any advertising copy; brief vita of translator. **Deadline:** 15 May 1999. **Notification:** fall 1999.

Lewis Galantiere Literary Translation Prize

Types of material: translations of full-length plays and one-acts. **Frequency:** biennial. **Remuneration:** $1000; up to $500 expenses to attend ATA annual conference. **Guidelines:** translation from any language except German published in U.S. by American publisher during 2 years before deadline as single volume or in collection. **Submission procedure:** no submission by translator; publisher nominates translation and submits 2 copies of book plus 10 consecutive pages of original, extra jacket and any advertising copy; brief vita of translator. **Deadline:** 15 May 1998. **Notification:** fall 1998.

Anna Zornio Memorial Children's Theatre Playwriting Award

Department of Theater and Dance; University of New Hampshire;
  Paul Creative Arts Center; 30 College Rd; Durham, NH 03824-3538;
  (603) 862-3046, FAX 862-0298
Julie Brinker

Types of material: plays and musicals for young audiences. **Frequency:** every 4 years. **Remuneration:** $1000; production by UNH Theatre in Education Program in May 1998. **Guidelines:** U.S. or Canadian resident; unpublished work not produced professionally and not more than 1 hour long; prefers single or unit set; 2-submission limit; write for rules. **Submission procedure:** script with brief synopsis, character breakdown and statement of design/technical considerations; SASP for acknowledgment of receipt; include cassette for musical. **Deadline:** 1 Sep 1997. **Notification:** Jun 1998.

The Annual Blank Theatre Company Young Playwrights Festival

1301 Lucile Ave; Los Angeles, CA 90026-1519; (213) 662-7734;
  E-mail btc@primenet.com; Web http://www.primenet.com/~portal/
Ginnie Held, *Producer*

Types of material: full-length plays, one-acts, plays for young audiences, musicals, solo pieces, operas. **Frequency:** annual. **Remuneration:** workshop production for approximately 9 playwrights; some winning scripts subsequently receive full production. **Guidelines:** playwright 19 years of age or younger as of deadline date; original play of any length on any subject; send SASE in late Jan 1998 for guidelines. **Submission procedure:** script with cover sheet containing name, date of birth, home address, phone number, and name of school (if any). **Deadline:** Apr 1998 (exact date TBA). **Notification:** May 1998.

ASF Translation Prize

The American-Scandinavian Foundation; 725 Park Ave; New York, NY 10021;
  (212) 879-9779, FAX 249-3444; E-mail agyongy@amscan.org
Publishing Office

Types of material: translations. **Frequency:** annual. **Remuneration:** $2000; publication of excerpt in *Scandinavian Review*, $500 for runner-up. **Guidelines:** unpublished translation from a Scandinavian language into English of work written by a Scandinavian author after 1800; manuscript must be at least 50 pages long if prose, 25 pages if poetry, and must be conceived as part of a book; write for guidelines. **Submission procedure:** 4 copies of translation, 1 of original; permission letter from copyright holder. **Deadline:** 1 Jun 1998. **Notification:** fall 1998.

AT&T/EAST WEST PLAYERS NEW VOICES PLAYWRITING COMPETITION

East West Players; 4424 Santa Monica Blvd; Los Angeles, CA 90029;
(213) 660-0366, FAX 666-0896; Web http://home.earthlink.net~ewplayers
Ken Narasaki, *Literary Manager*

Types of material: full-length plays, plays for young audiences, musicals. **Frequency:** annual. **Remuneration:** 1st prize $1000, reading, possible workshop or production; 2nd prize $500, reading, possible workshop or production. **Guidelines:** English-language play not produced professionally; prefers Asian-Pacific writers and works with Asian-Pacific themes and cast. **Submission procedure:** 2 copies of script, cast list, cover letter, SASP for confirmation of receipt and $15 fee. **Deadline:** 1 Apr 1998. **Notification:** 1 Jul 1998.

ATTIC THEATRE ENSEMBLE'S ONE-ACT MARATHON

Attic Theatre Centre; 6562½ Santa Monica Blvd; Hollywood, CA 90038;
(213) 469-3786, FAX 463-9571
James Carey, *Producing Artistic Director*

Types of material: one-acts. **Frequency:** annual. **Remuneration:** 1st prize $200 and production; 2nd prize $100 and production. **Guidelines:** previously unproduced one-act no longer than 45 minutes; no adaptations. **Submission procedure:** script, brief synopsis, character breakdown, resume with cover letter and $10 fee. **Deadline:** 15 Oct 1997. **Notification:** 1 Dec 1997. **Dates:** March 1998.

BAKER'S PLAYS HIGH SCHOOL PLAYWRITING CONTEST

Baker's Plays; 100 Chauncy St; Boston, MA 02111; (617) 482-1280,
FAX 482-7613
Raymond Pape, *Associate Editor*

Types of material: full-length plays, one-acts, plays for young audiences, musicals. **Frequency:** annual. **Remuneration:** 1st prize $500 and publication; 2nd prize $250; 3rd prize $100. **Guidelines:** high school student, sponsored by high school drama or English teacher; prefers play which has been produced or given public reading; write for guidelines. **Submission procedure:** script with signature of sponsoring teacher. **Deadline:** 31 Jan 1998. **Notification:** May 1998.

BEVERLY HILLS THEATRE GUILD–
JULIE HARRIS PLAYWRIGHT AWARD

2815 North Beachwood Dr; Los Angeles, CA 90068-1923; (213) 465-2703
Marcella Meharg, *Coordinator*

Types of material: full-length plays, solo pieces. **Frequency:** annual. **Remuneration:** $5000 1st prize plus $2000 to help finance production in Los Angeles area within 1 year; $2000 2nd prize; $1000 3rd prize. **Guidelines:** U.S. citizen; 1 submission, not previously submitted, published, produced or optioned, or winner of major competition; send SASE for guidelines. **Submission procedure:** completed entry form and script. **Deadline:** 1 Nov 1997. **Notification:** Jun 1998.

BIENNIAL PROMISING PLAYWRIGHT AWARD
Colonial Players, Inc; 108 East St; Annapolis, MD 21401
Contest Coordinator

Types of material: full-length plays, bills of 2 related one-acts, adaptations. **Frequency:** biennial. **Remuneration:** $750; production (playwright must be available to attend rehearsals). **Guidelines:** resident of DC, DE, MD, PA, VA or WV; play, not produced professionally, suitable for arena stage; between 90–120 minutes; 2-set limit; cast limit of 10; only adaptations of material in public domain; send SASE for guidelines. **Submission procedure:** script and SASP for acknowledgment of receipt. **Deadline:** 31 Dec 1998; no submission before 1 Sep 1998. **Notification:** Jun 1999.

CALIFORNIA PLAYWRIGHTS COMPETITION
South Coast Repertory; Box 2197; Costa Mesa, CA 92628; (714) 957-2602, FAX 545-0391
John Glore, *Literary Manager*

Types of material: full-length plays. **Frequency:** biennial. **Remuneration:** 1st prize: $3000; staged reading; possible production with royalty; travel and housing to attend rehearsals and opening; 2nd prize: cash award of approximately $2000. **Guidelines:** playwright whose principal residence is in CA; play not professionally produced or optioned; previous entries ineligible; 2-submission limit. **Submission procedure:** completed entry form, script, synopsis of no more than 300 words and brief bio including information on CA residency. **Deadline:** 1 Dec 1997. **Notification:** Mar 1998.

CALIFORNIA YOUNG PLAYWRIGHTS CONTEST
Playwrights Project; 1450 Frazee Rd, Suite 215; San Diego, CA 92108; (619) 298-9242, FAX 298-9244
Deborah Salzer, *Director*

Types of material: full-length plays, one-acts, musicals, solo pieces. **Frequency:** annual. **Remuneration:** $100, production or staged reading, travel and housing to attend rehearsals to each of several winners (5 in 1996); all entrants receive written evaluation of work. **Guidelines:** CA writer or collaborating writers under 19 years of age as of deadline date; work at least 10 pages long; previous submissions ineligible; write for guidelines. **Submission procedure:** script, cover letter and brief bio; script will not be returned. **Deadline:** 1 Apr 1998. **Notification:** late fall 1998.

CENTER THEATER INTERNATIONAL PLAYWRIGHTING CONTEST
1346 West Devon Ave; Chicago, IL 60660; (773) 508-0200
Dale Calandra, *Literary Manager*

Types of material: full-length plays, solo pieces. **Frequency:** annual. **Remuneration:** $300; possible production; winner and runners-up receive listings in mailing sent to all TCG theatres. **Guidelines:** unpublished play, not produced or optioned; cast limit of 8, minimal technical requirements; send SASE for rules. **Submission procedure:** completed entry form, script, 1-page synopsis, character breakdown, resume, $15 fee per submission and SASE for response; script will not be returned. **Deadline:** TBA (15 Aug in 1997).

CHICANO/LATINO LITERARY CONTEST

Department of Spanish and Portuguese; University of California at Irvine; Irvine, CA 92697; (714) 824-5443, -6901
Juan Bruce-Novoa, *Director*

Types of material: full-length plays. **Frequency:** every 4 years. **Remuneration:** $1000 1st prize, publication, travel to attend award ceremony; $500 2nd prize; $250 3rd prize. **Guidelines:** U.S. citizen or resident; unpublished play written in Spanish or English; 1-submission limit; send SASE for guidelines. **Submission procedure:** 2 copies of bound script, minimum 100 typed double-spaced pages. **Deadline:** 30 Apr 1998. **Notification:** Oct 1998.

CLAUDER COMPETITION FOR EXCELLENCE IN PLAYWRITING

Box 383259; Cambridge, MA 02238-3259; (617) 322-3187
Betsy Carpenter, *Director*

Types of material: full-length plays. **Frequency:** biennial. **Remuneration:** $2500 1st prize; production by professional New England theatre; $500 prize and staged reading for several runners-up. **Guidelines:** resident of or student attending school or college in CT, MA, ME, NH, RI or VT; play not produced professionally and minimum 45 minutes long; write for guidelines. **Submission procedure:** script and production history, if any. **Deadline:** summer 1999; exact date TBA. **Notification:** TBA.

COE COLLEGE NEW WORKS FOR THE STAGE COMPETITION

Department of Theatre Arts; 1220 First Ave NE; Cedar Rapids, IA 52402; (319) 399-8689, FAX 399-8557; E-mail swolvert@coe.edu
Susan Wolverton, *Chair, Playwriting Festival*

Types of material: full-length plays, plays for young audiences. **Frequency:** biennial, contingent on funding. **Remuneration:** $325; staged reading; travel, room and board for 1-week residency during Jan term. **Guidelines:** unproduced, unpublished play dealing with theme of Playwriting Festival and Symposia (theme different each year); festival includes workshops and public discussions; no translations, adaptations or musicals; send SASE for guidelines. **Submission procedure:** script only. **Deadline:** 1 May 1998. **Notification:** 1 Nov 1998.

COLUMBUS SCREENPLAY DISCOVERY AWARDS
Christopher Columbus Society; 433 North Camden Dr, Suite 600;
Beverly Hills, CA 90210; (310) 288-1881, FAX 288-0257;
E-mail writing@screenwriters.com; Web http://screenwriters.com
Carlos de Abreu and Janice Pennington, *Co-Founders*

Types of material: screenplays. **Frequency:** annual. **Remuneration:** Discovery of the Month Award: up to 3 scripts a month selected for development and may be referred to industry professionals; all winners become eligible for Discovery of the Year Award: up to 3 scripts a year optioned by society for up to $10,000. **Guidelines:** unproduced feature screenplay not under current option; write for guidelines. **Submission procedure:** screenplay, completed application, release form and $45 fee; screenplay will not be returned. **Deadline:** last day of each month for monthly selection; 1 Dec each year for annual cycle.

CONNECTIONS
Delaware Theatre Company; 200 Water St; Wilmington, DE 19801-5030
Cleveland Morris, *Artistic Director*

Types of material: full-length plays, musicals. **Frequency:** biennial. **Remuneration:** $10,000 1st prize; staged reading; possible full production with travel to rehearsals, housing and royalties; $500 each to 2nd and 3rd prize winners. **Guidelines:** full-length play, which has not received full professional production, that deals with interracial dynamics in America. **Submission procedure:** 3 copies of script with production history, if any, and brief bio. **Deadline:** 1 Apr 1998. **Notification:** Aug 1998.

THE CUNNINGHAM PRIZE FOR PLAYWRITING
The Theatre School; DePaul University; 2135 North Kenmore;
Chicago, IL 60614-4111; (773) 325-7938, FAX 325-7920
Lara Goetsch, *Public Relations Director*

Types of material: full-length plays, plays for young audiences, musicals, solo pieces. **Frequency:** annual. **Remuneration:** $5000. **Guidelines:** Chicago-area playwright; play which "affirms the centrality of religion, broadly defined, and the human quest for meaning, truth and community"; write for guidelines. **Submission procedure:** script and brief statement making connection to purpose of prize. **Deadline:** 1 Dec 1997. **Notification:** 1 Mar 1998.

DALE WASSERMAN DRAMA AWARD
Council for Wisconsin Writers; Box 55322; Madison, WI 53705; (608) 233-2484, FAX 833-8808
Russell King, *Treasurer*

Types of material: full-length plays, one-acts, translations, adaptations, plays for young audiences, musicals, solo pieces, operas. **Frequency:** annual. **Remuneration:** $1000. **Guidelines:** current or former WI resident; work produced during preceding calendar year. **Submission procedure:** completed entry form, script and $15 fee. **Deadline:** 1 Jan 1998.

DAVID JAMES ELLIS MEMORIAL AWARD

Theatre Americana; Box 245; Altadena, CA 91003; (818) 683-1740
Playreading Committee

Types of material: full-length plays. **Frequency:** annual. **Remuneration:** $500 to best of 4 plays selected for production; color videotape of produced play. **Guidelines:** unpublished original play, not more than 2 hours in length; prefers American writers and plays on the American scene; 2-submission limit; send SASE for guidelines. **Submission procedure:** script and resume. **Deadline:** 1 Feb 1998.

DAYTON PLAYHOUSE FUTUREFEST

1301 East Siebenthaler Ave, Box 1958; Dayton, OH 45414; (937) 277-0144, FAX 277-9539
Tina McPhearson, *Managing Director*

Types of material: full-length plays, solo pieces. **Frequency:** annual. **Remuneration:** 3 plays selected for full production, 3 for reading at Jul 1998 FutureFest weekend; travel and housing to attend production; judges view full productions and award $1000 1st prize, $500 to 5 runners-up. **Guidelines:** unproduced, unpublished play; send SASE or fax number for guidelines. **Submission procedure:** script and resume. **Deadline:** 30 Sep 1997. **Notification:** Apr 1998.

DEEP SOUTH WRITERS CONFERENCE

c/o English Department; Box 44691; University of Southwestern Louisiana; Lafayette, LA 70504-4691; FAX 482-6195; E-mail wxf8424@usl.edu
Willard Fox, *Director*

James H. Wilson Full-Length Play Award

Types of material: full-length plays, solo pieces. **Frequency:** annual. **Remuneration:** $300 1st prize, $100 2nd prize. **Guidelines:** original, unpublished play (no adaptations or musicals) not produced commercially. **Submission procedure:** send SASE for guidelines. **Deadline:** 15 Jul 1998. **Notification:** Sep 1998.

Paul T. Nolan One-Act Play Award

Types of material: one-acts, solo pieces. **Frequency:** annual. **Remuneration:** $200 1st prize, $100 2nd prize; possible publication in DSWC *Chapbook.* **Guidelines:** original, unpublished play (no adaptations or musicals) less than 50 pages long, not produced commercially; publication rights to winning plays reserved until 1 Jun 1999. **Submission procedure:** send SASE for guidelines. **Deadline:** 15 Jul 1998. **Notification:** Sep 1998.

110 / PRIZES

Dorothy Silver Playwriting Competition

Jewish Community Center of Cleveland; 3505 Mayfield Rd;
　　Cleveland Heights, OH 44118; (216) 382-4000, ext 275, FAX 382-5401
Elaine Rembrandt, *Director of Cultural Arts*

Types of material: full-length plays. **Frequency:** annual. **Remuneration:** $1000 (including $500 to cover residency expenses); staged reading; possible production. **Guidelines:** unproduced play that provides fresh and significant perspective on the range of Jewish experience. **Submission procedure:** script only. **Deadline:** 15 Dec 1997. **Notification:** Aug 1998.

Dramafest 2000

Lodi Arts Commission; 125 South Hutchins St, Suite D; Lodi, CA 95240;
　　(209) 333-6895
Cyndi Olagaray, *Arts Coordinator*

Types of material: full-length plays, plays for young audiences, musicals. **Frequency:** biennial. **Remuneration:** $1000 for full-length play or musical, $1000 for play for young audiences; production; travel, housing and board to attend rehearsals. **Guidelines:** unproduced, unpublished work; write for guidelines. **Submission procedure:** completed entry form and script. **Deadline:** 1 Apr 1999; no submission before 1 Jan 1999. **Notification:** fall 1999.

Dramarama

The Playwrights' Center of San Francisco; Box 460466;
　　San Francisco, CA 94146-0466; (415) 626-4603, FAX 863-0901;
　　E-mail playctrsf@aol.com
Sheppard Kominers, *Chairman*

Long Play Contest

Types of material: full-length plays, solo pieces. **Frequency:** annual. **Remuneration:** up to 4 scripts given 4–5 rehearsals and staged readings at fall festival; $500 prize awarded on basis of readings. **Guidelines:** unproduced play minimum 60 minutes; send SASE for guidelines and application. **Submission procedure:** see guidelines; submission requirements include $25 fee. **Deadline:** 16 Mar 1998. **Dates:** Oct 1998.

Short Play Contest

Types of material: one-acts, solo pieces. **Frequency:** annual. **Remuneration:** up to 4 scripts given 4–5 rehearsals and staged readings at fall festival; $500 prize awarded on basis of readings. **Guidelines:** unproduced play maximum 60 minutes; send SASE for guidelines and application. **Submission procedure:** see guidelines; submission requirements include $25 fee. **Deadline:** 16 Mar 1997. **Dates:** Oct 1998.

DRURY COLLEGE ONE-ACT PLAY COMPETITION
Drury College; 900 North Benton Ave; Springfield, MO 65802; (417) 873-7430
Sandy Asher, *Writer-in-Residence*

Types of material: one-acts. **Frequency:** biennial. **Remuneration:** $300 1st prize, 2 runners-up receive $150; possible production; winners recommended to the Open Eye Theater (see entry in Production). **Guidelines:** unproduced, unpublished play 20–45 minutes long; prefers small cast, 1 set; 1 submission; send SASE for guidelines. **Submission procedure:** script only. **Deadline:** 1 Dec 1998. **Notification:** 1 Apr 1999.

DUBUQUE FINE ARTS PLAYERS
NATIONAL ONE-ACT PLAYWRITING CONTEST
1321 Tomahawk Dr; Dubuque, IA 52003; (319) 583-6748
Jennie G. Stabenow, *Coordinator*

Types of material: one-acts, one-act adaptations. **Frequency:** annual. **Remuneration:** $600 1st prize, $300 2nd prize, $200 3rd prize; possible production for all 3 plays. **Guidelines:** unproduced, unpublished play maximum 35 pages and 40 minutes long; prefers cast limit of 5, 1 set; no submission limit; only adaptations of material in public domain; send SASE for guidelines. **Submission procedure:** completed entry form, 2 copies of script, 1-paragraph synopsis and $10 fee per submission; optional SASE for critique and optional SASP for acknowledgment of receipt. **Deadline:** 31 Jan 1998; no submission before 1 Nov 1997. **Notification:** 30 Jun 1998.

EMERGING PLAYWRIGHT AWARD
Playwrights' Preview Productions; 17 East 47th St;
 New York, NY 10017; (212) 421-1380
David Sheppard, Jr., *Literary Manager*

Types of material: full-length plays, one-acts. **Frequency:** annual. **Remuneration:** $500; production; travel to attend rehearsals. **Guidelines:** play unproduced in New York; submissions from minority playwrights and plays with ethnically diverse casts encouraged. **Submission procedure:** script, production history (if any) and bio. **Deadline:** ongoing; best submission time Jul–Aug and Dec.

THE FESTIVAL OF EMERGING AMERICAN THEATRE (FEAT)
COMPETITION
The Phoenix Theatre; 749 North Park Ave; Indianapolis, IN 46202;
 (317) 635-7529, FAX 635-7529 (call first)
Bryan Fonseca, *Producing Director*

Types of material: full-length plays, one-acts, solo pieces. **Frequency:** annual. **Remuneration:** $750 for full-length play, $375 for one-act; 2 full-production slots will be filled, each with a full-length play or a bill of one-acts; housing to attend rehearsals. **Guidelines:** unpublished play not professionally produced and suitable for theatre with 150-seat and 75-seat houses that produces contemporary, issue-oriented works; moderate cast size and production demands; availability of playwright for rehearsals a consideration; 1 submission. **Submission procedure:** script, production history, 1- or 2-page synopsis, bio and $5 entry fee; optional SASE for critique. **Deadline:** 28 Feb 1998. **Notification:** May/Jun 1998.

Festival of Firsts Playwriting Competition
Sunset Center; Box 1950; Carmel, CA 93921; (408) 624-3996
Director

Types of material: full-length plays. **Frequency:** annual. **Remuneration:** up to $1000; possible production. **Guidelines:** unproduced play; send SASE for guidelines. **Submission procedure:** completed entry form, script, cast list, synopsis and $15 entry fee. **Deadline:** 31 Aug 1998; no submission before 15 Jun 1997.

The Francesca Primus Prize
Denver Center Theatre Company; 1050 13th St; Denver, CO 80204;
(303) 893-4000, FAX 825-2117; E-mail bsevy@star.dcpa.org
Bruce K. Sevy, *Associate Artistic Director/New Play Development*

Types of material: full-length plays. **Frequency:** annual. **Remuneration:** $2000–3000; workshop; reading as part of Denver Center Theatre Company U.S. WEST Theatrefest (see Development); travel and housing to attend rehearsals; possible full production. **Guidelines:** plays by women only. **Submission procedure:** script, cover letter and SASE for response. **Deadline:** 1 Jan 1998. **Notification:** Mar–Apr 1998.

George Hawkins Playwriting Contest
The Ensemble Theatre; 3535 Main St; Houston, TX 77002; (713) 520-0055, FAX 520-1269
Eileen Morris, *Artistic Director*

Types of material: one-acts and musicals for young audiences. **Frequency:** annual. **Remuneration:** $500 1st prize; production; travel and housing to attend final week of rehearsals; 2nd and 3rd prizewinners receive staged reading. **Guidelines:** original work, not professionally produced, that illuminates the African-American experience for young people aged 6–18; prefers works maximum 45 minutes long with cast limit of 7 and simple set and props; write for guidelines. **Submission procedure:** completed entry form and script. **Deadline:** 20 Apr 1998; no submission before 1 Dec 1997. **Notification:** 20 Jun 1998.

George Houston Bass Play-Rites Festival and Memorial Award
Rites and Reason Theatre; Box 1148; Brown University; Providence, RI 02912;
(401) 863-3558, FAX 863-3559; E-mail sheila_grant@brown.edu
Elmo Terry-Morgan *Artistic Director*

Types of material: full-length plays, one-acts, musicals, solo pieces. **Frequency:**

annual. **Remuneration:** 4 winners receive $250, staged reading at festival, travel and housing to attend rehearsals; winner of best play of festival receives $1000, workshop production, housing and travel to attend rehearsals. **Guidelines:** unproduced, unpublished work not previously awarded any other prize; plays 60–75 minutes long dealing with theme of cultural diversity; 1-submission limit. **Submission procedure:** script only; include cassette for musicals. **Deadline:** 1 Apr 1998. **Notification:** Jun 1998. **Dates:** Oct 1998.

GEORGE R. KERNODLE PLAYWRITING CONTEST

Department of Drama; 619 Kimpel Hall; University of Arkansas;
 Fayetteville, AR 72701; (501) 575-2953
Director

Types of material: one-acts. **Frequency:** annual. **Remuneration:** $300 1st prize, $200 2nd prize, $100 3rd prize; possible staged reading or production. **Guidelines:** U.S. or Canadian playwright; unproduced, unpublished play, not more than 1 hour long; cast limit of 8; 3-submission limit; write for guidelines. **Submission procedure:** script with statement that play has not received full production, $3 fee per submission and optional SASE or SASP for acknowledgment of receipt. **Deadline:** 1 Jun 1998; no submission before 1 Jan 1998. **Notification:** 1 Nov 1998.

GILMAN AND GONZALEZ-FALLA THEATRE FOUNDATION MUSICAL THEATRE AWARD

109 East 64th St; New York, NY 10021; (212) 734-8011
Janet Weis, *Coordinator*

Types of material: musicals. **Frequency:** annual. **Remuneration:** $25,000. **Guidelines:** writer(s) must have had a musical produced by commercial or nonprofit theatre; contact foundation for guidelines. **Submission procedure:** see guidelines. **Deadline:** 30 Sep 1997.

GILMORE CREEK PLAYWRITING COMPETITION

St. Mary's University of Minnesota; 700 Terrace Heights, #78;
 Winona, MN 55987; (507) 457-1606, FAX 457-1752;
 E-mail bpevitts@smumn.edu
Robert Pevitts, *Dean, School of Performing Arts*

Types of material: full-length plays, translations, adaptations, plays for young audiences, musicals, solo pieces. **Frequency:** biennial. **Remuneration:** $2500; production; stipend to cover travel, room and board for 2-week residency. **Guidelines:** full-length work not produced professionally. **Submission procedure:** completed application and script. **Deadline:** 15 Jan 1999. **Notification:** 15 May 1999.

GOSHEN COLLEGE PEACE PLAYWRITING CONTEST

Goshen College; 1700 South Main St; Goshen, IN 46526; (219) 535-7393,
FAX 535-7618; E-mail laurendf@goshen.edu
Lauren Friesen, *Director of Theatre*

Types of material: one-acts. **Frequency:** biennial. **Remuneration:** $500; production; room and board to attend rehearsals and/or production. **Guidelines:** 1 unproduced submission, 30–50 minutes long, exploring a contemporary peace theme. **Submission procedure:** script only. **Deadline:** 31 Dec 1998. **Notification:** 1 May 1999.

GREAT PLAINS PLAY CONTEST

University Theatre; 317 Murphy Hall; University of Kansas;
Lawrence, KS 66045; (913) 864-3381, FAX 864-5251
Delbert Unruh, *Director*

Types of material: full-length plays, musicals and operas for adult and young audiences. **Frequency:** annual. **Remuneration:** $2000 1st prize, production, $500 to cover travel and housing; $500 2nd prize. **Guidelines:** play not previously professionally produced dealing with any historical or contemporary aspect of the Great Plains; 2nd prize gives theatre option to produce work. **Submission procedure:** script only. **Deadline:** 1 Sep 1997. **Notification:** 15 Jan 1998.

GREAT PLATTE RIVER PLAYWRIGHTS' FESTIVAL

University of Nebraska-Kearney Theatre; Kearney, NE 68849-5260;
(308) 865-8406, FAX 865-8806; E-mail greenj@platte.unk.edu
Jeffrey Green, *Artistic Director*

Types of material: full-length plays, one-acts, plays for young audiences, musicals. **Frequency:** annual. **Remuneration:** $500 1st prize, $300 2nd prize, $200 3rd prize; production; travel and housing to attend rehearsals. **Guidelines:** unproduced, unpublished original work; submission of works-in-progress for possible development encouraged. **Submission procedure:** script with cover letter; include cassette for musical. **Deadline:** 1 Apr 1998. **Notification:** 31 Jul 1998.

THE GREGORY KOLOVAKOS AWARD

PEN American Center; 568 Broadway; New York, NY 10012; (212) 334-1660,
FAX 334-2181; E-mail pen@echonyc.com
John Morrone, *Awards Coordinator*

Types of material: translations. **Frequency:** biennial. **Remuneration:** $2000. **Guidelines:** award to U.S. writer, critic or translator whose work has made a sustained contribution over time to the cause of Latin American literatures, as well as their Iberian counterparts, in English; primarily recognizes work from Spanish but contributions from other Hispanic languages also considered; candidate must be nominated by editor or colleague; write for guideline. **Submission procedure:** letter from nominator documenting candidate's qualifications with particular attention to depth and vision of his or her work;

candidate's vita; supporting materials may be requested from finalists. **Deadline:** 1 Dec 1997. **Notification:** finalists mid-Dec 1997; winner mid-May 1998.

HAROLD MORTON LANDON TRANSLATION AWARD
The Academy of American Poets; 584 Broadway, Suite 1208;
   New York, NY 10012; (212) 274-0343
India Amos, *Program Director*

Types of material: translations. **Frequency:** annual. **Remuneration:** $1000. **Guidelines:** U.S. citizen; published translation of verse, including verse drama, from any language into English verse; book published in 1997. **Submission procedure:** 3 copies of book (no manuscripts). **Deadline:** 31 Dec 1997.

HENRICO THEATRE COMPANY
ONE-ACT PLAYWRITING COMPETITION
The County of Henrico; Division of Recreation and Parks; Box 27032;
   Richmond, VA 23273; (804) 672-5115, FAX 672-5284
J. Larkin Brown, Cultural Arts Coordinator

Types of material: one-act plays, musicals and solo pieces. **Frequency:** annual. **Remuneration:** $250 and production 1st prize; $125, possible production and video for runner-up. **Guidelines:** unproduced, unpublished work; no controversial themes; prefers small cast, simple set; write for guidelines. **Submission procedure:** 2 copies of script. **Deadline:** 1 Jul 1998. **Notification:** 31 Dec 1998.

HRC'S ANNUAL PLAYWRITING CONTEST
Hudson River Classics, Inc; Box 940; Hudson, NY 12534; (518) 828-1329
W. Keith Hedrick, *President*

Types of material: full-length plays, one-acts, solo pieces. **Frequency:** annual. **Remuneration:** $500; staged reading; room, board and travel to attend performance. **Guidelines:** 60–90-minute unpublished play by New York State playwright. **Submission procedure:** script and $5 fee. **Deadline:** 1 Jun 1998; no submission before 1 Mar 1998. **Notification:** 15 Nov 1998.

INNER CITY CULTURAL CENTER COMPETITION
Box 272; Los Angeles, CA 90028; (213) 627-7670, FAX 622-5881

Types of material: one-acts, translations, adaptations, plays for young audiences, musicals, solo pieces, operas. **Frequency:** annual. **Remuneration:** cash award ($1000 1st prize, $500 2nd prize, $250 3rd prize) or paid professional internship with film studio to winner (past winners awarded internships with Warner Brothers and Universal Studios). **Guidelines:** fully mounted productions compete in series of elimination rounds; maximum 40 minutes running time; small cast, minimal set; translations and adaptations must be of unpublished work; write for guidelines. **Submission procedure:** completed application and $45 fee. **Deadline:** 21 Jul 1998. **Dates:** Jul–Oct 1998.

Jackie White Memorial National Children's Playwriting Contest
309 Parkade Blvd; Columbia, MO 65202; (573) 874-5628
Betsy Phillips, *Director*

Types of material: plays and musicals to be performed by young actors. **Frequency:** annual. **Remuneration:** $250; production by Columbia Entertainment Company Children's Theatre School; room, board and partial travel to attend performance; all entrants receive written evaluation. **Guidelines:** unpublished original work, 60–90 minutes in length, with 20–30 speaking characters of all ages, at least 10 developed in some detail, to be played by students aged 10–15; send SASE for guidelines. **Submission procedure:** completed entry form, script, character description, act/scene synopsis, resume and $10 fee; include cassette for musical. **Deadline:** 1 Jun 1998. **Notification:** 30 Aug 1998.

James D. Phelan Award in Literature
Intersection for the Arts/The San Francisco Foundation; 446 Valencia St;
    San Francisco, CA 94103; (415) 626-2787, FAX 626-1636;
    E-mail intrsect@thecity.sfsu.edu
Awards Coordinator

Types of material: full-length plays, one-acts, plays for young audiences. **Frequency:** annual. **Remuneration:** $2000. **Guidelines:** unpublished play-in-progress; author CA born and aged 20–35 years as of 31 Jan 1998. **Submission procedure:** completed application and script. **Deadline:** 31 Jan 1998; no submission before 15 Nov 1997. **Notification:** 15 Jun 1998.

Jane Chambers Playwriting Award
c/o ATHE; Suite 300; 200 North Michigan Ave; Chicago, IL 60601;
    (937) 775-4128
Mary Donahoe, *Coordinator*

Types of material: full-length plays, one-acts, solo pieces, performance-art texts. **Frequency:** annual. **Remuneration:** $1000; student submissions eligible for $250 Student Award; both winners receive listing in mailing sent to all TCG theatres. **Guidelines:** work by a woman that reflects a feminist perspective and contains a majority of roles for women; special interest in works by and about women from a diversity of positions in respect to race, class, sexual preference, physical ability, age and geographical region; experimentation with dramatic form encouraged; 1-submission limit; award administered by the Association for Theatre in Higher Education (see Organizations); send SASE for guidelines and application. **Submission procedure:** completed application form, script, synopsis and resume; if possible, letter of endorsement by theatre professional familiar with writer's work; optional SASP for acknowledgment of receipt. **Deadline:** 15 Feb 1998. **Notification:** 30 May 1998.

JEWEL BOX THEATRE PLAYWRIGHTING AWARD

3700 North Walker; Oklahoma City, OK 73118-7099; (405) 521-1786,
FAX 525-6562
Charles Tweed, *Production Director*

Types of material: full-length plays, solo pieces. **Frequency:** annual. **Remuneration:** $500; possible production. **Guidelines:** unproduced full-length play of strong ensemble nature with emphasis on character rather than spectacle; send SASE in Oct for guidelines and forms. **Submission procedure:** completed entry form, playwright's agreement, $5 fee and 2 copies of script. **Deadline:** 15 Jan 1998. **Notification:** Apr 1998.

JOHN GASSNER MEMORIAL PLAYWRITING AWARD

The New England Theatre Conference; c/o Department of Theatre;
Northeastern University; 306 Huntington Ave; Boston, MA 02115;
(617) 424-9275, FAX 424-1057; E-mail netc@world.com

Types of material: full-length plays. **Frequency:** annual. **Remuneration:** $1000 1st prize, $500 2nd prize; staged reading at NETC annual convention; possible publication. **Guidelines:** New England resident or NETC member; unpublished play that has not had professional full production and is not under consideration for publication or professional production; 1-submission limit. **Submission procedure:** script with cover page, cast list with character descriptions, brief synopsis and statement that play has not been published or professionally produced and is not under consideration; SASP for acknowledgment of receipt; $10 fee, except for NETC members. **Deadline:** 15 Apr 1998. **Notification:** 1 Sep 1998 (winners only).

KATHERINE AND LEE CHILCOTE AWARD

Cleveland Public Theatre; 6415 Detroit Ave; Cleveland, OH 44102;
(216) 631-2727, FAX 631-2575; E-mail cpt@en.com
Terence Cranendonk, *Director, New Plays Festival*

Types of material: full-length plays, one-acts. **Frequency:** annual. **Remuneration:** 10–12 plays receive staged reading at Jan festival; of those, 2 chosen to receive award of $2000; 1 given full production. **Guidelines:** unproduced play; to be eligible for award, play must be chosen for inclusion in New Plays Festival (see Cleveland Public Theatre in Production); write for guidelines. **Submission procedure:** script and $10 fee (waivable). **Deadline:** 1 Sep 1997. **Notification:** 1 Dec 1997 for festival; 1 Jan 1998 for award.

Kennedy Center American College Theater Festival: Michael Kanin Playwriting Awards Program

The John F. Kennedy Center for the Performing Arts;
    Washington, DC 20566-0001; (202) 416-8850, FAX 416-8802
John Lion, *Producing Director*

Anchorage Press Theater for Youth Playwriting Award

Types of material: full-length plays, adaptations, musicals. **Frequency:** annual. **Remuneration:** $1000; publication by Anchorage Press with royalties; $1,250 fellowship to attend either the New Visions/New Voices Festival (see Development) or the National Youth Theatre Symposium (see Waldo M. and Grace C. Bonderman IUPUI Playwriting Competition for Young Audiences in this section). **Guidelines:** play on theme appealing to young people from kindergarten–12th grade produced by an ACTF-participating college or university; writer enrolled as full-time student at college or university during year of production or during either of the 2 years preceding the production; write for KC/ACTF brochure. **Submission procedure:** college or university which has entered production of work in ACTF registers work for awards program. **Deadline:** 1 Dec 1997. **Dates:** 27 Apr–5 May 1998.

The Fourth Freedom Forum Playwriting Award

Types of material: full-length plays. **Remuneration:** 1st prize: for playwright, $5000 plus all-expense-paid 2-week residency at Sundance Theatre Laboratory (see Development), which includes consultation with Sundance directors and dramaturgs and reading by Lab actors; $1500 to producing college or university; 2nd prize: $2500 to playwright; $1000 to producing college or university. **Guidelines:** play on themes of world peace and international disarmament; produced by an ACTF-participating college or university; writer enrolled as full-time student at college or university during year of production or during either of 2 years preceding the production; write for KC/ACTF brochure. **Submission procedure:** college or university which has entered production of work in ACTF registers work for awards program. **Deadline:** 1 Dec 1997. **Dates:** 27 Apr–5 May 1998.

The KC/ACTF Musical Theater Award

Types of material: musicals. **Frequency:** annual. **Remuneration:** $1000 for lyrics; $1000 for music; $1000 for book; $1000 to producing college or university. **Guidelines:** original and copyrighted work produced by an ACTF-participating college or university; at least 50% of writing team must be enrolled as full-time student(s) at college or university during year of production or during either of the 2 years preceding the production; write for KC/ACTF brochure. **Submission procedure:** college or university which has entered production of work in ACTF registers work for awards program. **Deadline:** 1 Dec 1997. **Dates:** 27 Apr–5 May 1998.

The Lorraine Hansberry Playwriting Award

Types of material: full-length plays. **Frequency:** annual. **Remuneration:** 1st prize: $2500, all-expenses-paid fellowship to attend playwrights retreat and publication of play by Dramatic Publishing Company (see Publication); $750 to producing college or university; 2nd prize: $1000 to playwright; $500 to producing college or university. **Guidelines:** play dealing with the black experience produced by an ACTF-participating college or university; writer enrolled as full-time student at college or university during year of production or during either of the 2 years preceding the production; write for KC/ACTF brochure. **Submission procedure:** college or university which has entered production of work in ACTF registers work for awards program. **Deadline:** 1 Dec 1997. **Dates:** 27 Apr–5 May 1998.

The National AIDS Fund Award for Playwriting

Types of material: full-length plays, adaptations, musicals. **Frequency:** annual. **Remuneration:** $2500 plus fellowship to attend Bay Area Playwrights Festival (see Development). **Guidelines:** play concerning personal and social implications of HIV/AIDS produced by an ACTF-participating college or university; writer enrolled as full-time student at college or university during year of production or during either of the 2 years preceding the production; write for KC/ACTF brochure. **Submission procedure:** college or university which has entered production of work in ACTF registers work for awards program. **Deadline:** 1 Dec 1997. **Dates:** 27 Apr–5 May 1998.

The National Student Playwriting Award

Types of material: full-length plays, adaptations, musicals. **Frequency:** annual. **Remuneration:** $2500; production at Kennedy Center during festival; publication by Samuel French with royalties; offer of William Morris Agency management contract; fellowship to attend Sundance Theatre Laboratory (see Development); Dramatists Guild membership (see Membership and Service Organizations). **Guidelines:** work must be produced by an ACTF-participating college or university; writer enrolled as full-time student at college or university during year of production or during either of the 2 years preceding the production; write for KC/ACTF brochure. **Submission procedure:** college or university which has entered production of work in ACTF registers work for awards program. **Deadline:** 1 Dec 1997. **Dates:** 27 Apr–5 May 1998.

The Short Play Awards Program

Types of material: one-acts, one-act adaptations. **Frequency:** annual. **Remuneration:** up to 3 awards: $1000; publication by Samuel French; Dramatists Guild membership (see Membership and Service Organizations). **Guidelines:** one-act must be produced by an ACTF-participating college or university; writer enrolled as full-time student at college or university during year of production or during either of the 2 years preceding the production; simple production demands (minimal setup and strike time); write for KC/ACTF brochure. **Submission procedure:** college or university which has entered production of work in ACTF registers work for awards program. **Deadline:** 1 Dec 1997. **Dates:** 27 Apr–5 May 1998.

KUMU KAHUA PLAYWRITING CONTEST

Department of Theatre and Dance; University of Hawaii at Manoa;
1770 East-West Rd; Honolulu, HI 96822; (808) 956-2588, FAX 956-4234
Dennis Carroll, *Theatre and Dance*

Hawai'i Prize

Types of material: full-length plays. **Frequency:** annual. **Remuneration:** $500. **Guidelines:** play set in HI or dealing with some aspect of HI experience; unproduced play; previous entries ineligible. **Submission procedure:** write for entry brochure. **Deadline:** 1 Jan 1998. **Notification:** 1 May 1998.

Pacific/Rim Prize

Types of material: full-length plays. **Frequency:** annual. **Remuneration:** $400. **Guidelines:** play set in or dealing with Pacific Islands, Pacific Rim or Pacific/Asian-American experience; unproduced play; previous entries ineligible. **Submission procedure:** write for entry brochure. **Deadline:** 1 Jan 1998. **Notification:** 1 May 1998.

Resident Prize

Types of material: full-length plays, one-acts. **Frequency:** annual. **Remuneration:** $200; reading and/or production if playwright present. **Guidelines:** play on any topic by HI resident; unproduced play; previous entries ineligible. **Submission procedure:** write for entry brochure. **Deadline:** 1 Jan 1998. **Notification:** 1 May 1998.

L. ARNOLD WEISSBERGER PLAYWRITING COMPETITION

New Dramatists; 424 West 44th St; New York, NY 10036; (212) 757-6960
Coordinator

Types of material: full-length plays. **Frequency:** annual. **Remuneration:** $5000. **Guidelines:** 1 unpublished submission, not produced professionally; write for guidelines. **Submission procedure:** play must be nominated, then playwright submits script with optional SASP for acknowledgment of receipt. **Deadline:** 31 May 1998; no submission before 15 Sep 1997. **Notification:** May 1999.

LAMIA INK! INTERNATIONAL ONE-PAGE PLAY COMPETITION

Box 202, Prince St Station; New York, NY 10012
Cortland Jessup, *Editor*

Types of material: 1-page plays. **Frequency:** annual. **Remuneration:** $200; reading in New York City and publication in magazine (see Lamia Ink! in Publication) for winner and 11 other best plays. **Guidelines:** 3-submission limit; send SASE for guidelines. **Submission procedure:** script, SASE for response and $1 fee per submission. **Deadline:** 15 Mar 1998. **Notification:** 15 May 1998.

Lawrence S. Epstein Playwriting Award
115 Hatteras Rd; Barnegat, NJ 08005-2814
Lawrence S. Epstein, *Director*

Types of material: full-length plays, bills of related one-acts. **Frequency:** annual. **Remuneration:** $250. **Guidelines:** unproduced play. **Submission procedure:** script and optional $1 fee to help cover expenses. **Deadline:** 31 Mar 1998; no submission before 1 Jan 1998. **Notification:** Dec 1998.

The Lee Korf Playwriting Awards
The Original Theatre Works; Burnight Center; Cerritos College;
   11110 Alondra Blvd; Norwalk, CA 90650-6298;
   (310) 860-2451, ext 2638, FAX 467-5097
Gloria Manriquez, *Production Coordinator*

Types of material: full-length plays, musicals, theatre pieces, extravaganzas. **Frequency:** annual. **Remuneration:** $750; production. **Guidelines:** special interest in works with multicultural themes. **Submission procedure:** send SASE for guidelines and application. **Deadline:** 1 Sep 1997. **Notification:** 1 Apr 1998.

The Little Theatre of Alexandria National One-Act Playwriting Competition
Little Theatre of Alexandria; 600 Wolfe St; Alexandria, VA 22314;
   (703) 683-5778
Chairman, Playwriting Competition

Types of material: one-acts. **Frequency:** annual. **Remuneration:** $350 1st prize, $250 2nd prize, $150 3rd prize; possible production. **Guidelines:** U.S. citizen; 1 unpublished, unproduced submission; prefers plays with running times of 20–60 minutes, few scenes and 1 set. **Submission procedure:** script, synopsis, character descriptions and $5 fee; send SASE for guidelines. **Deadline:** 28 Feb 1998; no submission before 1 Sep 1997. **Notification:** Sep 1998.

Live Oak Theatre's Harvest Festival of New American Plays
719 Congress Ave; Austin, TX 78701; (512) 472-5143, FAX 472-7199;
   E-mail liveoak@eden.com; Web http://www.austinlink.com/arts/liveoak.html
Michael Hankin, *Associate Director*

Types of material: full-length plays, solo pieces. **Frequency:** annual. **Remuneration:** $1000 Best New American Play Award; $500 Larry L. King Playwriting Award for Outstanding Texas Playwright; $500 for University of Texas student "who makes outstanding contribution towards new play development"; staged reading in fall festival; possible full production. **Guidelines:** U.S. resident; 1 submission, not produced professionally. **Submission procedure:** script and $15 fee. **Deadline:** 1 Apr 1998. **Notification:** fall 1998.

Lois and Richard Rosenthal New Play Prize
Cincinnati Playhouse in the Park; Box 6537; Cincinnati, OH 45206;
(513) 345-2242
Charles Towers, *Associate Artistic Associate*

Types of material: full-length plays, musicals. **Frequency:** annual. **Remuneration:** $10,000; production; travel and housing to attend rehearsals. **Guidelines:** 1 unpublished submission, not produced professionally. **Submission procedure:** no scripts; 5 pages of dialogue, 2-page maximum abstract including synopsis, character breakdown and playwright's bio, submitted by playwright or agent. **Deadline:** 1 Feb 1998; no submission before 15 Oct 1997. **Notification:** 2 months; 6 months if script is requested.

Los Angeles Designers' Theatre Commissions
Box 1883; Studio City, CA 91614-0883; (213) 650-9600 (voice),
(818) 769-9000 (TDD), (818) FAX 985-9200
Richard Niederberg, *Artistic Director*

Types of material: full-length plays, bills of related one-acts, translations, adaptations, plays for young audiences, musicals, solo pieces, operas. **Frequency:** ongoing. **Remuneration:** negotiable commissioning fee; possible travel to attend rehearsals if developmental work is needed. **Guidelines:** commissioning program for work with commercial potential which has not received professional full production, is not under option and is free of commitment to specific director, actors or other personnel; large casts and multiple sets welcome; prefers controversial material. **Submission procedure:** proposal or synopsis and resume; include cassette for musical; materials will not be returned. **Deadline:** ongoing. **Notification:** at least 4 months.

Love Creek Annual Short Play Festival
Love Creek Productions; c/o 79 Liberty Pl; Weehawken, NJ 07087-7014
Cynthia Granville-Callahan, *Festival Literary Manager/Chair, Reading Committee*

Types of material: one-acts. **Frequency:** annual. **Remuneration:** minimum of 40 finalists receive mini-showcase production in New York City during festival; $300 prize for best play of festival. **Guidelines:** unpublished play not produced in NYC area within past year; maximum length of 40 minutes; cast of 2 or more, simple sets and costumes; 2-submission limit; prefers women in major roles; festival centered around specific themes; upcoming festivals include "Fear of God: Religion in the '90s," gay and lesbian themes, political plays; send SASE for guidelines. **Submission procedure:** script with letter giving theatre permission to produce play if chosen and specifying whether Equity showcase is acceptable. **Deadline:** ongoing. **Dates:** year-round.

THE MARC A. KLEIN PLAYWRITING AWARD
Department of Theater Arts; Case Western Reserve University; 10900 Euclid Ave;
Cleveland, OH 44106-7077; (216) 368-4868, FAX 368-5184;
E-mail ksg@po.cwru.edu
John Orlock, *Chair, Reading Committee*

Types of material: full-length plays, bills of related one-acts. **Frequency:** annual. **Remuneration:** $1000, including $500 to cover residency expenses; production. **Guidelines:** student currently enrolled at U.S. college or university; work, endorsed by faculty member of university theatre department, that has not received professional full production or trade-book publication. **Submission procedure:** completed entry form and script. **Deadline:** 15 May 1998. **Notification:** 1 Aug 1998.

MARGARET BARTLE PLAYWRITING AWARD
Community Children's Theatre; 8021 East 129th Terr;
Grandview, MO 64030-2114; (816) 761-5775
Blanche Sellens, *Chairman, Playwriting Contest*

Types of material: plays and musicals for young audiences. **Frequency:** annual. **Remuneration:** $500. **Guidelines:** unpublished, unproduced work 55–60 minutes long, suitable for grades 1–6; 8-character limit; all parts played by adult women. **Submission procedure:** script only; include cassette for musical. **Deadline:** 31 Jan 1998. **Notification:** Apr 1998.

MARVIN TAYLOR PLAYWRITING AWARD
Sierra Repertory Theatre; Box 3030; Sonora, CA 95370; (209) 532-3120,
FAX 532-7270; E-mail srt@mlode.com;
Web http://www.mlode.com/~nsierra/srt
Dennis Jones, *Producing Director*

Types of material: full-length plays, adaptations, musicals, solo pieces. **Frequency:** annual. **Remuneration:** $500; possible production. **Guidelines:** 1 submission that has received no more than 2 productions or staged readings; cast limit of 15, prefers 6; not more than 2 sets. **Submission procedure:** script only. **Deadline:** 31 Aug 1997. **Notification:** Mar 1998.

MAXIM MAZUMDAR NEW PLAY COMPETITION
Alleyway Theatre; 1 Curtain Up Alley; Buffalo, NY 14202-1911; (716) 852-2600,
FAX 852-2266; E-mail alleywayth@aol.com
Joyce Stilson, *Dramaturg*

Types of material: full-length plays, one-acts, musicals. **Frequency:** annual. **Remuneration:** $400, production with royalty, and travel and housing to attend rehearsals for full-length play or musical; $100 and production for one-act play or musical. **Guidelines:** unproduced full-length work minimum 90 minutes long with cast limit of 10 and unit set or simple set, or unproduced one-act work less than 60 minutes long with cast limit of 6 and simple set; prefers work with unconventional setting that explores the boundaries of theatricality; limit of 1 submission in each category. **Submission procedure:** script and resume; $5 fee per playwright. **Deadline:** 1 Jul 1998. **Notification:** 1 Oct 1998 for finalists; 1 Feb 1998 for winners.

MCLAREN MEMORIAL COMEDY PLAYWRITING COMPETITION

Midland Community Theatre; 2000 West Wadley Ave; Midland, TX 79705; (915) 682-2544, FAX 682-6136
Mary Lou Cassidy, *Coordinator*

Types of material: full-length plays, one-acts, translations, adaptations, plays for young audiences, musicals, solo pieces. **Frequency:** annual. **Remuneration:** 4 finalists chosen for staged readings; winner receives $400, full production, housing while attending rehearsals. **Guidelines:** comedies only; prefers work that has not received professional full production but will consider work with 1 nonprofit-theatre production. **Submission procedure:** script and $5 fee. **Deadline:** 31 Jan 1998; no submission before 1 Dec 1997. **Notification:** 16 May 1998.

MIDWEST THEATRE NETWORK ORIGINAL PLAY COMPETITION/ ROCHESTER PLAYWRIGHT FESTIVAL

5031 Tongen Ave NW; Rochester, MN 55901; (507) 281-1472
Joan Sween, *Executive Director/Dramaturg*

Types of material: full-length plays, collections of one-acts, plays for young audiences, musicals, full-length solo pieces, satirical revues. **Frequency:** biennial. **Remuneration:** 4–8 awards of $1000 each (contingent on funding); full production at 1 of 7 cooperating theatres; possible travel, room and board to attend performance. **Guidelines:** unpublished work that has not received professional production; send SASE for guidelines and entry form. **Submission procedure:** 1 completed entry form with each script; $15 fee; include cassette for musical. **Deadline:** 15 Nov 1997. **Notification:** Mar 1998.

MIDWESTERN PLAYWRIGHTS FESTIVAL

The University of Toledo; Department of Theatre, Film and Dance; Toledo, OH 43606-3390; (419) 537-2202, FAX 530-8439
John S. Kuhn, *Festival Director*

Types of material: full-length plays, translations, adaptations, musicals. **Frequency:** annual. **Remuneration:** winner receives $1000, staged reading in fall 1998, production at Toledo Repertoire Theatre in spring 1999, and travel, room and board for reading and 2-week residency during production; 1st runner-up receives $350 and staged reading; 2nd runner-up receives $150 and staged reading. **Guidelines:** resident of IL, IN, MI or OH; 1 full-length, 2-act submission not published or produced professionally; cast limit of 10; prefers 1 set; write for guidelines. **Submission procedure:** 2 copies of script, 1-page synopsis, resume and cover letter. **Deadline:** 1 May 1998. **Notification:** 1 Aug 1998.

Mildred and Albert Panowski Playwriting Award
Forest A. Roberts Theatre; Northern Michigan University; Marquette, MI 49855; (906) 227-2553, FAX 227-2567
James A. Panowski, *Director*

Types of material: full-length plays, adaptations, solo pieces. **Frequency:** annual. **Remuneration:** $2000; production; travel, room and board for 1-week residency. **Guidelines:** 1 unpublished, unproduced submission; rewrites of previous entries ineligible; production will be entered in Kennedy Center American College Theater Festival (see entry in this section) if playwright is eligible; write for guidelines. **Submission procedure:** completed entry form and script. **Deadline:** 21 Nov 1997. **Notification:** Apr 1998.

The Mill Mountain Theatre New Play Competition: The Norfolk Southern Festival of New Works
1 Market Square SE, 2nd Floor; Roanoke, VA 24011-1437; (540) 342-5730, FAX 342-5745
Jo Weinstein, *Literary Manager*

Types of material: full-length plays, one-acts, musicals, solo pieces. **Frequency:** annual. **Remuneration:** $1000; staged reading with possibility of production; travel stipend and housing for limited residency. **Guidelines:** U.S. resident; 1 unproduced, unpublished submission; cast limit of 10; no 10-minute plays; send SASE for guidelines. **Submission procedure:** agent submission or script with professional recommendation by director, literary manager or dramaturg; include cassette for musical. **Deadline:** 1 Jan 1998; no submission before 1 Oct 1997. **Notification:** Aug 1998.

Morton R. Sarett National Playwriting Competition
Department of Theatre; University of Nevada, Las Vegas;
   4505 Maryland Pkwy, Box 455036; Las Vegas, NV 89154-5036;
   (702) 895-3666
Corrine A. Bonate, *Coordinator*

Types of material: full-length plays, musicals. **Frequency:** biennial. **Remuneration:** $3000; production; travel and housing to attend rehearsals and opening performance. **Guidelines:** unpublished, unproduced play or musical; no adaptations; send SASE for guidelines. **Submission procedure:** completed application, 2 copies of script and 50-word synopsis. **Deadline:** 15 Dec 1997; no submission before 1 Sep 1997. **Notification:** Jun 1998.

Moving Arts Premiere One-Act Competition
1822 Hyperion Ave; Los Angeles, CA 90027; (213) 665-8961, FAX 665-1816;
   E-mail movnarts@primenet.com; Web http://www.primenet.com/~movnart
Rebecca Rasmussen, *Director of One-Act Competition*

Types of material: one-acts. **Frequency:** annual. **Remumeration:** $200; production. **Guidelines:** play not previously produced in L.A. area; cast limit of 8; single set;

playwrights previously produced by Moving Arts ineligible. **Submission procedure:** script and $8 fee. **Deadline:** Feb 28, 1998. **Notification:** Jun 1998.

MRTW SCRIPT CONTEST

Midwest Radio Theatre Workshop; KOPN Radio; 915 East Broadway;
  Columbia, MO 65201; (573) 874-5676, FAX 499-1662;
  E-mail mrtw@mrtw.org; Web http://www.mrtw.org/mrtw
Sue Zizza, *Executive Director*

Types of material: short radio plays. **Frequency:** annual. **Remuneration:** $800 to be divided among 2–4 winners; possible radio production for local broadcast and national distribution via satellite and tape sales; scholarship to attend May 1998 Midwest Radio Theatre Workshop (see Development); publication in MRTW Scriptbook. **Guidelines:** original radio play 15–30 minutes long (no adaptations) by established or emerging writer; special interest in plays by women, gay and lesbian writers and writers of color and in issue-oriented plays on contemporary themes; 1 submission; write for guidelines. **Submission procedure:** 3 copies of script in radio format and cover letter indicating if play has been produced; $10 fee. **Deadline:** 15 Nov 1997. **Notification:** 1 Mar 1998.

NANTUCKET SHORT PLAY FESTIVAL AND COMPETITION

Nantucket Theatrical Productions; Box 2177; Nantucket, MA 02584;
  (508) 228-5002
Jim Patrick, *Literary Manager*

Types of material: one-acts. **Frequency:** annual. **Remuneration:** $200; 1 or more staged readings for winning play and selected additional plays as part of summer festival. **Guidelines:** unpublished play which has not received Equity production; maximum length of 1 hour; simple production demands; send SASE for guidelines. **Submission procedure:** script and $5 fee. **Deadline:** 1 Jan 1998. **Notification:** 1 May 1998. **Dates:** Jul 1998.

NATIONAL CHILDREN'S THEATRE FESTIVAL

Actors' Playhouse at the Miracle Theatre; 280 Miracle Mile;
  Coral Gables, FL 33134; (305) 444-9293, ext. 603, FAX 444-4181
Thomas Pender, *Education Director*

Types of material: works for young audiences. **Frequency:** annual. **Remuneration:** awards in each of 2 categories (plays and musicals): $500–1000 prize plus production, travel and housing to attend fall festival. **Guidelines:** unpublished play for young people aged 12–17, 45–60 minutes long, with cast limit of 6 (may play multiple roles) and minimal sets suitable for touring; or unpublished musical for young people aged 5–12, 45–60 minutes long, with cast limit of 8 (may play multiple roles) and minimal sets suitable for touring; translations and adaptations eligible only if writer owns copyright to material; special interest in works dealing with social issues including multiculturalism in today's society; write for guidelines. **Submission procedure:** completed entry form, script and $10 fee;

include score and cassette for musical. **Deadline:** 30 Jun 1998. **Notification:** Sep 1998. **Dates:** Nov 1998.

NATIONAL HISPANIC PLAYWRITING CONTEST

Arizona Theatre Company; Box 1631; Tucson, AZ 85702; (602) 884-8210, FAX 628-9123
Literary Manager

Types of material: full-length plays, adaptations. **Frequency:** annual. **Remuneration:** $1000; staged reading; travel, room and board to attend rehearsals and performance. **Guidelines:** playwright of Hispanic heritage residing in U.S., territories or Mexico; 1 unproduced submission written in English or in Spanish with English translation with Hispanic-American themes or setting. **Submission procedure:** script (with English translation if original in Spanish), 1-page cover letter including production history, if any, and bio. **Deadline:** 1 Sep 1997. **Notification:** spring 1998.

NATIONAL PLAY AWARD

Box 286; Hollywood, CA 90078; (213) 465-9517, FAX (310) 652-2543; E-mail nrtf@aol.com
Raul Espinoza, *Project Director*

Types of material: full-length plays. **Frequency:** annual. **Remuneration:** $5000. **Guidelines:** original unpublished play, not produced with paid Equity cast, that has not won major award or been previously submitted to NPA. **Submission procedure:** script and $25 fee (check payable to National Repertory Theatre Foundation). **Deadline:** 31 Mar 1998; no submission before 1 Jan 1998. **Notification:** 1 Sep 1998 for finalists; 31 Dec 1998 for winner.

NATIONAL TEN-MINUTE PLAY CONTEST

Actors Theatre of Louisville; 316 West Main St; Louisville, KY 40202-4218; (502) 584-1265, FAX 584-1265
Michael Bigelow Dixon, *Literary Manager*
Liz Engelman, *Assistant Literary Manager*

Types of material: 10-minute plays. **Frequency:** annual. **Remuneration:** Heideman Award of $1000; possible production with royalty. **Guidelines:** U.S. citizen or resident; play 10 pages long or less which has not had Equity production; 2-submission limit; previous entries ineligible; write for guidelines. **Submission procedure:** script only. **Deadline:** 1 Dec 1997. **Notification:** fall 1998.

NEW AMERICAN COMEDY (NAC) FESTIVAL

Ukiah Players Theatre; 1041 Low Gap Rd; Ukiah, CA 95482; (707) 462-1210
Lesley Currier, *NAC Producer*

Types of material: full-length plays. **Frequency:** biennial. **Remuneration:** 2 awards: $1000; staged reading; up to $400 travel, housing and $25 per diem to attend 2-week festival. **Guidelines:** unproduced, unpublished comedy; prefers small cast, simple set; playwright must be available to participate in 2-week developmental process during festival; write for guidelines. **Submission procedure:** completed application, script with 1-page summary of plot, scenic requirements, character breakdown and estimated running time; optional resume. **Deadline:** 31 Sep 1997. **Notification:** 1 Feb 1998. **Dates:** May 1998.

NEW CHRISTIAN PLAYS AWARD
Ensemble Theatre Company/Colorado Christian University;
    180 South Garrison St; Lakewood, CO 80226; (303) 238-5386, ext 131;
    E-mail prdorn@aol.com
Patrick Rainville Dorn, *Literary Manager*

Types of material: full-length plays, one-acts, adaptations, plays for young audiences, musicals, solo pieces. **Frequency:** annual. **Remuneration:** $200 1st prize; possible production and publication in *Christian Drama Magazine* or *Encore Performance Publishing* for winner and 3 finalists. **Guidelines:** unpublished play that is "good theatre with a Christian worldview and not preachy or didactic"; send SASE for guidelines. **Submission procedure:** script and $15 fee. **Deadline:** 1 Jun 1998. **Notification:** 1 Sep 1998.

NEW LINE THEATRE MUSICAL THEATRE COMPETITION
3649 Dunnica Ave, #2E; St. Louis, MO 63116; (314) 773-6526
Scott Miller, *Artistic Director*

Types of material: one-act musicals. **Frequency:** annual. **Remuneration:** $750; production; possible travel and housing to attend rehearsals. **Guidelines:** unproduced work maximum 50 minutes long; must deal with social or political issue; cast limit of 8; unit set. **Submission procedure:** 3 copies of script, 1 copy each of score for 2 songs, cassette of entire score, and resume(s). **Deadline:** 15 Oct 1997. **Notification:** 31 Dec 1997. **Dates:** Feb or Mar 1998.

NEW PROFESSIONAL THEATRE WRITERS FESTIVAL
424 West 42nd St, 3rd Floor; New York, NY 10036;
    (212) 290-8150, FAX 290-8202; E-mail newprof@aol.com
Kenneth Johnson, *Literary Manager*

Types of material: full-length plays. **Frequency:** annual. **Remuneration:** 3 awards of $2000; excerpts performed at Oct gala; seminars and mentoring. **Guidelines:** special interest in African-American women writers. **Submission procedure:** script, resume and SASP for acknowledgment of receipt. **Deadline:** 1 Jun 1998. **Notification:** Sep 1998.

New Women Playwright's Contest
Off Center Theater; Tampa Bay Performing Arts Center; Box 518;
 Tampa, FL 33601-0518; (813) 222-1087, FAX 222-1057;
 E-mail tbpac@cent.com
Karla Hartley, *Artistic Associate*

Types of material: full-length plays. **Frequency:** annual. **Remuneration:** 1st prize $1000, full production, travel and housing to attend rehearsals and performance; 2nd prize $100, staged reading, possible travel and housing; 3rd prize $50, reading. **Guidelines:** unproduced comedies by and about women with small casts at least 50% female; prefers plays depicting "strong, intelligent, contemporary women with keen senses of humor." **Submission procedure:** script, synopsis and $15 fee. **Deadline:** 12 Sep 1997. **Notification:** Dec 1997.

New York City High School Playwriting Contest
Young Playwrights Inc; 321 West 44th St, Suite 906; New York, NY 10036;
 (212) 307-1140, FAX 307-1454; E-mail writeaplay@aol.com
Sheri M. Goldhirsch, *Artistic Director*

Types of material: full-length plays, one-acts. **Frequency:** annual. **Remuneration:** $500. **Guidelines:** New York City high school student; writers under 18 years of age automatically entered in Young Playwrights Festival National Playwriting Contest (see listing in this section); write for guidelines. **Submission procedure:** script with playwright's name, date of birth, home address, phone number, school and grade on title page. **Deadline:** 1 Apr 1998. **Notification:** 1 Jun 1998.

Oglebay Institute Towngate Theatre Playwriting Contest
Oglebay Institute; Stifel Fine Arts Center; 1330 National Rd;
 Wheeling, WV 26003; (304) 242-7700, FAX 242-7700
Performing Arts Department

Types of material: full-length plays. **Frequency:** annual. **Remuneration:** $300; production; partial travel to attend performances. **Guidelines:** unpublished, unproduced play; simple set. **Submission procedure:** script and resume. **Deadline:** 30 Dec 1997. **Notification:** 1 May 1998.

Pacific Northwest Writers Conference Literary Contest
2033 Sixth Ave, Suite 804; Seattle, WA 98121;
 (206) 443-3807, FAX 441-8262; E-mail pnwriterscons@halcyon.com;
 Web http://www.reporters.net/pnwc
Shirley Bishop, *Executive Director*

Types of material: one-acts. **Frequency:** annual. **Remuneration:** 3 prizes awarded to writers chosen from 13 categories, 1 of which is playwriting; $300 1st prize, $200 2nd prize, $150 3rd prize; all finalists receive written critiques; award-winning play receives reading at summer conference. **Guidelines:** unpublished, unproduced play; maximum 40 pages long and cast limit of 4; 1-submission limit per category per writer; send SASE for guidelines and registration form. **Submission procedure:** completed registration form, 2 copies of script submitted anonymously with separate sheet giving 1-sentence plot summary and playwright's name and contact information; $30 fee for nonmembers or $20 fee for members; include SASE for critique and SASP for acknowledgment of receipt. **Deadline:** TBA (15 Feb in 1997). **Notification:** Jul 1998.

PAUL GREEN PLAYWRIGHTS PRIZE

North Carolina Writers' Network; Box 954; Carrboro, NC 27510;
E-mail nc_writers@unc.edu; Web http://sunsite.unc.edu/ncwn

Types of material: full-length plays, one-acts, solo pieces. **Frequency:** annual. **Remuneration:** $500, possible production. **Guidelines:** unpublished, unproduced play; send SASE for guidelines. **Submission procedure:** 2 copies of script, synopsis and $10 fee for nonmembers or $7.50 fee for members; do not list name on manuscript, include separate cover sheet with title, name and contact information; include SASE for winners list. **Deadline:** 30 Sep 1997. **Notification:** Jan 1998.

PEN CENTER USA WEST LITERARY AWARDS

672 South Lafayette Park Pl, Suite 41; Los Angeles, CA 90057;
(213) 365-8500, FAX 365-9616
Rachel Hall, *Administrative Coordinator*

Types of material: full-length plays, screenplays, teleplays. **Frequency:** annual. **Remuneration:** $500 award in each of several categories, including drama, screenwriting and television writing. **Guidelines:** writer residing west of Mississippi River; only full-length (original or adapted) screenplays and teleplays; script first produced during 1997 calendar year. **Submission procedure:** 4 copies of script with cover letter giving title of work, author's name and state of residence, name of producer and production dates. **Deadline:** 31 Dec 1997.

PEN–BOOK-OF-THE-MONTH CLUB TRANSLATION PRIZE

PEN American Center; 568 Broadway; New York, NY 10012;
(212) 334-1660, FAX 334-2181; E-mail pen@echonyc.com
John Morrone, *Program Coordinator*

Types of material: translations. **Frequency:** annual. **Remuneration:** $3000. **Guidelines:** book-length translation from any language into English published in U.S. during current calendar year. **Submission procedure:** 3 copies of book. **Deadline:** 15 Dec 1997. **Notification:** May 1998.

PERISHABLE THEATRE WOMEN'S PLAYWRITING FESTIVAL

Box 23132; Providence, RI 02903; (401) 331-2695, FAX 331-7811;
Web http://www.ids.net/~as220/perishable/home.html
Kathleen Jenkins, *Festival Director*

Types of material: one-act plays. **Frequency:** annual. **Remuneration:** 3 awards of $200; production. **Guidelines:** unproduced one-act, less than 1 hour in length, by woman playwright. **Submission procedure:** script and resume. **Deadline:** 31 Dec 1997. **Notification:** 31 Mar 1998.

PLAYHOUSE ON THE SQUARE NEW PLAY COMPETITION

Playhouse on the Square; 51 South Cooper St; Memphis, TN 38104;
 (901) 725-0776, 726-4498
Jackie Nichols, *Executive Director*

Types of material: full-length plays, musicals. **Frequency:** annual. **Remuneration:** $500; production. **Guidelines:** unproduced work; small cast; full arrangement for piano for musical; prefers southern playwrights. **Submission procedure:** script only. **Deadline:** 1 Apr 1997.

PLAYWRIGHTS FIRST AWARD

c\o The National Arts Club; 15 Gramercy Park South; New York, NY 10003;
 (212) 249-6299

Types of material: full-length plays. **Frequency:** annual. **Remuneration:** $1000 for best play; reading for selected plays; useful introductions to theatre professionals. **Guidelines:** 1 unproduced play written within last 2 years (no adaptations or translations). **Submission procedure:** script and resume. **Deadline:** 15 Oct 1997. **Notification:** May 1998.

PLAYWRIGHTS' THEATER OF DENTON PLAYWRITING COMPETITION

Box 732; Denton, TX 76202-0732
Mark Pearce, *Artistic Director*

Types of material: full-length plays, one-acts, solo pieces. **Frequency:** annual. **Remuneration:** $1000. **Submission procedure:** script and $15 fee (check payable to Sigma Corporation). **Deadline:** 15 Dec 1997.

QRL POETRY SERIES AWARDS

Quarterly Review of Literature; Princeton University; 26 Haslet Ave;
 Princeton, NJ 08540
Renée Weiss, *Co-Editor*

Types of material: full-length plays, one-acts, translations. **Frequency:** annual. **Remuneration:** $1000; publication in QRL Poetry Series; 100 complimentary paperback copies. **Guidelines:** up to 6 awards a year for poetry and poetic drama only; play 50–100 pages in length; send SASE for guidelines. **Submission procedure:** submissions accepted in Nov and May only; must be accompanied by $20 subscription for books published in series.

Renato Poggioli Award

PEN American Center; 568 Broadway; New York, NY 10012; (212) 334-1660,
FAX 334-2181; E-mail pen@echonyc.com
John Morrone, *Program Coordinator*

Types of material: translations. **Frequency:** annual. **Remuneration:** $3000. **Guidelines:** book-length translation from Italian into English by promising young translator; work-in-progress eligible. **Submission procedure:** curriculum vitae, sample of translation and original Italian text. **Deadline:** 5 Jan 1998. **Notification:** May 1998.

Reva Shiner Full-Length Play Contest

Bloomington Playwrights Project; 308 South Washington St;
Bloomington, IN 47401; (812) 334-1188
Kathy Fletcher, *Artistic Director*

Types of material: full-length plays, musicals. **Frequency:** annual. **Remuneration:** $500; staged reading; production. **Guidelines:** unpublished, unproduced work 75–150 minutes long, suitable for production in small 65-seat theatre; welcomes innovative works; small-scale musicals; simple set; write for guidelines. **Submission procedure:** script, cover letter and $5 fee; include cassette for musical. **Deadline:** 15 Jan 1998. **Notification:** Apr 1998.

Robert Bone Memorial Playwriting Award

The Playwrights' Project; Sammons Center for the Arts, #12;
3630 Harry Hines Blvd; Dallas, TX 75219; (214) 497-1752
Priscilla Sample, *Artistic Director*

Types of material: full-length plays, musicals. **Frequency:** annual. **Remuneration:** $500; all entries receive 1-page written critique. **Guidelines:** resident of AR, AZ, CO, NM, OK or TX; unproduced play; 1-submission limit. **Submission procedure:** script, synopsis, bio and $15 fee; optional SASE for critique; optional SASE for acknowledgment of receipt; include cassette for musical. **Deadline:** 1 May 1998. **Notification:** Aug 1998.

Robert J. Pickering Award
for Playwriting Excellence

Coldwater Community Theater; c/o 89 South Division; Coldwater, MI 49036;
(517) 279-7963
J. Richard Colbeck, *Chairman, Play Selection Committee*

Types of material: full-length plays, plays for young audiences, musicals, solo pieces. **Frequency:** annual. **Remuneration:** 1st prize $300, production and housing to attend performance; 2nd prize $100; 3rd prize $50. **Guidelines:** unproduced play. **Submission procedure:** script only. **Deadline:** 31 Dec 1997. **Notification:** 1 Feb 1998.

SAM EDWARDS DEAF PLAYWRIGHTS COMPETITION
New York Deaf Theatre; 305 Seventh Ave, 11th Floor;
New York, NY 10001-6008; (212) 924-9535 (teletypewriter);
E-mail nydt@juno.com
Robert DeMayo, *Artistic Director*

Types of material: full-length plays, one-acts. **Frequency:** annual. **Remuneration:** $400 for full-length play, $200 for one-act; possible full or workshop production or staged reading. **Guidelines:** unproduced play by deaf playwright; write for guidelines. **Submission procedure:** completed application, script, short synopsis and bio; fee of $10 for U.S. playwright, $15 for non-U.S. playwright. **Deadline:** 31 Dec 1997. **Notification:** Aug 1998.

SCHOLASTIC WRITING AWARDS
555 Broadway; New York, NY 10012; (212) 343-6892

Types of material: for high school seniors only, portfolios of 3–8 pieces (fiction, poetry, drama, etc.); for students grades 7–12, individual pieces in various categories, including drama (stage, film, television and radio scripts). **Frequency:** annual. **Remuneration:** $5000 scholarship towards college tuition for author of each of 5 best portfolios; $1000 merit award, to be applied toward tuition for New York University's Tisch School of the Arts dramatic writing program, for best work in any category by high school senior; cash prizes totaling $25,000 awarded to several top students in each category, including dramatic writing. **Guidelines:** portfolio totaling not more than 50 pages; for dramatic category, unpublished script not more than 30 minutes long; write for further information by 1 Oct 1997. **Submission procedure:** completed application and portfolio or script. **Deadline:** mid-Jan 1998; exact date TBA. **Notification:** May 1998.

SHORT GRAIN CONTEST
Grain Magazine; Box 1154; Regina, SK S4P 3B4; Canada; (306) 244-2828, FAX 244-0255; E-mail grain.mag@sk.sympatico.ca;
Web http://www.sasknet.com/corporate/skwriter
Steven Ross Smith, *Business Manager*

Types of material: monologues. **Frequency:** annual. **Remuneration:** $500 1st prize, $300 2nd prize, $200 3rd prize (Canadian dollars); winners and honorable mentions receive payment for publication in magazine. **Guidelines:** unpublished, unproduced monologue not submitted elsewhere; 500-word maximum; write for guidelines. **Submission procedure:** U.S. and international entries: entry form and $24 fee; Canadian entries: entry form and $20 fee for first 2 entries ($5 fee for each additional entry); fee includes 1-year subscription. **Deadline:** 31 Jan 1998. **Notification:** 30 Apr 1998.

Shubert Fendrich Memorial Playwriting Contest

Pioneer Drama Service; Box 4267; Englewood, CO 80155-4267; (303) 779-4035, FAX 779-4315; E-mail piodrama@aol.com

Lynne Zborowski, *Editor*

Types of material: full-length plays, one-acts, translations, adaptations, plays for young audiences, musicals. **Frequency:** annual. **Remuneration:** publication with $1000 advance on royalties (10% book royalty, 50% performance royalty). **Guidelines:** produced, unpublished work not more than 90 minutes long; subject matter and language appropriate for schools and community theatres; prefers works with a preponderance of female roles and minimal set requirements; all entries considered for publication; send SASE for guidelines. **Submission procedure:** script with proof of production (e.g., program, reviews); include score or cassette for musical. **Deadline:** 1 Mar 1998 (scripts received after deadline will be considered for 1999 contest).

Siena College International Playwrights Competition

Department of Creative Arts; Siena College; 515 Loudon Rd; Loudonville, NY 12211-1462; (518) 783-2381, FAX 783-4293; E-mail maciag@siena.edu

Gary Maciag, *Director of Theatre*

Types of material: full-length plays. **Frequency:** biennial. **Remuneration:** $2000; production; $1000 to cover residency expenses. **Guidelines:** play that has had no previous workshop or full production; prefers play suitable for college audience and featuring characters suitable for college-age performers; prefers small cast; playwright must be available for 6-week residency in Jan/Feb 1999. **Submission procedure:** send SASE for application form and guidelines after 1 Nov 1997; mail completed application with letter-size SASE in advance of script. **Deadline:** 30 Jun 1998; no submission before 1 Feb 1998. **Notification:** 30 Sep 1998.

Source Theatre Company
1998 Literary Prize

1835 14th St NW; Washington, DC 20009; (202) 462-1073

Keith Parker, *Literary Manager*

Types of material: full-length plays, one-acts, musicals, solo pieces. **Frequency:** annual. **Remuneration:** $250; workshop production in Washington Theatre Festival (see theatre's entry in Production). **Guidelines:** work not produced professionally. **Submission procedure:** script, synopsis, resume and letter-size SASE for response; materials will not be returned. **Deadline:** 15 Jan 1998. **Notification:** 15 May 1998.

South Carolina Playwrights' Festival
Trustus Theatre; Box 11721; Columbia, SC 29211; (803) 771-9153,
    FAX 771-9153
Jayce T. Tromsness, *Literary Manager*

Types of material: full-length plays, one-acts, solo pieces. **Frequency:** annual. **Remuneration:** 1st prize of $500 and production with travel and housing to attend opening; 2nd prize of $250 and staged reading; one-acts eligible only for $50 prize and reading as part of Late Night series. **Guidelines:** play not produced professionally; cast limit of 8; prefers 1 set; full-length play not less than 80 minutes long; send SASE for guidelines and application. **Submission procedure:** completed application. **Deadline:** 1 Feb 1998; no submission before 1 Jan 1998. **Notification:** 1 Jun 1998.

South Florida Writers Contest
South Florida Chapter National Writers Association; Box 570415;
    Miami, FL 33257-0415; (305) 235-2867
Charles Aye, *President*

Types of material: full-length plays, one-acts. **Frequency:** annual. **Remuneration:** 1st prize $250, stage reading; 2nd prize $100, stage reading. **Guidelines:** unpublished, unproduced work. **Submission procedure:** script, cover letter and $10 fee. **Deadline:** 15 Jan 1998. **Notification:** Apr 1998.

Southeastern Theatre Conference New Play Project
Box 9868; Greensboro, NC 27429-0868; (910) 272-3645
James I. Schempp, *Coordinator*

Types of material: full-length plays, bills of related one-acts. **Frequency:** annual. **Remuneration:** $1000; staged reading at SETC Annual Convention; travel, room and board to attend convention; submission of work by SETC to O'Neill Center for favored consideration for National Playwrights Conference (see Development). **Guidelines:** resident of state in SETC region (AL, FL, GA, KY, MS, NC, SC, TN, VA, WV); unproduced work; bills of one-acts bound in 1 cover; limit of 1 full-length submission or bill of one-acts. **Submission procedure:** completed application and script. **Deadline:** 1 Jun 1998. **Notification:** Nov 1998.

Southern Playwrights Competition
228 Stone Center; Jacksonville State University; Jacksonville, AL 36265;
    (205) 782-5411, FAX 782-5441; E-mail swhitton@jsucc.jsu.edu
Steven J. Whitton, *Coordinator*

Types of material: full-length plays, solo pieces. **Frequency:** annual. **Remuneration:** $1000; production; housing to attend rehearsals. **Guidelines:** native or resident of AL, AR, FL, GA, KY, LA, MS, NC, SC, TN, TX, VA or WV; 1 unpublished original submission that deals with the southern experience and has not received Equity production; write for guidelines. **Submission procedure:**

completed entry form, script and synopsis. **Deadline:** 15 Feb 1998. **Notification:** 1 May 1998.

SUMMERFIELD G. ROBERTS AWARD

The Sons of the Republic of Texas; 1717 8th St; Bay City, TX 77414;
(409) 245-6644, FAX 245-6644
Melinda Williams

Types of material: full-length plays. **Frequency:** annual. **Remuneration:** $2500 given to work from 1 of several genres, including playwriting. **Guidelines:** play about living in the Republic of Texas, completed during calendar year preceding deadline. **Submission procedure:** 5 copies of script; scripts will not be returned. **Deadline:** 15 Jan 1998. **Notification:** early Apr 1998.

THE SUSAN SMITH BLACKBURN PRIZE

3239 Avalon Pl; Houston, TX 77019; (713) 308-2842
Emilie S. Kilgore, *Board of Directors*

Types of material: full-length plays. **Frequency:** annual. **Remuneration:** $5000 1st prize plus signed Willem de Kooning print, made especially for Blackburn Prize; $2000 2nd prize; $500 to each of 8–10 other finalists. **Guidelines:** woman playwright of any nationality writing in English; unproduced play or play produced within one year of deadline. **Submission procedure:** no submission by playwright; professional artistic director, literary manager or dramaturg invited to nominate play and submit 2 copies of script; playwright may bring script to attention of eligible nominator; send 55¢-postage SASE for guidelines and list of theatres eligible to nominate. **Deadline:** 20 Sep 1997. **Notification:** Jan 1998 for finalists; Feb 1998 for winners.

SWTA ANNUAL NEW PLAY CONTEST

Southwest Theatre Association; University of Texas at El Paso; Theatre Arts Dept;
500 West University Ave; El Paso, TX 79968-0549; (915) 747-7854
FAX 747-5438
Michael Wright, *New Plays Committee*

Types of material: full-length plays, one-acts, adaptations. **Frequency:** annual. **Remuneration:** $200 1st prize; staged reading at SWTA convention in Nov 1998; publication in SWTA journal, *Theatre Southwest*. **Guidelines:** unproduced, unpublished play. **Submission procedure:** script, brief synopsis, character breakdown and $10 fee (check payable to SWTA); letter of recommendation helpful. **Deadline:** 1 Mar 1998.

TADA! SPRING STAGED READING SERIES/NEW PLAY PROJECT

120 West 28th St; New York, NY 10001; (212) 627-1732, FAX 243-6736;
E-mail tada@ziplink.net; Web http://www.tadatheater.com
Janine Nina Trevens, *Artistic Director*

Types of material: one-acts for young audiences. **Frequency:** annual. **Remuneration: 5 awards of $200 and staged reading. **Guidelines:** unproduced, unpublished one-act by professional or student playwright; prefers plays not more than 1 hour long; majority of roles must be for child actors who do not play adult characters; prefers works with human characters, as opposed to "animal" plays. **Submission procedure:** script and character breakdown. **Deadline:** 1 Jul 1998. **Notification:** Sep 1998.

TENNESSEE WILLIAMS/NEW ORLEANS LITERARY FESTIVAL ONE-ACT PLAY COMPETITION

Metro College Conference Services, ED 122; University of New Orleans; New Orleans, LA 70148; (504) 581-1144

Types of material: one-acts. **Frequency:** annual. **Remuneration:** $1000; reading in spring 1998 festival; production in spring 1999 festival. **Guidelines:** unpublished play on an American subject, not more than 1 hour long and not produced professionally. **Submission procedure:** script with SASE for notification and $15 fee (check payable to University of New Orleans); script will not be returned; write for guidelines before submitting work. **Deadline:** 1 Dec 1997.

THEATER AT LIME KILN REGIONAL PLAYWRITING CONTEST

Lime Kiln Arts; 14 South Randolph St; Lexington, VA 24450; (540) 463-7088, FAX 463-1082; E-mail limekiln@cfw.com
Eleanor Connor, *Community Liaison/Dramaturg*

Types of material: full-length plays, one-acts, musicals. **Frequency:** annual. **Remuneration:** $1000 1st prize, $500 2nd prize; possible staged reading. **Guidelines:** unproduced, unpublished work relating to the Appalachian region; plays with music encouraged; write for guidelines. **Submission procedure:** script, short synopsis, history of play and bio; include letter-size SASE if notification is desired. **Deadline:** 30 Sep 1997. **Notification:** spring 1998 (if SASE is enclosed).

THEATRE CONSPIRACY ANNUAL NEW PLAY CONTEST

Theatre Conspiracy, Inc; 10091 McGregor Blvd; Ft. Myers, FL 33919; (941) 936-3239
Bill Taylor, *Artistic Director*

Types of material: full-length plays. **Frequency:** annual. **Remumeration:** $500; production. **Guidelines:** play not previously produced; cast limit of 6; simple production demands. **Submission procedure:** script, 1-page synopsis, character breakdown, technical requirements, bio and $10 fee. **Deadline:** 10 Jan 1998. **Notification:** Apr 1998. **Dates:** late Jul–early Aug 1998.

THEATRE MEMPHIS NEW PLAY COMPETITION
630 Perkins St Extended; Memphis, TN 38117-4799; (901) 682-8323,
    FAX 763-4096
Chair, New Play Competition

Types of material: full-length plays. **Frequency:** triennial. **Remuneration:** cash award, exact amount TBA ($1500 in 1996); award may be split between 2 winners; possible production with travel and housing to attend performance. **Guidelines:** original work not produced with royalty payment prior to deadline date; send SASE for guidelines after 1 Jul 1998. **Submission procedure:** script submitted anonymously with detached title page giving playwright's name and address; resume. **Deadline:** 1 Jul 1999. **Notification:** Dec 1999.

THEODORE WARD PRIZE FOR AFRICAN-AMERICAN PLAYWRIGHTS
Columbia College Chicago Theater/Music Center; 72 East 11th St;
    Chicago, IL 60605; (312) 663-1600, ext 6136, FAX 663-9591;
    E-mail chigochuck@aol.com
Chuck Smith, *Facilitator*

Types of material: full-length plays, translations, adaptations, full-length solo pieces. **Frequency:** annual. **Remuneration:** 1st prize $2000, production, travel and housing to attend rehearsals; 2nd prize $500, staged reading; 3rd prize, staged reading at Goodman Theatre. **Guidelines:** U.S. resident of African-American descent; 1 full-length submission not professionally produced; translations and adaptations of material in public domain only; write for guidelines. **Submission procedure:** script, short synopsis, production history and brief resume. **Deadline:** 1 Jul 1998; no submission before 1 Apr 1998. **Notification:** Nov 1998.

THRESHOLD THEATER METAPHYSICAL PLAY CONTEST
1907 Cannonwood Ln; Austin, TX 78745; (512) 448-4373
Jennifer Mellett, *Executive Director*

Types of material: full-length plays. **Frequency:** annual. **Remuneration:** $200. **Guidelines:** play, not professionally produced, whose theme involves two contrasting levels of theatrical reality (e.g. the dead and the living, waking and dreaming, body and soul, material and nonmaterial) and the crossing of the "threshold" between them; 100–135 minutes long; must have at least 3 substantial speaking roles and maximum cast of 8; prefers 1 set; write for guidelines by 1 Jan 1998. **Submission procedure:** script, synopsis, resume and $15 fee. **Deadline:** 1 Apr 1998. **Notification:** 31 Mar 1999.

TOWNGATE THEATRE PLAYWRITING CONTEST
Oglebay Institute; Stifel Fine Arts Center; 1330 National Rd;
    Wheeling, WV 26003, (304) 242-7700

Types of material: full-length plays. **Frequency:** annual. **Remuneration:** $300; production; partial travel expenses. **Guidelines:** unproduced, unpublished play;

no musicals; no submission limit. **Submission procedure:** script only. **Deadline:** 1 Jan 1998. **Notification:** 1 May 1998.

TOWSON STATE UNIVERSITY PRIZE FOR LITERATURE
Towson State University; Towson, MD 21252; (410) 830-2128
Dean, College of Liberal Arts

Types of material: book or book-length manuscript; all literary genres eligible, including plays. **Frequency:** annual. **Remuneration:** $1000. **Guidelines:** work published within 3 years prior to submission or scheduled for publication within the year; author no more than 40 years of age, MD resident for 3 years and at time prize awarded. **Submission procedure:** publisher or playwright submits completed application and 5 copies of work; write for guidelines. **Deadline:** 15 May 1998. **Notification:** 1 Dec 1998.

UNICORN THEATRE NATIONAL PLAYWRIGHTS' AWARD
3820 Main St; Kansas City, MO 64111; (816) 531-7529, FAX 531-0421
Herman Wilsen, *Literary Assistant*

Types of material: full-length plays. **Frequency:** no set dates. **Remuneration:** $1000; production; possible travel and residency. **Guidelines:** unpublished play not produced professionally; special interest in social issues; contemporary (post-1950) themes and settings only; cast limit of 10; 2-submission limit. **Submission procedure:** no scripts; send synopsis, at least 10 pages of dialogue, character breakdown, resume, letter of inquiry and SASE for response. **Deadline:** ongoing. **Notification:** 4 weeks; 4–6 months if script is requested.

UNIVERSITY OF LOUISVILLE GRAWEMEYER AWARD FOR MUSIC COMPOSITION
Grawemeyer Music Award Committee; School of Music; University of Louisville;
 Louisville, KY 40292; (502) 852-6907, FAX 852-0520;
 E-mail mlgreeoi@ulkyum.louisville.edu
Paul Brink, *Chair*

Types of material: works in major musical genres, including music-theatre works and operas. **Frequency:** annual. **Remuneration:** $150,000 (paid in 5 annual installments of $30,000). **Guidelines:** work premiered during previous 5 years; entry must be sponsored by professional music organization or individual; write for guidelines. **Submission procedure:** completed application, score, cassette, supporting materials and $30 fee submitted jointly by composer and sponsor. **Deadline:** 26 Jan 1998. **Notification:** late spring 1998.

URBAN STAGES AWARD
17 East 47th St; New York, NY 10017; (212) 421-1380
David Sheppard, Jr., *Literary Manager*

Types of material: one-acts. **Frequency:** annual. **Remuneration:** $200, 4–6 "radio style" staged readings in libraries throughout New York City's boroughs.

Guidelines: play which has not been produced in New York; maximum 1 hour long with cast limit of 5; special interest in minority playwrights and ethnically diverse casts; send SASE for guidelines. **Submission procedure:** script, production history and author bio. **Deadline:** 15 Jun 1998.

VERMONT PLAYWRIGHTS AWARD
The Valley Players; Box 441; Waitsfield, VT 05673-0441; (802) 496-3751
Jennifer Howard, *Coordinator*

Types of material: full-length plays. **Frequency:** annual. **Remuneration:** $1000; probable production. **Guidelines:** resident of ME, NH or VT; unproduced, unpublished play, suitable for community group, that has not won playwriting competition; moderate production demands; send SASE for guidelines. **Submission procedure:** completed entry form and 2 copies of script. **Deadline:** 1 Feb 1998.

VERY SPECIAL ARTS PLAYWRIGHT DISCOVERY PROGRAM
(Formerly Very Special Arts Young Playwrights Program)
Education Office; The John F. Kennedy Center for the Performing Arts; Washington, DC 20566; (800) 933-8721 (voice), 737-0645 (TTY), FAX 737-0725; E-mail saraq@vsarts.org
Elena Widder, *Program Manager, Program Development*

Types of material: full-length plays, one-acts. **Frequency:** annual. **Remuneration:** scholarship; professional production at Kennedy Center; travel, room and board to attend performance. **Guidelines:** play dealing with some aspect of disability by writer with a disability, aged 25 and under; write for guidelines. **Submission procedure:** 2 copies of script and short bio. **Deadline:** Apr 1998; exact date TBA.

WALDO M. AND GRACE C. BONDERMAN IUPUI PLAYWRITING COMPETITION FOR YOUNG AUDIENCES
IUPUI University Theatre; 425 University Blvd, Suite 309; Indianapolis, IN 46202; (317) 274-2095, FAX 278-1025; E-mail dwebb@indyunix.iupui.edu
Mark McCreary, *Literary Manager*

Types of material: plays for young audiences. **Frequency:** biennial. **Remuneration:** 4 prizes of $1000; 1 week of developmental work culminating in showcase reading at National Youth Theatre Playwriting Symposium; travel, room and board for residency. **Guidelines:** well-crafted play with strong storyline, compelling characters and careful attention to language; unpublished play at least 45 minutes long and not previously produced by Equity company; writer must be available for week-long residency. **Submission procedure:** send SASE for entry form and guidelines. **Deadline:** 1 Sep 1998. **Notification:** Dec 1998. **Dates:** first week of May 1999.

WE DON'T NEED NO STINKIN' DRAMAS
(Formerly Mixed Blood Versus America)
Mixed Blood Theatre Company; 1501 South 4th St; Minneapolis, MN 55454; (612) 338-0937
David Kunz, *Script Czar*

Types of material: full-length comedies, musical comedies. Frequency: annual. Remuneration: $2000 if theatre chooses to produce play; $1000 if not. Guidelines: unproduced, unpublished work by U.S. citizen who has had at least 1 work produced or workshopped professionally or by educational institution; 2-submission limit (dual entries must be sent under separate cover); plays minimum 65 pages long about race issues, sports or with a political edge; write for guidelines. If interested in MBTC but not sure if work is suitable, send brief cover letter and 1-page-maximum synopsis to MBTC. Submission procedure: script; resume optional. Deadline: 15 Mar 1998. Notification: fall 1998.

WEST COAST ENSEMBLE CONTESTS
Box 38728; Los Angeles, CA 90038; (310) 449-1447, FAX 453-2254
Les Hanson, *Artistic Director*

West Coast Ensemble Full-Length Play Competition

Types of material: full-length plays. Frequency: annual. Remuneration: $500; production; royalty on any performances beyond 8-week run. Guidelines: 1 submission not produced in southern CA; cast limit of 12. Submission procedure: script with SASE or SASP for acknowledgment of receipt. Deadline: 31 Dec 1997. Notification: within 6 months of deadline.

West Coast Ensemble Musical Stairs

Types of material: musical theatre works. Frequency: annual. Remuneration: $500; production; royalty on any performances beyond 8-week run. Guidelines: 1 unpublished musical submission not produced in southern CA; all genres and styles eligible, including pop, rock, country and western, etc.; cast limit of 12. Submission procedure: script, cassette of music (include score and lead sheets if available). Deadline: 30 Jun 1998. Notification: within 6 months.

WHITE BIRD ANNUAL PLAYWRITING CONTEST
White Bird Productions; Box 20233, Columbus Circle Station;
    New York, NY 10023; (718) 788-5984
Kathryn Dickinson, *Artistic Director*

Types of material: full-length plays, one-acts. Frequency: annual. Remuneration: $200; staged reading; possible travel to attend rehearsals. Guidelines: play whose theme, plot and/or central idea deals in a general or specific way with the environment; 2-submission limit. Submission procedure: script and resume. Deadline: 15 Feb 1998. Notification: Jun 1998.

WICHITA STATE UNIVERSITY PLAYWRITING CONTEST
University Theatre; Wichita State University; Wichita, KS 67260-0153;
(316) 689-3368, FAX 689-3951
Leroy Clark, *Contest Director*

Types of material: full-length plays, bills of related one-acts. **Frequency:** annual. **Remuneration:** production; expenses for playwright to attend production. **Guidelines:** unpublished, unproduced work at least 90 minutes long by student currently enrolled at U.S. college or university; write for guidelines. **Submission procedure:** script only. **Deadline:** 15 Feb 1998. **Notification:** 15 Apr 1998.

WRITER'S DIGEST WRITING COMPETITION
1507 Dana Ave; Cincinnati, OH 45207-1005; (513) 531-2690, ext 580
Competition Coordinator

Types of materials: full-length plays, screenplays, teleplays. **Frequency:** annual. **Remuneration:** Grand Prize: $1000, expenses-paid trip to New York City to meet with editors and agents; $500 1st prize, $250 2nd prize, $100 3rd prize, each with $100 worth of Writer's Digest books; $50 4th prize with current *Writer's Market* and 1-year subscription to *Writer's Digest* magazine; $25 5th prize with 1-year subscription to *Writer's Digest* magazine. **Guidelines:** unproduced, unpublished work, not accepted by publisher or producer at time of submission; previous entries ineligible; send SASE for guidelines. **Submission procedure:** completed entry form, first 15 pages of script, 1-page synopsis and indication of projected market for work, and $10 fee. **Deadline:** 30 May 1998. **Notification:** fall 1998.

YEAR-END-SERIES (Y.E.S.) NEW PLAY FESTIVAL
Department of Theatre; Northern Kentucky University;
Highland Heights, KY 41099; (606) 572-6362, FAX 572-5566;
E-mail mking@nku.edu
Michael King, *Project Director*

Types of material: full-length plays, adaptations, musicals. **Frequency:** biennial. **Remuneration:** 3 awards of $400; production; travel and expenses to attend late rehearsals and performance; 1 award of $100; staged reading; travel and expenses to attend reading. **Guidelines:** unproduced work in which majority of roles can be handled by students; small orchestra for musicals; 1-submission limit. **Submission procedure:** completed application and script. **Deadline:** 15 Oct 1998. **Notification:** Jan 1999. **Dates:** 17–27 Apr 1999.

Young Playwrights Festival National Playwriting Contest
Young Playwrights Inc.; 321 West 44th St, Suite 906; New York, NY 10036;
(212) 307-1140; E-mail writeaplay@aol.com
Sheri M. Goldhirsch, *Artistic Director*

Types of material: full-length plays, one-acts. **Frequency:** annual. **Remuneration:** staged reading or production with royalty; travel and residency; 1-year Dramatists Guild membership (see Membership and Service Organizations). **Guidelines:** playwright 18 years of age or younger as of 15 Oct 1997; submissions from playwrights of all backgrounds encouraged; write for guidelines. **Submission procedure:** script with playwright's name, date of birth, home address and phone number on title page. **Deadline:** 15 Oct 1997.

Publication

What is listed in this section?

Those who are primarily or exclusively play publishers and who consider work of unpublished writers. In addition, we list literary magazines and other small presses which have indicated they publish plays.

How can I determine the best places to submit my play?

Think of these publishers as highly individual people looking for very particular kinds of material, which means you should find out as much as possible about their operations before submitting scripts. One of the best ways to do research is by contacting the Council of Literary Magazines and Presses: 154 Christopher St, Suite 3C; New York, NY 10014-2839; (212) 741-9110. Ask for *The 1997–98 Directory of Literary Magazines* ($12.95 paper, plus $3.05 for 1st-class postage and handling), a descriptive listing of hundreds of magazines, including many which say they publish plays. You may be able to look at copies of some of these in a local library or bookstore. Other leads may be found in the *1997–98 International Directory of Little Magazines and Small Presses* (Dustbooks; Box 100; Paradise, CA 95967; (916) 877-6110; $32.95 paper, $47.95 cloth, plus $6.00 shipping and handling). You can also write to individual publishers listed here and ask for style sheets, catalogues, sample copies, etc. Don't forget that when publishers say they accept unsolicited scripts, they *always* require you to enclose an SASE for return of the manuscript.

Alabama Literary Review
253 Smith Hall; Troy State University; Troy, AL 36082; (334) 670-3307
FAX 670-3519
Theron Montgomery, *Chief Editor*

Types of material: full-length plays, one-acts, translations, adaptations, solo pieces. **Remuneration:** 3 complimentary copies (more on request); $5–10 a page when funds are available. **Guidelines:** biannual literary journal publishing 2–3 plays a year; plays less than 50 pages long, less than 30 pages preferred. **Submission procedure:** accepts unsolicited scripts. **Response time:** 2–3 months.

Amelia Magazine
329 "E" St; Bakersfield, CA 93304; (805) 323-4064;
E-mail amelia@lightspeed.net
Frederick A. Raborg, Jr., *Editor*

Types of material: one-acts, including translations and solo pieces. **Remuneration:** $150 prize; 10 complimentary copies. **Guidelines:** winner of annual Frank McClure One-Act Play Award published in magazine; unpublished play maximum 45 minutes long. **Submission procedure:** submit script, including note of any productions, and $15 fee. **Deadline:** 15 May 1998. **Notification:** 15 Sep 1998.

American Theatre
Theatre Communications Group; 355 Lexington Ave; New York, NY 10017-0217; (212) 697-5230
Jim O'Quinn, *Editor in Chief*
Wendy Weiner, *Play Editor*

Types of material: full-length plays, one-acts, translations, adaptations, plays for young audiences. **Remuneration:** fee for one-time serial rights; 25 complimentary copies. **Guidelines:** national magazine publishing 5 plays a year; significant works from the contemporary world theatre. **Submission procedure:** no unsolicited scripts; submissions at play editor's request only.

American Writing: A Magazine
4343 Manayunk Ave; Philadelphia, PA 19128
Alexandra Grilikhes, *Editor*

Types of material: translations, solo pieces, short experimental theatre pieces, performance pieces, performance artists' in-process notes and diaries. **Remuneration:** 3 complimentary copies. **Guidelines:** biannual literary/arts journal publishing 1 or 2 theatrical works a year; seeks new writing that takes risks and explores new forms; interested in "the voice of the loner"; 10,000 words maximum. **Submission procedure:** accepts unsolicited scripts. **Response time:** 3–6 months.

ANCHORAGE PRESS
Box 8067; New Orleans, LA 70182; (504) 283-8868, FAX 866-0502
Orlin Corey, *Editor*

Types of material: works for young audiences, including full-length plays, one-acts, translations, adaptations and musicals. **Remuneration:** negotiated royalty. **Guidelines:** specialty house publishing quality works for young audiences only; works produced at least 3 times. **Submission procedure:** accepts unsolicited scripts with proof of production. **Response time:** 45–90 days.

ARAN PRESS
1320 South 3rd St; Louisville, KY 40208-2306; (502) 636-0115
Tom Eagan, *Editor and Publisher*

Types of material: full-length plays, one-acts, translations, adaptations, solo pieces. **Remuneration:** 10% book royalty, 50% production royalty; playwright contributes to publishing costs: $300 for full-length play, $150 for one-act. **Guidelines:** plays suitable for marketing to community, college and university, summer stock, dinner and professional theatres. **Submission procedure:** accepts unsolicited scripts; prefers letter of inquiry with SASE for response. **Response time:** 2 weeks.

ART CRAFT PUBLISHING COMPANY
Box 1058; Cedar Rapids, IA 52406; (319) 364-6311, FAX 364-1771;
    E-mail editor@hitplays.com; Web http://www.hitplays.com
C. Emmett McMullen, *Editor and Publisher*

Types of material: plays for young audiences, including full-length plays, one-acts and musicals. **Remuneration:** outright purchase or performance royalty; complimentary copies. **Guidelines:** works suitable for middle school and junior and senior high school market. **Submission procedure:** accepts unsolicited scripts. **Response time:** 1–2 months.

ARTE PÚBLICO PRESS
University of Houston; Houston, TX 77204-2090; (713) 743-2841, FAX 743-2847
Nicolás Kanellos, *Publisher*

Types of material: full-length plays, one-acts, adaptations, plays for young audiences, musicals. **Remuneration:** negotiated royalty; complimentary copies. **Guidelines:** unpublished works in English or Spanish by Hispanic writers only. **Submission procedure:** accepts unsolicited scripts. **Response time:** 6 months.

ASIAN PACIFIC AMERICAN JOURNAL
37 Saint Marks Pl, Suite B; New York, NY 10003-7801; (212) 228-6718,
    FAX 228-7718; E-mail aaww@panix.com;
    Web http://www.panix.com./~aaww
Editors

Types of material: one-acts. **Remuneration:** 2 complimentary copies. **Guidelines:**

biannual literary journal publishing work by and/or of interest to Asian-Americans; plays maximum 4000 words. **Submission procedure:** accepts unsolicited scripts; send 2 copies of script. **Response time:** 3 months.

AUDREY SKIRBALL-KENIS PLAY COLLECTION
630 West 5th St.; Los Angeles, CA 90071; (213) 228-7327, FAX 228-7339
Tom Harris, *Project Director*

Types of material: full-length plays, one-acts, translations, adaptations, plays for young audiences, musicals, solo pieces, performance-art texts. **Remuneration:** descriptive listing of work in Southern California Unpublished Plays Collection, catalogue of plays housed in Central Library in downtown Los Angeles. **Guidelines:** plays must be unpublished and professionally produced in Southern California; all scripts meeting criteria are accepted. **Submission procedure:** accepts unsolicited scripts.

BAKER'S PLAYS
100 Chauncy St; Boston, MA 02111; (617) 482-1280, FAX 482-7613
Raymond Pape, *Associate Editor*

Types of material: full-length plays, one-acts, plays for young audiences, musicals, chancel dramas. **Remuneration:** negotiated book and production royalty. **Guidelines:** prefers produced plays; prefers plays suitable for high school, community and regional theatres; "Plays from Young Authors" division features plays by high school playwrights. **Submission procedure:** accepts unsolicited scripts with resume; include press clippings if play has been produced. **Response time:** 2–6 months. **Special programs:** Baker's Plays High School Playwriting Contest (see Prizes).

THE BELLINGHAM REVIEW
The Signpost Press; Mail Stop 9053; Western Washington University;
    Bellingham, WA 98225
Robin Hemley, *Editor*

Types of material: one-acts, solo pieces. **Remuneration:** 1 complimentary copy; 1-year subscription. **Guidelines:** biannual small-press periodical featuring short plays, fiction, poetry and creative nonfiction; unpublished plays less than 10,000 words long. **Submission procedure:** accepts unsolicited scripts; submit 1 Sep–1 May only. **Response time:** 4 months.

BLIZZARD PUBLISHING
73 Furby St; Winnipeg, MB R3C 2A2; Canada;
    (204) 775-2923, (800) 694-9256, FAX (204) 775-2947;
    E-mail atwood@blizzard.mb.ca
Peter Atwood, *Managing Editor*

Types of material: full-length plays, one-acts, translations, adaptations, plays for young audiences. **Remuneration:** advance against royalties; 10% book royalty; complimentary copies. **Guidelines:** publishes 11 plays a year and critical literature on theatre; special interest in contemporary or provocative themes and educational works; write for guidelines. **Submission procedure:** no unsolicited scripts; synopsis and letter of inquiry; submit Mar–Nov only. **Response time:** 4 months.

BROADWAY PLAY PUBLISHING, INC.
56 East 81st St; New York, NY 10028-0202; (212) 772-8334, FAX 772-8358; E-mail BroadwayPl@aol.com

Types of material: full-length plays. **Remuneration:** 10% book royalty, 80% amateur royalty, 90% stock royalty; 10 complimentary copies. **Guidelines:** major interest is in original, innovative work by American playwrights; no historical or autobiographical plays. **Submission procedure:** no unsolicited scripts; letter of inquiry. **Response time:** 3 months.

CALLALOO
Department of English; University of Virginia; Bryan Hall; Charlottesville, VA 22903; (804) 924-6637, FAX 924-1478
Charles H. Rowell, *Editor*

Types of material: one-acts, including translations. **Remuneration:** complimentary copies and offprints; payment when grant money is available. **Guidelines:** journal of Afro-American and African arts and letters published by Johns Hopkins University Press. **Submission procedure:** accepts unsolicited scripts. **Response time:** 6 months.

COLLAGES & BRICOLAGES
Box 86; Clarion, PA 16214; (814) 226-5799; E-mail fortis@vaxa.clarion.edu
Marie-José Fortis, *Editor*

Types of material: one-acts. **Remuneration:** 2 complimentary copies. **Guidelines:** annual journal of international writing publishing poetry, fiction, drama and criticism, including 1–5 plays a year; for 1998 issue, works on theme of "Racial and Cultural Tensions" only; minimalist plays; avant-garde and feminist work; innovative plays less than 30 pages long. **Submission procedure:** accepts unsolicited scripts. **Deadline:** 15 Dec for 1998 issue. **Response time:** 2 weeks–3 months.

CONFRONTATION
English Department; C.W. Post College of Long Island University; Greenvale, NY 11548; (516) 299-2391, FAX 299-2735; E-mail mtucker@eagle.liunet.edu
Martin Tucker, *Editor*

Types of material: one-acts. **Remuneration:** $15–75; 1 complimentary copy. **Guidelines:** general magazine for "literate" audience; unpublished plays. **Submission procedure:** accepts unsolicited scripts. **Response time:** 8–10 weeks.

CONTEMPORARY DRAMA SERVICE
Meriwether Publishing, Ltd; 885 Elkton Dr; Colorado Springs, CO 80907
(719) 594-4422, FAX 594-9916
Arthur L. Zapel, *Executive Editor*

Types of material: one-acts, adaptations, plays for young audiences, musicals, readers' theatre, monologues. **Remuneration:** book royalties or payment for amateur and professional performance rights. **Guidelines:** publishes works suitable for teenage, high school and college market, as well as collections of scenes and practical books on theatre arts; no works for preteen audiences; prefers comedies; prefers produced works; special interest in works by authors with name recognition. **Submission procedure:** accepts unsolicited scripts; send $2 for sample catalogue and guidelines. **Response time:** 2 months.

CRAZYQUILT QUARTERLY
Box 632729; San Diego, CA 92163-2729; (619) 688-1023, FAX 688-1753
Marsh Cassady, *Drama Editor*

Types of material: one-acts, including solo pieces. **Remuneration:** 2 complimentary copies. **Guidelines:** quarterly literary journal publishing 4–6 plays a year; one-act plays not more than 30 pages long. **Submission procedure:** accepts unsolicited scripts. **Response time:** 2 months.

DESCANT
Box 314, Station P; Toronto, Ontario; Canada M5S 2S8; (416) 593-2557
Mary Myers, *Managing Editor*

Types of material: full-length plays, one-acts, performance-art texts. **Remuneration:** $100 honorarium; 1 complimentary copy (additional copies at 40% discount). **Guidelines:** quarterly literary magazine publishing an average of 2 plays a year; unpublished plays. **Submission procedure:** accepts unsolicited scripts. **Response time:** 6 months.

THE DRAMATIC PUBLISHING COMPANY
311 Washington St; Box 129; Woodstock, IL 60098; (815) 338-7170,
   FAX 338-8981; E-mail 75712.3621@compuserve.com;
   Web http://www.dramaticpublishing.com
Linda Habjan, *Editor*

Types of material: full-length plays, one-acts, translations, adaptations, plays for young audiences, musicals, monologues. **Remuneration:** standard royalty; 10 complimentary copies (33% discount on additional copies). **Guidelines:** works for professional, stock and amateur markets; at least 10 minutes long; prefers produced plays. **Submission procedure:** accepts unsolicited scripts. **Response time:** 4–8 months.

Dramatics Magazine

3368 Central Pkwy; Cincinnati, OH 45225; (513) 559-1996, FAX 559-0012;
E-mail pubs@one.net
Don Corathers, *Editor*

Types of material: full-length plays, one-acts and solo pieces for young audiences. **Remuneration:** payment for 1-time publication rights; complimentary copies. **Guidelines:** educational theatre magazine; plays suitable for high school production; prefers produced plays. **Submission procedure:** accepts unsolicited scripts. **Response time:** 2–3 months.

Dramatists Play Service

440 Park Ave South; New York, NY 10016; (212) 683-8960, FAX 213-1539;
E-mail postmaster@dramatists.com;
Web http://www.dramatists.com/dramatists
Stephen Sultan, *President*

Types of material: full-length plays, one-acts, translations, adaptations, plays for young audiences, musicals. **Remuneration:** usually advance against royalties; 10% book royalty, 80% amateur royalty, 90% stock royalty; 10 complimentary copies. **Guidelines:** works for stock and amateur market; prefers works produced in New York City. **Submission procedure:** no unsolicited scripts; letter of inquiry. **Response time:** 3–5 months.

Earth's Daughters

Box 41, Central Park Station; Buffalo, NY 14215; (716) 837-7778

Types of material: full-length plays, one-acts, translations, adaptations, plays for young audiences, solo pieces. **Remuneration:** 2 complimentary copies. **Guidelines:** triannual feminist literary and art periodical with focus on experience and creative expression of women; publishes play excerpts with occasional issue devoted to complete text of play. **Submission procedure:** accepts unsolicited scripts. **Response time:** 2 months.

Eldridge Publishing Company

Box 1595; Venice, FL 34284-1595; (800) HI-STAGE; E-mail info@histage.com;
Web http://www.histage.com
Nancy S. Vorhis, *Editor*

Types of material: full-length plays, one-acts, musicals. **Remuneration:** outright purchase of religious material only; all other works, 10% book royalty, 50% amateur and educational royalty; complimentary copies (50% discount on additional copies). **Guidelines:** publishes 50–75 plays and musicals a year for school, church and community theatre; comedies, mysteries or serious drama. **Submission procedure:** accepts unsolicited scripts; if possible, include cassette for musicals. **Response time:** 2 months.

Encore Performance Publishing
Box 692; Orem, UT 84057; (801) 225-0605
Michael C. Perry, *President*

Types of material: full-length plays, one-acts, translations, adaptations, plays for young audiences, musicals, solo pieces. **Remuneration:** 10% book royalty, 50% performance royalty; 10 complimentary copies (discount on additional copies). **Guidelines:** publishes 10–30 plays and musicals a year; works must have had at least 2 amateur or professional productions; special interest in works with strong family or Judeo-Christian message and in Christmas, Halloween and other holiday plays. **Submission procedure:** no unsolicited scripts; synopsis, production information and letter of inquiry; best submission time May–Aug. **Response time:** 2–4 weeks letter; 2–3 months script.

Freelance Press
Box 548; Dover, MA 02030; (508) 785-8250, FAX 785-8291
Narcissa Campion, *Managing Editor*

Types of material: musicals. **Remuneration:** 10% book royalty, 70% performance royalty; 1 complimentary copy. **Guidelines:** unpublished issue-oriented musicals and musical adaptations of classics; approximately 1 hour long, suitable for performing by young people only. **Submission procedure:** accepts unsolicited scripts. **Response time:** 3 months.

Heuer Publishing Company
Box 248; Cedar Rapids, IA 52406; (319) 364-6311, FAX 364-1771;
    E-mail editor@hitplays.com; Web http://www.hitplays.com
C. Emmett McMullen, *Editor and Publisher*

Types of material: works for young audiences, including full-length plays, one-acts and musicals. **Remuneration:** outright purchase or performance royalty; complimentary copies. **Guidelines:** works suitable for middle school and junior and senior high school markets. **Submission procedure:** accepts unsolicited scripts. **Response time:** 1–2 months.

I. E. Clark Publications
Box 246; Schulenburg, TX 78956-0246; (409) 743-3232
Donna Cozzaglio, *Editorial Department*

Types of material: full-length plays, one-acts, translations, adaptations, plays for young audiences, musicals. **Remuneration:** book and performance royalties. **Guidelines:** publishes for worldwide professional, amateur and educational market; prefers produced works. **Submission procedure:** accepts unsolicited scripts; cassette or videotape must accompany musical; include proof of production with reviews and photos for produced works; send $3 for catalogue; send SASE for submission guidelines. **Response time:** 2–6 months.

KALLIOPE, A JOURNAL OF WOMEN'S ART
Florida Community College; 3939 Roosevelt Blvd; Jacksonville, FL 32205
Mary Sue Koeppel, *Editor*

Types of material: one-acts, including solo pieces. **Remuneration:** 3 complimentary copies or free 1-year subscription. **Guidelines:** triannual journal of women's art publishing short fiction, poetry, artwork, photography, interviews, reviews and an average of 1 play a year; unpublished plays, less than 25 pages long, by women only; no trite themes or erotica. **Submission procedure:** accepts unsolicited scripts. **Response time:** 3–6 months.

THE KENYON REVIEW
Kenyon College; Gambier, OH 43022; (614) 427-5202, FAX 427-5417;
E-mail kenyonreview@kenyon.edu
David H. Lynn, *Editor*

Types of material: one-acts (including solo pieces), excerpts from full-length plays. **Remuneration:** cash payment; 2 complimentary copies. **Guidelines:** literary journal publishing an average of 2 plays a year; unproduced, unpublished works maximum 30 pages long. **Submission procedure:** accepts unsolicited scripts (typed and double-spaced only) with SASE for response. **Response time:** 3 months.

LAMIA INK!
Box 202, Prince St Station; New York, NY 10012
Cortland Jessup, *Editor*

Types of material: very short monologues and performance pieces; 1-page plays for contest (see below). **Remuneration:** 4 complimentary copies. **Guidelines:** triannual "art rag" magazine; experimental theatre pieces maximum 5 pages long, prefers 2–3 pages; special interest in Japanese, Pacific Rim and Native American writers, and poets' theatre, performance poems, theatre manifestos and essays. **Submission procedure:** accepts unsolicited scripts with SASE for response. **Deadline:** 30 Sep for Dec issue; 30 Dec for Feb issue; 30 Mar for May issue. **Response time:** 2–3 weeks after deadline. **Special programs:** Lamia Ink! International One-Page Play Competition (see Prizes).

LILLENAS DRAMA RESOURCES
Lillenas Publishing Company; Box 419527; Kansas City, MO 64141;
(816) 931-1900, (800) 877-0700, FAX 753-4071
Paul M. Miller, *Consultant/Editor*

Types of material: full-length plays, one-acts, musicals, collections of sketches, skits, playlets, recitations. **Remuneration:** outright purchase or royalty. **Guidelines:** unpublished "creatively conceived and practically producible scripts and outlines that provide church and school with an opportunity to glorify God and his creation in drama." **Submission procedure:** accepts unsolicited scripts; send SASE for contributor's guidelines and current need sheet. **Response time:** 3 months.

NEW PLAYS
Box 5074; Charlottesville, VA 22905; (804) 979-2777;
E-mail patwhitton@aol.com
Patricia Whitton, *Publisher*

Types of material: plays for young audiences. **Remuneration:** 10% book royalty, 50% performance royalty. **Guidelines:** innovative material not duplicated by other sources of plays for young audiences; produced plays, directed by someone other than author. **Submission procedure:** accepts unsolicited scripts. **Response time:** at least 1-2 months.

PACIFIC REVIEW
English Department; California State University; 5500 University Pkwy; San Bernardino, CA 92407-2397; (909) 880-5894
James Brown and Juan Delgado, *Faculty Editors*

Types of material: one-acts, including solo pieces. **Remuneration:** 2 complimentary copies. **Guidelines:** annual literary journal; plays maximum 25 pages long. **Submission procedure:** accepts unsolicited scripts; submit 1 Sep–1 Feb only. **Response time:** 3 months.

PAJ BOOKS
Box 260, Village Station; New York, NY 10014-0260; (212) 243-3885,
FAX 243-3885; E-mail pajpub@aol.com
Bonnie Marranca and Gautam Dasgupta, *Editors*

Types of material: full-length plays, one-acts, translations, solo pieces. **Remuneration:** royalty and/or fee. **Guidelines:** plays and critical literature on the performing arts from the international repertoire published by John Hopkins University Press; special interest in translations. **Submission procedure:** no unsolicited scripts; synopsis and letter of inquiry. **Response time:** 1-2 months.

PERFORMING ARTS JOURNAL
Box 260, Village Station; New York, NY 10014-0260; (212) 243-3885,
FAX 243-3885; E-mail pajpub@aol.com
Bonnie Marranca and Gautam Dasgupta, *Co-Publishers and Editors*

Types of material: short full-length plays, one-acts, translations, solo pieces. **Remuneration:** fee. **Guidelines:** publishes plays and critical essays on the performing arts from the international repertoire; special interest in translations; plays less than 40 pages long. **Submission procedure:** no unsolicited scripts; synopsis and letter of inquiry. **Response time:** 1-2 months.

PIONEER DRAMA SERVICE
Box 4267; Englewood, CO 80155-4267; (303) 779-4035, FAX 779-4315;
E-mail piodrama@aol.com

Types of material: full-length plays, one-acts, plays for young audiences, musicals.

Remuneration: royalty. **Guidelines:** produced work suitable for educational theatre, including melodramas and Christmas plays. **Submission procedure:** accepts unsolicited scripts; prefers synopsis and letter of inquiry. **Response time:** 2 weeks letter; 3–4 months script. **Special programs:** Shubert Fendrich Memorial Playwriting Contest (see Prizes).

PLAYERS PRESS
Box 1132; Studio City, CA 91614-0132; (818) 789-4980
Robert W. Gordon, *Senior Editor*

Types of material: full-length plays, one-acts, translations, adaptations, plays for young audiences, musicals, solo pieces, monologues, scenes, teleplays, screenplays. **Remuneration:** cash option and/or outright purchase or royalty; complimentary copies (additional copies at 20% discount). **Guidelines:** theatre press publishing technical and reference books and scripts; produced works for professional, amateur and educational markets. **Submission procedure:** accepts unsolicited scripts with proof of production, resume and 2 business-size SASEs; prefers synopsis, proof of production, resume and letter of inquiry with SASE for response. **Response time:** 1–6 weeks letter; 1–6 months script.

PLAYS ON TAPE
Box 5789; Bend, OR 97708-5789; (541) 923-6246, FAX 923-9679;
    E-mail theatre@playsontape.com; Web http://www.playsontape.com
Literary Dept.

Types of material: full-length plays, one-acts. **Remuneration:** $1000 plus 15% royalty for full-length plays; negotiable fee and royalty for shorter works; 10 complimentary copies of audiotape. **Guidelines:** audiobook company marketing primarily to bookstores; "works that do not diminish in quality due to restrictions of audiotape" only; prefers non-naturalistc "bizarre" plays that take risks and have contemporary themes; special interest in works by women and minorities. **Submission procedure:** accepts unsolicited scripts; prefers synopsis, letter of inquiry and up to 10 pages of dialogue with SASE or e-mail address for response; send SASE for guidelines. **Response time:** 3 months.

PLAYS, THE DRAMA MAGAZINE FOR YOUNG PEOPLE
120 Boylston St; Boston, MA 02116-4615; (617) 423-3157,
    FAX (no submissions) 423-2168; Web http://www.channel1.com/plays
Elizabeth Preston, *Managing Editor*

Types of material: one-act plays for young audiences, including adaptations of material in the public domain. **Remuneration:** payment on acceptance. **Guidelines:** publishes about 70 plays and programs a year; prefers work 20–30 minutes long for junior and senior high, 15–20 minutes for middle grades, 8–15 minutes for lower grades; no religious plays. **Submission procedure:** accepts unsolicited original scripts; letter of inquiry for adaptations; prefers format used in magazine (send SASE for style sheet). **Response time:** 2 weeks.

POEMS & PLAYS
English Department; Middle Tennessee State University; Murfreesboro, TN 37132;
(615) 898-2712, FAX 898-5098
Gay Brewer, *Editor*

Types of material: one-acts and short plays, including solo pieces. **Remuneration:** 1 complimentary copy. **Guidelines:** annual magazine of poetry and short plays published Apr and including an average of 2–3 plays in each issue; unpublished works; prefers works not more than 10 pages long. **Submission procedure:** accepts unsolicited scripts; submissions read 1 Oct–15 Jan only; sample issue $6. **Response time:** 1–2 months. **Special programs:** Tennessee Chapbook Prize: annual award for one-act (or combination of short plays) maximum 24–30 pages long; winning script published as interior chapbook in magazine; playwright receives 50 complimentary copies; submit script and $10 for reading fee and copy of next issue; *deadline:* 15 Jan 1998; no submissions before 1 Oct 1997.

PRISM INTERNATIONAL
Creative Writing Program; University of British Columbia;
Buch E462–1866 Main Mall; Vancouver, BC; Canada V6T 1Z1;
(604) 822-2514, FAX 822-3616; E-mail prism@unixg.ubc.ca;
Web http://www.arts.ubc.ca/crwr/prism/prism.html
Melanie Little and Sioux Browning, *Co-Editors*

Types of material: one-acts (including translations and solo pieces), excerpts from full-length plays. **Remuneration:** $20–30 per printed page; 1-year subscription. **Guidelines:** quarterly literary magazine; unpublished plays, maximum 40 pages long; send SASE for guidelines. **Submission procedure:** accepts unsolicited scripts, include copy or original with translations. **Response time:** 2–4 months.

PROVINCETOWN ARTS/PROVINCETOWN ARTS PRESS
650 Commercial St; Provincetown, MA 02657; (508) 487-3167, FAX 487-8634
Christopher Busa, *Editor and Publisher*

Types of material: one-acts, translations, solo pieces, performance-art texts. **Remuneration:** $50–300; 2 complimentary copies. **Guidelines:** annual magazine focusing broadly on artists and writers who inhabit or visit the tip of Cape Cod, and publishing an average of 1 play a year; also small press publishing 1 play or collection of plays a year; especially interested in performance-art texts; unpublished plays not more than 30 pages long. **Submission procedure:** accepts unsolicited scripts; submissions read Sep–Mar. **Response time:** 2 months.

RAG MAG
Box 12; Goodhue, MN 55027; (612) 923-4590
Beverly Voldseth, *Editor and Publisher*

Types of material: full-length plays, one-acts, solo pieces. **Remuneration:** 1 complimentary copy. **Guidelines:** biannual small-press literary magazine publishing artwork, prose and poetry, and interested in receiving play submis-

156 / PUBLICATION

sions; for Oct issue, works on theme "families" only; innovative character plays; prefers short one-acts but will consider longer plays with a view to publishing extracts or scenes. **Submission procedure:** accepts unsolicited short one-acts; send maximum 10-page sample, bio and letter of inquiry for longer plays; submit Mar–May only; send SASE for guidelines. **Response time:** 1–2 months.

RESOURCE PUBLICATIONS, INC.
160 East Virginia St, #290; San Jose, CA 95112-5848; (408) 286-8505, FAX 287-8748; E-mail mdrnlitrgy@aol.com; Web http://www.rpinet.com
Nick Wagner, *Editorial Director*

Types of material: plays 7–15 minutes long. **Remuneration:** royalty. **Guidelines:** unpublished plays or collections of plays suitable for youth ministry, education, counseling and therapy. **Submission procedure:** accepts unsolicited scripts. **Response time:** 2 months.

ROCKFORD REVIEW
Box 858; Rockford, IL 61105
David Ross, *Editor*

Types of material: one-acts, including solo pieces. **Remuneration:** one-acts selected for publication eligible for quarterly "Editor's Choice" prize of $25 (winner invited to reading and reception as guest of honor in Jun); 1 complimentary copy. **Guidelines:** quarterly journal publishing poetry, fiction, satire, artwork and an average of 4–5 plays a year; one-acts not more than 10 pages long, preferably of a satirical nature; interested in work that provides new insight into the human dilemma ("to cope or not to cope"). **Submission procedure:** accepts unsolicited scripts; sample copy $5. **Response time:** 1–2 months.

SAMUEL FRENCH
45 West 25th St; New York, NY 10010-2751; (212) 206-8990
Lawrence Harbison and William Talbot, *Editors*

Types of material: full-length plays, one-acts, plays for young audiences, musicals, solo pieces. **Remuneration:** 10% book royalty; 10 complimentary copies (40% discount on additional copies). **Guidelines:** "Many of our publications have never been produced in New York; these are generally comprised of light comedies, mysteries, mystery-comedies, a handful of one-acts and plays for young audiences, and plays with a preponderance of female roles; however, do not hesitate to send in your Future Pulitzer Prize Winner." **Submission procedure:** accepts unsolicited scripts. **Response time:** 2–4 months.

SCRIPTS AND SCRIBBLES
141 Wooster St; New York, NY 10012-3163; (212) 473-6695, FAX 473-6695
Daryl Chin, *Consulting Editor*

Types of material: full-length plays, one-acts, solo pieces, performance-art texts or scenarios. **Remuneration:** 25 complimentary copies. **Guidelines:** series initiated to publish texts for nontraditional theatre work and works produced outside New York City. **Submission procedure:** no unsolicited scripts; synopsis and letter of inquiry. **Response time:** 6 months.

SINISTER WISDOM
Box 3252; Berkeley, CA 94703
Akiba Onada-Sikwoia, *Editor*

Types of material: one-acts, excerpts from full-length plays (3000 words maximum). **Remuneration:** 2 complimentary copies. **Guidelines:** lesbian quarterly of art and literature; works by lesbians reflecting the diversity of lesbians; no heterosexual themes; send SASE for current themes. **Submission procedure:** accepts unsolicited scripts. **Response time:** 2–9 months.

SMITH AND KRAUS
Box 127; Lyme, NH 03768; (603) 795-4331, FAX 795-4427
Marisa Smith, *President*

Types of material: full-length plays, one-acts, translations, adaptations, plays for young audiences, solo pieces, monologues. **Remuneration:** usually fee or royalty; at least 10 complimentary copies. **Guidelines:** theatre press publishing works of interest to theatrical community, especially to actors, including collections of monologues and an average of 50 full-length plays a year. **Submission procedure:** no unsolicited scripts; synopsis and letter of inquiry. **Response time:** 2–4 months.

STET MAGAZINE
Box 75; Cambridge, MA 02238-0075; (508) 264-4938, FAX 264-4938
Cassandra Oxley, *Editor and Publisher*

Types of material: one-acts, solo pieces, performance-art texts. **Remuneration:** 2 complimentary copies. **Guidelines:** biannual literary magazine publishing an average of 2 plays a year; unpublished works maximum 20 pages long; special interest in short pieces and in innovative, experimental work. **Submission procedure:** accepts unsolicited scripts with bio; sample copy $4. **Response time:** 2–3 months.

SUN & MOON PRESS
6026 Wilshire Blvd; Los Angeles, CA 90036; (213) 857-1115;
E-mail djmess@sunmoon.com; Web www.sunmoon.com
American Theater and Literature Program (ATL)

Types of material: full-length plays, one-acts, translations. **Remuneration:** royalty; 10 complimentary copies. **Guidelines:** press publishing average of 10 single-play volumes a year including 2 winners of American Theater and Literature Program Contest; unpublished plays. **Submission procedure:** accepts unsolicited script for prize only, submit with $25 fee. **Response time:** 2–6 months.

THEATER
222 York St; New Haven, CT 06520; (203) 432-1568, FAX 432-8336;
E-mail theater.magazine@yale.edu;
Web http://www.yale.edu/drama/publications/theater
Erika Munk, *Editor*

Types of material: full-length plays, one-acts, translations, adaptations, solo pieces. **Remuneration:** maximum fee of $150; complimentary copies. **Guidelines:** triannual theatre journal publishing an average of 2 plays in each issue; special interest in experimental, innovative work; "no standard psychological realism or TV-script clones." **Submission procedure:** accepts unsolicited scripts with resume. **Response time:** 3–6 months.

THEATREFORUM
Theatre Department; University of California–San Diego;
9500 Gilman Dr; La Jolla, CA 92093-0344; (619) 534-6598, FAX 534-1080;
E-mail theatreforum@ucsd.edu
Jim Carmody, Adele Edling Shank and Theodore Shank, *Editors*

Types of material: full-length plays, translations, adaptations, solo pieces. **Remuneration:** varies by length; 10 complimentary copies. **Guidelines:** biannual international journal focusing on innovative work. **Submission procedure:** no unsolicited scripts; professional recommendation. **Response time:** 3 months.

THIS MONTH ON STAGE
Box 62; Hewlett, NY 11557-0062; (800) 536-0099; E-mail tmonstage@aol.com
Editorial Department

Types of material: full-length plays, one-acts, translations, adaptations, libretti, solo pieces. **Remuneration:** $1; 2 complimentary copies. **Guidelines:** monthly theatre magazine; special interest in short plays and one-acts; accepted scripts must be available in electronic form. **Submission procedure:** accepts unsolicited scripts with resume, cover letter and SASE for response; send SASE for guidelines. **Response time:** 12–18 months.

TOMORROW MAGAZINE
Box 148486; Chicago, IL 60614; E-mail audrelv@tezcat.com
Tim W. Brown, *Editor*

Types of material: one-acts, monologues, solo pieces, performance-art texts. **Remuneration:** 1 complimentary copy. **Guidelines:** biannual magazine publishing all literary genres, including an average of 1–2 plays a year; works maximum 15 pages long; special interest in comedy. **Submission procedure:** accepts unsolicited scripts; sample copy $5. **Response time:** 3 weeks–3 months.

UBU REPERTORY THEATER PUBLICATIONS
See Membership and Service Organizations.

UNITED ARTS
141 Wooster St; New York, NY 10012-3163; (212) 473-6695, FAX 473-6695
Daryl Chin, *Editor*

Types of material: one-acts, translations, solo pieces, performance-art texts, scenarios, manifestos. **Remuneration:** complimentary copies. **Guidelines:** journal of analysis and opinion covering visual arts, film, video, theatre and dance, published 3–4 times a year by University Arts Resources; nontraditional, avant-garde plays. **Submission procedure:** accepts unsolicited scripts; prefers synopsis and letter of inquiry. **Response time:** 6 months.

VENTANA PRODUCTIONS/PUBLICATIONS
Box 191973; San Francisco, CA 94119; (415) 522-8989
Vicky Simmons, *Literary Manager*

Types of material: full-length plays, one-acts, monologues. **Remuneration:** 10% book royalty, 90% production royalty; 10 complimentary copies. **Guidelines:** independent production company and small press publishing original single- and multiple-play volumes; prefers produced plays or plays with significant accomplishments. **Submission procedure:** no unsolicited scripts; synopsis and letter of inquiry. **Response time:** 3 months. **Special programs:** Ventana Publications Play Award: annual award for full-length or one-act play with significant accomplishments; winning script receives publication and public reading, playwright receives book and performance royalties and 10 complimentary copies; submit script with proof of production/accomplishments and $10 fee; send SASE for guidelines; *deadline:* 15 Feb 1998.

Development

What's in this section?

Conferences, festivals, workshops and programs whose primary purpose is to develop plays and playwrights, including a substantial number devoted to music-theatre. Also listed are some playwright groups and membership organizations whose main activity is play development. Developmental organizations such as New Dramatists whose many programs cannot be adequately described in the brief format used in this section are listed in Membership and Service Organizations. Some programs listed in Prizes also include a developmental element.

How can I get into these programs?

Keep applying to those for which you are convinced your work is suited. If you're turned down one year, you may be accepted the next on the strength of your latest piece. If you're required to submit a script with your application, don't forget your SASE!

ABINGDON THEATRE COMPANY
Box 110; Radio City Station; New York, NY 10101-0110; (212) 802-8383, FAX 206-6242; Web http://www.longbow.com/abingdon/
Ray Atherton, *Literary Manager*

Open to: playwrights. **Description:** year-round workshop for approximately 8 writers; biweekly in-house readings; 10 plays receive 12 hours of rehearsal and staged readings; of those, 4 plays selected for workshop production; of those, 2 plays selected for main stage production. **Financial arrangement:** stipend for main stage production. **Guidelines:** play unproduced in New York. **Application procedure:** script only. **Deadline:** ongoing. **Notification:** 6 months.

ACADEMY THEATRE NEW PLAY DEVELOPMENT PROGRAM
501 Means St NW; Atlanta, GA 30318; (404) 525-4111, FAX 688-8009;
  E-mail academytheatre@mindspring.com;
  Web http://www.mindspring.com/~academytheatre
Robert Waterhouse, *Artistic Education Director*

Open to: playwrights. **Description:** year-round program of 6–8 week workshops; 8–10 plays developed each workshop in collaboration with actors, directors and dramaturgs, culminating in readings and staged readings; playwright receives access to theatre's studio spaces and conference room for independent rehearsals and readings. **Financial arrangement:** $100–160 fee per workshop. **Guidelines:** resident of metro-Atlanta area or Southeast region. **Application procedure:** 10-page dialogue sample of work-in-progress, synopsis, bio and letter of inquiry. **Deadline:** ongoing.

ALCAZAR SCRIPTS IN PROGRESS
650 Geary St; San Francisco, CA 94102; (415) 441-6655, FAX 441-9567
Alan Ramos, *Script Supervisor*

Open to: playwrights, composers, solo performers, screenwriters. **Description:** 1 play developed through 3-month process, including 2 staged readings; possible full production with 4 weeks of rehearsal. **Financial arrangement:** room and board; royalties, if produced. **Guidelines:** unproduced play. **Application procedure:** script and resume. **Deadline:** 31 Dec 1997. **Notification date:** 28 Feb 1998. **Dates:** Jun–Sep 1998.

ASCAP MUSICAL THEATRE WORKSHOP
1 Lincoln Plaza; New York, NY 10023; (212) 621-6234
Michael A. Kerker, *Director of Musical Theatre*

Open to: composers, lyricists. **Description:** 10-session workshop under the direction of Stephen Schwartz; works presented to panels of musical theatre professionals. **Financial arrangement:** $500 Bernice Cohen Musical Theatre Fund Award given to most promising participating individual or team. **Guidelines:** write for press release. **Application procedure:** resume and cassette of 4 theatrical songs (no pop songs). **Deadline:** 15 Mar 1998; no submission before 1 Jan 1998. **Notification:** Jan 1999. **Dates:** Apr–May 1999.

ASHLAND NEW PLAYS FESTIVAL

ArtWork Enterprises, Inc.; Box 453; Ashland, OR 97520; (541) 858-7164

Open to: playwrights. **Description:** up to 6 new works given 16–20 hours of rehearsal with actors, director and dramaturg, culminating in 2 public readings. **Financial arrangement:** $250 stipend; travel and housing. **Guidelines:** resident of CA, ID, MT, NV, OR or WA; previously unproduced full-length play; cast limit of 10; 1-submission. **Application procedure:** script and double-spaced, 1-page maximum synopsis **Deadline:** 15 Sep 1997. **Notification:** Feb 1998. **Dates:** Mar or Apr 1998.

ASIAN AMERICAN THEATER COMPANY
NEW PLAYS & PLAYWRIGHTS DEVELOPMENT PROGRAM

1840 Sutter St, Suite 207; San Francisco, CA 94115; (415) 440-5545
Karen Amano, *Artistic Director*

Open to: playwrights. **Description:** developmental workshop for 2–4 plays, leading to staged reading or production; plays not selected for workshop considered for inclusion in series of 8–10 readings presented each season. **Financial arrangement:** free. **Guidelines:** American, Canadian or U.K. playwright of Asian-Pacific descent writing in English; prefers plays depicting Asian-Pacific American perspective. **Application procedure:** script, synopsis and character breakdown. **Deadline:** ongoing. **Dates:** TBA.

A.S.K. THEATER PROJECTS

(Formerly Audrey Skirball-Kenis Theatre)
11845 West Olympic Blvd, Suite 1250 West; Los Angeles, CA 90064;
 (310) 478-3200, FAX 478-5300; E-mail askplay@primenet.com;
 Web http://www.primenet.com/~askplay
Mead K. Hunter, *Director of Literary Programs*

Open to: playwrights, solo performers. **Description:** 15–20 plays receive public staged readings; of those, 2–3 selected for workshop production. **Financial arrangement:** playwright receives $150 for staged reading, $1000 for workshop production. **Guidelines:** full-length play-in-progress not produced or scheduled for production. **Application procedure:** script submissions accepted only from agents or with professional recommendation; playwrights may submit synopsis, sample pages and resume. **Deadline:** ongoing. **Notification:** 4–6 months.

BAY AREA PLAYWRIGHTS FESTIVAL

The Playwrights Foundation; Box 460357; San Francisco, CA 94114;
 (415) 263-3986
Jayne Wenger, *Artistic Director*

Open to: playwrights. **Description:** 6–9 scripts given dramaturgical attention and

2 rehearsed readings separated by 5–6 days for rewrites during 2-week festival at Magic Theatre; prefestival weekend retreat for initial brainstorming with directors and dramaturgs. **Financial arrangement:** small stipend, travel. **Guidelines:** unproduced original full-length play only. **Application procedure:** script and resume. **Deadline:** 1 Feb 1998. **Notification:** May 1998. **Dates:** prefestival weekend Aug 1998; festival Sep 1998.

BMI–LEHMAN ENGEL MUSICAL THEATRE WORKSHOP
Broadcast Music, Inc.; 320 West 57th St; New York, NY 10019; (212) 830-2515, FAX 262-2824; E-mail jb@bmi.com
Norma Grossman, *Director, Musical Theatre*

Open to: composers, librettists, lyricists. **Description:** 2-year program of weekly workshop meetings; showcase presentations to invited members of entertainment industry each year. **Financial arrangement:** free. **Application procedure:** completed application and work samples. **Deadline:** 1 May 1998 for librettists; 1 Aug 1998 for composers and lyricists.

BROADWAY TOMORROW
191 Claremont Ave, Suite 53; New York, NY 10027; (212) 864-4736
Elyse Curtis, *Artistic Director*

Open to: composers, librettists, lyricists. **Description:** new musicals presented in concert with writers' involvement. **Financial arrangement:** free. **Guidelines:** resident of NY metropolitan area. **Application procedure:** submissions accepted with professional recommendation from past participant only; cassette of 3 songs with description of 3 scenes in which they occur, synopsis, resume, reviews if available and SASE for response. **Deadline:** 31 Aug 1998.

CAC PLAYWRIGHT'S UNIT
Contemporary Arts Center; Box 30498; New Orleans, LA 70190; (504) 523-1216, FAX 528-3828
Pamela Marquis, *Theatre Coordinator*

Open to: playwrights. **Description:** 9-month workshop for 8–10 writers; participants' works developed and given staged readings. **Financial arrangement:** write or call for information. **Guidelines:** writer living in New Orleans area. **Application procedure:** script only. **Deadline:** ongoing. **Dates:** Sep–May.

CARNEGIE MELLON DRAMA'S SHOWCASE OF NEW PLAYS
Carnegie Mellon Drama; College of Fine Arts; Pittsburgh, PA 15213; (412) 268-3284, FAX 621-0281; E-mail mc1f@andrew.cmu.edu
Frank Gagliano, *Artistic Director* (submissions)
Mary Lou Chlipala, *Managing and Literary Director* (phone inquiries)

Open to: playwrights, translators, solo performers. **Description:** 4 playwrights each brought in for 2 weeks to work on play with director and Equity company of actors, culminating in 2 public script-in-hand performances. **Financial arrange-

ment: $1000 stipend, travel and housing. **Guidelines:** full-length play, bill of related one-acts, or one-act which writer is developing into full-length play; program seeks "plays of risk; no subjects are taboo; all forms are acceptable; the more audacious and the richer the language, the better." **Application procedure:** scripts accepted only from agents or when accompanied by a letter of recommendation from literary manager or artistic director of a major theatre. **Deadline:** 1 Dec 1997. **Notification:** Apr 1998. **Dates:** Jul 1998.

CHARLOTTE FESTIVAL/NEW PLAYS IN AMERICA
Charlotte Repertory Theatre; 201 South College St, Suite 2040; Charlotte, NC 28244; (704) 333-8587
Claudia Carter Covington, *Literary Manager*
Carol Bellamy, *Literary Associate*

Open to: playrights, translators. **Description:** 4 plays each given 12–16 hours of rehearsal with Equity company, culminating in 2 public staged readings, during week-long festival; some scripts subsequently receive full production as part of theatre's regular season. **Financial arrangement:** honorarium, travel, housing. **Guidelines:** only full-length plays and translations that have not received professional production. **Application procedure:** script only. **Deadline:** ongoing.

THE CHESTERFIELD FILM COMPANY/WRITER'S FILM PROJECT
8205 Santa Monica Blvd, #200; Los Angeles, CA 90046; (213) 683-3977, FAX (310) 260-6116; Web http://www.infoboard.com/chesterfield

Open to: playwrights, screenwriters. **Description:** up to 5 writers annually chosen for year-long screenwriting workshop meeting 3–5 times a week; writer creates 2 feature-length screenplays; company intends to produce best of year's work. **Financial arrangement:** $20,000 stipend. **Guidelines:** current and former writing-program students encouraged to apply; write or call for information. **Application procedure:** 2 copies of completed application, writing samples and $39.50 fee. **Deadline:** 15 Oct 1997. **Dates:** Jun 1998–May 1999.

CORNERSTONE DRAMATURGY AND DEVELOPMENT PROJECT
The Penumbra Theatre Company; 270 North Kent St; St. Paul, MN 55102-1794; (612) 224-4601, FAX 224-7074
Lou Bellamy, *Artistic Director*

Open to: playwrights. **Description:** 1 playwright a year offered main stage production with possible 3–4 week residency; 1 playwright offered 4-week workshop-residency culminating in staged reading; 3 playwrights offered staged reading. **Financial arrangement:** varies according to needs of project. **Guidelines:** full-length play dealing with the African-American and/or Pan African experience which has not received professional full production; one-acts considered; write for guidelines. **Application procedure:** script and resume. **Deadline:** ongoing.

DENVER CENTER THEATRE COMPANY
U S WEST THEATRE FEST
1050 13th St; Denver, CO 80204; (303) 893-4000
Bruce K. Sevy, *Associate Artistic Director/New Play Development*

Open to: playwrights. **Description:** new plays receive workshops and rehearsed readings during spring festival; most plays given 15–30 hours of rehearsal, culminating in 1 public presentation. **Financial arrangement:** stipend, travel, housing. **Guidelines:** unproduced full-length play only; no plays for young audiences, musicals, one-acts or solo pieces. **Application procedure:** write for guidelines. **Deadline:** Jan 1998. **Dates:** late May–early Jun.

DIAMOND HEAD THEATRE ORIGINALS
520 Makapuu Ave; Honolulu, HI 96816; (808) 734-8763, FAX 735-1250
John Rampage, *Artistic Director*

Open to: playwrights. **Description:** ongoing playwrights' workshop led by Jim Hutchison in which playwrights meet regularly to develop their scripts through reading and discussion; monthly public readings of works-in-progress. **Financial arrangement:** participant pays $5 a session. **Application procedure:** attend workshop session; check date and time of sessions (currently every other Wednesday 7–10 p.m.).

DRAMA LEAGUE NEW DIRECTORS–NEW WORKS SERIES
The Drama League of New York; 165 West 46th St, Suite 601;
    New York, NY 10036; (212) 302-2100, FAX 302-2254;
    E-mail dlny@echonyc.com
Roger T. Danforth, *Artistic Director*

Open to: playwright-director teams. **Description:** 3 projects each summer receive 4 weeks of rehearsal space in New York City; development ranges from exploratory rehearsals to workshop production according to needs of collaborative team. **Financial arrangement:** $1000 for each team. **Application procedure:** proposal describing project submitted jointly by playwright and director; bios; write or call for guidelines. **Deadline:** 15 Feb 1998.

5TH ANNUAL WOMEN AT THE DOOR STAGED READING SERIES
Famous Door Theatre Company; 3212 North Broadway; Chicago, IL 60657;
    (773) 404-8283, FAX 404-8317; E-mail fdoor@tezcat.com;
    Web http://www.tezcat.com/~fdoor
Laura T. Fisher, *Artistic Producer*

Open to: playwrights. **Description:** 4 plays receive 4 4-hour rehearsals with professional actors and director, culminating in staged readings; of those, 1 play selected for full production. **Guidelines:** American woman playwright; full-length play that has not been professionally produced; 1 submission. **Financial arrangement:** free; possible housing. **Application procedure:** 1-page synopsis, first scene or first 10 pages of play and resume. **Deadline:** 15 Sep 1997. **Notification:** finalists 15 Oct 1997; winners 2 Jan 1998 **Dates:** April–May 1998.

FIRST STAGE

Box 38280; Los Angeles, CA 90038; (213) 850-6271, FAX 850-6295
Dennis Safren, *Literary Manager*

Open to: playwrights, solo performers, screenwriters. **Description:** organization providing year-round developmental services using professional actors, directors and dramaturgs; weekly staged readings of plays and screenplays followed by discussions; bimonthly playwriting and screenwriting workshops; periodic dramaturgy workshops; annual short-play marathon. **Financial arrangement:** subscription of $120 a year or $35 a quarter for resident of Los Angeles, Orange or Ventura counties; $58 annual subscription for nonresident; nonmember may submit script for reading. **Application procedure:** script only. **Deadline:** ongoing.

THE 42ND STREET WORKSHOP

432 West 42nd St; New York, NY 10036; (212) 362-9592
Michelle Bouchard, James DeMarse and Sam Schacht, *Artistic Directors*

Open to: playwrights, screenwriters. **Description:** writers meet weekly to develop scripts through in-house readings and critique; approximately 30 works a year receive staged readings; 3–4 works receive showcase productions. **Financial arrangement:** $25 monthly fee. **Application procedure:** script and letter of reference from company member. **Deadline:** 1 Sep 1997. **Notification:** 1 Nov 1997. **Dates:** ongoing.

THE FRANK SILVERA WRITERS' WORKSHOP

Box 1791; Manhattanville Station; New York, NY 10027; (212) 662-8463,
    FAX 662-8469 (call first); E-mail playrite@artswire.org
Garland Lee Thompson, *Founding Executive Director*

Open to: playwrights. **Description:** resident program of the Harlem Victoria Five Theatre; program includes Monday series of readings of new plays by new and established writers, followed by critiques; Wednesday seminars conducted by master playwrights; staged readings and 2–3 Equity showcase productions a year. **Financial arrangement:** $35 annual fee plus $10 per Wednesday class; Monday-night readings free. **Guidelines:** interested in new plays by writers of all colors and backgrounds. **Application procedure:** Sep open house; submitting script and attending a Monday-night session encouraged; call for information.

FREDERICK DOUGLASS CREATIVE ARTS CENTER WRITING WORKSHOPS

270 West 96th St; New York, NY 10025; (212) 864-3375,
    FAX 864-3474 (call first)
Fred Hudson, *Artistic Director*

Open to: playwrights, screenwriters, television writers. **Description:** 4 cycles a year of 8-week workshops; beginning and advanced playwriting; latter includes readings and possible productions; also film and television writing workshops; weekly meetings. **Financial arrangement:** $125 fee per workshop; author of play given staged reading receives $50, author of produced play receives $500. **Application procedure:** contact FDCAC for information. **Deadline:** Sep 1997 for 1st cycle; Jan 1998 for 2nd cycle; May 1998 for 3rd cycle; Jul 1998 for 4th cycle; call for exact dates. **Dates:** Oct–Dec 1997; Jan–Mar 1998; Apr–Jun 1998; Jul–Sep 1998.

FREE PLAY READING SERIES AND PLAYWRIGHT DEVELOPMENT WORKSHOP

American Renaissance Theatre of Dramatic Arts; 10 West 15th St, Suite 325; New York, NY 10011; (212) 924-6862, FAX 255-2598
Rich Stone, *Artistic Director*

Open to: playwrights. **Description:** up to 5 plays-in-progress given 2 rehearsals and a public reading, followed by audience critique; some scripts may subsequently receive full production; playwright also attends workshop addressing each of the plays and the "business" of playwriting. **Financial arrangement:** free. **Guidelines:** unproduced play; resident of New York city area. **Application procedure:** synopsis, 10 sample pages and SASE for response. **Deadline:** 15 Jan 1998. **Notification:** 30 Mar 1998. **Dates:** May/June 1998 (exact dates TBA).

THE GENESIUS GUILD PROGRAMS FOR THE DEVELOPMENT OF NEW PLAYS & MUSICALS

Box 2273; New York, NY 10108; (212) 946-5625, FAX 229-9188;
E-mail tomorr@interport.net
Peter Coston, *Literary Manager* (Plays)
Thomas Morrissey, *Artistic Director* (Musicals)

Open to: playwrights, translators, composers, librettists, lyricists, solo performers. **Description:** program offering range of developmental services including weekly in-house readings; staged readings; workshop and showcase productions; development process varies according to needs of script. **Financial arrangement:** free. **Guidelines:** emerging or established playwright. **Application procedure:** 1- or 2-page synopsis, scene breakdown, cast requirements, production needs, cassette for musical and bio or resume. **Deadline:** ongoing. **Dates:** Sep–May.

HAROLD PRINCE MUSICAL THEATRE PROGRAM

The Directors Company; 311 West 43rd St, Suite 206; New York, NY 10036; (212) 246-5877, FAX 265-7482
HPMTP Selection Committee

Open to: playwrights, composers, librettists, lyricists, screenwriters. **Description:** program supports creation, development and production of new musicals; writers and composers work collaboratively with director under guidance of TDC Artistic Staff and Harold Prince; process includes monthly meetings, reading series, 4 weeks of rehearsal, presentation for invited audience in New York City, and possible future full production at Denver Center Theatre Company. **Financial arrangement:** writer paid fee for option on first production; commissioning fees, residencies and fellowships available. **Guidelines:** full-length musical or operetta that has not received professional New York production. **Application procedure:** script with at least 1 complete act, tape of score, synopsis, resume, 3 letters of recommendation and letter of interest. **Deadline:** ongoing. **Notification date:** Apr 1998. **Dates:** fall 1997–Jun 1998.

HEDGEROW HORIZONS
146 Rose Valley Rd; Rose Valley, PA 19065; (610) 565-4211
Walt Vail, *Literary Manager*

Open to: playwrights. **Description:** 5 full-length plays and 4 one-acts each given 2 rehearsals and 1 public reading; of these, 1 play selected for 3–5 days of rehearsal, culminating in at least 1 performance. **Financial arrangement:** free. **Guidelines:** playwright must be resident of DE, PA or NJ; play not professionally produced. **Application procedure:** script and resume. **Deadline:** 31 Mar 1998. **Notification:** 30 Apr 1998. **Dates:** 10–30 May 1998.

HISPANIC PLAYWRIGHTS PROJECT
South Coast Repertory; Box 2197; Costa Mesa, CA 92628-2197;
   (714) 957-2602, ext. 215
Juliette Charillo, *Project Director*

Open to: playwrights. **Description:** up to 3 scripts given 6-day workshop with director, dramaturg and professional cast, culminating in public reading and discussion; playwright meets with director and dramaturg prior to workshop. **Financial arrangement:** honorarium, travel, housing. **Guidelines:** Hispanic-American playwright; unproduced play preferred but produced play which would benefit from further development will be considered; play must not be written entirely in Spanish; no musicals. **Application procedure:** script, synopsis and bio. **Deadline:** 15 Mar 1998. **Notification:** 10 May 1998. **Dates:** preworkshop meeting weekend of 13 Jun 1998; workshop 28 Jul–9 Aug 1998.

THE ISIDORA AGUIRRE PLAYWRIGHTING LAB
El Teatro de la Esperanza; Box 40578; San Francisco, CA 94140-0578;
   (415) 255-2320, FAX 255-8031
Program Manager

Open to: playwrights. **Description:** 1–3 plays developed through individual sessions and weekly seminars with professional dramaturg over 6-week period, culminating in public staged reading; possible future full production for 1 or more plays. **Financial arrangement:** stipend to cover room and board. **Guidelines:** Chicano/Latino playwright; full-length play-in-progress reflective of or adaptable to the Chicano experience; prefers bilingual plays, but accepts monolingual plays in Spanish or English; prefers cast limit of 6 (doubling allowed) and set suitable for touring, but will consider larger-cast plays with nontourable sets; write for guidelines. **Application procedure:** 3 copies of script and resume (material will not be returned). **Deadline:** 15 Mar 1998. **Notification:** 15 May 1998. **Dates:** Jun–Jul 1998.

KEY WEST THEATRE FESTIVAL
Box 992; Key West, FL 33041; (302) 292-3725, FAX 293-0845;
  E-mail theatrekw@aol.com
Joan McGillis, *Artistic Director*

Open to: playwrights, translators, solo performers. **Description:** up to 8 plays given staged readings and 5 plays given full productions during 10-day festival, which also includes workshops and seminars. **Financial arrangement:** travel and housing. **Guidelines:** unproduced full-length play, one-act, musical, work for young audiences. **Application procedure:** script, resume and letter of recommendation. **Deadline:** ongoing. **Dates:** 2–12 Oct 1997.

L. A. BLACK PLAYWRIGHTS
5926 5th Ave; Los Angeles, CA 90043; (213) 292-9438
James Graham Bronson, *President*

Open to: playwrights, librettists, lyricists. **Description:** group meets every second Sunday for guest speakers, private and public readings, and showcases. **Financial arrangement:** free. **Guidelines:** resident of Los Angeles area; members mainly but not exclusively black; prefers produced playwright. **Application procedure:** submit full-length play. **Deadline:** ongoing. **Dates:** year-round.

THE LEHMAN ENGEL MUSICAL THEATRE WORKSHOP
6425 Hollywood Blvd; Hollywood, CA 90028; (213) 465-9142;
  E-mail jsparksco@aol.com
John Sparks, *Co-Director*

Open to: composers, librettists, lyricists. **Description:** Sep–Jun workshop; in-house staged readings; skeletal productions (Equity contract). **Financial arrangement:** 1st-year workshop members pay dues of $500, which include nonrefundable application fee (see below); in subsequent years, members pay dues of $300. **Application procedure:** completed application; 1-page resume; cassette of 3 songs or equivalent for composer; 3 lyrics for lyricist; short scene for librettist; nonrefundable $25 fee. **Deadline:** 1 Aug 1998. **Notification:** Sep 1998. **Dates:** Sep 1998–Jun 1999.

THE LOFT FEST '98—FESTIVAL OF SHORTS
Box 173405; Tampa, FL 33672; (813) 275-9400, FAX 222-1057
Kelly Smith, *Artistic Director*

Open to: playwrights, solo performers. **Description:** 10 10-minute plays and/or monologues and 4–6 one-acts each given full production during 6-week festival. **Financial arrangement:** $100 honorarium for one-act, $50 for 10-minute play or monologue. **Guidelines:** unproduced one-act, 10-minute play or monologue. **Application procedure:** script, synopsis, letter of interest and $5 fee per submission (material will not be returned). **Deadline:** 31 Mar 1998. **Notification:** 31 May 1998. **Dates:** Jul–Aug 1998.

LONG WHARF THEATRE STAGE II WORKSHOPS
222 Sargent Dr; New Haven, CT 06511; (203) 787-4284, FAX 776-2287
Sari Bodi, *Literary Analyst*

Open to: playwrights, translators, composers, librettists, lyricists. **Description:** 2 scripts given 3 weeks of rehearsal, 3 weeks of performance with playwright in residence; optional discussion after performance with audience members, who complete comment sheets (no critics); unit set, costumes and props from stock. **Financial arrangement:** stipend. **Application procedure:** script and professional recommendation, or agent submission. **Deadline:** ongoing. **Notification:** 6 months. **Dates:** Sep–May.

MANHATTAN PLAYWRIGHTS UNIT
338 West 19th St, #6B; New York, NY 10011-3982; (212) 989-0948
Saul Zachary, *Artistic Director*

Open to: playwrights, screenwriters. **Description:** developmental workshop meeting weekly for in-house readings and discussions of members' works-in-progress; end-of-season series of staged readings of new plays. **Financial arrangement:** free. **Guidelines:** produced or published writer. **Application procedure:** letter of inquiry, resume and SASE for response. **Deadline:** ongoing.

MARK TAPER FORUM DEVELOPMENTAL PROGRAMS
135 North Grand Ave; Los Angeles, CA 90012; (213) 972-7574
Pier Carlo Talenti, *Associate Literary Manager*

Asian Theatre Workshop (ATW)

Open to: playwrights, solo performers. **Description:** ongoing developmental program including Asian Pacific American Friends of Center Theatre Group (APAF) Reading Series; discussions with outside theatre artists; workshop productions. **Financial arrangement:** honorarium. **Guidelines:** Asian-Pacific playwright. **Application procedure:** script and resume. **Deadline:** ongoing.

Blacksmyths

Open to: playwrights, solo performers. **Description:** ongoing developmental program including writers' group, staged readings and workshops. **Financial arrangement:** honorarium. **Guidelines:** African-American playwright; resident of Los Angeles area. **Application procedure:** script and resume. **Deadline:** ongoing.

Latino Theatre Initiative (LTI)

Open to: playwrights, solo performers. **Description:** ongoing developmental program including staged readings and workshops. **Financial arrangement:**

remuneration varies. **Guidelines:** Latino playwright. **Application procedure:** script and resume. **Deadline:** ongoing.

New Work Festival

Open to: playwrights, solo performers. **Description:** 16–18 plays given workshops (2 weeks of rehearsal, 2 public presentations) or rehearsed readings. **Financial arrangement:** remuneration varies. **Guidelines:** unproduced, unpublished play. **Application procedure:** brief synopsis, 5–10 sample pages and resume. **Deadline:** 30 Apr 1998.

Other Voices Project

Open to: playwrights, solo performers. **Description:** ongoing developmental program including community and professional development; staged readings; workshops; Summer Chautauqua: biennial week-long seminar. **Financial arrangement:** remuneration varies. **Guidelines:** disabled playwright; program designed to increase presence of disabled community in mainstream theatre. **Application procedure:** script and resume; call for guidelines for Summer Chautauqua. **Deadline:** call for information.

THE MAXWELL ANDERSON PLAYWRIGHTS SERIES

Box 671; West Redding, CT 06896; (203) 938-2770
Bruce Post, *Dramaturg*

Open to: playwrights. **Description:** 10 new plays a year each given staged reading with professional director and actors, followed by audience discussion. **Financial arrangement:** stipend. **Guidelines:** unproduced play. **Application procedure:** script only. **Deadline:** ongoing.

MIDWEST RADIO THEATRE WORKSHOP

KOPN Radio; 915 East Broadway; Columbia, MO 65201; (573) 874-5676, FAX 499-1662; E-mail mrtw@mrtw.org; Web http://www.mrtw.org/mrtw
Sue Zizza, *Executive Director*

Open to: playwrights, radio writers. **Description:** annual program of 6-day radio-theatre workshops for writers, actors, directors and sound designers: 55 participants of all disciplines take workshops in production, direction, acting, writing and engineering; commissioned plays or scripts selected through MRTW Script Contest (see Prizes) produced for radio broadcast and live performance with audience. **Financial arrangement:** $200–300 fee for each workshop; some partial and full scholarships available based on financial need and experience, with priority given to women and people of color; possibility of free housing in community. **Application procedure:** completed registration form with deposit; write for information. **Deadline:** 1 Apr 1998 for scholarship applications; most workshops filled at least 1 month before starting date. **Dates:** May 1998.

MUSICAL THEATRE WORKS
440 Lafayette St; New York, NY 10003; (212) 677-0040, FAX 598-0105
Jacqueline A. Siegel, *Executive Director*

Open to: composers, librettists, lyricists. **Description:** new composers, librettists and lyricists work with established musical-theatre professionals to develop projects through meetings, informal readings, staged readings and full Off Broadway productions. **Financial arrangement:** free. **Guidelines:** completed unproduced work. **Application procedure:** script and cassette of music. **Deadline:** ongoing.

NATIONAL MUSIC THEATER CONFERENCE
O'Neill Theater Center; 234 West 44th St, Suite 901;
   New York, NY 10036-3909; (212) 382-2790, FAX 921-5538
Paulette Haupt, *Artistic Director*
Michael E. Nassar, *Associate Director*

Open to: composers, librettists, lyricists. **Description:** development period of 2–4 weeks at O'Neill Center, Waterford, CT for new music-theatre works of all genres, traditional and nontraditional; some works developed privately, others presented as staged readings. **Financial arrangement:** stipend, round-trip travel from NYC, room and board. **Guidelines:** U.S. citizen; unproduced work; adaptations acceptable if rights have been obtained. **Application procedure:** send SASE for guidelines and application form after 15 Sep 1997. **Deadline:** 1 Mar 1998; no submission before 1 Nov 1997. **Dates:** Aug 1998.

NATIONAL MUSIC THEATER NETWORK
1697 Broadway, Suite 902; New York, NY 10019; (212) 664-0979,
   FAX 664-0978
Timothy Jerome, *President*

Open to: composers, librettists, lyricists. **Description:** national screening of submitted musical theatre works; written evaluations sent to all writers; descriptive listings of recommended works published in catalogue distributed to producers/theatres and 12 of these given staged readings in annual "Broadway Dozen," a showcase for potential producers. **Financial arrangement:** free. **Guidelines:** completed work with original music which has not received a major production. **Application procedure:** completed application and $45 fee; write for details. **Deadline:** ongoing.

NATIONAL PLAYWRIGHTS CONFERENCE
O'Neill Theater Center; 234 West 44th St, Suite 902; New York, NY 10036-3909;
   (212) 382-2790, FAX 921-5538
Lloyd Richards, *Artistic Director*
Mary F. McCabe, *Managing Director*

Open to: playwrights, screenwriters, television writers. **Description:** 4-week conference at O'Neill Center, Waterford, CT; 9–12 plays developed and presented as staged readings; 1–3 screenplays/teleplays developed and read; preconference weekend for initial reading and planning. **Financial arrangement:** stipend, travel, room and board. **Guidelines:** U.S. citizen or resident; unoptioned and unproduced work; no adaptations or translations. **Application procedure:** send SASE for guidelines after 15 Sep 1997. **Deadline:** 1 Dec 1997. **Notification:** Apr 1998. **Dates:** preconference weekend TBA; conference Jul 1998.

THE NEW HARMONY PROJECT LABORATORY

613 North East St; Indianapolis, IN 46202; (317) 464-9405, FAX 635-4201
Jeffrey L. Sparks, *Executive Director*
Jim Houghton, *Artistic Director*

Open to: playwrights, composers, librettists, screenwriters, television writers. **Description:** 4–6 scripts given up to 2 weeks of intensive development with professional community of directors, actors, producers, dramaturgs and musical directors. **Financial arrangement:** stipend of $200–400, depending on length of stay; travel, room and board. **Guidelines:** narrative works that "emphasize the dignity of the human spirit and the worth of the human experience." **Application procedure:** 10-page writing sample, project proposal and statement of artistic purpose. **Deadline:** 15 Nov 1997. **Notification:** 15 Mar 1998. **Dates:** 14 May–31 May 1998.

NEW VISIONS/NEW VOICES

The Kennedy Center–Youth and Family Programs; 2700 F Street NW; Washington, DC 20566; (202) 416-8880, FAX 416-8802;
E-mail kpkovac@mail.kennedy-center.org
Kim Peter Kovac, *Program Manager*

Open to: playwrights. **Description:** up to 8 plays given rehearsals and staged readings. **Guidelines:** previously unproduced plays for young and family audiences; playwright must be sponsored by theatre; call for information and application. **Financial arrangement:** small stipend. **Application procedure:** sponsoring theatre submits completed application and supporting materials. **Deadline:** 1 Oct 1997. **Notification:** 15 Jan 1998. **Dates:** 11–18 May 1998.

NEW VOICES PLAY DEVELOPMENT PROGRAM

Plowshares Theatre Company; Fisher Building Station; Box 11399; Detroit, MI 48211; (313) 862-4386, FAX 274-3671;
E-mail garydarnel@aol.com or worf@voyager.net
Gary Anderson, *Producing Artistic Director*

Open to: playwrights, translators, solo performers. **Description:** up to 6 plays-in-progress given 2 weeks of rehearsal with professional company of actors, directors and dramaturgs, culminating in 2 staged readings followed by audience discussion; program provides marketing assistance following development; possible future full production. **Financial arrangement:** some travel stipends available. **Guidelines:** African-American playwright; unproduced play addressing the African-American experience. **Application procedure:** completed application, synopsis and resume. **Deadline:** 31 Oct 1997. **Notification date:** Mar 1998. **Dates:** Jul 1998.

NEW WORKS FOR A NEW WORLD
c/o Department of Theater; University of Massachusetts; 112 Fine Arts Center; Amherst, MA 01003; (413) 545-3490; E-mail vscott@theater.umass.edu
Lucy Burns, *Literary Manager*

Open to: playwrights, composers, librettists, lyricists, solo performers. **Description:** 4 plays developed over 2-week residency with actors, director and dramaturg, culminating in staged reading. **Guidelines:** special interest in works by writers of color and plays that "reflect the diversity of American culture." **Financial arrangement:** $1500 stipend; travel and housing. **Application procedure:** send SASE for guidelines. **Deadline:** 1 Jun 1998. **Notification:** late fall 1998. **Dates:** Jul 1999.

NEW YORK FOUNDATION FOR THE ARTS SPONSORSHIP PROGRAM
155 Ave of the Americas, 14th Floor; New York, NY 10013-1507; (212) 366-6900, FAX 366-1778; E-mail nyfaafp@artswire.org
Kevin Duggan, *Assistant Director of Artists' Services*

Open to: playwrights, translators, composers, librettists, lyricists, solo performers, screenwriters, radio and television writers. **Description:** program supports development, production and distribution of creative new projects by individual artists, both emerging talents and established professionals, with strong emphasis on independent film and video but also including radio, literature, performance art, theatre, music, dance and visual arts; as sponsoring organization for nonprofit status, NYFA provides fiscal management assistance and proposal reviews with focus on fundraising counsel; program does not offer grants. **Financial arrangement:** as a service fee, NYFA retains 8% of grants and contributions it receives on behalf of a project; $50 contract fee payable on signing. **Guidelines:** majority of sponsored artists located in NY metropolitan area; solid project proposal with realistic budget (most selected projects budgeted at not less than $25,000); selection based on artistic excellence, uniqueness and fundability of project, and on artist's previous work and proven ability to complete proposed work. **Application procedure:** write for application form and further information. **Deadline:** 7 Nov 1997; contact NYFA for 1998 deadlines. **Notification:** 3 months.

NEWGATE THEATRE NEW PLAY DEVELOPMENT
134 Mathewson St; Providence, RI 02906; E-mail af891@osfn.org
David J. Lima, *Literary Manager*

Open to: playwrights, solo performers. **Description:** organization providing year-round developmental services; bimonthly meetings for local playwrights; 4–8 scripts each season receive staged reading, in some cases leading to workshop production; 2–6 plays receive workshop productions in annual Short Play Festival. **Financial arrangement:** small stipend and possible housing for main stage production. **Guidelines:** resident of southern New England. **Application procedure:** script, resume and SASE for response. **Deadline:** 1 Feb 1998 for reading; 1 Jun 1998 for festival. **Dates:** Short Play Festival Sep 1998.

THE NEXT STAGE

The Cleveland Play House; Box 1989; Cleveland, OH 44106-0189;
    (216) 795-7010, ext 207, FAX 795-7005
Scott Kanoff, *Literary Manager/Dramaturg*

Open to: playwrights. **Description:** 3-tier developmental program: stage one: The Playwrights Unit, ongoing playwrights' workshop; new plays developed through discussion and readings; members attend rehearsals, performances and all other theatre programming. Stage two: Next Stage Festival: in Oct, 4–8 plays each given 2–3 days of rehearsal with Play House company, culminating in public reading. Stage three: at least 1 play developed in stages one or two offered main stage production. **Financial arrangement:** for stage one: possible stipend for expenses; for stage two: stipend, transportation and housing; for stage three: royalties, transportation and housing. **Guidelines:** for stage one, resident of Northern Ohio area, produced or unproduced full-length play; for stage two, unproduced full-length play. **Application procedure:** script, resume and letter of inquiry. **Deadline:** for stage one, submit 1–30 Apr only; for stage two, submit 1 May–30 Jun only.

OFF-OFF BROADWAY ORIGINAL SHORT PLAY FESTIVAL

45 West 25th St; New York, NY 10010-2751; (212) 206-8990, FAX 206-1429
William Talbot, *Festival Coordinator*

Open to: playwrights. **Description:** festival production hosted by Love Creek Productions on Theatre Row in New York City; possible publication by Samuel French. **Financial arrangement:** free. **Guidelines:** one-acts or segments of full-length plays less than 40 minutes long only; play must have been developed and produced by theatre, professional school or college that has playwriting program; send SASE for application after Jan 1998. **Application procedure:** no submission by playwright; completed application submitted by organization producing work. **Deadline:** Feb–Mar 1998; exact date TBA. **Notification:** within 2 weeks. **Dates:** late spring 1998.

OLD PUEBLO PLAYWRIGHTS

Box 767; Tucson, AZ 85702; (520) 297-3384, FAX 887-6741;
    E-mail 4stern@vnet.ibm.com
Chris Stern, *Member*

Open to: playwrights, translators, screenwriters, radio writers, television writers. **Description:** members meet weekly to develop scripts; staged readings at annual New Play Festival. **Financial arrangement:** $24 annual dues. **Application procedure:** submit writing sample at weekly meeting. **Deadline:** ongoing. **Dates:** ongoing.

ONE ACTS IN PERFORMANCE

Polaris North c/o Diane Martella; 1265 Broadway, Room 803;
   New York, NY 10001; (212) 684-1985
Diane Martella, *Treasurer/Co-sponsor*

Open to: playwrights. **Description:** approximately every 2 months, 3–5 plays given brief rehearsal period, culminating in workshop production followed by informal audience discussion. **Guidelines:** unproduced one-act play not more than 30 minutes long; 4-character maximum; single set. **Financial arrangement:** free. **Application procedure:** script only. **Deadline:** ongoing. **Notification:** 2 weeks. **Dates:** ongoing.

PLAYFORMERS

20 Waterside Plaza, Apt 11G; New York, NY 10010; (212) 213-9835
John Fritz, *Executive Director*

Open to: playwrights. **Description:** playwrights' support group meeting 1 or 2 times a month Sep–Jun for readings of works-in-progress and critiques. **Financial arrangement:** $15 initiation fee on acceptance; $90 annual dues. **Guidelines:** playwright invited to attend meetings as guest before applying for membership. **Application procedure:** script and resume. **Deadline:** ongoing.

PLAYLABS

The Playwrights' Center; 2301 Franklin Ave East; Minneapolis, MN 55406-1099;
   (612) 332-7481
Elissa Adams, *Artistic Director*

Open to: playwrights, solo performers. **Description:** 4–6 new works given 2 weeks of development with playwright's choice of professional director, dramaturg and Twin Cities actors, culminating in staged reading followed by audience discussion. **Financial arrangement:** travel, housing and per diem. **Guidelines:** U.S. citizen or permanent resident; unproduced, unpublished play, solo performance piece or mixed-media piece; full-length works preferred; writer must be available to attend entire conference and preconference weekend. **Application procedure:** completed application and script; send SASE for application after 15 Oct 1997. **Deadline:** 15 Dec 1997. **Notification:** 1 May 1998. **Dates:** preconference weekend May/June 1998 (exact dates TBA); conference 26 Jul–9 Aug 1998.

PLAYQUEST

Arena Stage; 6th & Maine Ave, SW; Washington, DC 20024; (202) 554-9066,
   FAX 488-4056
Cathy Madison, *Literary Manager*

Open to: playwrights. **Description:** 2–5 plays each year developed in text-intensive workshop with playwright in residence, culminating in a mini-season of minimally staged public performances. **Financial arrangement:** varies. **Guidelines:** unproduced full-length play, translation or adaptation; special interest in works for a multicultural company and works by writers of color. **Submission procedure:**

synopsis, bio and letter of inquiry. **Deadline:** ongoing (spring–early summer best time to submit). **Notification:** 1 day letter; 6 months script, if requested.

PLAYS-IN-PROGRESS FESTIVALS OF NEW WORKS
615 4th St; Eureka, CA 95501; (707) 443-3724
Susan Bigelow-Marsh, *Executive Director*

Open to: playwrights. **Description:** 5 scripts each given full production and 8–10 scripts each given 3–4 weeks of development with actors and directors, culminating in staged reading followed by discussion, in spring or fall festival of new work; ongoing development and Monday night reading series for local writers. **Financial arrangement:** negotiable; housing. **Guidelines:** primarily CA writers; 1 out-of-state writer selected for each festival; unproduced, unpublished play. **Application procedure:** script and resume. **Deadline:** 1 Mar 1998; 1 Jul 1998. **Dates:** Sep 1998; May 1999.

PLAYWORKS FESTIVAL
Theatre Department; Fox Fine Arts Center; University of Texas at El Paso;
El Paso, TX 79968-0549; (915) 747-5146, -7854, FAX 747-5438;
E-mail mwright@utep.edu
Michael Wright, *Head of Playwriting and Directing*

Open to: playwrights, solo performers. **Description:** 3 playwrights each given 3-week residencies to write new play, culminating in public presentation of work-in-progress followed by critique; possible future full production. **Financial arrangement:** stipend TBA (amount contingent on funding); travel and housing. **Guidelines:** student playwright enrolled in U.S. college or university; submissions from Latin-American and Native American playwrights especially encouraged. **Submission procedure:** work sample, proposal for script to be developed in residence and names of at least two faculty references. **Deadline:** 31 Jan 1998. **Notification:** 1 Apr 1998. **Dates:** Jun 1998.

PLAYWRIGHTS' CENTER OF SAN FRANCISCO STAGED READINGS
Box 460466; San Francisco, CA 94146-0466; (415) 626-4603, FAX 863-0901;
E-mail playctrsf@aol.com
Sheppard B. Kominers, *Chairman of the Board*

Open to: playwrights. **Description:** developmental program meeting weekly for 1 staged reading, monthly for reading and discussion of works-in-progress. **Financial arrangement:** $45 annual fee plus $3 per reading and $3–5 per works-in-progress meeting; non-members can attend meetings for higher fees. **Application procedure:** completed application. **Deadline:** ongoing.

Playwrights Forum
Box 11488; Washington, DC 20008-0688; (301) 816-0569, FAX 816-0569;
   E-mail playforum@aol.com
Ernest Joselovitz, *President*

Open to: playwrights. **Description:** ongoing developmental program including 3-tier range of membership options: Forum 2, professional playwriting groups meeting biweekly; Forum 1, workshop program offering three 3-month sessions a year for apprentice playwrights; and Associate membership offering participation in many of Forum's auxiliary programs but not in workshops; depending on type of membership, members variously eligible for in-house and public readings, Musical Theatre Wing, special classes including Rewrites and Screenwriting, production observerships, free theatre tickets, annual conference, organization's newsletter and handbook, and new published series of members' scripts. **Financial arrangement:** for Forum 2, $90 every 4 months; for Forum 1, $90 per 15-week session; Associate membership $25 a year. **Guidelines:** resident of mid-Atlantic area only; for Forum 2, prefers produced playwright or former Forum 1 participant, willing to make long-term commitment; send SASE for further information. **Application procedure:** for Forum 2, script and bio; for Forum 1, send SASE or call for information; for Associate membership, send annual fee. **Deadline:** for Forum 2, ongoing; for Forum 1, 10 Sep 1997, 10 Jan 1998, 10 May 1998. **Notification:** 4 weeks.

Playwrights' Kitchen Ensemble
c/o Coronet Theatre; 368 North La Cienega; Los Angeles, CA 90048;
   FAX (310) 838-8430
Dan Lauria, *Artistic Director*

Open to: playwrights. **Description:** 1 play per week given staged reading by celebrity actors and directors for audience including theatre, film and TV professionals. **Financial arrangement:** free. **Guidelines:** play unproduced in Los Angeles. **Application procedure:** script only. **Deadline:** submit 1 Sep–31 Dec only.

Playwrights' Platform
164 Brayton Rd; Boston, MA 02135; (617) 254-4482
Beverly Creasey, *President*

Open to: playwrights. **Description:** ongoing developmental program including weekly workshop held at Massachusetts College of Art, staged readings, summer festival of full productions, dramaturgical and referral services. **Financial arrangement:** playwright receives percentage of gate for festival productions; participants encouraged to become members of organization ($15 annual dues). **Guidelines:** MA resident only; unpublished, unproduced play; write for membership information. **Application procedure:** letter of inquiry only. **Deadline:** ongoing.

PLAYWRIGHTS' PREVIEW PRODUCTIONS
17 East 47th St; New York, NY 10017; (212) 421-1380
Frances Hill, *Artistic Director*
David Sheppard, Jr., *Literary Manager*

Open to: playwrights. **Description:** 8–12 plays receive staged readings, some chosen for full production or further development; see also Urban Stages Award and Emerging Playwright Award in Prizes. **Financial arrangement:** free. **Guidelines:** play not produced in NY metropolitan area. **Application procedure:** script, production history, bio and SASE for response. **Deadline:** ongoing; best submission times Jul, Aug, Dec. **Dates:** Oct–Nov, Feb–Mar.

PLAYWRIGHTS THEATRE OF NEW JERSEY
NEW PLAY DEVELOPMENT PROGRAM
33 Green Village Rd; Madison, NJ 07940; (201) 514-1787
Kate McAteer, *Literary Manager*

Open to: playwrights. **Description:** new plays developed through sit-down readings, staged readings and productions; liaison with other producing theatres provided. **Financial arrangement:** playwright receives royalty. **Guidelines:** unproduced play by American playwright; write for brochure. **Application procedure:** script and developmental history, if any; resume and SASP for acknowledgment of receipt. **Deadline:** submit 1 Sep–30 Apr only.

PLAYWRIGHTS WEEK
The Lark Theatre Company; 395 Riverside Dr, Suite 12B;
   New York, NY 10025; (212) 246-2676
Attn: Literary Department

Open to: playwrights, solo performers. **Description:** 8 plays-in-progress given up to 15 hours of rehearsal, culminating in staged reading followed by optional audience discussion or critique; at least 1 script receives subsequent full production. **Financial arrangement:** possible travel and housing. **Application procedure:** script only. **Deadline:** 31 Dec 1997. **Notification date:** 10 Mar 1998. **Dates:** 11–17 May 1998.

PRIMARY STAGES COMPANY
584 Ninth Ave; New York, NY 10036; (212) 333-7471, FAX 333-2025
Andrew Leynse, *Literary Manager*

Open to: playwrights, solo performers. **Description:** organization committed to developing new plays through readings, workshops and full productions. **Financial arrangement:** varies. **Guidelines:** play or musical, not produced in New York City, by American playwright. **Application procedure:** letter of inquiry and SASE for response. **Deadline:** ongoing.

PUERTO RICAN TRAVELING THEATRE PLAYWRIGHTS' WORKSHOP
141 West 94th St; New York, NY 10025; (212) 354-1293, FAX 307-6769
Allen Davis III, *Director*

Open to: playwrights, solo performers. **Description:** 3 units, 1 for professional playwrights, 2 for beginners; weekly meetings; spring staged reading series; City "In Sight" showcase production series. **Financial arrangement:** free. **Guidelines:** resident of New York City area; Latino or other minority playwright or playwright interested in multicultural theatre. **Application procedure:** for professional unit, submit full-length play; beginners contact director. **Deadline:** 30 Sep 1997. **Notification:** within 2 weeks. **Dates:** Oct 1997–Jul 1998.

REMEMBRANCE THROUGH THE PERFORMING ARTS NEW PLAY DEVELOPMENT
3300 Bee Caves Rd, Suite 650; Austin, TX 78746; (512) 329-9118, FAX 329-9118
Marla Macdonald, *Director of New Play Development*

Open to: playwrights, solo performers. **Description:** 8 playwrights chosen annually for winter and spring developmental workshops, culminating in work-in-progress productions in fall; plays subsequently given referral to nationally recognized theatres for world premieres. **Financial arrangement:** free. **Guidelines:** resident of TX; full-length play that has not received Equity production. **Application procedure:** script, synopsis and resume. **Deadline:** ongoing.

THE RICHARD RODGERS AWARDS
American Academy of Arts and Letters; 633 West 155th St; New York, NY 10032-7599; (212) 368-5900, FAX 491-4615
Attn: Richard Rodgers Awards

Open to: playwrights, composers, librettists, lyricists. **Description:** 1 or more works a year given full production, studio/lab production or staged reading by nonprofit theatre in New York City; writer(s) participate in rehearsal process. **Financial arrangement:** free. **Guidelines:** U.S. citizen or permanent resident; new work by writer/composer not already established in musical theatre; innovative, experimental material encouraged; 1 submission; previous submissions ineligible. **Application procedure:** send SASE for application and information. **Deadline:** 3 Nov 1997. **Notification:** Feb 1998.

THE SCHOOLHOUSE
Owens Rd; Croton Falls, NY 10519; (914) 234-7232, FAX 234-4196
Douglas Michael, *Literary Manager*

Open to: playwrights. **Description:** about 6 plays a year receive development with director and actors, culminating in public reading and possible full production; ongoing weekly writer's group. **Financial arrangement:** small fee to help offset costs. **Guidelines:** resident of Westchester or Putnam counties, NY or Fairfield

County, CT, who can participate in program; prefers full-length plays. **Application procedure:** script or excerpt (at least 10 pages) and letter of inquiry. **Deadline:** ongoing. **Notification:** 1 month.

THE SCRIPTEASERS
3404 Hawk St; San Diego, CA 92103-3862; (619) 295-4040, FAX 299-2084
Jonathan Dunn-Rankin, *Corresponding Secretary*

Open to: playwrights, screenwriters, television writers. **Description:** writers, directors and actors meet every other Friday evening in private home for cold readings of new scripts, followed by period of constructive criticism; 1 or 2 rehearsed staged readings a year presented at local theatres as showcases. **Financial arrangement:** donations of $1 accepted at each reading. **Guidelines:** membership by invitation only; guest writer must attend at least 2 readings before submitting script; unproduced script by new or established writer who is resident of San Diego County; write or call for guidelines. **Submission procedure:** see guidelines. **Deadline:** ongoing.

SHENANDOAH INTERNATIONAL PLAYWRIGHTS RETREAT
ShenanArts; Rt 5, Box 167-F; Staunton, VA 24401; (540) 248-1868, FAX 248-7728; E-mail shenarts@cfw.com
Robert Graham Small, *Director*
Kathleen Tosco, *Managing Director*

Open to: playwrights, screenwriters. **Description:** 5-week retreat for 4–6 American writers and 6 international writers at Pennyroyal farm in Shenandoah Valley; program geared to facilitate major rewrite or new draft of existing script; personal writing balanced by workshops and staged readings with professional company of dramaturgs, directors and actors. **Financial arrangement:** fellowships cover costs. **Guidelines:** competitive admission based on submitted work. **Application procedure:** 2 copies of completed draft of script to be worked on at retreat; personal statement of applicant's background as a writer; SASP for acknowledgment of receipt; call or write for guidelines. **Deadline:** 1 Feb 1998. **Notification:** after 10 Jun 1998. **Dates:** Jul–Aug 1998.

SOUTHERN APPALACHIAN PLAYWRIGHTS' CONFERENCE
Southern Appalachian Repertory Theatre; Box 620; Mars Hill, NC 28754-0620; (704) 689-1384, FAX 689-1211; E-mail sart@mhc.edu
Dianne J. Chapman, *Assistant Managing Director*

Open to: playwrights. **Description:** up to 5 writers selected to participate in annual 3-day conference at which 1 work by each writer is given informal reading and critiqued by panel of theatre professionals; 1 work selected for production as part of summer 1998 season. **Financial arrangement:** room and board; writer of work selected for production receives $500 honorarium. **Guidelines:** unproduced, unpublished play. **Application procedure:** script with cast list and synopsis; resume. **Deadline:** 31 Oct 1997. **Dates:** Apr 1998.

STAGES REPERTORY THEATRE

3201 Allen Pkwy, #101; Houston, TX 77019; (713) 527-0240,
FAX 527-8669
Rob Bundy, *Artistic Director*

Texas Playwrights Festival

Open to: playwrights. **Description:** 2 plays chosen for development with dramaturg, director and actors over period of 7–30 days, culminating in staged readings. **Financial arrangement:** small stipend, contingent on funding. **Guidelines:** TX native or resident or non-TX playwright writing on TX theme; play not produced professionally; prefers small cast. **Application procedure:** script only. **Deadline:** 31 Jan 1998. **Notification:** May 1998. **Dates:** Jun 1998.

Women's Repertory Project

Open to: playwrights. **Description:** 6 plays chosen for development with professional actors and director over period of 1 week, culminating in presentation of scenes. **Financial arrangement:** stipend. **Guidelines:** woman playwright. **Application procedure:** script only. **Deadline:** 31 Dec 1997; no submission before 1 Oct 1997. **Dates:** Mar 1998.

SUMMERNITE, NEW PLAY STUDIO

Stevens Bldg; Northern Illinois University; DeKalb, IL 60115-2854;
(815) 753-8258, FAX 753-8415
Gene Terruso, *Artistic Director*

Open to: playwrights. **Description:** up to 10 plays receive staged readings during 15-week program; 2 plays chosen for subsequent full production. **Financial arrangement:** royalties for plays chosen for production. **Guidelines:** full-length play or one-act not previously produced in Chicago area. **Application procedure:** synopsis. **Deadline:** 1 Sep 1997. **Notification date:** 1 Dec 1997. **Dates:** May–Aug 1998.

THE SUNDANCE INSTITUTE
FEATURE FILM PROGRAM

225 Santa Monica Blvd, 8th Floor; Santa Monica, CA 90401; (310) 394-4662,
FAX 394-8353; E-mail sundance@deltanet.com

Open to: playwrights, screenwriters, filmmaking teams (e.g., writer/director). **Description:** program includes 5-day Screenwriters Labs each Jan and Jun offering participants one-on-one problem-solving sessions with professional screenwriters; 3-week Filmmakers Lab in Jun in which projects are explored through work with directors, writers, actors, cinematographers, producers, editors and other resource personnel; network/advisory service offers practical and creative assistance to selected projects. **Financial arrangement:** travel, room and board for at least 1 writer/filmmaker per project; possible room and board for additional members of team. **Guidelines:** "compelling, original narrative feature film scripts (they can be based on a true story or be adaptations of plays, novels, short stories, etc.)

which represent the unique vision of the writer and/or director"; special interest in supporting new talent and artists in transition (e.g., theatre artist who wants to work in film, writer who wants to direct); send SASE for guidelines. **Submission procedure:** completed application, cover letter, first 5 pages of screenplay, synopsis, bios of project participants and $25 fee; after review process, applicants who pass 1st round of selection will be asked to send full screenplay. **Deadline:** May 1998 for all 1999 programs (exact date TBA).

THE SUNDANCE THEATRE LABORATORY

225 Santa Monica Blvd, 8th Floor; Santa Monica, CA 90401; (310) 394-4662, FAX 394-9893
Philip Himberg, *Producing Director*

Open to: playwright-director teams. **Description:** 8–12 scripts workshopped for 10–20 days. **Financial arrangement:** travel, room and board. **Guidelines:** full-length play, one-act, musical, solo piece, new adaptation and/or translation of classic material; plays can be for young or adult audiences. **Application procedure:** send SASE for guidelines and application. **Deadline:** 15 Dec 1997. **Notification:** Apr 1998. **Dates:** Jul 1998.

THE TEN-MINUTE MUSICALS PROJECT

Box 461194; West Hollywood, CA 90046; (213) 656-8751
Michael Koppy, *Producer*

Open to: composers, librettists, lyricists, solo performers. **Description:** up to 10 brief pieces selected during annual cycle for possible inclusion in full-length anthology-musicals to be produced at Equity theatres in U.S. and Canada; occasionally some pieces workshopped using professional actors and director. **Financial arrangement:** $250 royalty advance with equal share of licensing royalties when produced. **Guidelines:** complete work with a definite beginning, middle and end, 7–14 minutes long, in any musical style or genre; adaptations of strongly structured material in the public domain, or for which rights have been obtained, are encouraged; cast of 2–9, prefers 6–9; write for guidelines. **Application procedure:** script, lead sheets and cassette of sung material. **Deadline:** 31 Aug 1998. **Notification:** 30 Nov 1998.

THEATRE ARTISTS WORKSHOP OF WESTPORT

17 Morningside Dr S; Westport, CT 06880; (203) 227-5836
Admissions Committee

Open to: playwrights, composers, librettists, lyricists. **Description:** laboratory where professional writers can exercise their craft and develop projects in collaboration with member directors, actors and allied theatre artists; ongoing workshop meetings; work presented for peer evaluation. **Financial arrangement:** annual membership dues and contributions of $220; $50 initiation fee. **Guidelines:** serious, theatre-oriented writer of professional caliber. **Application procedure:** completed application and 3 copies of script. **Deadline:** ongoing.

The Theatre-Studio Playtime Series
750 Eighth Ave, #200; New York, NY 10036; (212) 719-0500
A. M. Raychel, *Artistic Director/Producer*

Open to: playwrights, solo performers. **Description:** program to develop plays through staged readings and full productions; playwright receives free rehearsal and performance space. **Financial arrangement:** free. **Application procedure:** script only. **Deadline:** ongoing.

Theatreworks/USA Commissioning Program
Theatreworks/USA; 890 Broadway, 7th Floor; New York, NY 10003;
(212) 677-5959, FAX 353-1632
Barbara Pasternack, *Associate Artistic Director*

Open to: composers, librettists, lyricists. **Description:** step commissioning process, possibly leading to 2-week developmental workshop and production. **Financial arrangement:** free. **Guidelines:** works dealing with issues relevant to target audiences; special interest in historical/biographical subject matter and musical adaptations of fairy tales and traditional or contemporary classics; 1 hour long; cast of 5 actors, set suitable for touring. **Application procedure:** prefers treatment with sample scenes, lyric sheets and cassette of music; will accept script only. **Deadline:** ongoing. **Notification:** 6 months.

The Tuesday Group
202 President St, #2; Brooklyn, NY 11231; (212) 462-9135
William Gadea, *Coordinator*

Open to: playwrights. **Description:** group meets every 2 weeks to read and discuss members' works; some plays workshopped with resident directors and ensemble. **Financial arrangement:** $60 fee per trimester. **Application procedure:** writing sample and letter of inquiry with SASE for response. **Deadline:** ongoing. **Notification:** 2 months.

University of Alabama New Playwrights' Program
Department of Theatre and Dance; University of Alabama; Box 870239;
Tuscaloosa, AL 35487-0239; (205) 348-9032, FAX 348-9048;
E-mail pcastagn@woodsquad.as.ua.edu
Paul C. Castagno, *Director and Dramaturg*

Open to: playwrights, composers, librettists, lyricists, solo performers. **Description:** opportunity for writer to develop unproduced script or to pursue further development of produced work, culminating in full production; writer may visit campus several times during rehearsal process and is required to offer limited playwriting workshops during visit(s); recent MFA playwrights encouraged to apply; production considered for entry in the Kennedy Center American College Theater Festival (see Prizes). **Financial arrangement:** substantial stipend, travel and expenses. **Guidelines:** writer with some previous experience and script that has had some development; special interest in works with southern themes.

Application procedure: script or synopsis and cover letter. **Deadline:** submit Aug–Mar only. **Notification:** 6 months. **Dates:** fall–spring. **Other programs:** department will also consider one-acts for festival by its directing students and writers' proposals for workshops with its playwriting and acting students.

Westbeth Playwright Program
Westbeth Theatre Center; 151 Bank St; New York, NY 10014; (212) 691-2272
Craig Carlisle, *Director*

Open to: playwrights, solo performers. **Description:** program to develop full-length plays through critiques, story conferences and staged readings; possible production by Westbeth Theatre Center or through referral to other producing organizations. **Financial arrangement:** free. **Guidelines:** contemporary themes; cast limit of 8, minimal set; welcomes work by minority playwrights; send SASE for guidelines. **Application procedure:** synopsis and resume. **Deadline:** ongoing. **Notification:** 4–6 months.

Williamstown Theatre Festival
100 East 17th St., 3rd Floor; New York, NY 10003; (212) 228-2286, FAX 228-9091
Michael Ritchie, *Producer*

Open to: playwrights, composers, librettists, lyricists. **Description:** 4 plays each season given public reading. **Financial arrangement:** stipend, travel and housing. **Guidelines:** American playwright; play not professionally unproduced. **Application procedure:** work sample. **Deadline:** submit 1 Sep 1997–28 Feb 1998 only.

Women Playwrights Project
Centenary Stage Company; 400 Jefferson St; Hackettstown, NJ 07840; (908) 979-0900, FAX 813-1984
Catherine Rust, *Project Director*

Open to: playwrights. **Description:** 1 play given 1 week of rehearsal with professional actors and director, followed by staged reading and possible main stage production. **Financial arrangement:** $200 honorarium; travel, room and board. **Guidelines:** woman playwright; full-length play preferred. **Application procedure:** script only. **Deadline:** 1 Nov 1997. **Notification:** 1 Dec 1997. **Dates:** Mar 1998.

WOMEN'S WORK
New Perspectives Theatre Company; 750 Eighth Ave, Suite 601;
  New York, NY 10036; (212) 730-2030
Melody Brooks, *Artistic Director*

Open to: playwrights. **Description:** 2 playwrights chosen for 6–9 month residency to develop full-length play. **Financial arrangement:** free. **Guidelines:** woman playwright; previously unproduced full-length play; special interest in works by writers of color; call for application and guidelines. **Application procedure:** completed application and script. **Deadline:** 1 Jun 1998. **Notification:** 15 Jul 1998. **Dates:** ongoing.

Career Opportunities

- Agents
- Fellowships and Grants
- Emergency Funds
- State Arts Agencies
- **Colonies and Residencies**
- **Membership and Service Organizations**

Agents

I'm wondering whether or not I should have an agent. Where can I get information to help me decide?

Write to the Association of Authors' Representatives at 10 Astor Pl, 3rd Floor; New York, NY 10003. Send a check or money order for $7 and a 55¢ SASE to receive the AAR's brochure describing the role of the literary agent and how to find an agent, and its membership list and canon of ethics. See Useful Publications for books you can consult on the subject. Ask fellow playwrights what they think.

How do I select the names of appropriate agents to contact?

All of the agents listed here represent playwrights. (In some cases, the name of the agency contains the name of the agent.) The Dramatists Guild also has a list of agents available to its members, and provides advice on relationships with agents (see Membership and Service Organizations). You may come across names that appear on none of these lists, but be wary, especially if someone tries to charge you a fee to read your script. Again, talk to other playwrights about their experiences. Look at copies of scripts for the names of agents representing specific playwrights. See what kinds of plays various agents handle in order to make an intelligent guess as to whether they would be interested in representing you and your work.

190 / AGENTS

How do I approach an agent?

Do not telephone, do not drop in, do not send manuscripts. Write a brief letter describing your work and asking if the agent would like to see a script. Enclose your professional resume; it should show that you have had work produced or published and make clear that you look at writing as an ongoing career, not an occasional hobby. If you're a beginning writer who's just finished your first play, you'd probably do better to work on getting a production rather than an agent.

ABE NEWBORN ASSOCIATES
1365 York Ave, #25G; New York, NY 10021; (212) 861-4635
Abe Newborn, Joyce Newborn, *Agents*

THE AGENCY
1800 Ave of the Stars, Suite 400; Los Angeles, CA 90067; (310) 551-3000
Dino Carlaftes, Jeffrey Laymun, Nick Mechanic, Jerome Zeitman, *Agents*

AGENCY FOR THE PERFORMING ARTS
888 Seventh Ave, Suite 602; New York, NY 10106; (212) 582-1500
Leo Bookman, *Agent*

ALAN BRODIE REPRESENTATION LTD.
211 Piccadilly; London W1V 9LD; England; 441-71-917-2871
Alan Brodie, Sarah McNair, *Agents*

ANN ELMO AGENCY
60 East 42nd St; New York, NY 10165; (212) 661-2880
Mari Cronin, Letti Lee, *Agents*

THE BARBARA HOGENSON AGENCY, INC.
165 West End Ave, Suite 19C; New York, NY 10023; (212) 874-8084

BERMAN, BOALS & FLYNN
225 Lafayette St, Suite 1207; New York, NY 10012; (212) 966-0339
Lois Berman, Judy Boals, Jim Flynn, *Agents*

BERTHA KLAUSNER INTERNATIONAL LITERARY AGENCY
71 Park Ave; New York, NY 10016; (212) 685-2642

THE BETHEL AGENCY
360 West 53rd St, Suite BA; New York, NY 10019; (212) 664-0455
Lewis Chambers, *Agent*

Bret Adams Ltd.
448 West 44th St; New York, NY 10036; (212) 765-5630
Bret Adams, Bruce Ostler, *Agents*

Don Buchwald & Associates
10 East 44th St; New York, NY 10017; (212) 867-1200
Shelly Reid, *Agent*

The Dramatic Publishing Company
311 Washington St; Box 129; Woodstock, IL 60098; (815) 338-7170
Linda Habjan, Dana Wolworth (musicals), *Agents*

Elisabeth Marton Agency
1 Union Square, Room 612; New York, NY 10003-3303; (212) 255-1908
Tonda Marton, *Agent*

Fifi Oscard Associates
24 West 40th St, 17th Floor; New York, NY 10018; (212) 764-1100
Carmen LaVia, Kevin McShane, Fifi Oscard, Peter Sawyer, *Agents*

Flora Roberts
157 West 57th St; New York, NY 10019; (212) 355-4165
Sarah Douglas, Flora Roberts, *Agents*

Freida Fishbein Associates
Box 723; Bedford, NY 10506; (914) 234-7232
Douglas Michael, *Agent*

The Gersh Agency
130 West 42nd St; New York, NY 10036; (212) 997-1818
Scott Yoselow, *Agent*

Graham Agency
311 West 43rd St; New York, NY 10036; (212) 489-7730
Earl Graham, *Agent*

Harden-Curtis Associates
850 Seventh Ave, Suite 405; New York, NY 10019; (212) 977-8502
Mary Harden, *Agent*

Harris Agency
156 Fifth Ave, Suite 617; New York, NY 10010; (212) 924-6269
Joy Harris, *Agent*

Helen Merrill
435 West 23rd St, Suite 1A; New York, NY 10011; (212) 691-5326
Clyde Kuemmerle, Helen Merrill, *Agents*

International Creative Management
40 West 57th St; New York, NY 10019; (212) 556-5600
Bridget Aschenberg, Mitch Douglas, *Agents*

The Joyce Ketay Agency
1501 Broadway, Suite 1908; New York, NY 10036; (212) 354-6825
Joyce P. Ketay, Carl Mulert, *Agents*

The Kopaloff Company
6440 West Olympic Blvd; Los Angeles, CA 90048; (213) 782-1854
Don Kopaloff, *Agent*

Lantz Agency
888 Seventh Ave; New York, NY 10106; (212) 586-0200
Robert Lantz, *Agent*

Paramuse Artists Associates
1414 Ave of the Americas; New York, NY 10019; (212) 758-5055
Shirley Bernstein, *President*

The Parness Agency
11693 San Vincenti, Suite 202; Los Angeles, CA 90049; (310) 820-4524
Leslie Parness, *Agent*

Peregrine Whittlesey Agency
345 East 80th St, #31F; New York, NY 10021; (212) 737-0153

Robert A. Freedman Dramatic Agency
1501 Broadway, Suite 2310; New York, NY 10036; (212) 840-5760
Robert A. Freedman, Selma Luttinger, *Agents*

The Roberts Company
10345 West Olympic Blvd, Penthouse; Los Angeles, CA 90064; (310) 552-7800
Nancy Roberts, *Agent*

Rosenstone/Wender
3 East 48th St, 4th Floor; New York, NY 10017; (212) 832-8330
Ronald Gwiazda, Howard Rosenstone, Phyllis Wender, *Agents*

Samuel French
45 West 25th St; New York, NY 10010-2751; (212) 206-8990
Lawrence Harbison, *Editor*

SHUKAT COMPANY, LTD.
340 West 55th St, Suite 1A; New York, NY 10019; (212) 582-7614
Scott Shukat, Patricia McLaughlin, *Agents*

STEPHEN PEVNER, INC.
248 West 73rd St, 2nd Floor; New York, NY 10023; (212) 496-0474

THE SUSAN GURMAN AGENCY
865 West End Ave, #15A; New York, NY 10025; (212) 864-5243

SUSAN SCHULMAN LITERARY AGENCY
454 West 44th St; New York, NY 10036; (212) 713-1633

THE TANTLEFF OFFICE
375 Greenwich St, Suite 603; New York, NY 10013; (212) 941-3939
Charmani Ferenczi, Jack Tantleff, *Agents*

WILLIAM MORRIS AGENCY
1325 Ave of the Americas; New York, NY 10019; (212) 586-5100
Peter Franklin, George Lane, Owen Laster, Biff Liff, Mary Meagher, Gilbert Parker, *Agents*

WRITERS & ARTISTS AGENCY
19 West 44th St, Suite 1000; New York, NY 10036; (212) 391-1112
Jeff Berger, William Craver, Greg Wagner, *Agents*

Fellowships and Grants

Can I apply directly to all the programs listed in this section?

No. You will see that a number of the grant programs we list must be applied to by a producing or presenting organization. However, you should be aware that these programs exist so that you can bring them to the attention of organizations with which you have a working relationship. All or most of the funds disbursed directly benefit the individual artist since they go to cover commissioning fees, residencies and other expenses related to the creation of new works.

How can I enhance my chances of winning an award?

Start early. This is so important that we give full listings to the increasing number of awards offered in alternate years, even when the deadline falls outside the period this *Sourcebook* covers. Use the Submission Calendar in the back of this book to help you plan your campaign. In the case of all awards for which you can apply directly, write for guidelines and application forms months ahead. Study the guidelines carefully and follow them meticulously. Don't hesitate to ask for advice and assistance from the organization to which you are applying. Submit a well thought-out, excellently written, neatly typed application—and make sure it arrives in the organization's office by the deadline. (Never assume, without checking, that the deadline is the postmark date.) Apply for as many awards as you qualify for; once you have written the first grant proposal, you can often, with little additional work, adapt it to fit others' guidelines.

THE ALFRED HODDER FELLOWSHIP

The Council of the Humanities; 122 East Pyne; Princeton University; Princeton, NJ 08544-5264; (609) 258-4717, FAX 258-2783

Open to: playwrights, translators. **Frequency:** annual. **Remuneration:** $42,000 fellowship. **Guidelines:** emerging artist; writer spends academic year at Princeton pursuing independent project; prefers writer who has published 1 critically acclaimed book. **Application procedure:** maximum 10-page work sample, 2–3 page project proposal, resume and SASE for response. **Deadline:** 15 Nov 1997.

THE AMERICAN-SCANDINAVIAN FOUNDATION

725 Park Ave; New York, NY 10021; (212) 879-9779, FAX 249-3444;
  E-mail grants@amscan.org
Exchange Division

Open to: playwrights, translators, composers, librettists, lyricists. **Frequency:** annual. **Remuneration:** $3000–15,000. **Guidelines:** grants and fellowships for research and study in Scandinavian countries; U.S. citizen or permanent resident with undergraduate degree. **Application procedure:** completed application, supplementary materials and $10 fee. **Deadline:** 1 Nov 1997. **Notification:** Mar 1998.

ARTIST TRUST

1402 Third Ave, Suite 404; Seattle, WA 98101-2118; (206) 467-8734,
  FAX 467-9633; E-mail arttrust@eskimo.com
Marschel Paul, *Director*

Fellowships

Open to: playwrights, composers, librettists, lyricists, screenwriters, radio and television writers. **Frequency:** awards rotate among disciplines. **Remuneration:** $5000 award. **Guidelines:** WA resident only; practicing professional artist of exceptional talent and demonstrated ability; award based on creative excellence and continuing dedication to an artistic discipline; send SASE for guidelines. **Application procedure:** completed application and work sample. **Deadline:** late spring 1998 for playwrights; exact dates TBA (14 Jun in 1996); late spring 1999 (13 Jun in 1997) for composers, librettists, lyricists, screenwriters, radio and television writers.

GAP (Grants for Artist Projects)

Open to: playwrights, composers, librettists, lyricists, screenwriters, radio and television writers. **Frequency:** annual. **Remuneration:** grant of up to $1200. **Guidelines:** WA resident only; grant for the initiation, continuation or completion of specific creative project undertaken by individual artist; award based on quality of work as represented by supporting material and on creativity and feasibility of proposed project; write for guidelines. **Application procedure:** completed application and work sample. **Deadline:** 28 Feb 1998.

Artists-in-Berlin Programme
German Academic Exchange Service (DAAD); 950 Third Ave, 19th Floor;
New York, NY 10022; (212) 758-3223

Open to: playwrights, composers. **Frequency:** annual. **Remuneration:** monthly grant to cover living costs and rent during 1-year residency in Berlin (6 months in exceptional cases); workspace provided or paid for; travel for writer and any members of immediate family who will be staying in Berlin for period of residency; health and accident insurance; in some cases specific projects such as readings or publications can be subsidized. **Guidelines:** to enable 15–20 internationally known and qualified young artists to pursue own work while participating in the cultural life of the city and making contact with local artists; must reside in Berlin for period of grant; German nationals and foreign writers who are resident in Germany ineligible; write for guidelines. **Application procedure:** completed application; samples of published work, preferably in German, otherwise in English or French, (no manuscripts) for playwrights; scores, records, tapes or published work for composers. **Deadline:** 31 Dec 1997. **Notification:** May 1998. **Dates:** residency begins between 1 Jan and 30 Jun 1999.

Arts International
Institute of International Education; 809 United Nations Plaza;
New York, NY 10017-3580; (212) 984-5370, FAX 984-5574

Cintas
Esther McGowan, *Program Officer*

This fellowship program is open to individuals (including playwrights, translators and composers) of Cuban descent or citizenship living outside Cuba. Award rotates among disciplines; discipline for 1998–1999 fellowship TBA; call after Dec 1997 for information.

Fund for U.S. Artists at International Festivals and Exhibitions
(see also NEA International Program in this section)
Laura Moore, *Program Officer*
E-mail thefund@iie.org

Open to: performing artists and groups, including solo performers and theatre companies. **Frequency:** triannual. **Remuneration:** grants of up to $25,000 (most grants $500–10,000) to cover foreign travel, housing, per diem and production costs. **Guidelines:** U.S. citizen or permanent resident who has been invited to international festival. **Application procedure:** completed application; copy of invitation from festival; full budget showing all costs of participation in festival and festival's contribution to these costs; work sample; bio. **Deadline:** 2 Sep 1997; 15 Jan 1998; 1 May 1998.

Inroads
Vanessa Palmer, *Associate Director*
E-mail ainternational@iie.org

Open to: performing artists and organizations. **Frequency:** annual. **Remuneration:** grants of $20,000–30,000. **Guidelines:** funds to be used for short-term planning residencies for partnership between artists in different disciplines; 1 artist must be U.S. resident, 1 must be resident of Africa, Asia, Latin America, the Middle East, the Pacific Islands or the Caribbean; project must be under umbrella of U.S. host organization. **Application procedure:** write for guidelines and application. **Deadline:** Apr 1998 (exact date TBA).

ASIAN CULTURAL COUNCIL
1290 Ave of the Americas; New York, NY 10104; (212) 373-4300

ACC Residency Program in Asia

Open to: playwrights, composers, librettists, lyricists. **Frequency:** annual. **Remuneration:** amount varies. **Guidelines:** to support American artists, scholars, and specialists undertaking collaborative research, teaching or creative residencies at cultural and educational institutions in East and Southeast Asia. **Application procedure:** write describing project and requesting application. **Deadline:** 1 Feb 1998.

Japan-United States Arts Program

Open to: playwrights, composers, librettists, lyricists. **Frequency:** annual. **Remuneration:** amount varies. **Guidelines:** to support residencies in Japan for American artists for a variety of purposes, including creative activities (other than performances), research projects, professional observation tours and specialized training. **Application procedure:** write describing project and requesting application. **Deadline:** 1 Feb 1998.

ATLANTA BUREAU OF CULTURAL AFFAIRS
675 Ponce de Leon Ave; Atlanta, GA 30308; (404) 817-6815, FAX 817-6827
Sophia Lyman, *Project Adminstrator*

Artists Project

Open to: playwrights, composers, librettists, lyricists. **Frequency:** annual. **Remuneration:** grant of up to $3000. **Guidelines:** practicing professional artist resident in city of Atlanta for at least 1 year prior to deadline. **Application procedure:** write for guidelines and application. **Deadline:** Nov 1997; exact date TBA. **Notification:** 3 months.

Mayor's Fellowships in the Arts

Open to: playwrights, composers, librettists, lyricists. **Frequency:** awards rotate among disciplines. **Remuneration:** $6600 award. **Guidelines:** practicing professional artist resident in city of Atlanta for at least 3 consecutive years prior to deadline; playwright may apply under literary or theatre arts; composer, librettist, lyricist applies under music. **Application procedure:** write for guidelines and application. **Deadline:** Feb 2000 for playwrights (exact date TBA). **Notification:** 3 months.

BRODY ARTS FUND
California Community Foundation; 606 South Olive St, Suite 2400;
   Los Angeles, CA 90014-1526; (213) 242-7489; Web http://www.calfund.org
Program Secretary

Open to: playwrights, composers, librettists, lyricists, solo performers, screenwriters, radio and television writers. **Frequency:** awards rotate among disciplines. **Remuneration:** fellowship of $5000. **Guidelines:** L.A. county resident; emerging artist; prefers artist in "expansion arts" field (minority, inner-city, rural and tribal arts); write for guidelines; application available in spring of application year. **Application procedure:** completed application and supporting materials. **Deadline:** Mar 1999; exact dates TBA. **Notification:** Jun 1999.

BUNTING FELLOWSHIP PROGRAM
The Mary Ingraham Bunting Institute of Radcliffe College; 34 Concord Ave;
   Cambridge, MA 02138; (617) 495-8212, FAX 495-8136
Fellowships Coordinator

Open to: playwrights, composers, librettists. **Frequency:** annual. **Remuneration:** $36,000 1-year fellowship. **Guidelines:** to provide opportunity and support for professional woman of demonstrated accomplishment and exceptional promise to complete substantial project in her field; full-time appointment; fellow required to reside in Boston area and expected to present work-in-progress in public colloquia during year; office or studio space, auditing privileges and access to libraries and other resources of Radcliffe and Harvard provided; call or write for guidelines and application. **Application procedure:** completed application with $45 fee. **Deadline:** 15 Oct 1997. **Notification:** Apr 1998. **Dates:** 15 Sep 1998–15 Aug 1999.

BUSH ARTIST FELLOWSHIPS
The Bush Foundation; E-900 First National Bank Bldg; 332 Minnesota St;
   St. Paul, MN 55101; (612) 227-5222
Julie Dalgleish, *Program Director*

Open to: playwrights, composers, screenwriters. **Frequency:** awards rotate biennially among disciplines. **Remuneration:** $36,000 in equal monthly installments for 12–18 months. **Guidelines:** MN, ND, SD or western WI resident at least 25 years old who is not a student; playwright must have had at least 1 play given full production or workshop production for which admission was charged; screenwriter must have had 1 public staged reading or workshop production for which admission was charged, or screenplay sale or option. **Application procedure:** write for guidelines and application. **Deadline:** next deadline for playwrights, composers and screenwriters Oct 1998; exact date TBA. **Notification:** Apr 1999.

DOBIE-PAISANO FELLOWSHIP

University of Texas at Austin; Main Bldg 101; Austin, TX 78712;
   (512) 471-7213, FAX 471-7620; E-mail aslate@mail.utexas.edu
Audrey Slate, *Coordinator*

Open to: playwrights. **Frequency:** annual. **Remuneration:** $7200 stipend to cover 6-month residency at 265-acre ranch; free housing; families welcome. **Guidelines:** native Texan, or playwright who has lived in TX for at least 2 years or has published work about TX; ordinarily 2 writers selected each year. **Application procedure:** write for application after 1 Oct 1997. **Deadline:** 23 Jan 1998. **Notification:** May 1998.

THE DON AND GEE NICHOLL FELLOWSHIPS IN SCREENWRITING

Academy of Motion Picture Arts and Sciences; 8949 Wilshire Blvd;
   Beverly Hills, CA 90211-1972; (310) 247-3059;
   Web http://www.oscars.org/
Greg Beal, *Program Coordinator*

Open to: playwrights, screenwriters. **Frequency:** annual. **Remuneration:** up to 5 fellowships of $25,000. **Guidelines:** playwright, screenwriter or fiction writer who has not worked as a professional screenwriter for theatrical films or television or sold screen or television rights to any original story, treatment, stage play, screenplay or teleplay; 1st-round selection based on submission of original screenplay or screen adaptation of writer's own original work, 100–130 pages, written in standard screenplay format; send SASE for guidelines after 1 Jan 1998. **Application procedure:** completed application, screenplay and $30 application fee. **Deadline:** 1 May 1998. **Notification:** 1st-round selection Aug 1998; winners late Oct 1998.

ELECTRONIC ARTS GRANT PROGRAM

Experimental Television Center; 109 Lower Fairfield Rd;
   Newark Valley, NY 13811; (607) 687-4341, FAX 687-4341
Sherry Miller Hocking, *Program Director*

Finishing Funds

Open to: media artists, including writers and composers, involved in creation of film, audio, video or computer-generated time-based works. **Frequency:** annual. **Remuneration:** 20–25 grants of up to $500. **Guidelines:** resident of NY State; funds to be used to assist completion of work which is time-based in conception and execution and is to be presented as tape or installation; work must be completed before 30 Sep 1998; write for guidelines. **Application procedure:** 3 copies of completed application, project description, work samples and resume. **Deadline:** 15 Mar 1998. **Notification:** 6 weeks.

Presentation Funds

Open to: not-for-profit organizations presenting audio, film, video or computer-generated time-based works. **Frequency:** ongoing. **Remuneration:** grant of approximately $150–300 to assist presentation of work and artist's involvement in activities related to presentation. **Guidelines:** New York State organization; event must be open to public and should emphasize work of NY State artist(s); write for guidelines. **Application procedure:** individual may not apply; completed application and supporting materials submitted by organization well in advance of event. **Notification:** 15th of month following month of submission.

FULBRIGHT SCHOLAR AWARDS
Council for International Exchange of Scholars (CIES); 3007 Tilden St NW,
   Suite 5M; Washington, DC 20008-3009; (202) 686-7877, FAX 362-3442;
   E-mail cies1@ciesnet.cies.org; Web http://www.cies.org

Open to: scholars and professionals in all areas of theatre and the arts, including playwrights, translators, composers, librettists and lyricists. **Frequency:** annual. **Remuneration:** grant for university lecturing or research in one of more than 100 countries for 2–9 months; amount varies with country of award; travel; maintenance allowance for living costs of grantee and possibly family. **Guidelines:** U.S. citizen; MFA, Ph.D. or comparable professional qualifications; university or college teaching experience for lecturing awards; for selected countries, proficiency in a foreign language. **Application procedure:** completed application. **Deadline:** 1 Aug 1998. **Notification:** up to 11 months, depending on country; average 8 months.

FUND FOR NEW AMERICAN PLAYS
The John F. Kennedy Center for the Performing Arts; 2700 F St NW;
   Washington, DC 20566; (202) 416-8024, FAX 416-8026;
   E-mail mwoodward@mail.kennedy-center.org;
   Web http://kennedy-center.org
Max Woodward, *Manager*

Open to: not-for-profit professional theatres. **Frequency:** annual. **Remuneration:** $10,000 grant to playwright whose work theatre is producing, plus grant (amount dependent on quality of proposal and need) to theatre (7 in 1996); occasional $2,500 Roger L. Stevens award to playwright whose work shows "extraordinary promise" (1 in 1996). **Guidelines:** grant to theatre covers living and travel expenses for playwright during minimum 4 weeks of rehearsal and during any necessary additional rehearsals and rewrites in course of run; grant also covers expenses exceeding theatre's budget allocation for hiring of director, designer and guest actors; limit of 1 proposal per theatre; translations and musicals ineligible; write for guidelines. **Application procedure:** playwright may not apply; proposal and supporting materials submitted by theatre. **Deadline:** 16 Mar 1998.

GEORGE BENNETT FELLOWSHIP
Phillips Exeter Academy; Exeter, NH 03833-1104
Charles Pratt, *Coordinator, Selection Committee*

Open to: playwrights. **Frequency:** annual. **Remuneration:** academic-year stipend of $5000; free room and board for fellow and family. **Guidelines:** individual who is seriously contemplating or pursuing a career as a writer and who needs time and freedom from material considerations to complete a project in progress; committee favors writers who have not yet been produced commercially or at a major not-for-profit theatre; fellow expected to make self and talents available in informal and unofficial way to students interested in writing; send SASE for guidelines and application (no phone inquiries). **Application procedure:** completed application, work sample, statement concerning work-in-progress, names of 2 references and $5 fee. **Deadline:** 1 Dec 1997. **Notification:** 15 Mar 1998. **Dates:** Sep 1998–Jun 1999.

INSTITUTE OF INTERNATIONAL EDUCATION
809 United Nations Plaza; New York, NY 10017-3580; (212) 984-5330;
   Web http://www.iie.org/fulbright
U.S. Student Programs Division

Open to: playwrights, translators, composers, librettists, lyricists. **Frequency:** annual. **Remuneration:** fellowship or grant; amount varies with country of award. **Guidelines:** specific opportunities for study abroad in the arts; write for brochure. **Application procedure:** completed application and supporting materials. **Deadline:** 23 Oct 1997. **Notification:** Jan 1998.

THE JAPAN FOUNDATION
152 West 57th St, 39th Floor; New York, NY 10019; (212) 489-0299,
   FAX 489-0409; Web http://www.jfny.org/jfny/index.html
Artists Fellowship Program

Open to: specialists in the fields of fine arts, performing arts, music, journalism and creative writing, including playwrights, composers, librettists, lyricists and screenwriters. **Frequency:** annual. **Remuneration:** monthly stipend of ¥370,000 (about $3500) or ¥430,000 (about $4000), depending on grantee's professional career; travel; other allowances. **Guidelines:** U.S. citizen or permanent resident; fellowship of 2–6 months, not to be held concurrently with another major grant, to support project substantially related to Japan. **Application procedure:** write for guidelines and application, stating theme of project, present position and citizenship. **Deadline:** 1 Dec 1997. **Notification:** late Mar/early Apr 1998. **Dates:** between 1 Apr 1998 and 31 Mar 1999.

JOHN SIMON GUGGENHEIM MEMORIAL FOUNDATION
90 Park Ave; New York, NY 10016; (212) 687-4470, FAX 697-3248;
   E-mail fellowships@gf.org

Open to: playwrights, composers. **Frequency:** annual. **Remuneration:** 1-year fellowship (in 1996, 158 fellowships with average grant of $28,480). **Guidelines:** citizen or permanent resident of U.S. or Canada; recipient must demonstrate exceptional creative ability; grant to support research in any field of knowledge or creation in any of the arts under the freest possible conditions. **Application procedure:** write for information. **Deadline:** 1 Oct 1997. **Notification:** Mar 1998.

THE KLEBAN AWARD

c/o Zissu, Stein & Mosher; 270 Madison Ave, Suite 1410; New York, NY 10016; (212) 683-5320
Alan J. Stein, *Secretary*

Open to: TBA (librettists and/or lyricists). **Frequency:** annual. **Remuneration:** TBA ($100,000 each to lyricist and librettist, payable in installments of $50,000 a year, in 1996-97). **Guidelines:** applicant whose work has received a full or workshop production, or who has been a member or associate of a professional musical workshop or theatre group (e.g., ASCAP or BMI workshop or Dramatists Guild Musical Theater Development Program); writer whose work has been performed on the Broadway stage for a cumulative period of 2 years ineligible; write for guidelines. **Application procedure:** completed application and work sample. **Deadline:** TBA (27 Sep in 1996).

MANHATTAN THEATRE CLUB PLAYWRITING FELLOWSHIPS

453 West 16th St; New York, NY 10011; (212) 645-5590, FAX 691-9106; E-mail 76735,3316@compuserve.com
Alyse Rothman, *Literary Assistant*

Open to: playwrights. **Frequency:** annual. **Remuneration:** $10,000 fellowship. **Guidelines:** New York-based playwright who has completed formal education and can demonstrate financial need; writers from diverse cultural groups encouraged to apply; fellowship includes commission for new play, production assistantship, 1-year residency at MTC; send SASE for further information. **Application procedure:** sample script, resume, statement of purpose and letter of recommendation from theatre professional or professor. **Deadline:** TBA.

THE MARY ROBERTS RINEHART AWARDS

English Department; MSN 3E4; George Mason University; Fairfax, VA 22030-4444; (703) 993-1185
Director, Writing Program

Open to: playwrights. **Frequency:** biennial. **Remuneration:** grant; amount varies with fund's income (currently around $900). **Guidelines:** playwright who lacks financial means to complete a definitely projected work; playwrights who have had a play professionally produced or published, or who have previously received a Rinehart Fund Grant, are ineligible. **Application procedure:** playwright may not apply; nominations accepted from established authors, editors, agents or writing program faculty members. **Deadline:** 30 Nov 1998. **Notification:** Mar 1999.

Mature Women Scholarship Award
The National League of American Pen Women; 1300 17th St NW; Washington, DC 20036-1973; (202) 785-1997
National Scholarship Chairman

Open to: playwrights, composers, librettists, lyricists. **Frequency:** biennial. **Remuneration:** $1000 grant. **Guidelines:** American woman aged over 35; 3 awards (1 in art, 1 in music, 1 in letters) to further creative goals of women at age when encouragement can lead to realization of long-term purposes; NLAPW members ineligible; send SASE after 1 Aug 1997 for guidelines. **Application procedure:** work sample; statement of purpose for which money will be used; statement that applicant is over age 35 and is not a member of NLAPW; and $8 fee. **Deadline:** 15 Jan 1998. **Notification:** Jun 1998.

The McKnight Interdisciplinary Fellowship Grant
Intermedia Arts, Minnesota; 2822 Lyndale Ave. South; Minneapolis, MN 55408; (612) 871-4444, FAX 871-6927; E-mail allstaff@intermediaarts.org
Sandy Agustin, *Community Programs Manager*

Minnesota Fellowship

Open to: interdisciplinary artists. **Frequency:** annual. **Remuneration:** $12,000 fellowship. **Guidelines:** resident of MN for 1 year before application; mid-career interdisciplinary artists; fellowship and technical support to pursue educational/presentational activity during 18-month fellowship period; send SASE for guidelines after Oct 1997. **Application procedure:** completed application, 1-page maximum artist statement, 10-page maximum work sample, resume and optional SASP for acknowledgment of receipt. **Deadline:** 16 Jan 1998. **Notification:** spring 1998.

National McKnight Interdisciplinary Fellow in Residence

Open to: interdisciplinary artists. **Frequency:** biennial. **Remuneration:** $10,000 artist's fee; up to $4000 in travel expenses. **Guidelines:** artists with accomplished body of work; must have teaching and/or mentoring experience; must be able to be in Minneapolis for at least 4 weeks (not necessarily consecutive) during 2000; send SASE for guidelines. **Application procedure:** letter of intent no more than 2 pages in length describing artist's body of interdisciplinary work, teaching and/or mentoring experience and previous residency experience; resume. **Deadline:** Jun 1999. **Notification:** Jul 1999.

Meet The Composer Grant Programs
2112 Broadway, Suite 505; New York, NY 10023; (212) 787-3601

International Creative Collaboration
Pablo Martinez, *Program Manager*

Open to: opera, theatre, dance and music-theatre companies, arts presenters and musical organizations. **Frequency:** annual. **Remuneration:** up to $75,000 for commissioning, residency and travel costs. **Guidelines:** U.S. organizations apply for funds to support multidisciplinary collaborations up to 3 years in length between U.S.-based composers, librettists, playwrights or choreographers and artists from Africa, Middle East, Asia, Pacific Islands, Latin America or Caribbean; priority given to projects involving composers; call or write for guidelines. **Application procedure:** individual may not apply; performing organization submits letter of intent before making formal application. **Deadline:** TBA.

Meet the Composer/Arts Endowment Commissioning Music/USA
Theodore Wiprud, *Program Manager*

Open to: opera, theatre and music-theatre companies, arts presenters, musical organizations, TV production companies and radio stations. **Frequency:** awards rotate among disciplines. **Remuneration:** commissioning grant of up to $30,000 to cover composer, librettist, TV writer and/or radio writer fees for opera or music-theatre work (amount dependent on scope and length of work). **Guidelines:** organizations that have been producing or presenting for at least 3 years; application may be from single organization for grants up to $10,000, or from consortium of organizations for grants up to $30,000; plans must involve full production of work and at least 4 performances for a single organization, or at least 6 for a consortium; write for guidelines. **Application procedure:** individual may not apply; 1 host organization submits completed application and supporting materials. **Deadline:** 15 Jun 1998. **Notification:** Aug 1998.

New Residencies
Theodore Wiprud, *Program Manager*

Open to: opera, theatre and music-theatre companies, arts presenters and musical organizations. **Frequency:** annual. **Remuneration:** grant for composer's salary ($40,000 per annum for 2 years; $20,000 towards 3rd-year salary, to be matched by host organizations); $15,000 toward institutional partnership building activities; possible $1500 for composer's relocation costs. **Guidelines:** 3–5 organizations, including at least 2 producing or presenting organizations and at least 1 human service or community organization, form Residency Partnership to sponsor 3-year composer residency; composer writes pieces for all host organizations and works at least 60 hours per month "making music a positive force in community life" through teaching, organizing cultural events, recruiting other composers to community work, etc; host organizations produce residency works, provide office space and logistical support and provide health insurance; write for guidelines. **Application procedure:** individual may not apply; performing organizations in Residency Partnership submit letter of intent with composer work samples before making formal application. **Deadline:** 15 Mar 1998 for letter of intent; 15 Jun 1998 for formal application. **Notification:** Sep 1998. **Dates:** residencies begin Jan 1999.

National Endowment for the Arts
International Program
1100 Pennsylvania Ave NW, Room 618; Washington, DC 20506;
(202) 682-5429, FAX 682-5602; E-mail thefund@iie.org
Pennie Ojeda, *Acting Director*

ArtsLink Collaborative Projects
All applications and inquiries to Citizen Exchange Council; 12 West 31st St; New York, NY 10001-4415; (212) 643-1985, FAX 643-1996; E-mail cecny@igc.apc.org

Open to: creative, interpretive and traditional artists, including playwrights, translators, composers, librettists, lyricists and solo performers. **Frequency:** annual. **Remuneration:** grant of up to $6000 (most grants $1500–3500). **Guidelines:** U.S. citizen or permanent resident; to enable individual artists or groups of up to 5 artists to work with their counterparts in Central or Eastern Europe, the former Soviet Union or the Baltics; mutually beneficial collaborative project that will enrich artists' work and/or create new work that draws inspiration from knowledge and experience gained in country visited; write for guidelines. **Application procedure:** completed application and supporting materials. **Deadline:** Mar 1998. **Notification:** 15 Jun 1998.

Fund for U.S. Artists at International Festivals and Exhibitions
(see also Arts International in this section)
All applications and inquiries to: Arts International; Institute of International Education; 809 United Nations Plaza; New York, NY 10017-3580; (212) 984-5370, FAX 984-5574; E-mail cecny@igc.apc.org

Open to: performing artists and groups, including solo performers and theatre companies. **Frequency:** triannual. **Remuneration:** grants of up to $25,000 (most grants $500–10,000) to cover foreign travel, housing, per diem and production costs. **Guidelines:** U.S. citizen or permanent resident who has been invited to international festival. **Application procedure:** completed application; copy of invitation from festival; full budget showing all costs of participation in festival and festival's contribution to these costs; work sample; bio. **Deadline:** 2 Sep 1997; 15 Jan 1998; 1 May 1998.

United States/Japan Creative Artists' Fellowships
All applications and inquiries to: Japan/U.S. Friendship Commission; 1120 Vermont Ave NW, Suite 925; Washington, DC 20005; (202) 275-7712; E-mail 72133.2433@compuserve.com

Open to: creative, interpretive or traditional artists, including playwrights, translators, composers, librettists and lyricists. **Frequency:** annual. **Remuneration:** monthly stipend to cover housing, living expenses and modest professional support services; roundtrip transportation for artist and family members; stipend to study Japanese language in U.S., if necessary. **Guidelines:** U.S. citizen or permanent resident; to enable established artist to pursue discipline in Japan for 6 consecutive months; artists who have spent more than 3 months in Japan ineligible. **Application procedure:** write or call for guidelines and application materials. **Deadline:** Jun 1998.

National Endowment for the Arts
Literature Program
1100 Pennsylvania Ave NW, Room 720; Washington, DC 20506;
(202) 682-5428; Web http://arts.endow.gov
Gigi Bradford, *Director*

Fellowships for Translators

Open to: translators. **Frequency:** annual. **Remuneration:** $20,000 fellowship. **Guidelines:** 1999 fellowship for translators of verse drama only; previously published translators of exceptional talent. **Application procedure:** write for guidelines and application. **Deadline:** mid-May 1998.

National Endowment for the Humanities
Public Programs
1100 Pennsylvania Ave NW; Washington, DC 20506; (202) 606-8269
Nancy Rogers, *Director*

Humanities Projects in Media
James J. Dougherty, *Assistant Director* (202) 606-8280

Open to: independent producers, radio and television writers. **Frequency:** annual. **Remuneration:** varies. **Guidelines:** support for planning, writing and/or production of television and radio projects focused on subjects and issues central to the humanities, and aimed at an adult national or broad regional audience; no historical dramatizations or adaptations of literary works; write for guidelines. **Application procedure:** submit draft proposal before making formal application. **Deadline:** 12 Jan 1998. **Notification:** Jul 1998.

National Endowment for the Humanities
Research and Education Programs
1100 Pennsylvania Ave NW; Washington, DC 20506; (202) 606-8200
James Herbert, *Director*

Collaborative Research
Margot Backas (202) 606-8209: E-mail: mbackas@neh.fed.us

Open to: translators. **Frequency:** annual. **Remuneration:** grant; amount varies according to project. **Guidelines:** U.S. citizen or resident for 3 years; money to support individual or collaborative projects to translate into English works that provide insight into the history, literature, philosophy and artistic achievements of other cultures and that make available to scholars, students, teachers and the public the thought and learning of those civilizations. **Application procedure:** completed application and supporting materials; write for guidelines. **Deadline:** 1 Sep 1997. **Notification:** Apr 1998.

NEW PLAY COMMISSIONS IN JEWISH THEATRE
National Foundation for Jewish Culture; 330 Seventh Ave, 21st Floor;
New York, NY 10001; (212) 629-0500
Judith Rosenbaum, *Grants Administrator*

Open to: North American not-for-profit theatres. **Frequency:** annual. **Remuneration:** grant of $1000–5000. **Guidelines:** 1 award a year to theatre that has completed at least 2 seasons of public performances and is commissioning new full-length play, adaptation, work for young audiences, musical or opera dealing substantively with issues of Jewish history, tradition, values or contemporary life; theatre must commit to presenting at least a public workshop production and/or staged reading of work, followed by discussion with audience; funds may be applied to commissioning fee, playwright's residency expenses or workshop costs; write for guidelines. **Application procedure:** completed proposal, cover sheet and supporting materials, submitted by theatre. **Deadline:** 30 Sep 1997. **Notification:** Dec 1998.

NEW YORK FOUNDATION FOR THE ARTS ARTISTS' FELLOWSHIPS
155 Ave of the Americas, 14th Floor; New York, NY 10013-1507;
(212) 366-6900, FAX 366-1778; E-mail nyfaafp@artswire.org
Penelope Dannenberg, *Director, Artists' Programs and Services*

Open to: playwrights, composers, librettists, screenwriters. **Frequency:** awards alternate biennially among disciplines. **Remuneration:** $7000 fellowship. **Guidelines:** NY State resident for 2 years prior to deadline; students ineligible. **Application procedure:** completed application and supporting materials; application seminars held each Sep. **Deadline:** next deadline for playwrights, composers, librettists and screenwriters fall 1997; exact date TBA.

PEW FELLOWSHIPS IN THE ARTS
The University of the Arts; 250 South Broad St, Suite 400;
Philadelphia, PA 19102; (215) 875-2285, FAX 875-2276
Melissa Franklin, *Director*

Open to: playwrights, composers, screenwriters. **Frequency:** annual; award rotates among disciplines. **Remuneration:** $50,000 fellowship. **Guidelines:** to give artists living in Southeastern PA the opportunity to dedicate themselves wholly to the development of their work for up to 2 years; students not eligible; call or write for application and guidelines. **Application procedure:** completed application and work sample. **Deadline:** Dec 1997; exact date TBA. **Notification:** Jun 1998.

PILGRIM PROJECT
156 Fifth Ave, Suite 400; New York, NY 10010; (212) 627-2288, FAX 627-2184
Davida Goldman, *Secretary*

Open to: playwrights, solo performers, individual producers and theatre companies. **Frequency:** ongoing. **Remuneration:** grant of $1000–7000. **Guidelines:**

grant towards cost of reading, workshop production or full production of play that deals with questions of moral significance; write for further information. **Application procedure:** script only. **Deadline:** ongoing.

The Playwrights' Center Grant Programs
2301 Franklin Ave East; Minneapolis, MN 55406-1099; (612) 332-7481
Carlos Cuesta, *Executive Director*

Jerome Playwright-in-Residence Fellowships

Open to: playwrights, solo performers. **Frequency:** annual. **Remuneration:** 5 1-year fellowships of $7000. **Guidelines:** U.S. citizen or permanent resident; emerging playwright whose work has not received more than 2 professional full productions; fellow must spend year in residence at Center, where fellow has access to developmental workshops, readings and other services; send SASE for guidelines. **Application procedure:** completed application and supporting materials. **Deadline:** 16 Sep 1997. **Notification:** 15 Jan 1998. **Dates:** 1 Jul 1998–30 Jun 1999.

Many Voices Multicultural Collaboration Grants

Open to: playwrights, translators, composers, librettists, solo performers, screenwriters. **Frequency:** annual, contingent on funding. **Remuneration:** $200–2000 grant to each of 2–4 teams. **Guidelines:** team of 2 or more artists of differing cultural backgrounds with commitment from MN organization to produce proposed collaborative work; team's lead artist must be MN playwright of color. **Application procedure:** send SASE for guidelines. **Deadline:** 1 Jul 1998. **Notification:** 15 Sep 1998. **Dates:** 1 Oct 1998–30 Jun 1999.

Many Voices Playwriting Residency Awards

Open to: playwrights, solo performers. **Frequency:** annual, contingent on funding. **Remuneration:** 8 awards: $750 stipend, playwriting-class scholarship, 1-year Playwrights' Center membership, opportunity to participate in culturally focused playwriting roundtables, dramaturgical assistance, workshop and public reading. **Guidelines:** MN resident of color. **Application procedure:** send SASE for guidelines. **Deadline:** 1 Jul 1998. **Notification:** 15 Sep 1998. **Dates:** 1 Oct 1998–30 Jun 1999.

McKnight Advancement Grants

Open to: playwrights, solo performers. **Frequency:** annual. **Remuneration:** 3 grants of $8500; up to $1500 per fellow for workshops and staged readings using Center's developmental program or for allocation to partner organization for joint development and/or production. **Guidelines:** U.S. citizen or permanent resident and legal MN resident since 1 May 1995; playwright of exceptional merit and potential who has had at least 2 plays fully produced by professional theatres; funds intended to significantly advance fellow's art and/or career and may be used to cover a variety of expenses, including writing time, residency at theatre or other arts organization, travel/study, production or presentation; fellow must designate 2 months of grant year during which he or she plans to participate actively in Center's programs, including weekly attendance at and critical participation in readings and workshops of other members' work; send SASE for guidelines after 1 Dec 1997. **Application procedure:** completed application and supporting materials. **Deadline:** 3 Feb 1998. **Notification:** 1 May 1998. **Dates:** 1 Jul 1998–30 Jun 1999.

McKnight Fellowships

Open to: playwrights, solo performers. **Frequency:** annual. **Remuneration:** 2 fellowships of $10,000; up to $2000 program allocation to cover reading/ workshop expenses; possible partial travel and living expenses for fellows living outside 150-mile radius of Twin Cities. **Guidelines:** U.S. citizen or permanent resident whose work has made significant impact on contemporary theatre and who has had at least 2 plays fully produced by professional theatres; fellow must spend 1 month in residence at Center, where fellow has access to developmental workshops, readings and other services; send SASE for guidelines after 15 Nov 1999. **Application procedure:** completed application and supporting materials. **Deadline:** 16 Jan 1998. **Notification:** 15 Apr 1998. **Dates:** 1 Jul 1998–30 Jun 1999.

PRINCESS GRACE AWARDS: PLAYWRIGHT FELLOWSHIP
Princess Grace Foundation–USA; 150 East 58th St, 21st Floor;
New York, NY 10155; (212) 317-1470, FAX 317-1473
(Ms.) Toby Boshak, *Executive Director*

Open to: playwrights. **Frequency:** annual. **Remuneration:** $7500 grant; 10-week residency with travel at New Dramatists, New York City (see entry in Membership and Service Organizations); inclusion of submitted script in New Dramatists' lending library and in its ScriptShare national script-distribution program for 1 year; possible publication with Dramatists Play Service. **Guidelines:** U.S. citizen or permanent resident; under ordinary circumstances, playwright not more than 30 years of age at time of application; award based primarily on artistic quality of submitted play and potential of fellowship to assist writer's growth; original, unproduced, unpublished play (no adaptations); eligibility requirements and application procedures currently under review; write for guidelines. **Application procedures:** see guidelines. **Deadline:** 31 Mar 1998.

TCG GRANT PROGRAMS
Theatre Communications Group; 355 Lexington Ave;
New York, NY 10017-0217; (212) 697-5230, FAX 983-4847
Emilya Cachapero, *Director of Grant Programs*

Extended Collaboration Grants
E-mail grants@tcg.org

Open to: not-for-profit theatres, in collaboration with playwrights. **Frequency:** annual, contingent on funding. **Remuneration:** grant of $5000 (4 awarded in 1996-97). **Guidelines:** augments normal development resources of TCG Constituent theatre by enabling playwright to develop work over an extended period of time in collaboration with director, designer, choreographer, composer and/or artist from another discipline; period of collaboration must exceed that which theatre would normally support; funds cover inter-city transportation within the U.S. and Canada and other expenses related to research and meetings among the collaborators. **Application procedure:** playwright may not apply; completed application submitted by artistic director of theatre. **Deadline:** late fall 1997 (contingent on funding).

National Theatre Artist Residency Program
E-mail ntarp@tcg.org

Category I: Residency Grants

Open to: playwrights, translators, composers, librettists, lyricists and other theatre artists in association with not-for-profit professional theatres. **Frequency:** annual (contingent on funding). **Remuneration:** approximately 10–14 grants of $50,000 or $100,000. **Guidelines:** experienced theatre artists who have created significant body of work and theatres with high artistic standards and organizational capacity to provide substantial support services to artists; funds cover compensation and residency expenses of 1 or 2 resident artists, working singly or in collaboration, during discrete periods used exclusively for residency-related activities that total at least 6 full months over 2-year period; proposals must be developed jointly by artists and institutions; theatres applying for $100,000 grant must have minimum operating budget of $500,000 in most recently completed fiscal year; theatres applying for $50,000 grant must have minimum operating budget of $250,000 in most recently completed fiscal year; write for guidelines. **Application procedure:** 2 copies of completed application and supporting materials. **Deadline:** write for 1998 deadlines.

Category II: Matching Grants

Open to: playwrights, translators, composers, librettists, lyricists and other theatre artists in association with not-for-profit professional theatres. **Frequency:** annual, contingent on funding. **Remuneration:** up to $50,000 in matching funds. **Guidelines:** matching funds to support the continuation of particularly fruitful partnerships; to be considered, applicants must meet Category I eligibility requirements. **Application procedure:** 2 copies of completed application and supporting materials. **Deadline:** write for 1998 deadlines.

NEA/TCG Theatre Residency Program for Playwrights

Open to: playwrights in association with not-for-profit professional theatres. **Frequency:** annual (contingent on funding). **Remuneration:** grant of $25,000 (12 awarded in 1997). **Guidelines:** playwrights must be citizens or permanent residents of U.S. at the time of application and have had at least one play published or produced within the last 5 years; theatres must have history of developing new work, high artistic standards and a minimum operating budget of $200,000 in the most recently completed fiscal year; a total of 6 months (not necessarily consecutive) must be dedicated to the development of a new work with the host theatre; call or write for application and guidelines. **Application**

procedure: intent to apply card, followed by completed application and supporting materials. **Deadline:** write for 1998 deadlines.

TRAVEL AND STUDY GRANT PROGRAM

c/o Jerome Foundation; West 1050, First National Bank Bldg; 332 Minnesota St; St. Paul, MN 55101-1312; (612) 224-9431, FAX 224-3439
Cynthia Gehrig, *President*

Open to: theatre artists and administrators, including playwrights, composers, librettists and lyricists. **Frequency:** annual. **Remuneration:** grant of up to $5000 for foreign or domestic travel. **Guidelines:** resident of Twin Cities metropolitan area; program funded by Dayton-Hudson, General Mills and Jerome Foundation to support short-term travel or period of significant professional development through travel and study for independent professional artist or staff member of not-for-profit organization; write for guidelines. **Application procedure:** completed application, work sample and resume. **Deadline:** Mar 1998.

U.S.-MEXICO FUND FOR CULTURE

Londres 16 P.B.; Col. Juárez México, DF; Mexico 06600; 52-5-592-5386,
    FAX 52-5-208-8943; E-mail usmexcult@laneta.apc.org;
    Web http://www.laneta.apc.org/usmexcult/intro.html
Beatriz Nava, *Assistant to the Coordinator*

Open to: playwrights, translators, librettists, lyricists, screenwriters, TV and radio writers, and producing organizations. **Frequency:** annual. **Remuneration:** grants of $2000-25,000. **Guidelines:** Mexican and North American artists and cultural institutions; program sponsored by Bancomer Cultural Foundation, the Rockefeller Foundation and Mexico's National Fund for Culture and the Arts to fund performing arts projects of excellence that reflect artistic and cultural diversity of Mexico and U.S. and encourage mutual collaboration between artists of both countries; media arts, script translation and adaptation of fiction, drama and poetry also considered; for brochure and application materials, send 78¢-postage SASE to U.S. Mexico Fund for Culture, c/o Benjamin Franklin Library, Laredo, TX 78044-3087. **Application procedure:** write for guidelines and application or see Web page. **Deadline:** 31 Mar 1998. **Notification:** Aug 1998.

VAN LIER PLAYWRITING FELLOWSHIP

New York Theatre Workshop; 79 East 4th St; New York, NY 10003;
    (212) 780-9037; FAX 460-8996
Chiori Miyagawa, *Artistic Associate*

Open to: playwrights. **Frequency:** annual. **Remuneration:** commission; amount of award varies. **Guidelines:** writer of color under 30 years of age and resident of New York City; must be available to attend monthly group meetings and 1-week summer retreat. **Application procedure:** cover letter and script. **Deadline:** call after 1 Jan 1998 for deadline.

The Walt Disney Studios Fellowship Program
500 South Buena Vista St; Burbank, CA 91521-0705; (818) 560-6894
Troy Nethercott, *Program Administrator*

Open to: playwrights, screenwriters, television writers. **Frequency:** annual. **Remuneration:** 1-year salary of $33,000 for up to 6 writers; travel and 1 month's housing for fellows from outside Los Angeles area. **Guidelines:** to enable writers to work full-time at developing their craft in Disney Studios features or television division; no previous film or TV writing experience necessary; writer with Writers Guild of America credits eligible but should apply through the Guild's Employment Access at (213) 782-4648; call for guidelines. **Application procedure:** completed application and notarized standard letter agreement with resume and writing sample (for feature division: screenplay approximately 120 pages long or full-length play; for TV division: 30-minute TV script approximately 45 pages long, full-length play, or one-act more than 24 pages long). **Deadline:** TBA (spring in 1997 with no submission before 1 Apr 1997); call for exact date. **Notification:** Aug 1998. **Dates:** fellowship year begins Oct 1998.

Emergency Funds

How do emergency funds differ from other sources of financial aid?

Emergency funds are for writers in severe *temporary* financial difficulties. Some funds give outright grants, others make interest-free loans. For support for anything other than a genuine emergency, turn to Fellowships and Grants.

THE AUTHORS LEAGUE FUND
330 West 42nd St, 29th Floor; New York, NY 10036; (212) 268-1208, FAX 564-8363
Susan Drury, *Administrator*

Open to: playwrights. **Type of assistance:** interest-free loan; no restriction on amount but request should be limited to immediate needs. **Guidelines:** published or produced working professional; must demonstrate real need. **Application procedure:** completed application and supporting materials. **Notification:** 2–4 weeks.

Carnegie Fund for Authors
1 Old Country Rd, Suite 113; Carle Place, NY 11514

Open to: playwrights. **Type of assistance:** emergency grant. **Guidelines:** playwright who has had at least 1 play or collection of plays published commercially in book form (anthologies excluded); emergency which has placed applicant in substantial verifiable financial need. **Application procedure:** write for application form.

The Dramatists Guild Fund
330 West 42nd St, 29th Floor; New York, NY 10036; (212) 268-1208
   FAX 564-8363
Susan Drury, *Administrator*

Open to: playwrights, composers, librettists, lyricists. **Type of assistance:** interest-free loan; no restriction on amount but request should be limited to immediate needs. **Guidelines:** published or produced working professional; must demonstrate real need. **Application procedure:** completed application and supporting materials. **Notification:** 2–4 weeks.

PEN Fund for Writers & Editors with AIDS
PEN American Center; 568 Broadway; New York, NY 10012; (212) 334-1660,
   FAX 334-2181; E-mail pen@echonyc.com
Program Coordinator

Open to: playwrights, translators, librettists, lyricists, screenwriters, television writers, radio writers. **Type of assistance:** grant or interest-free loan of up to $1000. **Guidelines:** emergency assistance for published and/or produced writer who is HIV-positive and having financial difficulties. **Application procedure:** completed application, work sample, documentation of financial emergency and resume. **Notification:** within 6–8 weeks.

PEN Writers Fund
PEN American Center; 568 Broadway; New York, NY 10012; (212) 334-1660,
   FAX 334-2181; E-mail pen@echonyc.com
Program Coordinator

Open to: playwrights, translators, librettists, lyricists, screenwriters, television writers, radio writers. **Type of assistance:** grant or interest-free loan of up to $500. **Guidelines:** emergency assistance for published and/or produced writer in financial difficulties. **Application procedure:** completed application, work sample, documentation of financial emergency and resume. **Notification:** within 6–8 weeks.

State Arts Agencies

What can my state arts agency do for me?

Possibly quite a bit—the only way to find out is to ask your agency for guidelines and study them carefully. State programs vary greatly and change frequently. Most have some sort of residency requirement, but eligibility is not always restricted to current residents, and may include people who were born in, raised in, attended school in or had some other association with the state in question.

What if my state doesn't give grants to individual artists?

A number of state arts agencies are restricted in this way. However, those with such restrictions, by and large, are eager to help artists locate nonprofit organizations that channel funds to individuals; you should ask specifically about this.

The New York State Council on the Arts, for example, is prohibited from funding individuals directly, and must contract with a sponsoring nonprofit organization when it awards grants to individual artists. Yet NYSCA has a number of ways of supporting the work of theatre writers. The Literature Program funds, in alternate years, translations, and writers' residencies in communities. The Individual Artists Program assists nonprofit organizations in commissioning works, including plays, music-theatre pieces; theatre and composers' commissions are also granted in alternate years. Moreover, NYSCA subgrants funds to the New York Foundation for the Arts, which in turn provides project development assistance for individual artists and creative teams (see NYFA Sponsorship

216 / STATE ARTS AGENCIES

Program in Development) and funds fellowships (see Fellowships and Grants). NYFA also assists residencies (see NYFA Artists in Residence Program in Colonies and Residencies).

At the least, every state has some kind of Artist-in-Education program; if you are able and willing to function in an educational setting you should certainly investigate this possibility.

ALABAMA STATE COUNCIL ON THE ARTS
201 Monroe St; Montgomery, AL 36130-1800; (334) 242-4076, FAX 240-3269
Al Head, *Executive Director*

ALASKA STATE COUNCIL ON THE ARTS
411 West 4th Ave, Suite 1E; Anchorage, AK 99501-2343; (907) 269-6610, FAX 269-6601; E-mail asca@alaska.net
Timothy Wilson, *Executive Director*

AMERICAN SAMOA COUNCIL ON CULTURE, ARTS AND HUMANITIES
Box 1540; Office of the Governor; Pago Pago, AS 96799; 011-684-633-4347, FAX 684-633-2059
(Mrs.) Fa'ailoilo Lauvao, *Executive Director*

ARIZONA COMMISSION ON THE ARTS
417 West Roosevelt St; Phoenix, AZ 85003; (602) 255-5882, FAX 256-0282; E-mail artscomm@prime.com
Shelley Cohn, *Executive Director*

ARKANSAS ARTS COUNCIL
1500 Tower Bldg; 323 Center St; Little Rock, AR 72201; (501) 324-9700, FAX 324-9154; E-mail info@dah.state.ar.us
Jim Mitchell, *Executive Director*

CALIFORNIA ARTS COUNCIL
1300 I St; Sacramento, CA 95814; (916) 322-6555, FAX 322-6575; E-mail cac@cwo.com
Barbara Pieper, *Executive Director*

COLORADO COUNCIL ON THE ARTS
750 Pennsylvania St; Denver, CO 80203; (303) 894-2617, FAX 894-2615; E-mail fran.holden@ossinc.net
Fran Holden, *Executive Director*

Connecticut Commission on the Arts
Gold Building; 755 Main St; Hartford, CT 06103; (860) 566-4770, FAX 566-6462
John Ostrout, *Executive Director*

Delaware Division of the Arts
Carvel State Office Bldg; 820 North French St, 5th Floor; Wilmington, DE 19801; (302) 577-8278, FAX 577-6561; E-mail pamsterdam@state.de.us
Peggy Amsterdam, *Director*

District of Columbia (DC) Commission on the Arts and Humanities
410 8th St NW, 5th Floor; Washington, DC 20004; (202) 724-5613, FAX 727-4135; E-mail carrien@tmn.com
Anthony Gittens, *Executive Director*

Florida Division of Cultural Affairs
Department of State, The Capitol; Tallahassee, FL 32399-0250; (904) 487-2980, FAX 922-5259; E-mail pfearington@mail.dos.state.fl.us
(Ms.) Peyton C. Fearington, *Executive Director*

Georgia Council for the Arts
530 Means St NW, Suite 115; Atlanta, GA 30318; (404) 651-7920, FAX 651-7922; E-mail gca@gwins.campus.mci.net
Caroline Ballard Leake, *Executive Director*

Guam Council on the Arts & Humanities Agency
Office of the Governor; Box 2950; Agana, GU 96910; 671-475-CAHA, FAX 671-472-ART1; E-mail arts@ns.gov.gu
Deborah Bordallo, *Executive Director*

State Foundation on Culture and the Arts (Hawaii)
44 Merchant St; Honolulu, HI 96813; (808) 586-0306, FAX 586-0308
Holly Richards, *Executive Director*

Idaho Commission on the Arts
Box 83720; Boise, ID 83720-0008; (208) 334-2119, FAX 334-2488; E-mail idarts@artswire.org
Margot H. Knight, *Executive Director*

Illinois Arts Council
State of Illinois Center; 100 West Randolph St, Suite 10-500; Chicago, IL 60601; (312) 814-6750, FAX 814-1471; E-mail ilarts@artswire.org
Kassie Davis, *Executive Director*

Indiana Arts Commission
402 West Washington St, Room 072; Indianapolis, IN 46204; (317) 232-1268, FAX 232-5595; E-mail inarts@aol.com
Dorothy Ilgen, *Executive Director*

Iowa Arts Council
Capitol Complex; 600 East Locust; Des Moines, IA 50319; (515) 281-4451, FAX 242-6498
William H. Jackson, *Executive Director*

Kansas Arts Commission
Jayhawk Tower; 700 Southwest Jackson, Suite 1004; Topeka, KS 66603; (913) 296-3335, FAX 296-4989
Eric Hayashi, *Executive Director*

Kentucky Arts Council
31 Fountain Pl; Frankfort, KY 40601; (502) 564-3757, FAX 564-2839; E-mail gcombs@arts.smag.state.ky.us
Gerri Combs, *Executive Director*

Louisiana Division of the Arts
Box 44247; Baton Rouge, LA 70804; (504) 342-8180, FAX 342-8173; E-mail arts@crt.state.la.us
James Borders, *Executive Director*

Maine Arts Commission
55 Capitol St; State House Station 25; Augusta, ME 04333; (207) 287-2724, FAX 287-2335; E-mail alden.wilson@state.me.us
Alden C. Wilson, *Executive Director*

Maryland State Arts Council
601 North Howard St, 1st Floor; Baltimore, MD 21201; (410) 333-8232, FAX 333-1062; E-mail msac@digex.net
Jim Backas, *Executive Director*

Massachusetts Cultural Council
120 Boylston St, 2nd Floor; Boston, MA 02116-4600; (617) 727-3668, FAX 727-0044; E-mail mary@art.state.ma.us
Mary Kelley, *Executive Director*

Michigan Council for the Arts & Cultural Affairs
1200 6th Ave, Executive Plaza; Detroit, MI 48226-2461; (313) 256-3731, FAX 256-3781; E-mail mcacal@artswire.org
Betty Boone, *Executive Director*

Minnesota State Arts Board
Park Square Court; 400 Sibley St, Suite 200; St. Paul, MN 55102;
(612) 215-1600, FAX 215-1602; E-mail msab@tc.umn.edu
Robert Booker, *Executive Director*

Mississippi Arts Commission
239 North Lamar St, 2nd Floor; Jackson, MS 39201; (601) 359-6030, -6040,
FAX 359-6008; E-mail bradley@arts.state.ms.us
Betsy Bradley, *Executive Director*

Missouri Arts Council
111 North 7th St, Suite 105; St. Louis, MO 63101; (314) 340-6845,
FAX 340-7215; E-mail mac@artswire.org
Flora Maria Garcia, *Executive Director*

Montana Arts Council
316 North Park Ave, Room 252; Helena, MT 59620-2201;
(406) 444-6430, FAX 444-6548; E-mail montana@artswire.org
Arlynn Fishbaugh, *Executive Director*

Nebraska Arts Council
Joslyn Castle Carriage House; 3838 Davenport; Omaha, NE 68131-2329;
(402) 595-2122, FAX 595-2334; E-mail lindanac@artswire.org
Jennifer S. Clark, *Executive Director*

Nevada State Council on the Arts
Capitol Complex; 602 North Curry St; Carson City, NV 89710; (702) 687-6680,
FAX 687-6688
Susan Boskoff, *Executive Director*

New Hampshire State Council on the Arts
40 North Main St, Phenix Hall; Concord, NH 03301; (603) 271-2789,
FAX 271-3584; lawrence@lilac.nhsl.lib.nh.us
Rebecca Lawrence, *Director*

New Jersey State Council on the Arts
20 West State St, 3rd Floor, CN 306; Trenton, NJ 08625-0306; (609) 292-6130,
FAX 989-1440; E-mail barbara@arts.sos.state.nj.us
Barbara Russo, *Executive Director*

New Mexico Arts Division
228 East Palace Ave; Santa Fe, NM 87501; (505) 827-6490, FAX 827-6043
Louis LeRoy, *Director*

New York State Council on the Arts
915 Broadway, 8th Floor; New York, NY 10010; (212) 387-7000, FAX 387-7164;
E-mail mroyce@nysca.org
Nicolette B. Clarke, *Executive Director*

North Carolina Arts Council
Department of Cultural Resources; Raleigh, NC 27611; (919) 733-2821,
FAX 733-4834; E-mail mregan@ncacmail.dcr.state.nc.us
Mary Regan, *Executive Director*

North Dakota Council on the Arts
418 East Broadway, Suite 70; Bismarck, ND 58501-4086; (701) 328-3954,
FAX 328-3963; E-mail ndca@artswire.org
Patsy Thompson, *Executive Director*

Commonwealth Council for Arts and Culture (Northern Mariana Islands)
Box 5553, CHRB; Saipan, MP 96950; 011-670-322-9982, -9983,
FAX 670-322-9028
Genevieve S. Cabrera, *Executive Director*

Ohio Arts Council
727 East Main St; Columbus, OH 43205; (614) 466-2613, FAX 466-4494;
E-mail jamig@mail.oac.ohio.gov
Wayne Lawson, *Executive Director*

Oklahoma Arts Council
Jim Thorpe Bldg; Box 52001-2001; Oklahoma City, OK 73152-2001;
(405) 521-2931, FAX 521-6418; E-mail okarts@artswire.org
Betty Price, *Executive Director*

Oregon Arts Commission
775 Summer St, NE; Salem, OR 97310; (503) 986-0087, FAX 986-0260;
E-mail christine.t.darcy@state.or.us
Christine D'Arcy, *Executive Director*

Pennsylvania Council on the Arts
Finance Bldg, Room 216; Harrisburg, PA 17120; (717) 787-6883, FAX 783-2538;
E-mail phorn@arts.cmicpol.state.pa.us
Philip Horn, *Executive Director*

Institute of Puerto Rican Culture
Box 4184; San Juan, PR 00902-4184; (787) 723-2115, FAX 724-8393
Dr. Luis Diaz Hernandez, *Executive Director*

Rhode Island State Council on the Arts
95 Cedar St, Suite 103; Providence, RI 02903-1034; (401) 277-3880,
FAX 521-1351; E-mail ride0600@ride.ri.net
Randall Rosenbaum, *Executive Director*

South Carolina Arts Commission
1800 Gervais St; Columbia, SC 29201; (803) 734-8696, FAX 734-8526;
E-mail surkamer@scsn.net
Suzette Surkamer, *Executive Director*

South Dakota Arts Council
Office of the Arts; 800 Governors Dr; Pierre, SD 57501-2294; (605) 733-3131,
FAX 773-6962; E-mail sdac@stlib.state.sd.us
Dennis Holub, *Executive Director*

Tennessee Arts Commission
Citizens Plaza, 401 Charlotte Ave; Nashville, TN 37243-0780; (615) 741-1701,
FAX 741-8559; E-mail btarleton@mail.state.tn.us
Bennett Tarleton, *Executive Director*

Texas Commission on the Arts
Box 13406, Capitol Station; Austin, TX 78711; (512) 463-5535, FAX 475-2699;
E-mail rah@arts.state.tx.us
John Paul Batiste, *Executive Director*

Utah Arts Council
617 East South Temple St; Salt Lake City, UT 84102; (801) 533-5895,
FAX 533-6196; E-mail bstephen@arts.state.ut.us
Bonnie Stephens, *Executive Director*

Vermont Arts Council
136 State St, Drawer 33; Montpelier, VT 05633-6001; (802) 828-3291,
FAX 828-3363; E-mail info@arts.uca.state.vt.us
Alex Aldrich, *Executive Director*

Virgin Islands Council on the Arts
41-42 Norre Gade; Box 103; St. Thomas, VI 00804; (809) 774-5984,
FAX 774-6206
John Jowers, *Executive Director*

Virginia Commission for the Arts
223 Governor St, 2nd Floor; Richmond VA 23219; (804) 225-3132,
FAX 225-4327; E-mail vacomm@artswire.org
Peggy Baggett, *Executive Director*

Washington State Arts Commission
Box 42675; Olympia, WA 98504-2675; (360) 753-3860, FAX 586-5351;
E-mail wsac@artswire.org
Karen Gose, *Executive Director*

West Virginia Commission on the Arts
1900 Kanawha Blvd E; Charleston, WV 25305; (304) 558-0240, FAX 558-2779;
E-mail cook_l_r@wvlc.wvnet.edu
Lakin Ray Cook, *Executive Director*

Wisconsin Arts Board
101 East Wilson St, 1st Floor; Madison, WI 53702; (608) 266-0190,
FAX 267-0380
George Tzougros, *Executive Director*

Wyoming Arts Council
2320 Capitol Ave; Cheyenne, WY 82002; (307) 777-7742, FAX 777-5499;
E-mail wyoarts@artswire.org
John G. Coe, *Executive Director*

Colonies and Residencies

What entries make up this section?

Though artist colonies that admit theatre writers constitute the majority of the listings, there are other kinds of residencies, such as artist-in-residence positions at universities, listed here as well. You can also find listings in the Development and Fellowships and Grants sections that could be considered residencies. Finally, we have included some "writers' rooms" where playwrights in need of a quiet place for uninterrupted work are welcome.

Note: you should assume that each deadline listed in this section is the date application materials must be *received*, unless you have ascertained that it is the postmark date.

THE ADAMANT PROGRAM

Box 73; Adamant, VT 05640-0073; (802) 223-2324, -3347, FAX 223-0915
Patricia Hutchinson, *Resident Manager*

Open to: playwrights, composers, screenwriters. **Description:** residencies of 2–8 weeks for artists, including writers, composers and visual artists, at retreat in small VT village of Adamant, near Montpelier; small individual studio in woods and private bedroom in 1 of 2 main houses; experimental theatre for the use of playwrights, grand pianos available for composers; lunch and dinner provided, residents make own breakfast and share housekeeping chores. **Financial**

arrangement: resident pays $25 a day towards cost of room, board and studio. **Guidelines:** creative artist with professional standing in field; less established artists of recognized ability also considered; write for guidelines. **Application procedure:** completed application, work sample, 3 references and $10 fee. **Deadline:** 30 May 1998. **Dates:** Sep–Oct.

ALDEN B. DOW CREATIVITY CENTER
Northwood University; 3225 Cook Rd; Midland, MI 48640-2398;
   (517) 837-4478, FAX 837-4468; E-mail creativity@northwood.edu
Carol B. Coppage, *Executive Director*

Open to: playwrights, translators, composers, librettists, lyricists, screenwriters. **Description:** 4 "Creativity Fellowships" each year for individuals working in any field, including the arts; 10-week summer residency at Northwood University, which provides environment for intense independent study; program includes interaction among fellows and formal presentation of work in Aug. **Financial arrangement:** travel, room, board, $750 for personal expenses and project materials. **Guidelines:** projects that are creative, original and have potential for impact on applicant's field; prefers 1 applicant per project; no accommodation for spouses or children. **Application procedure:** completed application, brief project description, budget, work sample, resume, and $10 application fee. **Deadline:** 31 Dec 1997. **Notification:** 1 Apr 1998. **Dates:** Jun–Aug 1998.

ALTOS DE CHAVON
c/o Parsons School of Design; 2 West 13th St, Room 707; New York, NY 10011;
   (212) 229-5370, FAX 229-5370; E-mail altos@spacelab.net
Stephen D. Kaplan, *Arts/Education Director*

Open to: playwrights, composers, screenwriters. **Description:** residencies of 3½ months for 15 artists a year, 1–2 of whom may be writers or composers, at nonprofit arts center located in tropical Caribbean surroundings 8 miles from town of La Romana in the Dominican Republic; efficiency studios or apartments with kitchenettes; small individual studios nearby; small visual-arts-oriented library; no typewriters for writers. **Financial arrangement:** $100 nonreturnable reservation fee; resident pays rent of $300 a month and provides own meals (estimated cost $20 a day). **Guidelines:** prefers Spanish-speaking artists who can use talents to benefit community, and whose work relates to Dominican or Latin American context; residents may teach workshops and are expected to contribute to group exhibition/performance at end of stay; write for further information. **Application procedure:** letter explaining applicant's interest in program, work sample and resume. **Deadline:** 1 Jul 1998. **Notification:** 15 Aug 1998. **Dates:** residencies start 1 Feb 1999, 1 Jun 1999, 1 Sep 1999.

APOSTLE ISLANDS NATIONAL LAKESHORE
Route 1, Box 4; Bayfield, WI 54814; (715) 779-3397, FAX 779-3049
Kate L. Miller, *Chief, Resources Education*

Open to: playwrights, composers, lyricists, solo performers. **Description:** 1 writer, poet, visual artist or choreographer at a time housed for 2–3 weeks on island in national park; cabin near beach and forest; no running water or electricity; resident must bring 2–3 week supply of food. **Financial arrangement:** free travel and housing. **Guidelines:** writer with accomplishment, artistic integrity and ability to relate to park through their work; must donate 1 work to park and communicate experience of residency through 1 program for public. **Application procedure:** completed application, project description, work sample, resume and cover letter. **Deadline:** 15 Jan 1998; no submission before 1 Oct 1997. **Notification:** 1 Mar 1998. **Dates:** Jun–Sep.

ATLANTIC CENTER FOR THE ARTS

1414 Art Center Ave; New Smyrna Beach, FL 32168; (904) 427-6975, (800) 393-6975, FAX (904) 427-5669; E-mail acansb@aol.com; Web http://www.atlantic-centerarts.org
Suzanne Fetscher, *Executive Director*
Nicholas Conroy, *Program Director*

Open to: playwrights, composers. **Description:** 6 3-week workshops each year offering writers; choreographers; media, visual and performing artists opportunity of concentrated study with internationally known Master Artists-in-Residence. **Financial arrangement:** resident pays $100 a week for tuition, $25 a day for private room with bath; limited scholarships available. **Application procedure:** Master Artist specifies submission materials and selects participants; write or call for brochure. **Deadline:** 4 months before residency. **Notification:** 3 months before residency. **Dates:** TBA; see brochure.

BLUE MOUNTAIN CENTER

Blue Mountain Lake, NY 12812; (518) 352-7391
Harriet Barlow, *Director*

Open to: playwrights, composers, librettists, lyricists, solo performers. **Description:** 4-week residencies for 14 writers, composers and visual artists at center in Adirondack Mountains. **Financial arrangement:** free room and board. **Guidelines:** artist whose work is aimed at a general audience and reflects social concerns. **Application procedure:** send SASE for information. **Deadline:** 1 Feb 1998. **Notification:** early Apr 1998. **Dates:** mid-Jun–late-Oct 1998.

BYRDCLIFFE ART COLONY

The Woodstock Guild; 34 Tinker St; Woodstock, NY 12498; (914) 679-2079, FAX 679-4529; E-mail wguild@mhu.net
Artists Residency Program

Open to: playwrights, translators, librettists, lyricists, solo performers, screenwriters. **Description:** 10 concurrent summer residencies of 1–4 4-week sessions for artists in all disciplines at historic 300-acre colony in the Catskill Mountains, 1½ miles from Woodstock village center, 90 miles north of New York City; private room and separate individual studio space in Villetta Inn, spacious turn-of-the-century mountain lodge; common dining room and living room; residents provide own meals, using community kitchen. **Financial arrangement:** resident pays fee of $500 per session; reductions offered to residents staying more than 1 session. **Guidelines:** proof of serious commitment to field of endeavor is major criterion for acceptance; professional recognition helpful but not essential; send SASE for further information. **Application procedure:** completed application, work sample, project description, resume, reviews and articles if available, contact information for 2 references and $5 fee. **Deadline:** 1 Apr (applications received after deadline considered for any space still available). **Dates:** Jun–Sep.

CAMARGO FOUNDATION
B.P. 75; 13260 Cassis; France; 33-42-01-1157, -1311
Michael Pretina, *Director*
U.S. Office:
125 Park Square Ct, 400 Sibley St, St. Paul, MN 55101

Open to: playwrights, translators, composers. **Description:** 11 concurrent residencies, most for scholars and teachers pursuing projects relative to Francophone culture, but also including 1 for writer, 1 for composer and 1 for visual artist, at estate in ancient Mediterranean fishing port 30 minutes from Marseilles; furnished apartments; music studio available for composer. **Financial arrangement:** free housing; residents provide own meals. **Guidelines:** resident outlines project to fellow colony members during stay and writes final report; families welcome when space available; write to U.S. office for guidelines. **Application procedure:** completed application, project description, bio and 3 letters of recommendation. **Deadline:** 1 Feb 1998. **Notification:** 5 Apr 1998. **Dates:** Sep–Dec; Jan–May.

CENTRUM ARTIST-IN-RESIDENCY PROGRAM
Fort Worden State Park; Box 1158; Port Townsend, WA 98368; (360) 385-3102, FAX 385-2470
Marlene Bennett, *Residency Coordinator*

Open to: playwrights, translators, composers, librettists, lyricists, solo performers, screenwriters, television writers. **Description:** 1-month residencies for writers, composers, poets, visual artists and choreographers at center near Victorian seaport in 440-acre Fort Worden State Park; self-contained cabins near beach and hiking trails; separate studio space. **Financial arrangement:** free; some stipends available. **Guidelines:** artist who has clear direction and substantial accomplishment in field. **Application procedure:** completed application, project description, work sample, resume and $15 fee. **Deadline:** 1 Oct 1997. **Notification:** 15 Nov 1997. **Dates:** Sep–May.

CHATEAU DE LESVAULT
58370 Onlay; Villapourçon; France; 33-3-86-843291, FAX -843578
Bibbi Lee, *Director*

Open to: playwrights, translators, librettists. **Description:** 5 concurrent winter residencies at 19th-century French château located in "le Morvan," a national park in western Burgundy 3½ hours from Paris, 3 hours from Geneva; large bedroom/studio with private bath; use of salon, library and grounds. **Financial arrangement:** resident pays Fr. 4500 (about $775) a month or Fr. 2500 (about $425) for 2 weeks, which covers room, utilities, and meals 7 days a week. **Application procedure:** brief description of project, maximum 3-page work sample, list of publications (if any) and 2 references; 50% deposit required 30 days before start of residency. **Deadline:** 90 days before proposed residency. **Dates:** Oct–Apr.

DJERASSI RESIDENT ARTISTS PROGRAM

2325 Bear Gulch Rd; Woodside, CA 94062-4405; (415) 747-1250,
    FAX 747-0105; E-mail djerassi@artswire.com
Charles Amirkhanian, *Executive Director*
Carol Law, *General Manager*

Open to: playwrights, translators, composers, librettists, lyricists, solo performers, screenwriters. **Description:** 6-week residencies for writers; choreographers; composers; media, visual and interdisciplinary artists and performers concurrently at 600-acre ranch in Santa Cruz mountains 1 hour south of San Francisco; interdisciplinary projects encouraged; collaborative projects considered. **Financial arrangement:** free room and board. **Guidelines:** emerging or established artist whose work has clear direction; send SASE for application. **Application procedure:** completed application, sample of published work or work-in-progress, resume and $25 fee. **Deadline:** 15 Feb 1998 for 1999 residencies. **Dates:** Apr–Oct.

DORLAND MOUNTAIN ARTS COLONY

Box 6; Temecula, CA 92593; (909) 676-5039; E-mail dorland@ez2.net;
    Web http://www.ez2.net/dorland/
Admissions

Open to: playwrights, composers, lyricists. **Description:** 1-month residencies for 6 writers, composers and visual artists concurrently in individual studios on 300-acre nature preserve 50 miles northeast of San Diego; no electricity. **Financial arrangement:** $50 processing fee upon scheduling, if accepted; resident pays rent of $300 a month. **Guidelines:** artist must demonstrate clear direction and accomplishment in field. **Application procedure:** send SASE for application and information. **Deadline:** 1 Sep 1997; 1 Mar 1998. **Notification:** 2 months.

DORSET COLONY FOR WRITERS

Box 519; Dorset, VT 05251; (802) 867-2223, FAX 867-0144;
    Web http://www.genghis.com/theatre.htm
John Nassivera, *Executive Director*

Open to: playwrights, composers, librettists, lyricists and collaborative teams. **Description:** residencies of 1 week–1 month at house located in historic village in southern VT. **Financial arrangement:** resident pays fee for housing according to means (suggested fee $95 a week); meals not provided; large, fully equipped kitchen. **Guidelines:** artist must demonstrate seriousness of purpose and have record of professional achievement (readings or productions of works); work sample may be requested from less established artist. **Application procedure:** letter of inquiry with description of proposed project and desired length and dates of stay; resume. **Deadline:** open. **Dates:** 10 Sep–20 May.

THE GELL WRITERS CENTER

c/o Writers & Books; 740 University Ave; Rochester, NY 14607; (716) 473-2590, FAX 729-0982
Joseph Flaherty, *Executive Director*

Open to: playwrights, translators, librettists, lyricists, solo performers, screenwriters, television writers. **Description:** 2 private bedrooms available in house surrounded by 23 acres of woodlands; workshops on creative writing sometimes available at extra cost; residents provide own meals. **Financial arrangement:** resident pays $35 a day (members of Writers & Books pay $25 a day). **Application procedure:** write or call for application and brochure. **Deadline:** ongoing. **Notification:** 1 week. **Dates:** year-round.

THE HAMBIDGE CENTER FOR CREATIVE ARTS AND SCIENCES

Box 339; Rabun Gap, GA 30568; (706) 746-5718, FAX 746-9933
Judith Barber, *Executive Director*

Open to: playwrights, translators, composers, librettists, lyricists. **Description:** residencies of 2 weeks–2 months for professionals in all areas of arts and humanities on 600 acres in northeast GA mountains; 8 private cottages with bedroom, kitchen, bathroom and studio/work area; evening meal provided Mon–Fri, May–Oct only; send SASE for guidelines. **Financial arrangement:** resident pays minimum of $125 a week toward total cost. **Application procedure:** completed application, work sample, resume, reviews, 3 letters of recommendation from professionals in applicant's field and $20 fee. **Deadline:** 1 Nov 1997 for Mar–Aug 1998; 1 May 1998 for Sep–Dec 1998. **Notification:** 2–3 months. **Dates:** Mar–Dec.

HAWTHORNDEN CASTLE
INTERNATIONAL RETREAT FOR WRITERS

Lasswade, Midlothian; Scotland EH18 1EG; 441-31-440-2180
Administrator

Open to: playwrights. **Description:** spring, summer and fall residencies of 4 weeks at medieval castle on secluded crag overlooking valley of the River Esk 8 miles south of Edinburgh; 5 writers in residence at any one time; fully furnished study-bedroom; communal breakfast and dinner, lunch brought to writer's room; typewriter rental and use of excellent libraries in Edinburgh can be arranged. **Financial arrangement:** free room and board. **Guidelines:** author of at least 1 published work. **Application procedure:** write for application and further information. **Deadline:** 30 Sep 1997. **Notification:** mid-Jan 1998. **Dates:** Feb–Dec 1998.

HEADLANDS CENTER FOR THE ARTS
944 Fort Barry; Sausalito, CA 94965; (415) 331-2787, FAX 331-3857
Kathryn Reasoner, *Executive Director*

Open to: playwrights, composers, librettists, lyricists, screenwriters, television writers. **Description:** residencies of 1–3 months for artists in all disciplines at center in national park on 13,000 acres of coastal wilderness across the bay from San Francisco; accommodation in 4-bedroom house with communal kitchen; evening meal provided in mess hall Sun–Thur; 11-month "live-out" residencies available for Bay Area artists only, providing studio space, 2 meals a week and access to center's facilities but no housing; all residents encouraged to interact with fellow artists in other media and with the environment. **Financial arrangement:** stipend of $500 a month, travel and free housing for artist from outside Bay Area; $2500 stipend and studio space for Bay Area artist. **Guidelines:** CA, NC or OH residents only; students ineligible. **Application procedure:** call or write for information (applications available Apr 1998). **Deadline:** 5 Jun 1998. **Dates:** Feb–Dec 1999.

HEDGEBROOK
2197 East Millman Rd; Langley, WA 98260; (360) 321-4786
Linda Bowers, *Director*

Open to: playwrights, librettists, solo performers. **Description:** residencies of 1 week–2 months for women writers of diverse cultural backgrounds working in all literary genres; 6 individual cottages on 30 wooded acres on Whidbey Island, near Seattle; writer furnishes own typewriter or computer. **Financial arrangement:** free room and board. **Guidelines:** woman writer of any age, published or unpublished; women of color encouraged to apply. **Application procedure:** send SASE for application; submit completed application, project description and work sample. **Deadline:** 1 Oct 1997 for winter–spring 1998; 1 Apr 1998 for summer–fall 1998. **Notification:** 2 months.

HELENE WURLITZER FOUNDATION OF NEW MEXICO
Box 545; Taos, NM 87571; (505) 758-2413, FAX 758-2559

Open to: playwrights, composers, screenwriters. **Description:** 12 studio/apartments available to writers, composers and poets (performing artists ineligible); length of residency flexible, usually 3 months. **Financial arrangement:** free housing and utilities; resident provides own meals; no financial aid; write or fax for application. **Application procedure:** completed application with project description, work sample and resume. **Deadline:** open. **Dates:** 1 Apr–30 Sep.

ISLE ROYALE NATIONAL PARK ARTIST-IN-RESIDENCE
800 East Lakeshore Dr; Houghton, MI 49931; (906) 482-0984 (general information), 487-7152 (Greg Blust), FAX 487-7170
Greg Blust, *Coordinator*

Open to: playwrights, composers, lyricists, solo performers. **Description:** 1 artist at a time housed for 2–3 weeks in cabin on remote island near Lake Superior; no electricity; resident must bring 2–3 week supply of food. **Financial arrangement:** free housing and transportation. **Guidelines:** writer with artistic integrity, ability to live in wilderness environment and to relate to park through their work; must donate 1 work to park and communicate experience of residency through programs for public. **Application procedure:** completed application form, project description, work sample and resume. **Deadline:** 15 Feb 1998. **Notification:** 15 Apr 1998. **Dates:** Jun–Sep.

THE JAMES THURBER WRITER-IN-RESIDENCE

The Thurber House; 77 Jefferson Ave; Columbus, OH 43215; (614) 464-1032, FAX 228-7445
Michael J. Rosen, *Literary Director*

Open to: playwrights. **Description:** 4 residencies a year, each for 1 academic quarter (2 for journalists, 1 for playwright, 1 for poet or fiction writer); writer teaches course at Ohio State University. **Financial arrangement:** $5000 stipend; 2-bedroom apartment provided. **Guidelines:** playwright who has had at least 1 play produced by a major theatre; teaching experience helpful; write or call for further information. **Application procedure:** letter of interest and curriculum vita. **Deadline:** 15 Dec 1997. **Notification:** within 2 months. **Dates:** winter or spring 1999.

THE JOHN STEINBECK WRITER'S ROOM

Long Island University–Southampton Campus Library; Southampton, NY 11968; (516) 287-8382, FAX 287-4049; E-mail sclibrary@sunburn.liunet.edu
Robert Gerbereux, *Library Director*

Open to: playwrights. **Description:** small room, space for 4 writers; carrel, storage space, access to reference material in room and to library. **Financial arrangement:** free. **Guidelines:** writer working under contract or with specific commitment. **Application procedure:** completed application.

LEIGHTON STUDIOS FOR INDEPENDENT RESIDENCIES

The Banff Centre for the Arts; Box 1020, Station 28; 107 Tunnel Mountain Dr; Banff, Alberta; Canada T0L 0C0; (403) 762-6180, (800) 565-9989, FAX (403) 762-6345; E-mail arts_info@banffcentre.ab.ca; Web http://www.banffcentre.ab.ca/cfaindex.html
Office of the Registrar

Open to: playwrights, composers, performance artists, film and television writers. **Description:** residencies of 1 week–3 months for writers, composers, musicians and visual artists at studios situated in mountains of Banff National Park; 8 specially designed studios, each with washroom and kitchenette; living accommodation (single room with bath) on Centre's main campus; nearby access to all amenities of Centre, including communal cafeteria, library and recreation complex. **Financial arrangement:** resident pays for studio, room and optional meals; discount on studio cost only available for those who demonstrate need.

Guidelines: artist who can demonstrate sustained contribution to own field and show evidence of significant achievement. **Application procedure:** write, e-mail or visit Web site for application and further information. **Deadline:** open; apply at least 6 months before desired residency. **Dates:** year-round.

THE MACDOWELL COLONY

100 High St; Peterborough, NH 03458-2485; (603) 924-3886, (212) 535-9690, FAX (603) 924-9142; Web http://www.macdowellcolony.org
Cheryl Young, *Executive Director*

Open to: playwrights, composers, film and video writers. **Description:** residencies of up to 2 months for writers, composers, visual artists, video/filmmakers, architects and interdisciplinary artists at 450-acre estate; studios and common areas accessible for those with mobility impairments. **Financial arrangement:** voluntary contributions accepted; travel grants available. **Guidelines:** admission based on talent. **Application procedure:** send SASE, call for application or download from Internet; submit completed application, work samples, names of 2 professional references and $20 fee; collaborating artists must apply separately. **Deadline:** 15 Sep 1997 for Jan–Apr 1998; 15 Jan 1998 for May–Aug 1998; 15 Apr 1998 for Sep–Dec 1998. **Notification:** 2 months.

MARY ANDERSON CENTER FOR THE ARTS

101 St. Francis Dr; Mount St. Francis, IN 47146; (812) 923-8602, FAX 923-3200; E-mail sry847@aol.com
Sarah Roberson Yates, *Executive Director*

Open to: playwrights, translators, composers, librettists, lyricists. **Description:** residencies of 2 weeks–3 months for 7 writers and visual artists concurrently at center on beautiful 400-acre wooded site with lake, 15 minutes from Louisville, KY; private studio/bedroom, communal kitchen and dining room. **Financial arrangement:** resident pays suggested minimum fee of $210 a week for room and board; possibility of funded residencies; write for information. **Guidelines:** formal education and production credits are not requirements but will be taken into consideration when applications are reviewed. **Application procedure:** completed application, project description, work sample, resume and 2 references. **Deadline:** open. **Dates:** year-round.

THE MILLAY COLONY FOR THE ARTS

East Hill Rd; Box 3; Austerlitz, NY 12017-0003; (518) 392-3103; Web http://www.millaycolony.org
Gail Giles, *Assistant Director*

Open to: playwrights, composers, screenwriters. **Description:** 1-month residencies for up to 5 writers, composers and visual artists concurrently at 600-acre estate in upstate NY; studio space and separate bedroom; colony accommodates artists with disabilities. **Financial arrangement:** free room, board and studio space. **Application procedure:** send SASE or e-mail to: application@millaycolony.org for application; submit completed application and supporting materials. **Deadline:** 1 Sep for

Feb–May; 1 Feb for Jun–Sep; 1 May for Oct–Jan. **Notification:** 12 weeks after deadline.

NANTUCKET PLAYWRIGHTS RETREAT
Box 2177; Nantucket MA 02584; (508) 228-5002
Jim Patrick, *Director*

Open to: playwrights. **Description:** new project of Nantucket Theatrical Productions (see also Nantucket Short Play Festival in Prizes) planned to start in winter of 1997–98; residencies of 1 week or longer will probably be offered with opportunity to have work-in-progress read and discussed with directors, actors and peers during stay. **Financial arrangement:** TBA. **Application procedure:** write for information. **Deadline:** open. **Dates:** probably Nov–Mar.

NEW YORK FOUNDATION FOR THE ARTS—ARTISTS IN RESIDENCE PROGRAM
155 Ave of the Americas, 14th Floor; New York, NY 10013-1507;
(212) 366-6900, ext 222, FAX 366-1778;
Web http://www.artswire.org/artswire/www/nyfa.html
Greg McCaslin, *Director, Education and Information*

Open to: schools and cultural organizations. **Description:** matching grants to assist schools and organizations that bring in artists, including playwrights, composers, librettists and lyricists, for residencies of 12 days–10 months; residency activities include artist-conducted student or teacher workshops, lecture-demonstrations, readings and performances. **Financial arrangement:** artist is paid by school or organization; recommended minimum fee of $250 a day. **Guidelines:** artist must be NY state resident. **Application procedure:** completed application from school or organization; individual artists may not apply but are encouraged to write for guidelines and to collaborate with eligible sponsors to set up residencies; artists may also contact program for information and for help in finding sponsors. **Deadline:** 2 Apr 1998; subsidiary deadlines for smaller grants in Oct, Nov, Feb and Jun each year. **Dates:** Sep 1998–Jun 1999.

NEW YORK MILLS ARTS RETREAT
24 North Main Ave, Box 246; New York Mills, MN 56567; (218) 385-3339,
FAX 385-3366; E-mail nymills@uslink.net
Kent Scheer, *Coordinator*

Open to: playwrights, translators, composers, librettists, lyricists, solo performers, screenwriters. **Description:** 1 artist at a time housed for 2–4 weeks in small farming community in north central Minnesota; housing ranges from bed and breakfast to private home; some meals provided. **Financial arrangement:** $750 stipend for 2 weeks, $1500 stipend for 4 weeks. **Guidelines:** emerging artist of demonstrated ability; must donate 8 hours per week during residency to community outreach. **Application procedure:** completed application form, project description, work sample, resume and 2 letters of recommendation. **Deadline:** 1 Oct 1997; 1 Apr 1998. **Notification:** 8 weeks after deadline. **Dates:** year-round.

NORCROFT
32 East First St. #330; Duluth, MN 55802; (218) 727-5199, FAX 727-3119
Jean Sramek, *Administrator*

Open to: playwrights, translators, librettists, film and television writers. **Description:** 4 concurrent residencies of 1–4 for women writers in all genres at remote lodge on shores of Lake Superior; private bedroom and separate individual "writing shed." **Financial arrangement:** free housing; groceries provided, resident does own cooking. **Guidelines:** women only; artist whose work demonstrates an understanding of and commitment to feminist change. **Application procedure:** completed application, five-page writing sample and description of project to be pursued at colony. **Deadline:** 1 Oct 1997. **Dates:** May–Oct.

RAGDALE FOUNDATION
1260 North Green Bay Rd; Lake Forest, IL 60045; (708) 234-1063, FAX 234-1075
Sonja Carlbord, *Director*

Open to: playwrights, composers, librettists, lyricists. **Description:** residencies of 2 weeks–2 months for writers and visual artists from all over the U.S. and abroad at estate situated on edge of prairie, 1 mile from center of town. **Financial arrangement:** resident pays $105 a week for room and board; partial or full fee waivers awarded on basis of financial need. **Guidelines:** admission based on quality of work submitted. **Application procedure:** send SASE for application; submit completed application, description of work-in-progress, work sample, resume, 3 references and $20 fee. **Deadline:** 15 Jan for Jun–Dec; 1 Jun for Jan–Apr. **Dates:** year-round except for May and last 2 weeks in Dec.

SNUG HARBOR CULTURAL CENTER
1000 Richmond Terr; Staten Island, NY 10301-9926; (718) 448-2500,
    FAX 442-8534
Rental Coordinator

Open to: playwrights, composers. **Description:** studio workspace in performing and visual arts center with theatre, art galleries, shops, museum, meeting rooms and banquet hall, located in 80-acre historic park. **Financial arrangement:** current monthly rental approximately $10 per sq. ft.; renewable 1-year lease; tenant must carry own insurance. **Guidelines:** professional artist. **Application procedure:** work sample with resume.

STUDIO FOR CREATIVE INQUIRY
Carnegie Mellon University; College of Fine Arts; Pittsburgh, PA 15213-3890;
    (412) 268-3454, FAX 268-2829; E-mail mmbm@andrew.cmu.edu
Marge Myers, *Assistant Director*

Open to: playwrights, translators, composers, librettists, lyricists, solo performers, screenwriters, television writers. **Description:** 25 short-term residencies of 2 weeks–3 months and 2 long-term residencies of 6 months–3 years concurrently for artists in all disciplines; residency provides studio facility located in Carnegie

Mellon's College of Fine Arts building, including office and meeting space, work area, computers, sound and video editing equipment; fellows may also use resources of university, including library. **Financial arrangement:** stipend; assistance in finding housing in community. **Guidelines:** writer interested in technology and interdisciplinary works; admission based on quality of work, clear statement of intention, experience with collaboration, and project feasibility. **Application procedure:** work sample, resume and letter of application. **Deadline:** open. **Notification:** 2 months. **Dates:** year-round.

THE TYRONE GUTHRIE CENTRE

Annaghmakerrig; Newbliss; County Monaghan; Ireland; 353-47-54003, FAX -54380; E-mail thetgc@indigo.ie
Bernard Loughlin, *Resident Director*

Open to: playwrights, composers, librettists, lyricists, screenwriters, television writers. **Description:** residencies of 3 weeks–3 months for artists in all disciplines from Ireland and abroad at former country home of Tyrone Guthrie, set amid 450 acres of forested estate overlooking large lake; private apartments; music room, rehearsal/performance space and extensive library. **Financial arrangement:** non-Irish artists pay about Irish £2000 (about $3025) a month for housing and meals; self-catering houses also available at reasonable rents. **Guidelines:** artist must show evidence of sustained dedication and a significant level of achievement; prefers artists with clearly defined projects; artist teams (e.g. writer/-director, composer/librettist) welcome; several weeks reserved each year for development of projects. **Application procedure:** write for application and further information.

UCROSS FOUNDATION RESIDENCY PROGRAM

2836 U.S. Hwy 14–16 East; Clearmont, WY 82835; (307) 737-2291, FAX 737-2322
Sharon Dynak, *Executive Director*

Open to: playwrights, translators, composers, librettists, lyricists. **Description:** residency of 2 weeks–2 months at "Big Red," restored historic site in the foothills of the Big Horn Mountains; 8 concurrent residencies for writers, composers and visual artists; opportunity to concentrate on own work without distraction and to present work to local communities, if desired. **Financial arrangement:** free room, board and studio space. **Guidelines:** criteria are quality of work and commitment. **Admission procedure:** completed application, project description and work sample; send SASE for application and further information. **Deadline:** 1 Oct for Feb–Jun; 1 Mar for Aug–Dec. **Notification:** 8 weeks.

VILLA MONTALVO ARTIST RESIDENCY PROGRAM

Box 158; Saratoga, CA 95071-0158; (408) 961-5818, FAX 961-5850; Web http://www.villamontalvo.org
Judy Moran, *Artist Residency Program Director*

Open to: playwrights, composers, screenwriters. **Description:** residencies of 1–3 months for 5 writers, musicians and visual artists concurrently at Mediterranean-style villa on 175 acres; rural setting close to major urban center. **Financial arrangement:** free housing; resident provides own meals, transportation; 4 fellowships available. **Guidelines:** spouses welcome; no children or pets. **Application procedure:** send SASE for application and guidelines. **Deadline:** 1 Sep for Apr–Sep; 1 Mar for Oct–Mar.

VIRGINIA CENTER FOR THE CREATIVE ARTS

Box VCCA, Mt. San Angelo; Sweet Briar, VA 24595; (804) 946-7236,
   FAX 946-7239; E-mail vcca@vcca.com
Director

Open to: playwrights, translators, composers, librettists, lyricists, solo performers, screenwriters. **Description:** residencies of 2 weeks–2 months for writers, composers, and visual and performance artists at 450-acre estate in Blue Ridge Mountains; separate studios and bedrooms; all meals provided. **Financial arrangement:** resident pays suggested minimum of $30 a day for room and board or as means allow; financial status not a factor in selection process. **Guidelines:** admission based on achievement or promise of achievement. **Application procedure:** completed application with work sample, resume and 2 recommendations. **Deadline:** 15 Sep for Jan–Apr; 15 Jan for May–Aug; 15 May for Sep–Dec. **Notification:** 2 months. **Dates:** year-round.

WILLIAM FLANAGAN MEMORIAL CREATIVE PERSONS CENTER

Edward F. Albee Foundation; 14 Harrison St; New York, NY 10013;
   (212) 226-2020

Open to: playwrights, translators, composers, librettists, screenwriters. **Description:** 1-month residencies for up to 5 writers, composers and visual artists concurrently at "The Barn" in Montauk, Long Island. **Financial arrangement:** free housing. **Guidelines:** admission based on talent and need. **Application procedure:** completed application, script (recording for composers) and supporting materials; write for information. **Deadline:** 1 Apr 1998; no submission before 1 Jan 1998. **Notification:** May 1998. **Dates:** 1 Jun–1 Oct 1998.

THE WRITERS ROOM

10 Astor Pl, 6th Floor; New York, NY 10003; FAX (212) 533-6059
Donna Brodie, *Executive Director*

Open to: playwrights, translators, composers, librettists, lyricists. **Description:** large room with 35 desks separated by partitions, space for 200 writers each quarter; open 24 hours a day year-round; kitchen, lounge and bathrooms, storage for files and typewriters, small reference library; monthly readings. **Financial arrangement:** $50 initiation fee; $175 fee for 3-month period. **Guidelines:** writer, emerging or established, must show seriousness of intent. **Application procedure:** completed application and references; all inquiries by mail (no visits without appointment).

The Writers' Studio

The Mercantile Library Association; 17 East 47th St; New York, NY 10017; (212) 755-6710, FAX 758-1387; E-mail mercantile_library@msn.com; Web http://www.bookpage.com/themerc
Harold Augenbraum, *Director*

Open to: playwrights, composers. **Description:** carrel space for 17 writers (3 reserved for writers of children's literature) in nonprofit, private lending library of 175,000 volumes; storage for personal computers or typewriters, library membership, access to special reference collection and rare collection of 19th-century American and British literature. **Financial arrangement:** $200 fee for 3 months, renewal possible for up to 1 year. **Guidelines:** open to all writers; unpublished writer must submit evidence of serious intent. **Application procedure:** completed application and work sample or project outline.

Yaddo

Box 395; Saratoga Springs, NY 12866-0395; (518) 584-0746, FAX 584-1312
Admissions Committee

Open to: playwrights, composers, performance artists, screenwriters. **Description:** residencies of 2 weeks–2 months for artists in all genres, working individually or as collaborative teams of up to 3 persons, at 19th-century estate on 400 acres; approximate total of 200 residents a year (15 concurrently Sep–May, 35 concurrently May–Labor Day). **Financial arrangement:** free room, board and studio space; contribution suggested to help underwrite cost of program. **Guidelines:** admission based on review by judging panels composed of artists in each genre; quality of work submitted is major criterion; send SASE for application and further information. **Application procedure:** completed application with work sample, resume, 2 letters of support, $20 fee and SASP for acknowledgment of receipt. **Deadline:** 15 Jan 1998 for mid-May 1998–Feb 1999; 1 Aug 1998 for 1 Nov 1998–mid-May 1999. **Notification:** 1 Apr 1998 for Jan deadline; 15 Oct 1998 for Aug deadline. **Dates:** year-round except early Sep.

Membership and Service Organizations

What's included here?

A number of organizations that exist to serve either the American playwright or a wider constituency of writers, composers and arts professionals. Some have a particular regional or special-interest orientation; some provide links to theatres in other countries. Taken together, these organizations represent an enormous range of services available to those who write for the theatre, and it is worth getting to know them.

THE ALLIANCE OF LOS ANGELES PLAYWRIGHTS
7510 Sunset Blvd, Suite 1050; Los Angeles, CA 90046-3418;
   (213) 957-4752
Hollis Evans, Monique Friedman and Michael Van Duzer, *Co-Chairs*

Founded in 1993, ALAP is a support and service organization dedicated to addressing the professional needs of the diverse Los Angeles playwriting community by facilitating creative programs nurturing the critical analysis of the theory and craft of playwriting, administering grants and fellowships, documenting and publishing the work of L.A. playwrights, creating an archive, and providing continuing advocacy for the playwright's voice in society. ALAP's programs and activities include general membership meetings; a voice-mail service which announces members' play readings, productions and other projects and provides information and referrals; a database of plays by L.A. playwrights to be made available to theatres and producers; a lab series; a community outreach program; and a quarterly newsletter. Dues are $29.95 a year (this sum is a donation and no playwright is turned away for lack of funds).

The Alliance of Resident Theatres/New York
131 Varick St, Room 904; New York, NY 10013-1410; (212) 989-5257,
   FAX 989-4880
Virginia P. Louloudes, *Executive Director*
Mary Harpster, *Deputy Director*

A.R.T./New York is the trade and service organization for the New York City nonprofit professional theatre, serving more than 250 New York theatre companies and professional affiliates (theatres outside NY, colleges and universities, and organizations providing services to the theatre field). Publications of interest include *Hot Seats*, which lists current productions in NYC, *Member Directory* ($5), and *Rehearsal and Performance Space Guide* ($15), which provides information on various theatre spaces currently available for rent.

Alternate ROOTS
1083 Austin Ave; Atlanta, GA 30307; (404) 577-1079, FAX 577-7991
Kathie deNobriga, *Development and Planning Director*

Alternate ROOTS is a service organization run by and for southeastern artists. Its mission is to support the creation and presentation of original performing art that is rooted in a particular community of place, tradition or spirit. It is committed to social and economic justice and the protection of the natural world and addresses these concerns through its programs and services. Founded in 1976, ROOTS now has more than 260 individual members across the 13 states of the Southeast, including playwrights, directors, choreographers, musicians, storytellers, clowns and new vaudevillians—both solo artists and representatives of 65 performing and presenting organizations. ROOTS aims to make artistic resources available to its members through workshops; to create appropriate distribution networks for the new work being generated in the region via touring, publications and liaison activity; and to provide opportunities for enhanced visibility and financial stability via publications and periodic performance festivals. Opportunities for member playwrights include readings and peer critiques of works-in-progress at the organization's annual meeting. Artists who are residents of the Southeast and whose work is consistent with the goals of ROOTS are accepted as new members after a year's provisional status. Annual membership dues are $50. The organization's meetings and workshops are open to the public and its triannual newsletter is available free to the public.

The American Alliance for Theatre & Education (AATE)
c/o Department of Theatre; Arizona State University; Box 872002;
   Tempe, AZ 85287-2002; (602) 965-6064 (Mon–Thur, 8:30–4:30),
   FAX 965-5351; E-mail aateinfo@asurm.inre.asu.edu
Barbara Salisbury Wills, *Executive Director*
Christy M. Taylor, *Acting Administrative Director*

AATE is a membership organization created in 1987 with the merger of the American Association of Theatre for Youth and the American Association for

Theatre in Secondary Education. AATE provides a variety of services to support the work of theatre artists and educators who work with young people and to promote theatre and drama/theatre education in elementary and secondary schools. To encourage the development and production of plays for young audiences the AATE Unpublished Play Reading Project annually selects and publicizes promising new plays in this field. AATE also sponsors annual awards for the best play for young people and the outstanding book relating to any aspect of the field published in the past calendar year; only the play or book's publisher may nominate a candidate for these awards. AATE's publications, which are free to members, include a quarterly newsletter with a Playwright's Page; the yearly *Youth Theatre Journal;* and the quarterly *STAGE of the Art.* Membership is open to all and costs $100 for organizations, $75 for individuals, $55 for retirees and $45 for students; please add $20 (U.S. funds) for foreign members (outside the U.S. and Canada).

THE AMERICAN FILM INSTITUTE
2021 North Western Ave; Box 27999; Los Angeles, CA 90027; (213) 856-7600, FAX 464-5217; E-mail www.afionline.org
Jean Picker Firstenberg, *Director*
James Hindman, *Co-Director*

East Coast Office:
The John F. Kennedy Center for the Performing Arts; Washington, DC 20566; (202) 828-4000

The American Film Institute is an independent not-for-profit organization established by the National Endowment for the Arts in 1967 to advance and preserve the art of the moving image and to encourage and develop new talent in the field. In pursuit of these goals, the AFI runs the Center for Advanced Film and Television Studies at its L.A. campus, coordinates the preservation of the nation's moving-image heritage through its National Center for Film and Video Preservation, and maintains the AFI National Theater at the Kennedy Center. AFI also sponsors festivals and touring programs and conducts workshops such as the Directing Workshop for Women. Of special interest to writers is AFI's annual Television Writers Summer Workshop, held in L.A., which provides 2–4 weeks of intensive advanced training for 10–12 competitively selected writers who have no major commercial television writing credits; participants pay a fee of $475; 3 full-tuition scholarships are available; interested writers should call (213) 856-7721 for guidelines and application information.

AMERICAN INDIAN COMMUNITY HOUSE
404 Lafayette St; New York, NY 10003; (212) 598-0100, FAX 598-4909
Rosemary Richmond, *Executive Director*
Jim Cyrus, *Director of Theatre*

American Indian Community House was founded in 1969 to encourage the interest of all U.S. ethnic groups in the cultural contributions of the American Indian, as well as to foster intercultural exchanges. The organization now serves the Native American population of the New York City region through a variety of social, economic and educational programs, and through cultural programs which include theatre events, an art gallery and a newsletter. Native Americans in the Arts, the performing arts component of the Community House, is committed to the development and production of works by Indian authors, and presents staged readings, workshop productions and full productions. The Community House also sponsors several other performing groups, including Spiderwoman Theatre, Coatlicue Theatre Company, the actors' group Off the Beaten Path, the Thunderbird American Indian Dancers, and the jazz-fusion and traditional singing group Ulali. A showcase for Native American artists is presented to agents and casting directors once or twice a year.

AMERICAN MUSIC CENTER

30 West 26th St, Suite 1001; New York, NY 10010-2011; (212) 366-5260, FAX 366-5265; E-mail center@amc.net; Web http://www.amc.net/amc
Deborah Atherton, *Acting Executive Director*

The American Music Center provides numerous programs and services for composers, performers and others interested in contemporary American music. The Jory Copying Assistance Program helps composers pay for copying music and extracting performance materials. The center's library contains more than 60,000 scores and recordings available for perusal by interested performers. The AMC provides information on competitions, publishers, performing ensembles, composers and other areas of interest in new music, and its publication *Opportunities in New Music* is updated annually. Membership is open to any person or organization wishing to support the center's promotion of the creation, performance and appreciation of American music. Annual dues are $55 for individuals ($35 for students and senior citizens). Members receive discounts on AMC publications, monthly "Opportunity Updates" and the option of participating in group health insurance. New members receive a free packet of information and articles of interest to the American composer. All members may vote in the annual board elections and attend the annual meeting.

AMERICAN TRANSLATORS ASSOCIATION (ATA)

1800 Diagonal Rd, Suite 220; Alexandria, VA 22314-2840;
(703) 683-6100, FAX (703) 683-6122;
E-mail 73564.2032@compuserve.com; Web http://www.atanet.org
Walter W. Bacak, Jr., *Executive Director*

Founded in 1959, the ATA is a national not-for-profit association which seeks to promote recognition of the translation profession; disseminate information for the benefit of translators and those who use their services; define and maintain professional standards; foster and support the training of translators and interpreters; and provide a medium of cooperation with persons in allied professions. Active membership is open to U.S. citizens and permanent residents who have professionally engaged in translating or closely related work and have passed an ATA accreditation examination or demonstrated professional attainment by other prescribed means. Those who meet these professional standards but are not U.S. citizens or residents may hold Corresponding membership; other interested persons may be Associate members. All members receive the monthly *ATA Chronicle* and a membership directory. Other publications include a *Translation Services Directory* containing professional profiles of Active members. ATA holds an annual conference and sponsors several honors and awards (see American Translators Association Awards in Prizes). Interested persons should write for a membership application. Annual dues are $95 for Active, Corresponding and Associate members; $40 for Associate-Students; $120 for institutions; and $175 for corporations.

ASCAP (AMERICAN SOCIETY OF COMPOSERS, AUTHORS AND PUBLISHERS)
1 Lincoln Plaza; New York, NY 10023; (212) 621-6234, FAX 724-9064
Michael A. Kerker, *Director of Musical Theatre*

ASCAP is a not-for-profit organization whose members are writers and publishers of musical works. It operates as a clearinghouse for performing rights, offering licenses that authorize the public performance of all the music of its composer, lyricist and music publishing members, and collecting license fees for these members. ASCAP also sponsors workshops for member and nonmember theatre writers (see ASCAP Musical Theatre Workshop in Development). Membership in ASCAP is open to any composer or lyricist who has been commercially recorded or "regularly published." Annual dues are $10 for individuals.

ASIAN AMERICAN ARTS ALLIANCE
74 Varick St, Suite 302; New York, NY 10013-1914; (212) 941-9208,
    FAX 941-7978; E-mail aaaajc@pipeline.com
Lillian Cho, *Executive Director*

Formed in 1983, Asian American Arts Alliance is a not-for-profit organization dedicated to increasing the support, recognition and appreciation of Asian-American arts. Alliance activities focus on relaying information, networking, providing advocacy services and pursuing related special projects. Ongoing services include information referrals; a resource library of books, journals, periodicals, files and other unique information on Asian-American culture and arts; and publications such as a directory of *Asian American Arts Organizations in New York & New Jersey* and *Beyond Boundaries National Resource Book.* Current initiatives include a 3-year Technical Assistance and Regrant Initiative (TARI) to help New York City Asian-American arts groups strengthen and grow and an Artist Series to provide a forum for discussion and exchange of ideas and resources among Asian-American artists. There are 7 membership levels: Starving Artist, $20; Mover & Shaker, $45; Arts Organization, $60; Project Leader, $100; Arts Patron, $250; Philanthropist, $500 and Leadership Council, $1000. Contributing members receive free library borrowing privileges, and are sent the monthlies *Asian American Arts Calendar* and *Asian American Arts Resources and Opportunities.* Members also receive discounts on advertising, special publications and events; additional services and savings are provided to members in the Project Leader, Arts Patron and Philanthropist categories.

A.S.K. Theater Projects

(Formerly The Audrey Skirball-Kenis Theatre)
11845 West Olympic Blvd, Suite 1250 W; Los Angeles, CA 90064;
(310) 478-3200, FAX 478-5300; E-mail askplay@primenet.com;
Web http://www.primenet.com/~askplay
Mead K. Hunter, *Director of Literary Programs*

Since 1989, A.S.K. Theater Projects has been an arts service organization dedicated to playwrights and new playwriting. Each year A.S.K. presents 15–20 rehearsed readings, out of which 2–3 plays are selected for workshop productions (see A.S.K. Theater Projects in Development). Allied programs supported by A.S.K. include: the A.S.K. Unpublished Plays Project, a repository of plays that premiered in southern California, housed in the L.A. Central Library; the international playwriting program at London's Royal Court Theatre; 3 playwright exchange programs, one each with the Playwrights' Center, the Royal Court and New Dramatists; the Audrey Skirball-Kenis Playwrights Program at Lincoln Center; the Mark Taper Forum's New Work Festival; the UCLA Playwriting Award and the UCLA Playwriting Fellowship; the Los Angeles Drama Critics Circle Ted Schmitt Award; the playscript publication in TCG's *American Theatre* magazine; and the *L.A. Weekly* Playwriting Award. A.S.K. sponsors symposiums, caucuses and playwriting labs, which serve as forums wherein issues may be explored or practical approaches to writing shared. A.S.K.'s publications include summary booklets of the symposium series entitled *Inventing the Future*; the *Directory of Los Angeles Playwright Groups*; the texts of plays given workshop productions; and *Parabasis*, a news magazine for, by and about playwrights. For additional information about programs and publications, contact A.S.K.

ASSITEJ/USA (International Association of Theatre for Children and Young People)

Box 22365; Seattle, WA 98122-0365; (206) 392-2147, FAX 443-0442;
E-mail assitej@aol.com
Dana Childs, *Membership Coordinator*

ASSITEJ/USA is a not-for-profit theatre agency which advocates the development of professional theatre for young audiences in the USA and facilitates interchange among theatre artists and scholars of the 60 member countries of ASSITEJ. ASSITEJ/USA sponsors festivals and seminars, operates an international playscript exchange and, with ASSITEJ/Japan, is founder of the Pacific-Asia Exchange Program. Members are theatres, institutions and individuals concerned for the theatre, young audiences and international goodwill. Members receive *Theatre for Young Audiences Today* and priority consideration for participation in national and international events. Membership costs $50 a year for individuals, $25 for students and retirees, $100–300 for organizations, depending on size of budget, and $30 for libraries. Write or call for membership application.

THE ASSOCIATED WRITING PROGRAMS
Tallwood House, Mail Stop 1E3; George Mason University; Fairfax, VA 22030; (703) 993-4301, FAX 993-4302; E-mail awp@gmu.edu
David Fenza, *Executive Director*

Founded in 1967, AWP serves the needs of writers, college and university writing programs, and students of writing by providing information services, job placement assistance, publishing opportunities, literary arts advocacy, and forums on all aspects of writing and its instruction. Writers not affiliated with colleges and universities but who support collective efforts to improve opportunities are also represented by AWP. The *AWP Chronicle*, published 6 times annually and available for $20 a year, includes listings of publishing opportunities, grants, awards and fellowships; interviews with writers; and essays on teaching creative writing. *The AWP Official Guide to Writing Programs* (8th edition, $25.95 postpaid) offers a comprehensive listing of writing programs and an expanded section on writing conferences, colonies and centers. Write or call AWP for information on membership requirements.

ASSOCIATION FOR THEATRE IN HIGHER EDUCATION (ATHE)
122 South Michigan Ave, Suite 1100; Chicago, IL 60603; (312) 431-9744, FAX 431-8697; E-mail athe@smtp.bmai.com
Jean Crotty, *Association Manager*

Founded in 1986, ATHE is an organization composed of individuals and institutions that provides vision and leadership for the profession and promotes excellence in theatre education. Membership services include insurance benefits, scholarships, annual professional awards including the Jane Chambers Playwriting Award (see Prizes) and assistance with issues such as tenure and alternate employment opportunities. Each year, members convene for the annual conference that brings together theatre scholars, educators and professionals from all over the world in workshops, performances, plenary sessions and group meetings. ATHE publishes several periodicals of interest to the theatre professional, including *ATHENEWS*, a quarterly newsletter that includes a list of teaching positions available at member organizations; *Theatre Topics*, a semiannual journal; *Theatre Journal*, a quarterly journal; a membership directory and pamphlets on various topics such as assessment guidelines for higher education theatre programs and tenure. There are 5 annual membership levels: Organizations, $195; 2-Person Households, $155; Individuals, $105; Retirees, $80; Students, $50. Members receive all publications.

THE ASSOCIATION OF HISPANIC ARTS
173 East 116th St; New York, NY 10029; (212) 860-5445, FAX 427-2787; E-mail aha1@artswire.com
Sandra Perez, *Executive Director of Programs*

A not-for-profit organization founded in 1975, AHA promotes the Latin American arts as an integral part of this country's cultural life. It acts as a clearinghouse for information on all the arts, including theatre, and 9 times a year publishes a newsletter, *Hispanic Arts News*, that provides information on playwriting contests, workshops, forums and other items of interest to Latin American artists. AHA also provides technical assistance to Latin American artists seeking funding.

ASSOCIATION OF INDEPENDENT VIDEO AND FILMMAKERS
304 Hudson St, 6th Floor; New York, NY 10013; (212) 807-1400,
 FAX 463-8519; E-mail aivffivf@aol.com; Web http://www.aivf.org
Ruby Lerner, *Executive Director*

The association is a national trade organization of 5000 independent film and video makers. The independent producer's advocate in Washington and within the entertainment industry, AIVF offers members a subscription to *The Independent Film & Video Monthly* magazine; group insurance for health, disability, production liability and equipment; and other benefits. AIVF's educational arm, the Foundation for Independent Video and Film (FIVF), publishes *The Independent* as well as books related to the field, runs a festival bureau and conducts public events on independent production issues.

BALTIMORE THEATRE PROJECT, INC.
45 West Preston St; Baltimore, MD 21201; (410) 539-3091, FAX 539-2137
Philip Arnoult, *Artistic Director*

Founded in 1971, Baltimore Theatre Project is a presenting theatre of new and innovative works, with special focus on Baltimore-area theatre companies. Additional services include workshops, roundtables, seminars, open auditions and a shared database of Balitmore-area affiliated artists. Membership is $25 and includes discounted tickets to participating Baltimore Theatre Project theatres and the monthly newsletter *Theatre Project Newsletter.*

BLACK THEATRE NETWORK
2603 Northwest 13th St, Suite 312; Gainesville, FL 32609; (352) 495-2116
 FAX 495-2051
Mikell Pinkney, *President*

Black Theatre Network (BTN) is a national network of professional artists, scholars and community groups founded in 1986 to provide an opportunity for the interchange of ideas; to collect and disseminate through its publications information regarding black theatre activity; to provide an annual national forum for the viewing and discussing of black theatre; and to encourage and promote black dramatists and the production of plays about the black experience. BTN members attend national conferences and workshops and receive complimentary copies of all BTN publications, which include the quarterly *BTN News*, listing conferences, contests, employment opportunities, BTN business matters and other items of interest from across the country; *Black Theatre Directory*, which contains over 800 listings of black theatre artists, scholars, companies, higher education programs and service organizations; *Dissertations Concerning Black Theatre: 1900–1994*, a listing of Ph.D. theses on black theatre; and *Black Theatre Connections*, a quarterly listing of jobs in educational and professional theatre. *Black Voices*, a catalogue of works by black playwrights, is available from BTN for $20.

Annual dues are $110 for organizations, $85 for individuals, $25 for retirees and students.

BMI (BROADCAST MUSIC INCORPORATED)
320 West 57th St; New York, NY 10019-3790; (212) 586-2000, FAX 262-2824
Jean Banks, *Senior Director, Musical Theater and Jazz*

BMI, founded in 1940, is a performing rights organization which acts as steward for the public performance of the music of its writers and publishers, offering licenses to music users. BMI monitors music performances and distributes royalties to those whose music has been used. Any writer whose songs have been published and are likely to be performed can join BMI at no cost. BMI also sponsors a musical theatre workshop (see BMI-Lehman Engel Musical Theatre Workshop in Development).

The BMI Foundation (President, Theodora Zavin) was established in 1984 to provide support for individuals in furthering their musical education and to assist organizations involved in the performance of music and music training.

BRITISH AMERICAN ARTS ASSOCIATION
116 Commercial St; London E1 6NF; England; 44-171-247-5385,
    FAX 44-171-247-5256
Jennifer Williams, *Executive Director*

A not-for-profit organization working in the field of arts and education, BAAA conducts research, organizes conferences, produces a quarterly newsletter and is part of an international network of arts and education organizations. As well as a specialized arts and education library, BAAA has a more general library which houses information on opportunities for artists and performers both in the UK and abroad. BAAA is not a grant-giving organization.

BROADWAY ON SUNSET
10800 Hesby St; North Hollywood, CA 91601; (818) 508-9270
Kevin Kaufman, *Executive Director*

Broadway on Sunset, a not-for-profit organization established in 1981, is sponsored by the National Academy of Songwriters (N.A.S.) (see entry in this section). The organization provides a structured developmental program for musical theatre writers (composers, lyricists, librettists) of all skill levels, which emphasizes a full understanding of the principles and standards of Broadway-level musical theatre craft, and provides writers opportunities to test their material at each level. Since its inception, Broadway on Sunset has presented more than 100 original musicals. There are no membership dues but writers may pay a nominal fee to participate in classes, readings and workshops. Writers and composers need to have access to the Los Angeles area to benefit fully from the workshops, although weekend intensive workshops may soon be offered for out-of-town writers.

Carolina Playwrights Center
Box 1705; Pinehurst, NC 28374; (910) 295-6896, FAX 295-1203
Carolyn Cole Montgomery, *Playwright-in-Residence*

Founded in 1989, CPC is a service organization for native or resident North/South Carolina member playwrights and some non-resident guest members. CPC provides staff to conduct research during play development, investigate production opportunities and provide administrative support. Additional services include a monthly play development program, and a playwright-producer program in which playwrights produce and market their plays from informal readings through to full production. Programs run from Sep–May. Basic membership services are available year-round; however CPC is currently not accepting new members. Annual dues are $100. Write or call for information.

Chicago Alliance for Playwrights (CAP)
Theatre Building; 1225 West Belmont; Chicago, IL 60657-3205;
 (773) 929-7367, ext 60, FAX 327-1404
Allan Chambers, *Board Member*

The Chicago Alliance for Playwrights is a service organization founded in 1990 to establish a network for Chicago-area playwrights and others committed to the development of new work for the stage. Members of the coalition include API Theatre, Chicago Dramatists Workshop, Columbia College New Musicals Project, New Tuners Theatre/Workshop, The Saints, Studio Z, Women's Theatre Alliance (see this section) and Writers Bloc. The alliance sponsors forums of interest to writers and publishes an annual directory of Chicago-area playwrights and their principal works. Write or call for membership details; annual dues are $25 for individuals and $100 for groups.

Chicago Dramatists Workshop
1105 West Chicago Ave; Chicago, IL 60622; (312) 633-0630, FAX 633-0610
Russ Tutterow, *Artistic Director*

Founded in 1979, Chicago Dramatists Workshop is dedicated to the development and advancement of playwrights and new plays. It employs a variety of programs to nurture the artistic and career development of both established and emerging playwrights. These programs include play readings, productions, classes, workshops, symposiums, discussions, panels, festivals, talent coordination, marketing services, collaborative projects with other theatres, national playwright exchanges and referrals to producers.

The Resident Playwright program seeks to nurture and promote the work and careers of dramatists who will make potentially significant contributions to the national theatre repertory. At no charge, Resident Playwrights benefit from the Workshop's fullest and longest-term support (a 3-year, renewable term), with full access to all of the Workshop's programs and services. Admittance to the program is selective, with emphasis on artistic and professional accomplishment or potential. While most Resident Playwrights are from the Chicago area, dramatists from around the country who are able to spend substantial time in Chicago may also apply; however, there are no stipends for travel or housing.

Interested playwrights should contact the Workshop for full information and details of the application procedure, which includes the submission of 2 plays, a resume and letters of recommendation and intent. *Deadline:* 1 Jun each year (no submission before 1 Apr).

The Playwrights' Network provides any U.S. playwright the opportunity to form an association with the Workshop. For an annual fee of $95, Network Playwrights receive written script critiques, consideration for all Workshop programs (including the annual New Voices Festival), class discounts, free admittance to Workshop events and other benefits.

Classes, Script Consultancies, the bimonthly 10-Minute Workshop and the biannual Deadline Workshop are open to all playwrights. A quarterly newsletter announces the Workshop's events and programs, and includes application procedures.

COLORADO DRAMATISTS

Box 101405; Denver, CO 80250; (303) 595-5600
Bob Woolsey, *President*

Founded in 1981, Colorado Dramatists, with chapters in Denver and Boulder, is a service organization for playwrights at all levels of development. In addition to bimonthly public readings, the organization sponsors small, private developmental groups; readings; workshops; seminars; an annual showcase; a mentoring program; and is in the process of developing a new play festival. Members receive a monthly newsletter, *The Colorado Theatre Guide*, and access to rehearsal space. Annual membership dues are $30 a year.

CORPORATION FOR PUBLIC BROADCASTING

901 E St NW; Washington, DC 20004-2037; (202) 879-9600, FAX 783-1019;
    Web http://www.cpb.org
Don Marbury, *Vice President, Programming*

The Corporation for Public Broadcasting, a private not-for-profit organization funded by Congress and by private sources, promotes and helps finance public television and radio. CPB provides grants to local public television and radio stations; conducts research in audience development, new broadcasting technologies and other areas. The corporation helped establish the Public Broadcasting Service and National Public Radio (see entries in this section). It supports public radio programming through programming grants to stations and other producers, and television programming by funding proposals made by stations and independent producers.

THE DRAMATISTS GUILD

1501 Broadway, Suite 701; New York, NY 10036; (212) 398-9366
    FAX 944-0420
Peter Stone, *President*
Richard Garmise, *Executive Director*

The Dramatists Guild, founded over 75 years ago, is a professional association established to advance the rights of playwrights, composers and lyricists. The Guild has more than 6000 members worldwide, from beginning writers to Broadway veterans. The Guild has 4 levels of membership: 1. Active ($125 a year): writers who have been produced on Broadway, Off-Broadway or on the main stage of a LORT theatre; 2. Associate ($75 a year): theatrical writers who have been produced in other venues or who have completed a full script; 3. Student ($35 a year): full-time students enrolled in an accredited writing degree program; 4. Estate ($125 a year): representatives of the estates of deceased authors. Membership benefits include a business affairs toll-free hotline, which offers advice on all theatre-related topics, including options, commissions, copyright procedures and contract reviews; model production contracts, which provide the best protection for the writer at all levels of production; collaboration, commission and licensing agreements; seminars led by experienced professionals concerning pressing topics for today's dramatist; access to a national health insurance program and a group term life insurance plan; free/discounted tickets to Off-Broadway/Broadway performances; and a meeting room that can accommodate more than 50 people for readings and backers auditions, available for a nominal rental fee.

The Guild publishes *The Dramatists Guild Newsletter*, issued 8 times a year with up-to-date business affairs articles and script opportunities; *The Dramatists Guild Quarterly*, a journal that contains interviews as well as articles on all aspects of theatre; *The Dramatists Guild Resource Directory*, an annual collection of contact information on producers, agents, contests, workshops and production companies. The periodicals are available to nonwriters on a subscription basis: Individual Subscribers ($50 a year): theatre-related individuals receive the *Quarterly* only; Institutional Subscribers ($135 a year): educational institutions, libraries and educational theatres receive all 3 periodicals and have access to audio tapes of Guild seminars; Professional Subscribers ($200 a year) receive all 3 periodicals. For further information contact Douglas Green, Membership Coordinator.

THE FIELD

161 Sixth Ave; New York, NY 10013; (212) 691-6969, FAX 255-2053;
    E-mail thefield@aol.com
Katherine Longstreth, *Executive Director*

The Field is a not-for-profit organization dedicated to helping independent performing artists develop artistically and professionally through a variety of performance opportunities, workshops, services and publications. The Field does not engage in curatorial activity; all artists are eligible to participate in its programs. Of special interest to New York metropolitan area playwrights wishing to produce their own work are programs such as the Performance Zone Festival, a showcase of works up to 50 minutes in length; Fielday, a showcase of 12-minute work; and Fieldwork, 10-week workshops for works-in-progress, guided by trained facilitators, culminating in performances. The Field assists artists with many aspects of producing their work, including grant writing, fundraising, project management, securing performance and rehearsal space, and cooperative promotional efforts. Publications include *Self-Production Guide; Funding Guide for Independent Artists; Space Chase Guide to New and Lesser Known Performance*

Opportunities, a listing of local performance spaces throughout New York City as well as out-of-town festivals, residencies and artist colonies; *Healing Guide*, a listing of artist-recommended healing practitioners who work on a sliding scale basis; and *Gone With The Field Guide*, a listing of performing possibilites for independent artists in 25 cites across the United States. All programs are available to members and non-members; members receive publications free, discounts on programs and may use the Field as an umbrella organization, falling under its nonprofit status. Annual membership costs $75; individual programs range in cost from $15–65. Field programs are also offered in Atlanta, Chicago, Dallas, Houston, Miami, Philadelphia, San Francisco, Seattle, Toronto and Washington D.C.

First Stage

Box 38280; Los Angeles, CA 90038; (213) 850-6271
Dennis Safren, *Literary Manager*

Founded in 1983, First Stage is a service organization for playwrights that holds staged readings, which are videotaped for the author's archival purposes; conducts workshops; provides referral services for playwrights; and publishes *First Stage Newsletter*. Services are free to nonmembers, except for workshops, which are available to members only. Membership dues are $35 per quarter or $120 per year; $58 per year for nonlocal members.

The Foundation Center

National Libraries:
1001 Connecticut Ave NW; Washington, DC 20036; (202) 331-1400
79 Fifth Ave; New York, NY 10003; (212) 620-4230, FAX 807-3677;
    Web http://www.fdncenter.org
Judith Margolin, *Director of Public Services, New York Library*

Field Offices:
312 Sutter St; San Francisco, CA 94108; (415) 397-0902
Hurt Bldg, Suite 150, Grand Lobby; 50 Hurt Plaza; Atlanta, GA 30303;
    (404) 880-0094
1422 Euclid, Suite 1356; Cleveland, OH 44115; (216) 861-1934

The Foundation Center is a nationwide service organization established and supported by foundations to provide a single authoritative source of information on foundation giving. It disseminates information on foundations through a public service program and through such publications as *The Foundation Directory* and *The Foundation Grants Index*. Of special interest is *Foundation Grants to Individuals*, which lists scholarships, fellowships, residencies, internships, grants, loans, awards, prizes and other forms of assistance available to individuals from approximately 3300 grantmakers (1997 edition $65). The center maintains 5 libraries and a national network of more than 205 cooperating collections. For the name of the collection nearest you or for more information about the center's programs, call toll free (800) 424-9836 or visit the website.

250 / MEMBERSHIP AND SERVICE ORGANIZATIONS

GREENSBORO PLAYWRIGHTS' FORUM

c/o City Arts; 200 North Davie St; Greensboro, NC 27401; (910) 373-5849, FAX 373-2659
Stephen D. Hyers, *Director*

GPF was founded in 1993 to facilitate a monthly gathering for playwrights to discuss works in progress, pool knowledge and encourage each other's artistic growth. Programs include cold and staged readings of member's plays and the annual North Carolina New Play Project Contest open to NC playwrights; winner receives $100 and workshop production. GPF also provides members with studio space for play development and publishes *New Play Catalog*, which lists plays written by members. Membership is open to anyone. Annual dues are $25.

THE HARBOR THEATRE LAB

(Formerly Playwrights Harbor)
c/o M & C Productions; 160 West 71st St, PHA; New York, NY 10023; (212) 787-1945
Stuart Warmflash, *Artistic Director*

The Harbor Theatre Lab, a not-for-profit organization founded in 1994, is a developmental workshop for 12 member theatre writers and a company of 30 actors cast specifically for writers' projects. Membership is available to playwrights, composers and librettists who have a body of work; are committed to rewrites and who work well in a supportive, professional atmosphere. The Lab meets every Monday in New York City for 3 hours and provides cold and/or rehearsed readings, followed by a short, playwright-driven critique from Lab members. Public readings of developed work are produced by the Harbor Theatre Company at least once during the season. Dues for the 1996–1997 season were $350. The organization is especially, but not exclusively, seeking minority playwrights.

HATCH-BILLOPS COLLECTION

491 Broadway, 7th Floor; New York, NY 10012-4412; (212) 966-3231
James V. Hatch, *Executive Secretary*

The Hatch-Billops Collection is a not-for-profit research library specializing in black American art and theatre history. It was founded in 1975 to collect and preserve primary and secondary resource materials in the black cultural arts; to provide tools and access to these materials for artists and scholars, as well as the general public; and to develop programs in the arts which use the collection's resources. The library's holdings include 1800 oral-history tapes; theatre programs; approximately 300 unpublished plays by black American writers from 1858 to the present; files of clippings, letters, announcements and brochures on theatre, art and film; slides, photographs and posters; and more than 4000 books and 400 periodicals. The collection also presents a number of salon interviews and films, which are open to the public; and publishes transcriptions of its annual "Artist and Influence" series of salon interviews, many of which are with playwrights. The collection is open to artists, scholars and the public by appointment only.

Hispanic Organization of Latin Actors (HOLA)
250 West 65th St; New York, NY 10023-6403; (212) 595-8286, FAX 799-6718;
E-mail holagram@aol.com
Manuel Alfaro, *Executive Director*

Founded in 1975, HOLA is a not-for-profit arts service organization for Hispanic performers and related artists. HOLA provides information, a 24-hour hotline, casting referral services, professional seminars and workshops. The organization publishes a biennial *Directory of Hispanic Talent* and a newsletter, *La Nueva Ola*, that lists job opportunities, grants and contests of interest to Hispanic artists. Members pay annual dues of $49.

Independent Feature Project
104 West 29th St, 12th Floor; New York, NY 10001-5310;
(212) 465-8200, FAX (212) 465-8525; E-mail ifpny@ifp.org;
Web http://www.ifp.org
Catherine Tait, *Executive Director*

The Independent Feature Project (IFP), a not-for-profit membership-supported organization, was founded in 1979 to encourage creativity and diversity in films produced outside the established studio system. The IFP produces the Independent Feature Film Market (IFFM), the premiere film event for U.S. independent cinema. The IFFM features 400 independent features, shorts, works-in-progress, documentaries and feature scripts. The IFP and IFP/West publish *Filmmaker*, a quarterly magazine. IFP also sponsors a series of screenings, professional seminars and industry showcases, including a conference on screenplay development. Group health insurance, a production insurance package, a Resource Program, publications, and a series of audiotapes of previous seminars and workshops are available to members. Membership dues start at $100 a year ($65 for students).

Institute for Contemporary East European and Slavic Drama and Theatre
Graduate Center of the City University of New York; Box 355;
33 West 42nd St; New York, NY 10036-8099; (212) 642-2231, -2235,
FAX 642-1977
Daniel C. Gerould, *Director*

The Institute for Contemporary East European and Slavic Drama and Theatre, under the auspices of the Center for Advanced Study in Theatre Arts (CASTA), publishes a triquarterly journal, *Slavic and East European Performance: Drama, Theatre, Film*, which is available by subscription ($10 a year, $15 foreign) and includes articles about current events in the East European and Slavic theatre, as well as reviews of productions and interviews with playwrights, directors and other theatre artists. The Institute also has available 2 annotated bibliographies of English translations of Eastern European plays written since 1945: *Soviet Plays in Translation* and *Polish Plays in Translation* ($5 each, $6 foreign). The institute is interested in hearing of published or unpublished translations for possible listing in updated editions of these bibliographies; translators may submit descriptive letters or scripts.

INSTITUTE OF OUTDOOR DRAMA

CB #3240; Nations Bank Plaza; University of North Carolina;
    Chapel Hill, NC 27599-3240; (919) 962-1328, FAX 962-4212;
    E-mail outdoor@unc.edu
Scott J. Parker, *Director*

The Institute of Outdoor Drama, founded in 1963, is a research and advisory agency of the University of North Carolina. It serves as a communications link between producers of existing outdoor dramas and is a resource for groups, agencies or individuals who wish to create new outdoor dramas or who are seeking information on the field. The institute provides professional consultation and conducts feasibility studies; holds annual auditions for summer employment in outdoor drama; sponsors conferences, lectures and symposiums; and publishes a quarterly newsletter, as well as information bulletins. Writers should note that the institute maintains a roster of available artists and production personnel, including playwrights and composers. It seeks to interest established playwrights and composers in participating in the creation of new outdoor dramas, and to encourage and advise new playwrights who wish to write for this specialized form of theatre.

INTERNATIONAL CENTER FOR WOMEN PLAYWRIGHTS

819 Forest Ave; Buffalo, NY 14209; (716) 882-9238, FAX (716) 883-6300
Deborah Kane and Camille Kazmierczak, *Co-Directors*

The ICWP supports women playwrights around the world, continuing the work begun with the First International Women Playwrights Conference, held in Buffalo in 1988. The center solicits new work at intervals, presents readings and channels work to production venues; it welcomes contact with theatre organizations seeking new plays by women. The center also publishes a periodical and newsletter which provide information about upcoming International Women Playwrights Conferences, and it handles communications for the International Advisory Committee, which determines sites and policies for these conferences. Basic membership dues are $20 (larger contributions are welcome); checks should be made out to the U.B. Foundation-ICWP.

INTERNATIONAL THEATRE INSTITUTE OF THE UNITED STATES (ITI/US)

47 Great Jones St; New York, NY 10012; (212) 254-4141, FAX (212) 254-6814
Martha W. Coigney, *Director*
Adam Thorburn, *Assistant Director*
Louis A. Rachow, *Library Director*

Now operating centers in 96 countries, ITI was founded in 1948 by UNESCO "to promote the exchange of knowledge and practice in the theatre arts." ITI assists foreign theatre visitors in the U.S. and American theatre representatives traveling abroad. The ITI International Theatre Collection is a reference library which documents theatrical activity in 146 countries and houses over 12,700 plays from 97 countries. American playwrights, as well as other theatre professionals, frequently use the collection to make international connections; to consult foreign theatre directories for names of producers, directors or companies with a view to submitting plays abroad; and to research the programs and policies of theatres or managements. ITI answers numerous requests from abroad about American plays and also provides information on rights to foreign plays to American producers, directors and literary managers. Building upon its commitment to theatre professionals, ITI recently began the University and Theatre Partner Programs in order to work more closely with institutions interested in international exchange.

THE INTERNATIONAL WOMEN'S WRITING GUILD
Box 810, Gracie Station; New York, NY 10028-0082; (212) 737-7536, FAX 737-9469; E-mail iwwg@iwwg.com; Web http://www.iwwg.com7
Hannelore Hahn, *Executive Director*

The International Women's Writing Guild, founded in 1976, is a network of women writers in the U.S., Canada and abroad. Playwrights, television and film writers, songwriters, producers and other women involved in the performing arts are included in its membership. Workshops are offered throughout the U.S. and annually at a week-long writing conference/retreat at Skidmore College in Saratoga Springs, NY. Members may also submit playscripts to theatres who have offered to read, critique and possibly produce IWWG members' works. *Network*, a 32-page newsletter published 6 times a year, provides a forum for members to share views and to learn about playwriting contests and awards, and theatre- and TV-related opportunities. The guild offers contacts with literary agents, group health insurance and other services to its members. Annual dues are $35 ($45 for foreign membership).

LA TELARAÑA
2626 North Mesa, #273; El Paso, TX 79902; E-mail tatiana@step.edu
tatiana de la tierra, *Director*

La telaraña supports Latina lesbian writers by providing information, referrals, access to resources and a connection to each other through *el telarañazo*, a newsletter that includes current news and information on contests, calls for writing submissions and retreats; and a networking/support list of members for members. Annual membership is $13.

LATIN AMERICAN THEATER ARTISTS
30 Grant Ave; San Francisco, CA 94108; (415) 439-2425, FAX 834-3360
Luis Oropeza, *Artistic Director*

Latin American Theater Artists is a performing and support organization. As a theatre, LATA "embraces Latino theatre from its indigenous roots in Spain and the Americas through its classical development and its contemporary expression."

LATA annually produces one full production, a reading series of both new and traditional Latin American plays and a children's show; LATA accepts new plays year-round. As an organization, LATA offers a casting and referral service to its dues-paying members, training workshops and a newsletter. LATA primarily serves Bay Area Latinos and Latinas, but is open for membership nationally. Annual dues are $25; checks should be made out to LATA.

LEAGUE OF CHICAGO THEATRES/ LEAGUE OF CHICAGO THEATRES FOUNDATION

67 East Madison Ave, Suite 2116; Chicago, IL 60603-3013; (312) 977-1730, FAX 977-1661

Founded in 1979, the League of Chicago Theatres/League of Chicago Theatres Foundation is a trade and service organization for Chicago theatre companies. It provides marketing, advocacy and membership services; and acts as an information clearinghouse, maintains resource files and publishes a bimonthly newsletter. The League's HOTTIX program sells half-price day-of-performance theatre tickets as well as full-price theatre and concert tickets.

LEAGUE OF PROFESSIONAL THEATRE WOMEN/NEW YORK

c/o Shari Upbin; 300 East 56th St., 2A; New York, NY 10022; (212) 583-0177 FAX 583-0549
Shari Upbin, *President*

Founded in 1979, the league is a not-for-profit organization of theatre professionals providing programs and services which promote women in all areas of professional theatre, create industry-related opportunities for women, and highlight contributions of theatre women, past and present. Through its salons, seminars, educational programs, social events, awards and festivals, the league links professional theatres with theatre women nationally and internationally and provides an ongoing forum for ideas, methods and issues of concern to the theatrical community and its audiences. Programs include the Lee Reynolds Award, given annually to a woman or women whose work for, in, about or through the medium of theatre has helped to illuminate the possibilities for social, cultural or political change; the annual Short Plays festival; the Oral History Project, which seeks to chronicle and document the contribution of significant theatre women; a membership directory; and panels discussing topics of interest to women theatre professionals with well-known experts in the field. Regular monthly meetings enable members to network, initiate programs and serve on committees. To be eligible for membership in the league, playwrights, composers, librettists and lyricists must have had a work presented in a First Class production in the U.S. or Canada; or in a New York City theatre under Equity's Basic Minimum Contract, excluding showcases; or at least 2 productions presented in a resident theatre, as defined under Equity's Minimum Basic Contract for Resident Theatres. All other theatre professionals must meet criteria listed in brochure. Annual dues are $75. For further details of membership eligibility and application procedure, write or call for Membership Information brochure.

LIPP (Lesbian-Identified Performance Project)
(Formerly LEND)
Box 1408; New York, NY 10276-1408; (212) 874-7900, ext 1103

Founded in 1993, LIPP (formerly known as LEND) is a service organization for lesbian playwrights and other artists. Programs include LIPPFest, an annual festival of staged readings and solo performance; the LOLAs, a biennial award program, including the Dyke Drama Award for an exceptional new play with significant lesbian content; and the Australian Playwrights Exchange, a short-term residency with Vitalstatistix Theatre in Adelaide, Australia. For all programs, apply by sending bio and indicating which program(s) interest you. *Deadline* for all programs: 15 Feb 1998.

Literary Managers and Dramaturgs of the Americas
Box 355–CASTA; CUNY Graduate Center; 33 West 42nd St;
    New York, NY 10036; (212) 642-2657, FAX 642-1977;
    E-mail ltimmel@email.gc.cuny.edu

LMDA is the professional service organization for American and Canadian literary managers and dramaturgs, founded in 1985 to affirm, examine and encourage these professions. Among the programs and services it offers are a free 800-number telephone job line; insurance coverage; the quarterly *LMDA Review*; the LMDA Script Exchange; the Production Diaries project; New Dramaturgs, which identifies and encourages new members of the profession and works to establish them in productive professional affiliations; and the University Program, which provides a liaison between training programs and the profession. Activities include public panels, symposiums and workshops, as well as membership-only meetings and an annual conference. Associate membership is open to playwrights, artistic directors, literary agents and other theatre professionals interested in dramaturgy. Dues are $45 for voting members, $35 for associates, $20 for students and $100 for institutional memberships.

Luminous Visions
267 West 89th St; New York, NY 10024; (212) 581-7455, FAX 581-3964
Carla Pinza, *Co-Founder and Artistic Director*

Founded in 1976, Luminous Visions is a multicultural, not-for-profit organization dedicated to developing the creative skills and culture of film and television writers, directors and actors seeking employment within the English-speaking film and television mainstream. The organization sponsors a weekly workshop for writers, an annual Writers Forum and a spring Stage Reading Festival.

MARY ANDERSON CENTER FOR THE ARTS
101 St. Francis Dr; Mount Saint Francis, IN 47146; (812) 923-8602,
    FAX 923-8602; E-mail sry847@aol.com
Sarah Roberson Yates, *Executive Director*

The Mary Anderson Center, founded in 1989, is a not-for-profit organization dedicated to providing artists with a quiet place where they can concentrate and work on their craft. Named after the 19th-century actress from Louisville who rose to become an international celebrity, the center is located on 400 acres in southern Indiana. The center's goal is to provide retreats and residencies for artists in many disciplines (see the organization's entry in Colonies and Residencies). As part of its outreach effort to the Midwest and the nation, the center sponsors symposiums, conferences and other gatherings which explore, in a multidisciplinary mode, topics of major interest to society and to artists. Contributors to the center receive a quarterly newsletter featuring center activities and news of area artists.

MEET THE COMPOSER
2112 Broadway, Suite 505; New York, NY 10023; (212) 787-3601,
    FAX 787-3745
Omus Hirshbein, *Director*

Meet The Composer, a national funding agency, was founded in 1974 to foster the creation, performance and dissemination of music by American composers and to broaden audiences for music of our time. A not-for-profit organization, Meet The Composer raises money from foundations, corporations, individual patrons and government sources, and designs programs that support all styles and genres of music—from folk, ethnic, jazz, electronic, symphonic and chamber to choral, music theatre, opera and dance. MTC provides artist fees to not-for-profit organizations that perform, present or commission original works. Its programs include Commissioning Music/USA, Composer/Choreographer Project, International Creative Collaborations, New Residencies (see Meet The Composer Grant Programs in Fellowships and Grants), the Meet the Composer Fund and Affiliate Network, New Music for Schools and NYC Composers AIDS Fund.

MIDWEST RADIO THEATRE WORKSHOP
KOPN; 915 East Broadway; Columbia, MO 65201; (573) 874-5676,
    FAX 499-1662; E-mail mrtw@mrtw.org; Web http://www.mrtw.org/mrtw
Sue Zizza, *Executive Director*

MRTW is a national resource center for radio theatre in the areas of writing, directing, acting and sound design. Founded in 1979, it is a project of KOPN Radio/New Wave Corporation, a not-for-profit community radio station serving central Missouri. MRTW holds an annual script contest (see MRTW Script Contest in Prizes) to identify and promote emerging and established radio writers. Winning scripts may be produced during one of a series of radio-theatre workshops held each year (see the organization's entry in Development). MRTW provides information and referral services and technical assistance to interested individuals and groups, distributes educational tapes and publishes an annual Scriptbook.

MISSOURI ASSOCIATION OF PLAYWRIGHTS
830 North Spoede Rd; St. Louis, MO 63141; (314) 567-6341
Jo Lovins, *President*

Missouri Association of Playwrights (M.A.P.) was founded in 1976 to assist playwrights in developing their skills. The association's activities include monthly meetings (Sep–Jun) at which members' scripts are presented as fully staged readings or workshops; guests from the theatrical arena speak; seminars on writing for the theatre are offered; and an annual full production of one-act plays is presented. Full productions and staged readings are open to works of M.A.P members only. Membership is open to all playwrights, but most members live in the greater St. Louis area (including southwest IL and out-state MO). Annual dues are $20.

NATIONAL ACADEMY OF SONGWRITERS
6255 Sunset Blvd, Suite 1023; Hollywood, CA 90028; (213) 463-7178 (in CA), (800) 826-7287 (outside CA), FAX (213) 463-2146;
E-mail nassong@aol.com; Web http://www.nassong
Randy Sharp, *President*

Founded in 1973, NAS is a not-for-profit organization dedicated to educating, assisting and protecting songwriters. Members may call a toll-free number for answers to questions about the music business, have songs evaluated by industry professionals and, as proof of authorship, deposit songs in the academy's SongBank. NAS sponsors seminars and workshops, produces the Salute to the Songwriter (of the year) awards concert and the Lifetime achievement awards dinner, and presents the Songwriters Expo every fall. Members receive the *Songwriters Musepaper* monthly and have access to listings of publishers and producers looking for new songs. Annual dues are $200 for Gold Membership (those who have a certified gold single or album), $125 for Pro Membership (those who have had at least 1 song commercially released and distributed) and $95 for General Membership.

NATIONAL ALLIANCE FOR MUSICAL THEATRE
330 West 45th St, Lobby B; New York, NY 10036-3854; (212) 265-5376, FAX 582-8730; E-mail namt@bway.net; Web http://www.bway.net/namt

The National Alliance for Musical Theatre is a service organization dedicated to supporting professional companies in their efforts to preserve and extend the American musical theatre as an art form. As part of its services, the Alliance annually publishes a Membership Directory with profiles of each member company, including details on those companies which develop and produce new works. The Alliance also produces an annual Festival of New Musicals in New York City, which aims to encourage further productions of the showcased works.

258 / MEMBERSHIP AND SERVICE ORGANIZATIONS

Works to be considered for the festival should be submitted to member theatres, not to the Alliance.

THE NATIONAL FOUNDATION FOR JEWISH CULTURE
330 Seventh Ave, 21st Floor; New York, NY 10001; (212) 629-0500, FAX 629-0508; E-mail nfjc@jewishculture.org
Richard A. Siegel, *Executive Director*

The National Foundation for Jewish Culture (NFJC) is the central cultural agency of the American Jewish community. Founded in 1960, the NFJC has been dedicated to the enhancement of Jewish life in America through the support and promotion of the arts and humanities. Rooted in the principle that memory, knowledge and creativity are essential to Jewish continuity, the NFJC encourages innovation and excellence in artistic, scholarly and communal expression of Jewish culture. For the past 30 years, the NFJC has been a leader in advancing Jewish scholarship and preserving the Jewish cultural heritage in America. In recent years, the NFJC's program has expanded to include supporting new creativity in the arts, as well as bringing Jewish culture to local communities throughout North America.

The NFJC provides programs and services to cultural institutions, local communities and individual artists and scholars in every region of the country. It serves as: advocate and coordinator for the fields of Jewish culture through its Council of American Jewish Museums, Council of Jewish Theatres, and Council of Archives and Research Libraries in Jewish Studies; sponsor of grants and awards to artists, scholars and major cultural institutions such as YIVO, Leo Baeck Institute, American Jewish Historical Society, Histadrut Ivrit and the Jewish Publication Society of America; cultural innovator through conferences, symposia, publications, media productions, traveling exhibitions, residencies and performances which promote an understanding and appreciation of contemporary Jewish life and culture; and presenter of the annual Jewish Cultural Achievement Awards recognizing outstanding contributions to Jewish life in America through the arts and scholarship.

THE NATIONAL LEAGUE OF AMERICAN PEN WOMEN, INC.
1300 17th St NW; Washington, DC 20036-1973; (202) 785-1997
Frances J. Carter, *National President*

Founded in 1897, NLAPW is a national membership organization for professional women writers, composers and visual artists. Its local branches meet monthly. It holds annual State Association meetings, a National Biennial Convention and a National Art Show, and sponsors the biennial Mature Women Scholarship Award (see Fellowships and Grants). Members, who receive a bimonthly magazine, *The Pen Woman*, and a National Roster, pay dues of $30 a year.

NATIONAL PUBLIC RADIO
635 Massachusetts Ave NW; Washington, DC 20001-3753; (202) 414-2399, FAX 414-3032; E-mail atrudeau@npr.org
Andy Trudeau, *Director, Program Acquisition and Production*

National Public Radio is a private not-for-profit membership organization which provides a national program service to its over 400 member noncommercial radio stations. It is funded by its member stations, the Corporation for Public Broadcasting and corporate grants. Among the programs available to member stations is *NPR Playhouse*, which presents 29-minute dramatic programs, series and serials. Writers should note that NPR does not itself read or produce plays. It acquires broadcast rights to produced packages. It will consider fully produced programs or works-in-progress on tape only.

NATIONAL THEATRE WORKSHOP OF THE HANDICAPPED
354 Broome St, Loft 5-F; New York, NY 10013; (212) 941-9511, FAX 941-9486
Rick Curry, *Founder and Artistic Director*

Founded in 1977, the National Theatre Workshop of the Handicapped (NTWH) is a training, production and advocacy organization serving physically disabled adults who are talented in the performing arts. It is one of the very few places in the country where new dramatic literature on themes of disability is regularly tested and produced. In addition to offering professional instruction in acting, music, voice and movement, and playwriting, NTWH maintains a professional repertory theatre company which showcases the talents of its students. To help serve the interests of the 43 million disabled Americans, NTWH solicits the participation of both playwrights with disabilities and the playwriting community at large in its annual Festival of Short Works. Playwrights wishing to submit scripts to the festival should write for guidelines; submissions are accepted throughout the year. Artists with disabilities who are interested in participating in NTWH's training programs should contact the workshop for information.

NEW DRAMATISTS
424 West 44th St; New York, NY 10036; (212) 757-6960, FAX 265-4738;
E-mail newdram@aol.com;
Web html://www.itp.tsoa.nyu.edu/~diana/ndintro.html
Paul Alexander Slee, *Executive Director*
Todd London, *Director of Artistic Programs*

New Dramatists is the nation's oldest playwright development center, designed to provide member playwrights with the resources they need to create plays for the American theatre. Rather than producing plays, New Dramatists aids playwrights in the development of their craft through play readings and workshops; dramaturgy; a resident director program; musical theatre development and training; ScriptShare (a national script distribution program); fellowships, awards and prizes; a free ticket program for Broadway and Off-Broadway productions; writing spaces and accomodations; and photocopying. All services are provided free of charge to members.

In addition, New Dramatists hosts several playwright exchanges, including the

Mary Lea Johnson Richards Exchange with Beit Lessin Theatre, Israel; the Brooks Atkinson Exchange/Max Weitzenhoffer Fellowship to the Royal National Theatre, England; the Brooks Atkinson Exchange/Clara Rotter Fellowship to the Royal Court Theatre, England; the Sumner Locke Elliott Exchange to the Australian National Playwrights Centre; and exchanges with the Tyrone Guthrie Center, County Monaghan, Ireland and A.S.K. Theater Projects, Los Angeles.

Membership is open to emerging playwrights living in the greater New York area, and to those living outside the area who demonstrate a willingness to regularly travel to New York and actively participate in the program. Playwrights interested in applying for membership should write for guidelines.

NEW ENGLAND THEATRE CONFERENCE

Department of Theatre, Northeastern University; 360 Huntington Ave;
    Boston, MA 02115; (617) 424-9275, FAX 424-1057;
    E-mail netc@world.com
Corey Boniface, *Manager of Operations*

Founded in 1952, New England Theatre Conference is a membership organization primarily but not exclusively for New England theatre people, including playwrights, teachers, students and theatre professionals. Services include an annual conference, publication of a member directory and annual summer theatre auditions. NETC also administers the John Gassner Memorial Playwriting Award (see Prizes). The organization publishes *New England Theatre Journal* and *NETC News*. Membership dues are $80 for groups, $30 for individuals and $20 for students.

NEW GEORGES

90 Hudson St, Suite 2E; New York, NY 10013; (212) 620-0113;
    E-mail newgeorges@aol.com
Susan Bernfield, *Artistic Director*

New Georges is a professional theatre organization that produces and develops new works by women and supports the creative efforts of emerging women theatre artists. The group's programs revolve around The Room, New Georges's workspace, and involve a loose network of affiliated artists. These include informal readings of works-in-progress and workshop presentations of pieces developed in The Room, as well as an annual season of new plays and performance pieces by women. Women playwrights interested in working with New Georges may submit a completed script or work-in-progress, together with a resume and cover letter.

NEW PLAYWRIGHTS FOUNDATION

c/o 608 San Vicente Blvd, #18; Santa Monica, CA 90402; (310) 393-3682
Jeffrey Lee Bergquist, *Artistic Director*

Founded in 1968, New Playwrights Foundation is a service organization for writers working in theatre, film, television and video. The foundation runs developmental workshops, holds readings, occassionally coproduces video and film projects and assists members in furthering their careers. Membership in NPF is limited to a maximum of 15 writers who must be able to attend meetings in Santa Monica every other Monday. Applicants for membership attend meetings before submitting materials to be reviewed by the group.

THE NEW YORK PUBLIC LIBRARY
FOR THE PERFORMING ARTS

40 Lincoln Center Plaza; New York, NY 10023-7498; (212) 870-1639,
FAX 787-3852; E-mail rtaylor@nypl.org
Bob Taylor, *Curator, The Billy Rose Theatre Collection*

The Billy Rose Theatre Collection, a division of the Library for the Performing Arts, is open to the public (aged 18 and over) and contains material on all aspects of theatrical art and the entertainment world, including stage, film, radio, television, circus, vaudeville and burlesque. The Theatre on Film and Tape Project (TOFT) is a special collection of films and videotapes of theatrical productions recorded during performance, as well as informal dialogues with important theatrical personalities. Tapes are available for viewing by appointment (call 870-1641) to students, theatre professionals and researchers.

NON-TRADITIONAL CASTING PROJECT

1560 Broadway, Suite 1600; New York, NY 10036;
(212) 730-4750 (voice), -4913 (TDD), FAX 730-4820
Sharon Jensen, *Executive Director*

Founded in 1986, the Non-Traditional Casting Project is a not-for-profit organization which exists to address and seek solutions to the problems of racism and exclusion in the theatre and related media, particularly as they relate to creative personnel: including, but not limited to, actors, directors, writers, designers and producers. The project works to advance the creative participation of artists of color and artists with disabilities through both advocacy and specific projects. Key NTCP programs include Artist Files/Artist Files Online, a national talent bank; roundtable discussions with industry leaders; forums; and a national Information and Consulting Service. In development is a 3-part series called *Resource Guides on Actors with Disabilities*. Writers of color and/or with disabilities, who are citizens or residents of the U.S. or Canada and have had at least one play given a professional production or staged reading should send a resume for inclusion in Artist Files/Artist Files Online, indicating their cultural identification and, in the case of disabled artists, any accommodation they may use; those interested in contacting listed artists will call them or their agents directly.

NORTHWEST PLAYWRIGHTS GUILD

408 Southwest 2nd Ave, Suite 427; Portland, OR 97204; (503) 222-7010;
E-mail bjscript@teleport.com;
Web http://www.teleport.com/~bjscript/nwpg.htm
Bill Johnson, *Office Manager*

Northwest Playwrights Guild is an information clearinghouse and support group for playwrights. The guild sponsors public readings, holds workshops and produces regional conferences on theatre that include the full production of original scripts. The guild publishes a quarterly, *Script*, that contains articles on theatre in the Northwest, as well as update newsletters that provide information on current script opportunities. Membership dues are $25 a year.

OLLANTAY CENTER FOR THE ARTS
Box 720636; Jackson Heights, NY 11372-0636; (718) 565-6499,
    FAX 446-7806
Pedro R. Monge-Rafuls, *Executive and Artistic Director*

Founded as a multidisciplinary Hispanic arts center in 1977, OLLANTAY has developed a Hispanic Heritage Center for the arts in America with a view to providing the knowledge and resources needed to pursue research and develop new programs and initiatives in the field. The center maintains a resource bank of video and audio tapes, slides, books, plays and articles, which may be consulted by writing for an appointment. OLLANTAY's Traveling Theater Program tours plays by local writers. Its unique Playwriting Workshop, an annual intensive course of 3–6 weeks, provides an opportunity for playwrights wishing to write in Spanish to work under the direction of major Latin American playwrights who reside outside the U.S. *OLLANTAY Theater Magazine* is a biannual journal in English and Spanish which gives local playwrights, critics and scholars the opportunity to share their knowledge and experience of Hispanic theatre within the framework of American and world drama. The magazine, which publishes at least one play in each issue, is available to subscribers. Annual subscription is $18 for individuals, $25 for organizations.

OPERA AMERICA
1156 15th St NW, Suite 810; Washington, DC 20005-3287; (202) 293-4466,
    FAX 393-0735; E-mail frontdesk@operaam.org
Krista Rimple, *Program Manager, The Next Stage*

Founded in 1970, OPERA America is the not-for-profit service organization for the professional opera field in North America and allied international members. OPERA America provides a variety of informational, technical and financial services to its membership, and serves as a resource to the media, funders, government agencies and the general public.

The Next Stage, a program of OPERA America, is a 3-year pilot program designed to increase the number of North American works in the standard repertory by providing financial, technical and informational assistance to professional opera companies for productions of existing, under-performed works by North American artists.

Application for grants awarded through the program are accepted only from Professional Company Members of OPERA America. Individual artists and other organizations may request information about the program.

PEN American Center
568 Broadway; New York, NY 10012; (212) 334-1660, FAX 334-2181;
   E-mail pen@echonyc.com
Karen Kennerly, *Executive Director*

PEN is an international association of writers. The American Center is the largest of the 130 centers which comprise International PEN. The 2800 members of PEN American Center are established North American writers and translators, and literary editors. PEN activities include the Freedom-to-Write program; monthly symposiums, readings and other public events; a prison writing program; and a translator-publisher clearinghouse. PEN's publications include *Grants and Awards Available to American Writers*, a biennially updated directory of prizes, grants, fellowships and awards (1996–97 edition $13 postpaid); and *The PEN Prison Writing Information Bulletin*. Among PEN's annual prizes and awards are the Gregory Kolovakos Award, PEN–Book-of-the-Month Club Translation Prize and the Renato Poggioli Award (see Prizes); and Writing Awards for Prisoners, awarded to the authors of the best fiction, nonfiction, drama and poetry received from prisoner-writers in the U.S. The PEN Writers Fund and the PEN Fund for Writers & Editors with AIDS assist writers (see Emergency Funds).

Playmarket
Box 9767; Wellington; New Zealand; 64-4-382-8462, FAX 64-4-382-8461;
   Web http://www.playmarket.org.nz
John McDavitt, *Executive Officer*
Susan Wilson, *Script Advisor*

Playmarket is a service organization for playwrights, established in 1973 as a result of a growing interest in plays by New Zealand writers and a need to find new writers. The organization runs a script advisory and critiquing service, arranges workshop productions of promising scripts, and serves as the country's principal playwrights' agency, preparing and distributing copies of scripts and negotiating and collecting royalties. Playmarket's publications include *The Playmarket Directory of New Zealand Plays and Playwrights*, and a script series *New Zealand Theatrescripts*.

The Playwrights' Center
2301 Franklin Ave East; Minneapolis, MN 55406-1099; (612) 332-7481
Carlo Cuesta, *Executive Director*

The Playwrights' Center is a service organization for playwrights. Its programs include: developmental services (cold readings and workshops using an Equity acting company); fellowships; exchanges with theatres and other developmental programs; a newsletter; the Jones one-act commissioning program; PlayLabs (see Development); playwriting classes; year-round programs for young writers; and the Many Voices program, designed to provide awards, education and lab services to new and emerging playwrights of color. The Center annually awards 5 Jerome Playwright-in-Residence Fellowships and 2 McKnight Fellowships, for which competition is open nationally; 3 McKnight Advancement Grants open to Minnesota playwrights; and 3 Many Voices Multicultural Collaboration Grants (see The Playwrights' Center Grant Programs in Fellowships and Grants). The annual

Young Playwrights Summer Conference, open to playwrights grades 8–12, offers 2 weeks of workshops and classes for 30 young writers, with daily workshops and readings of students' work; participants, who are selected on the basis of writing samples and recommendations, receive college credit; scholarships are available; applications are available 15 Dec 1997; *deadline:* 22 Apr 1998; *dates:* 12–25 Jul 1997.

A broad-based Center membership is available to any playwright or interested person. Benefits of general membership for playwrights include discounts on classes, applications for all Center programs, eligibility to apply for one-act commissions and script-development readings, and the Center's newsletter. Core (must be MN resident) and Associate Member Playwrights are selected by a review panel each spring, based on script submission. They have primary access to all Center programs and services, including developmental workshops and public readings. Write for Membership brochure. Membership applications are available 1 Feb 1998, *deadline:* 1 Apr 1998; *notification:* 1 Jul 1998.

THE PLAYWRIGHTS FOUNDATION
Box 460357; San Francisco, CA 94114; (415) 263-3986, FAX 771-5505
Belinda Taylor, *President*

The Playwrights Foundation provides developmental support to playwrights throughout the U.S., with emphasis on the northern California region. It produces the annual Bay Area Playwrights Festival (see Development). The foundation also sponsors a 10-minute play contest for members only and presents readings of the winning pieces at an annual benefit.

THE PLAYWRIGHTS' PROJECT
Sammons Center for the Arts, #12; 3630 Harry Hines Blvd; Dallas, TX 75219; (972) 497-1752
Priscilla Sample, *Director*

The Playwrights' Project was founded in 1990 as a service organization for playwrights from the north Texas area. The project holds biweekly group labs and in-house and public readings, organizes workshops and lecture series, publishes a newsletter and sponsors the annual Robert Bone Memorial Playwriting Award (see Prizes). While the group's resident playwrights pay annual dues of $50, no qualified playwright is excluded for lack of funds. New resident playwrights, who must be from the Dallas area or able to travel to meetings and events in Dallas, are selected annually; applicants should submit 1 full-length play, or 2 one-acts totaling a minimum of 60 minutes, a cover letter containing a brief synopsis of the play(s), a bio, an optional SASE for acknowledgment of receipt and $5 fee; *deadline:* 1 Jun 1998 for residencies starting in the fall of 1998.

PLAYWRIGHTS THEATRE OF NEW JERSEY
33 Green Village Rd; Madison, NJ 07940; (201) 514-1787, FAX 514-2060
John Pietrowski, *Producing Artistic Director*

Founded in 1986, the Playwrights Theatre of New Jersey is both a service organization for playwrights of all ages and a professional developmental theatre. In addition to its New Play Development Program (see Playwrights Theatre of New Jersey in Development), PTNJ sponsors a state-wide playwriting-in-the-schools program; a playwriting-for-teachers project; adult playwriting classes; children's creative dramatics classes; acting classes; and "special needs" playwriting projects which include work in housing projects and with senior citizens, teenage substance abusers, persons with physical disabilities and court-appointed youth, as well as a playwriting-in-prisons initiative. Young playwrights festivals are held in Madison and Newark, in addition to a statewide festival which is part of the New Jersey Young Playwrights Program. Gifted and talented playwriting symposiums, hosted by well-known playwrights, provide intensive 2-day experiences for up to 60 students from various school districts. With the New Jersey State Council on the Arts, PTNJ cosponsors the Writers-in-the-Schools Program, which teaches poetry and prose in schools and community centers statewide.

PLAZA DE LA RAZA

3540 North Mission Rd; Los Angeles, CA 90031; (213) 223-2475,
 FAX 223-1804; E-mail admin@plazaraza.org;
 Web http://www.plazaraza.org
Rose Cano, *Executive Director*

Founded in 1970, Plaza de la Raza is a cultural center for the arts and education, primarily serving the surrounding community of East Los Angeles. Of special interest to playwrights is the center's Nuevo L.A. Chicano TheatreWorks project, designed to discover, develop and present the work of Chicano playwrights. Initiated in 1989 and recurring approximately every 4 years, depending on funding, as part of the Nuevo L.A. Chicano Art Series cycle (Visual Arts, Music, Dance and Theatre), the project develops new one-acts through a 2-week workshop with director and actors, culminating in public readings; some plays are selected for subsequent full production. Latino playwrights who are California residents should contact the center for information on when and how to apply for the next round of the program. In addition to its playwrights' project, Plaza de la Raza conducts classes in drama, dance, music and the visual arts; provides resources for teachers in the community; and sponsors special events, exhibits and performances. Membership in Plaza de la Raza is open to all.

PROFESSIONAL ASSOCIATION OF CANADIAN THEATRES/ PACT COMMUNICATIONS CENTRE

415 Yonge St, 15th Floor; Toronto, Ontario; Canada; M5B 2E7;
 (416) 595-6455, FAX 595-6450; E-mail pact@mail.culturenet.ca
Pat Bradley, *Executive Director*
Rick Sherman, *Membership and Communications Coordinator*

PACT is the national service and trade association representing professional English-language theatres in Canada. PACT was incorporated in 1976 to work on behalf of its member theatres in the areas of advocacy, labor relations, professional development and communications. The members' newsletter *impact!* is published quarterly. PACT Communications Centre (PCC) was established in

1985 as the charitable wing of PACT in order to improve and expand communications and information services. PCC publishes *The Theatre Listing*, an annual directory of English-language Canadian theatres, rehearsal and performance spaces, government agencies and arts service organizations; and *Artsboard*, the monthly bulletin of employment opportunities in the arts in Canada.

PUBLIC BROADCASTING SERVICE
1320 Braddock Pl; Alexandria, VA 22314-1698; (703) 739-5000,
    FAX 739-8314, -8458; E-mail www@pbs.org
Corporate Communications

The Public Broadcasting Service is a private not-for-profit corporation that acquires and distributes programs to its 348 member stations. The PBS Programming Department can advise independent producers about the development of specific projects. Information about the preparation, presentation and funding of projects can be obtained from PBS. Printed materials such as the *PBS Packaging & Technical Guidelines* are also available.

THE PURPLE CIRCUIT
2025 Griffith Park Blvd, Suite 4; Los Angeles, CA 90039;
    (213) 666-0693 or 661-1982; E-mail purplecir@aol.com
Bill Kaiser, *Coordinator*

The Purple Circuit is a network of gay, lesbian, queer, bisexual and transsexual theatres, producers and performers, and "Kindred Spirits" (theatres which are not exclusively gay or lesbian in orientation but are interested in producing gay or lesbian material on a regular basis). The Purple Circuit publishes news, information and articles of interest to its constituency in its quarterly newsletter, *On the Purple Circuit*. *The Purple Circuit Directory* lists theatres and producers around the world, including "Kindred Spirits," that are interested in presenting gay, lesbian, bisexual and transsexual works. The Purple Circuit Hotline (213) 666-0693 provides information on gay and lesbian shows currently playing in California and advises travelers on shows around the US and abroad, as well as providing information for playwrights, journalists and others interested in promoting gay/lesbian/bisexual/transgender theatre and performance.

THE SCRIPTWRITERS NETWORK
11684 Ventura Blvd, #508; Studio City, CA 91604; (213) 848-9477
Bill Lundy, *Chair*

Though the Scriptwriters Network, founded in 1989, is predominantly an affiliation of film, television and corporate/industrial writers, playwrights are welcome. Meetings feature guest speakers; developmental feedback on scripts is available; and staged readings may be arranged in conjunction with other groups. The network sponsors members-only contests and publishes a newsletter. Prospective members submit a professionally formatted script and a completed application; membership is not based on the quality of the script. There is a $15 initiation fee, and dues are $60 a year.

The Songwriters Guild of America
1560 Broadway, Room 1306; New York, NY 10036; (212) 768-7902, FAX 768-9048; E-mail songnews@aol.com
George Wurzbach, *National Projects Director*

Head Office:
1500 Harbor Blvd; Weehawken, NJ 07087-6732; (201) 867-7603
Los Angeles Office:
6430 Sunset Blvd; Hollywood, CA 90028; (213) 462-1108
Nashville Office:
1222 16th Ave; Nashville, TN 37212; (615) 329-1782

The Songwriters Guild is a voluntary national association run by and for songwriters; all officers and directors are unpaid. Among its many services to composers and lyricists, the guild provides a standard songwriter's contract and reviews this and other contracts on request; collects writers' royalties from music publishers; maintains a copyright renewal service; conducts songwriting workshops and critique sessions with special rates for members; provides a songwriter collaboration service; issues news bulletins with essential information for writers; and offers a group medical and life insurance plan. Full members of the guild must be published songwriters and pay dues on a graduated scale from $70–400. Unpublished songwriters may become associate members and pay dues of $55 a year. Write for membership application.

S.T.A.G.E. (Society for Theatrical Artists' Guidance and Enhancement)
Box 214820; Dallas, TX 75221; (214) 630-7722, FAX 630-4468
Marilyn Pyeatt, *Executive Director*

Founded in 1981, S.T.A.G.E. acts as an information clearinghouse for theatre artists and theatre organizations in the north Texas region. The society maintains a library of plays, theatre texts and resource information; offers counseling on agents, unions, personal marketing and other career-related matters; posts listings of miscellaneous job opportunities; and maintains an audition callboard for regional opportunities in theatre and film; sponsors an actor's showcase, Noon Preview; sponsors annual general auditions; and produces Stages Festival of New Plays, the longest running new play festival in Dallas. Any playwright may submit to the festival, which seeks unproduced one-acts, not more than 30 minutes long, with minimal sets and props and preferably 8 or fewer characters; winning playwrights receive an honorarium and production; send SASE for guidelines; *deadline:* 15 Mar 1998. Members of S.T.A.G.E., who pay annual dues starting at $45 (for volunteers), $65 (for all others), receive a monthly publication, *CENTERSTAGE.*

Theatre Association of Pennsylvania (TAP)
Box 148; Mt. Gretna, PA 17064; (717) 964-1944, FAX 964-1945
Lisa Myers Sweeney, *Executive Director*

Founded in 1968, TAP is Pennsylvania's theatre service organization. Its membership includes theatres of every type, academic institutions, theatre training programs, and artists, educators and other individuals committed to the continuing development of quality theatre and the vital role that theatre plays in the life of the Commonwealth. TAP serves as the central information agency for its membership; sponsors festivals, conferences, workshops, playwriting competitions and auditions; administers granting programs; acts as a liaison with state and national organizations; and produces a variety of publications, including *TAPLINE* and *Essentials of a Theatre Curriculum*. Membership in TAP is open to all. Annual dues are $30 for individuals, $15 for students, and $45–275 for organizations.

THEATRE BAY AREA

657 Mission St, Suite 402; San Francisco, CA 94105; (415) 957-1557,
    FAX 957-1556; E-mail tba@best.com; Web http://www.theatrebayarea.org

TBA is a resource organization for San Francisco Bay Area theatre workers whose members include 3200 individuals and more than 260 theatre companies. Its programs include TIX Bay Area, San Francisco's half-price ticket booth; TIX By Mail, a half-price ticket catalog; professional workshops; and communications and networking services. Annual dues of $37 (add $12 for 1st-class postage) include a subscription to *Callboard*, a monthly magazine featuring articles, interviews and essays on the Northern California theatre scene, as well as information on play contests and festivals, and listings of production activity, workshops, classes, auditions, jobs and services. TBA also publishes *Theatre Directory of the Bay Area*, which includes entries of local theatre companies and listings of rehearsal and performance spaces; *Sources of Publicity* and *Sources of Funding*; and *Management Memo*, a monthly newsletter for theatre administrators and artistic directors. The Web site includes a playbill calendar, ticket information and sample *Callboard* articles.

THEATRE COMMUNICATIONS GROUP

355 Lexington Ave; New York, NY 10017-0217;
    (212) 697-5230, FAX 983-4847; E-mail: tcg@tcg.org
John Sullivan, *Executive Director*

Founded in 1961, TCG is the national organization for the American theatre. Its mission is to celebrate and inspire excellence in the artistry of theatre in America. To carry out this mission, TCG serves theatre artists and not-for-profit professional theatre organizations by recognizing and encouraging artistic diversity; providing a forum for open and critical examination of issues, standards and values; fostering interaction among theatre professionals; collecting, analyzing and disseminating information regarding the profession; and serving as the principal advocate for America's not-for-profit professional theatre. With a constituency of more than 300 theatres across America that reach a combined audience of more than 20 million people each year, TCG provides centralized services to aid the work of thousands in the field. Its chief programs include grants, fellowships and awards to theatre artists and institutions; conferences, workshops and roundtables; government affairs; surveys and research; and publications. (For more information, see *American Theatre* in Publication and TCG Grant Programs in Fellowships and Grants.)

In addition to *American Theatre* magazine, TCG publications of interest to theatre writers include *Theatre Profiles*, a biennial reference guide offering comprehensive statistical, historical and production information on more than 200 not-for-profit theatres; *Theatre Directory*, which provides complete contact information for more than 350 theatres and related arts organizations across the U.S.; *Stage Writers Handbook: A Complete Business Guide for Playwrights, Composers, Lyricists and Librettists*, by Dana Singer; and *ArtSEARCH*, a biweekly bulletin of job opportunities in the arts. The "Opportunities" column of *American Theatre* supplements information provided in this *Sourcebook*. TCG also publishes plays, translations and anthologies in book form, play texts in *American Theatre*, and books dealing with all aspects of theatre. (For further information, see Useful Publications, and Publications from TCG in the back of this book, or contact TCG for the current Publications catalogue.)

Individual Members receive a free subscription to *American Theatre* magazine, discounts on tickets to performances at more than 150 theatres nationwide, cost-savings on TCG resource materials, and discounts on all books from TCG and other select theatre publishers. Members are also eligible to apply for the TCG credit card, a no-annual fee MasterCard, and receive discounts from Budget Rent-A-Car, Airborne Express and the Hotel Reservation Network. Individual memberships are available to all theatre professionals, as well as to theatre enthusiasts, for $35 a year, $20 for students. (See membership application in the back of this book.)

THEATRE LA

644 South Figueroa St; Los Angeles, CA 90017; (213) 614-0556, FAX 614-0561;
E-mail theatrela@aol.com; Web http://www.theatrela.org
William Freimuth, *Executive Director*

A not-for-profit association of over 150 theatre producers, Theatre LA was founded in 1975 to unite, represent and promote theatre in greater Los Angeles. Theatre LA administers the annual Ovation Awards; provides cooperative advertising and insurance, a job bank and information and referral services for members; and runs a half-price ticket booth. Publications include *Theatre LA News*, a newsletter with information about advocacy and opportunities for playwrights; and *Opening Night Calendar*, which includes listings of member theatres' showtimes. Full membership in the organization is open only to theatre producers on an annual sliding scale of $220–$1200. Individuals may become associate members for $35 annually.

THE THEATRE MUSEUM

1E Tavistock St; London WC2E 7PA; England; 441-71-836-7891,
FAX 441-71-836-5148

The Theatre Museum, a branch of the Victoria & Albert Museum, is Britain's national museum of the performing arts. In addition to its regular displays, which feature 400 years of the history, technology, art and craft of theatre, and its

270 / MEMBERSHIP AND SERVICE ORGANIZATIONS

special exhibitions, the museum houses the U.K.'s largest archive of performing arts materials, including play texts, photographic and biographical files, theatre programs and reviews, and books about the theatre. The archive and study room is available by appointment (call during office hours) Tuesday to Friday, 10:30–1:00 p.m. and 2:00–4:30 p.m. The museum's innovative education department runs workshops and study days on theatre practice and set texts for children, students and teachers. The museum also runs a program of celebrity play readings, seminars and events to give visitors insight into current theatre production.

UBU REPERTORY THEATER

15 West 28th St; New York, NY 10001; (212) 679-7540, FAX 679-2033;
E-mail uburep@spacelab.net; Web http://www.nytheatre-wire.com
Françoise Kourilsky, *Artistic Director*

Ubu Repertory Theater, founded in 1982, is a not-for-profit theatre center dedicated to introducing translations of contemporary French-language plays to the English-speaking audience (see theatre's entry in Production). In addition to producing several plays a year, Ubu commissions translations and schedules reading programs, photography exhibits, panel discussions and workshops. Ubu publishes a series of contemporary plays by French-speaking playwrights in English translation, distributed nationally by TCG, and houses a French-English reference library of published plays and manuscripts.

VOLUNTEER LAWYERS FOR THE ARTS

1 East 53rd St, 6th Floor; New York, NY 10022;
(212) 319-2787 (administrative office), 319-2910 (Art Law Hotline),
FAX 752-6575
Amy Schwartzman, *Executive Director*

Volunteer Lawyers for the Arts arranges free legal representation and legal education for the arts community. Individual artists and not-for-profit arts organizations unable to afford private counsel are eligible for VLA's services; VLA can be especially useful to playwrights with copyright or contract problems. There is an administrative fee per referral of $30–50 for individuals, $50–100 for not-for-profit organizations and $250 for not-for-profit incorporation and tax exemption. VLA's education program offers biweekly seminars on not-for-profit incorporation and evening seminars held regularly to educate attorneys and artists in specific areas of art law. Publications include *Model Contracts for Independent Contractors: Sample Provisions and Job Descriptions* ($15 plus $4 postage and handling); and the *VLA Guide to Copyright for Visual Artists* ($5.95 plus $4 postage and handling). For more information about VLA's publications and the 40 VLA affiliates across the country, contact the New York office; referrals can be made to volunteer lawyer organizations nationwide.

Women's Theatre Alliance
Box 64446; Chicago, IL 60664-0446; (312) 408-9910
Jennifer Yeo, *President*

W.T.A. is a networking and resource organization for Chicago-area theatre artists including actors, directors, playwrights, producers, stage managers, technicians, designers and educators. Its mission is to advocate women's leadership in the Chicago-area theatre community; to create an empowering resource for women theatre artists to ensure that their voices are heard within that community; and to provide a support network for women theatre artists that will enable them to share their artistic diversity and learn from one another. In pursuit of these goals, W.T.A. holds quarterly meetings; sponsors informal readings, staged readings, play development workshops and an annual actors' showcase and new plays festival; and publishes a monthly newsletter. To join W.T.A., write or call for a Membership/Information Request Form. Membership dues are $30 a year.

The WOW Cafe
59–61 East 4th St; New York, NY 10003; (212) 777-4280

The WOW (Women's One World) Cafe is a women's theatre collective whose membership is primarily but not exclusively lesbian. WOW produces the work of women playwrights and performers. It has no permanent staff and its members are encouraged to participate in all aspects of the group's operations. In lieu of dues, members volunteer their services backstage on fellow members' productions in exchange for the opportunity to present their own work. Each show is produced by the member who initiates it. Women interested in becoming members of the WOW Cafe may attend one of the collective's regular meetings, which are scheduled every Tuesday at 6:30 PM.

Writers Guild of America, East (WGAE), AFL-CIO
555 West 57th St; New York, NY 10019-2967; (212) 767-7800
Mona Mangan, *Executive Director*

WGAE is the union for freelance writers in the fields of motion pictures, television and radio who reside east of the Mississippi River. The union negotiates collective bargaining agreements for its members and represents them in grievances and arbitrations under those agreements. It also makes credit determinations for the writing of its members. The guild gives annual awards, and sponsors a foundation which currently teaches film writing to disadvantaged high school students. WGAE participates in reciprocal arrangements with the International Affiliation of Writers Guilds and with its sister union, Writers Guild of America, West. The guild publishes a monthly newsletter, which is available to nonmembers by subscription; and a quarterly journal, *On Writing*. Write for information on WGAE's registration service for registering literary material, or call (212) 757-4360.

WRITERS GUILD OF AMERICA, WEST (WGAW)
7000 West 3rd St; Los Angeles, CA 90048-4329; (213) 951-4000, FAX 782-4800
Brian Walton, *Executive Director*

WGAw is the union for writers in the fields of motion pictures, television, radio and new media who write both entertainment and news programming. It represents its members in collective bargaining and other labor matters. It publishes a monthly magazine, *The Journal.* The Guild registers material, including screen- and teleplays, books, plays, poetry and songs. The library is open to the public Mon–Fri.

YOUNG PLAYWRIGHTS INC.
321 West 44th St, #906; New York, NY 10036; (212) 307-1140, FAX 307-1454;
E-mail writeaplay@aol.com
Sheri M. Goldhirsch, *Artistic Director*

Young Playwrights Inc. (YPI), founded in 1981 by Stephen Sondheim and other members of the Dramatists Guild, introduces young people to the theatre and encourages self-expression through the art of playwriting. YPI strives to identify, develop and encourage playwrights aged 18 years and younger; to develop new works for the theatre and to aid in the creation of the next generation of professional playwrights through the Young Playwrights Festival (see Prizes), the Young Playwrights Spring Conference, and the Urban Playwriting Retreat; to expose young people to theatre and playwriting through WRITING ON YOUR FEET! in-school playwriting workshops; to train teachers through the TEACHING ON YOUR FEET! Teacher Training Institute; to develop and serve audiences that reflect the complex makeup of our society and to create the next generation of theatregoers through the TAKE A GROWNUP TO THE THEATER! ticket subsidy program, student matinees and a discount voucher program; to bring the vital experience of professional theatre free of charge to neglected inner-city public schools, community organizations and youth centers through the Young Playwrights School Tour; and to serve as an advocate for young writers regardless of ethnicity, physical ability, sexual orientation or economic status, and to ensure that their voices are heard and acknowledged by a diverse community of artists and theatregoers.

Epilogue

- Useful Publications
- Submission Calendar
- Special Interests
- Index

Useful Publications

This is a selective listing of the publications that we think most usefully supplement the information given in the *Sourcebook*. Note that publications of interest to theatre writers are also described throughout this book, particularly in introductions to sections, in Membership and Service Organizations listings, and on the Related TCG Publications pages in the back. Before ordering you would be wise to find out if the prices given in all listings still pertain.

We have purposely left out any "how to" books on the art of playwriting because we do not want to promote the concept of "writing-by-recipe." However, we do recommend David Savran's *In Their Own Words: Contemporary American Playwrights*; *The Production Notebooks: Theatre in Process, Volume One*, edited by Mark Bly (see Related TCG Publications pages); and Dana Singer's *Stage Writers Handbook: A Complete Business Guide for Playwrights, Composers, Lyricists and Librettists* (see this section).

American Theatre

Theatre Communications Group; 355 Lexington Ave; New York, NY 10017-0217; (212) 697-5230, FAX 557-5817; E-mail custserv@tcg.org

1-year subscription/TCG membership $35, 2 years $70; single issue $4.95. This monthly magazine includes an "Opportunities" column which updates *Sourcebook* information between editions, announcing new grants and contests. A special Season Preview issue each October lists schedules for some 200 theatres nationwide, and monthly schedules are published in each issue. As part of its comprehensive coverage of all aspects of theatre, *American Theatre* regularly features articles and interviews dealing with theatre writers and their works, and publishes the complete texts of 5 new plays a year.

Back Stage
1515 Broadway, 14th Floor; New York, NY 10036; (212) 764-7300, FAX 536-5318;
  E-mail bstage96@aol.com

1-year subscription $79, 2 years $129; single issue $2.50, $3.75 by mail. This performing arts weekly includes industry news; reports from cities across the country; reviews; and columns, including "Playwrights' Corner." Though the primary focus is on casting, theatres and other producers sometimes run ads soliciting scripts; workshops and classes for playwrights are also likely to be advertised here.

A Handbook for Literary Translators
PEN American Center; 568 Broadway; New York, NY 10012; (212) 334-1660,
  FAX 334-2181; E-mail pen@echonyc.com

3rd edition, 1995. 35 pp, $2.50 (includes postage and handling) paper. Contents include "A Translator's Model Contract," "Negotiating a Contract," "Selected Resources" and "The Responsibilities of Translation."

Hollywood Scriptwriter
Box 10277; Burbank, CA 91510; (818) 845-5525; E-mail lgrantt@primenet.com

1-year subscription (11 issues) $44, 6 months $25; discount on renewals. This 10-page newsletter contains a "MARKETS for Your Work" section that includes "Plays Wanted" listings, as well as interviews and articles giving advice that is sometimes useful to playwrights as well as screenwriters. A list of back issues with a summary of the contents of each issue is available; call for information and a free sample.

The Individual's Guide to Grants by Judith B. Margolin
Plenum Press; 233 Spring St; New York, NY 10013; (212) 620-8051,
  (800) 221-9369, FAX (212) 647-1898; E-mail info@plenum.com;
  Web http://www.plenum.com

1983. 314 pp, $19.95 cloth. This comprehensive guide to individual grantseeking, written by a former director of the New York library of the Foundation Center, offers detailed advice on each step of the process.

Into Print: Guides to the Writing Life
Poets & Writers; 72 Spring St; New York, NY 10012; (212) 226-3586,
FAX 226-3963; E-mail pwsubs@aol.com; Web http://www.pw.org

1995. 212pp, $12.95 (plus $3.90 shipping and handling plus sales tax where applicable) paper. This book contains practical information on numerous topics of interest to theatre writers, including libel, permissions and trademarks, health insurance, writers' colonies, signing contracts and more. For more information, call, write or e-mail for Poets & Writers' catalogue.

Literary Agents: A Writer's Guide by Adam Begley
Poets & Writers; 72 Spring St; New York, NY 10012; (212) 226-3586,
FAX 226-3963; E-mail pwsubs@aol.com; Web http://www.pw.org

1993. 196 pp, $10 (plus $3.90 postage and handling plus sales tax where applicable) paper. This book contains several chapters exploring the functions of literary agents and the agent-writer relationship, and includes listings of 196 agencies which will consider unsolicited *queries* plus 37 more agencies which charge fees.

Literary Market Place 1998
R.R. Bowker; 121 Chanlon Rd; New Providence, NJ 07974; (908) 464-6800, (800) 521-8110, (888) BOWKER-2, FAX 771-7704

1995. 1942 pp, $189.95 (plus 7% shipping and handling plus sales tax where applicable) paper. This directory of the American book publishing industry gives contact information for book publishers and those in related fields, and includes a "Names & Numbers" index over 500 pages long. The 1998 *LMP* is due out in September 1997.

Market Insight...for Playwrights
Box 8598; Kansas City, MO 64114-0598; (800) 895-4720;
E-mail minsight@aol.com

1-year subscription $40 (12 issues), 6 months $25. This monthly newsletter for playwrights provides submission guidelines for theatres, residencies, publishers and contests, as well as updates on personnel changes at theatres, special programs for women writers, and more; call for a free sample.

Music, Dance & Theater Scholarships
Conway Greene Publishing Company; 1414 South Green Rd, Suite 206; South Euclid, OH 44121; (800) 977-2665

1995. 512 pp, $20.95 (plus $4.50 shipping and handling) paper. This guide provides information on more than 1800 theatre, music and dance conservatory and undergraduate programs, as well as more than 5000 professional and educational scholarship opportunities. It also includes detailed information on audition requirements, decision processes at individual schools, special scholarship stipulations and student profiles.

The National Playwrights Directory
O'Neill Theater Center; 305 Great Neck Rd; Waterford, CT 06385;
   (203) 443-5378, FAX 443-9653

1986. 507 pp, $20 (plus $3.50 postage and handling) cloth. With entries on 495 writers and an index of over 4000 plays, this book is a useful source of information.

Playhouse America!
Feedback Theatrebooks; 305 Madison Ave, Suite 1146; New York, NY 10165;
   (212) 687-4185, (800) 800-8671, FAX (207) 359-5532;
   E-mail feedback@hypernet.com;
   Web http://www.hypernet.com/prospero.html

1991. 300 pp, $16.95 (plus $3.00 postage and handling) paper. This directory contains the addresses and phone numbers of more than 3500 theatres across the country; it includes a cross-reference to specialty theatres (e.g., Dinner Theatres & Showboats, Military Theatres).

The Playwright's Companion, Mollie Ann Meserve, ed
Feedback Theatrebooks; 305 Madison Ave, Suite 1146; New York, NY 10165;
   (212) 687-4185, (800) 800-8671, FAX (207) 359-5532;
   E-mail feedback@hypernet.com;
   Web http://www.hypernet.com/prospero.html

1997. 416 pp, $20.95 (plus $3.00 postage and handling) paper. This annual guide for playwrights publishes submission guidelines for more than 1600 theatres, contests, publishers and special programs. The *Companion* includes useful tips on query letters, synopses, resumes and submission etiquette, as well as a list of state arts councils, agents, and playwriting programs in colleges and universities. The 1998 edition is due out in December 1997.

Poets & Writers Magazine
Poets & Writers; 72 Spring St; New York, NY 10012; (212) 226-3586,
   FAX 226-3963; E-mail pwsubs@aol.com; Web http://www.pw.org

1-year subscription (6 issues) $19.95, 2 years $38; single issue $3.95. Though primarily aimed at writers of poetry and fiction, this newsletter does include some announcements of grants and awards as well as other opportunities open to theatre writers.

Professional Playscript Format Guidelines and Sample
Feedback Theatrebooks; 305 Madison Ave, Suite 1146; New York, NY 10165;
   (212) 687-4185, (800) 800-8671, FAX (207) 359-5532;
   E-mail feedback@hypernet.com;
   Web http://www.hypernet.com/prospero.html

1991. 28 pp, $4.95 (plus $1.75 postage and handling) paper. This booklet provides detailed instructions for laying out a script in a professional manner.

USEFUL PUBLICATIONS / 279

Songwriter's Market, Cindy Laufenberg, ed
Writer's Digest Books; 1507 Dana Ave; Cincinnati, OH 45207; (513) 531-2690, FAX 531-7107; E-mail wdigest@aol.com

1997. 538 pp, $22.99 (plus $3 shipping and handling) paper. This annually updated directory, which lists contact information for more than 2200 song markets, includes a section on musical theatre. It also lists clubs, associations, contests and workshops of interest to songwriters. The 1998 edition is due out in September 1997.

Stage Directions Magazine
SMW Communications; Box 41202; Raleigh, NC 27629; (919) 872-7888,
FAX 872-6888; E-mail stagedir@aol.com;
Web http://www.stage-directions.com

1-year subscription $26 (10 issues), 2 years $48; single issue $3.50. This magazine provides information on royalty issues, play publishing, new play festivals and workshops/seminars for playwrights. A special Season Planner issue each November/December contains a directory of royalty houses.

Stage Writers Handbook: A Complete Business Guide for Playwrights, Composers, Lyricists and Librettists by Dana Singer
Theatre Communications Group; 355 Lexington Ave; New York, NY 10017-0217; (212) 697-5230, FAX 983-4847; E-mail custserv@tcg.org

1997. 328 pp, $16.95 (plus $3 shipping and handling for 1 book, $1 for each additional book) paper. This comprehensive guide, written by the Associate Director of the Dramatists Guild, covers such topics as: copyright, collaboration, underlying rights, marketing and self-promotion, production contracts, representation (agents and lawyers), publishers, authors' relationships with directors, and videotaping and electronic rights.

Theatre Directory 1997–98
Theatre Communications Group; 355 Lexington Ave; New York, NY 10017-0217; (212) 697-5230, FAX 983-4847; E-mail custserv@tcg.org

1997. 96 pp, $5.95 (plus $3 postage and handling for 1 book, $1 for each additional book) paper. TCG's annually updated directory provides complete contact information for more than 300 not-for-profit professional theatres—including new TCG Constituent and Associate theatres that join after this *Sourcebook* is published—and more than 50 arts resource organizations.

Theatre Profiles 12

Theatre Communications Group; 355 Lexington Ave; New York, NY 10017-0217; (212) 697-5230, FAX 983-4847; E-mail custserv@tcg.org

1996. 240 pp, $22.95 (plus $3 postage and handling for 1 book, $1 for each additional book) paper. Useful for finding out about this country's not-for-profit professional theatres, the 12th volume of this biennial series contains artistic profiles, production photographs, financial information and repertoire information for the 1993–95 seasons of 257 theatres.

U.S. Copyright Office publications

Register of Copyrights; Library of Congress; Washington, DC 20559; (202) 707-3000 for questions and advice

There are many ways to receive free circulars, including No. 1, "Copyright Basics." You can: call (202) 707-9100 to receive them by mail; call (202) 707-2600 and key in your fax number to receive them by fax; download them from the Internet at http://www.loc.gov/copyright. If you write for information instead, expect to wait a long time for a response.

The Writer

120 Boylston St; Boston, MA 02116-4615; (617) 423-3157, FAX 423-2168; Web http://www.channel1.com/thewriter/

1-year subscription (12 issues) $28, 2 years $52, 3 years $75. This monthly magazine announces contests in a "Prize Offers" column, and publishes a special "Where to Sell Manuscripts" section, which includes lists of play publishers, in the September issue.

A Writer's Guide to Copyright

Poets & Writers; 72 Spring St; New York, NY 10012; (212) 226-3586, FAX 226-3963; E-mail pwsubs@aol.com; Web http://www.pw.org

1990. 63 pp, $10 (plus $3.90 postage and handling plus sales tax where applicable) paper. This guide contains simply and clearly written information on copyright laws, authors' rights and the functions of the Copyright Office; it is illustrated with sample forms.

Writer's Market

Kirsten Holm, ed; Writer's Digest Books; 1507 Dana Ave; Cincinnati, OH 45207; (513) 531-2690, FAX 531-7107; E-mail wdigest@aol.com

1997. 1008 pp, $27.99 (plus $3 postage and handling plus sales tax where applicable) paper; it is also available on CD-ROM for $39.99. This annually updated directory lists 4000 places to sell what you write. It includes many opportunities for playwrights and screenwriters. The 1998 edition is due out in September 1997.

Submission Calendar

September 1997–August 1998

Included here are all *specified* deadlines contained in Production, Prizes, Publication, Development, Fellowships and Grants, Colonies and Residencies, and Membership and Service Organizations. Please note that suggested submission dates for theatres listed in Production are not included. There are always important deadlines that are not available at press time and so cannot be included here. The "Opportunities" and "CallBoard" columns of *American Theatre* are places to look for these.

September 1997

1   Anna Zornio Children's Theatre Award   *104*
1   Cleveland Public Theatre New Plays Festival   *26*
1   Dorland Mountain Arts Colony (1st deadline)   *227*
1   42nd Street Workshop   *166*
1   Great Plains Play Contest   *114*
1   Katherine and Lee Chilcote Award   *117*
1   Lee Korf Awards   *121*
1   Millay Colony for the Arts (1st deadline)   *231*
1   National Hispanic Playwriting Contest   *127*

1   NEH Collaborative Research grant   *206*
1   SummerNITE, New Play Studio   *182*
1   Villa Montalvo Residency Program (1st deadline)   *234*
2   Fund for Artist at International Festivals and Exhibitions   *196*
10 Playwrights Forum (1st deadline)   *178*
12 New Women Playwright's Contest   *129*
15 Ashland New Plays Festival   *162*
15 MacDowell Colony (1st deadline)   *231*
15 Virginia Center residencies (1st deadline)   *235*
15 Women at the Door Staged Reading Series   *165*
16 Jerome Fellowships   *208*
20 Susan Smith Blackburn Prize   *136*
30 Dayton Playhouse FutureFest   *109*
30 Gilman and Gonzalez-Falla Musical Theatre Award   *113*
30 Hawthornden Castle Retreat for Writers   *228*
30 Lamia Ink! (1st deadline)   *152*
30 New Play Commissions in Jewish Theatre   *207*
30 Paul Green Playwrights Prize   *130*
30 Puerto Rican Traveling Theatre Workshop   *180*
30 Theater at Lime Kiln Playwriting Contest   *137*
31 New American Comedy Festival   *127*

Contact for exact deadline during this month:
Douglass Center Workshops (1st deadline)   *166*

October 1997

1   Centrum Residency Program   *226*
1   Hedgebrook (1st deadline)   *229*
1   John Guggenheim Fellowships   *201*
1   New Visions/New Voices   *173*
1   New York Mills Arts Retreat (1st deadline)   *232*
1   Norcroft   *233*
1   Ucross Foundation Residency Program (1st deadline)   *234*
15 Attic Theatre Ensemble's One-Act Marathon   *105*
15 Bunting Fellowship Program   *198*
15 Chesterfield Film Company Project   *164*
15 New Line Theatre Musical Theatre Competition   *128*
15 Playwrights First Award   *131*
15 Year-End-Series Festival   *142*

15	Young Playwrights Festival Contest *143*
23	Institute of International Education *201*
31	New Voices Development Program *173*
31	Southern Appalachian Playwrights' Conference *181*

November 1997

1	American-Scandinavian Foundation grants *195*
1	Beverly Hills Theatre Guild Award *105*
1	Hambidge Center residencies (1st deadline) *228*
1	Women Playwrights Project *185*
3	Richard Rodgers Awards *180*
7	NYFA Sponsorship Program *174*
15	Hodder Fellowship *195*
15	Midwest Theatre Network Original Play Competition/Rochester Playwright Festival *124*
15	MRTW Script Contest *126*
15	New Harmony Project Laboratory *173*
21	Mildred and Albert Panowski Award *125*

Contact for exact deadline during this month:
Atlanta Artists Project   *197*

December 1997

1	Annual Marathon of One-Act Plays *34*
1	California Playwrights Competition *106*
1	Carnegie Mellon Drama's Showcase of New Plays *163*
1	Cunningham Prize *108*
1	DGP New Playwright Award *31*
1	Drama School Summerstages *76*
1	15 Minute Play Festival *92*
1	George Bennett Fellowship *201*
1	Gregory Kolovakos Award *114*
1	Japan Foundation grants *201*
1	KC/ACTF Michael Kanin Awards *118*
1	National Playwrights Conference *172*
1	National Ten-Minute Play Contest *127*
1	Tennessee Williams/New Orleans Literary Festival One-Act Competition *137*

15 Collages & Bricolages   *148*
15 Dorothy Silver Competition   *110*
15 James Thurber residency   *230*
15 Morton R. Sarett Competition   *125*
15 PEN–Book-of-the-Month Club Translation Prize   *130*
15 PlayLabs   *176*
15 Playwrights' Theater of Denton Competition   *131*
15 Sundance Theatre Laboratory   *183*
30 Lamia Ink! (2nd deadline)   *152*
30 Oglebay Institute Towngate Contest   *129*
31 Alcazar Scripts in Progress   *161*
31 Alden B. Dow Creativity Center   *224*
31 Artists-in-Berlin Programme   *196*
31 Flying Solo and Friends Festival   *8*
31 Harold Morton Landon Translation Award   *115*
31 PEN Center USA West Awards   *130*
31 Perishable Theatre Women's Playwriting Festival   *130*
31 Playwrights Week   *179*
31 Robert J. Pickering Award   *132*
31 Sam Edwards Deaf Playwrights Competition   *133*
31 West Coast Ensemble Full-Length Play Competition   *141*
31 Women's Repertory Project   *182*

Contact for exact deadline during this month:
Pew Fellowships in the Arts   *207*

January 1998

1   Dale Wasserman Drama Award   *108*
1   Francesca Primus Prize   *112*
1   Kumu Kahua Contest   *120*
1   Mill Mountain Theatre Competition   *125*
1   Nantucket Short Play Competition   *126*
1   Towngate Theatre Contest   *138*
5   Renato Poggioli Award   *132*
10 Playwrights Forum (2nd deadline)   *178*
10 Theatre Conspiracy Play Contest   *137*
12 NEH Humanities Projects in Media   *206*
15 Apostle Islands National Lakeshore   *224*
15 Free Reading Series and Development Workshop   *167*
15 Jewel Box Theatre Playwrighting Award   *117*

15   MacDowell Colony (2nd deadline)   *231*
15   Mature Women Scholarship Award   *203*
15   Poems & Plays' Tennessee Chapbook Prize   *155*
15   Ragdale Foundation residencies (1st deadline)   *233*
15   Reva Shiner Contest   *132*
15   Source Theatre Competition   *134*
15   South Florida Writers Contest   *135*
15   Summerfield G. Roberts Award   *136*
15   Virginia Center residencies (2nd deadline)   *235*
15   Washington Theatre Festival   *80*
15   Yaddo residencies (1st deadline)   *236*
16   McKnight Fellowships   *209*
16   McKnight Minnesota Fellowship   *203*
23   Dobie-Paisano Fellowship   *199*
26   University of Louisville Award for Music Composition   *139*
31   Baker's Plays High School Contest   *105*
31   Dubuque Fine Arts Players One-Act Contest   *111*
31   James D. Phelan Award   *116*
31   Margaret Bartle Playwriting Award   *123*
31   McLaren Comedy Playwriting Competition   *124*
31   PlayWorks Festival   *177*
31   Short Grain Contest   *133*
31   Texas Playwrights Festival   *182*

Contact for exact deadline during this month:
Denver Center Theatre Fest   *165*
Douglass Center Workshops (2nd deadline)   *166*
Scholastic Writing Awards   *133*

February 1998

1   Asian Cultural Council Japan-U.S. Program   *197*
1   Asian Cultural Council Residency Program in Asia   *197*
1   Bay Area Playwrights Festival   *162*
1   Blue Mountain Center   *225*
1   Camargo Foundation residencies   *226*
1   David James Ellis Award   *109*
1   Lois and Richard Rosenthal Prize   *122*
1   Men's Stories Short Play Festival   *8*
1   Millay Colony for the Arts (2nd deadline)   *231*
1   NewGate Theatre New Play Development (reading)   *174*

1	One World Premiere *32*
1	Owen Kelly Adopt-a-Playwright Program *32*
1	Shenandoah International Retreat *181*
1	South Carolina Playwrights' Festival *135*
1	TheatreVirginia New Voices for the Theatre *90*
1	Vermont Playwrights Award *140*
3	McKnight Advancement Grants *208*
15	Djerassi Resident Artists Program *227*
15	Drama League New Directors–New Works Series *165*
15	Isle Royale National Park Artist-in-Residence *229*
15	Jane Chambers Playwriting Award *116*
15	Lesbian-Identified Performance Project programs *255*
15	Southern Playwrights Competition *135*
15	Ventana Publications Award *159*
15	White Bird Contest *141*
15	Wichita State University Contest *142*
28	Artist Trust Grants for Artist Projects *195*
28	FEAT Competition *111*
28	Little Theatre of Alexandria One-Act Competition *121*
28	Moving Arts One-Act Competition *125*

Contact for exact deadline during this month:
Marilyn Bianchi Kids' Playwriting Festival *32*

March 1998

1	Dorland Mountain Arts Colony (2nd deadline) *227*
1	National Music Theater Conference *172*
1	Plays-in-Progress September Festival *177*
1	Shubert Fendrich Memorial Playwriting Contest *134*
1	SWTA New Play Contest *136*
1	Tomorrow's Playwrights *81*
1	Ucross Foundation Residency Program (2nd deadline) *234*
1	Villa Montalvo Residency Program (2nd deadline) *234*
15	ASCAP Musical Theatre Workshop *161*
15	Electronic Arts Grant Program Finishing Funds *199*
15	Hispanic Playwrights Project *168*
15	Isidora Aguirre Playwrighting Lab *168*
15	Lamia Ink! One Page Play Competition *120*
15	Meet the Composer Residencies (letter of intent) *204*
15	Stages Festival of New Plays *267*

15 We Don't Need No Stinkin' Dramas   *141*
16 Dramarama Long Play Contest   *110*
16 Dramarama Short Play Contest   *110*
16 Fund for New American Plays   *200*
20 Alaska Native Plays Contest   *103*
30 Lamia Ink! (3rd deadline)   *152*
31 Hedgerow Horizons   *168*
31 Lawrence S. Epstein Award   *121*
31 Loft Fest '98—Festival of Shorts   *169*
31 National Play Award   *127*
31 Princess Grace Fellowship   *209*
31 U.S.-Mexico Fund for Culture grants   *211*

Contact for exact deadline during this month:
NEA ArtsLink Collaborative Projects   *205*
Off-Off Broadway Original Short Play Festival   *175*
Travel and Study Grant Program   *211*

April 1998

1   AT&T/East West Players New Voices Competition   *105*
1   Byrdcliffe Art Colony   *225*
1   California Young Playwrights Contest   *106*
1   Connections   *108*
1   George Houston Bass Festival and Memorial Award   *112*
1   Great Platte River Playwrights' Festival   *114*
1   Hedgebrook (2nd deadline)   *229*
1   Live Oak Theatre Harvest Festival of New American Plays   *121*
1   Midwest Radio Theatre Workshop (scholarship applications)   *171*
1   New York City High School Contest   *129*
1   New York Mills Arts Retreat   *232*
1   Playhouse on the Square Competition   *131*
1   Playwrights' Center membership   *264*
1   Sarasota Festival of New Plays   *36*
1   Threshold Theater Metaphysical Play Contest   *138*
1   William Flanagan Memorial Center   *235*
2   NYFA—Artists in Residence Program   *232*
15 John Gassner Award   *117*
15 MacDowell Colony (3rd deadline)   *231*

20   George Hawkins Playwriting Contest   *112*
22   Playwrights' Center Young Playwrights Conference   *263*
30   Mark Taper Forum New Work Festival   *171*
30   Next Stage (stage one)   *175*

Contact for exact deadline during this month:
Annual Blank Theatre Company Young Playwrights Festival   *104*
Chicano/Latino Literary Contest   *107*
Inroads   *197*
Very Special Arts Playwright Discovery Program   *140*

May 1998

1   BMI Musical Theatre Workshop (librettists)   *163*
1   Coe College Competition   *107*
1   Don and Gee Nicholl Fellowships in Screenwriting   *199*
1   Hambidge Center residencies (2nd deadline)   *228*
1   Midwestern Playwrights Festival   *124*
1   Millay Colony for the Arts (3rd deadline)   *231*
1   Robert Bone Memorial Award   *132*
10   Playwrights Forum (3rd deadline)   *178*
15   Amelia Magazine's Frank McClure One-Act Award   *145*
15   Lewis Galantiere Literary Translation Prize   *103*
15   Marc A. Klein Award   *123*
15   Towson State University Prize   *139*
15   Virginia Center residencies (3rd deadline)   *235*
30   Adamant Program residencies   *223*
30   Writer's Digest Writing Competition   *142*
31   L. Arnold Weissberger Competition   *120*

Contact for exact deadline during this month:
Douglass Center Workshops (3rd deadline)   *166*
NEA Fellowships for Translators   *206*
Sundance Institute Feature Film Program   *182*

June 1998

1	ASF Translation Prize	*104*
1	Chicago Dramatists Workshop Resident Playwrights Program	*246*
1	George R. Kernodle Contest	*113*
1	HRC's Annual Contest	*115*
1	Jackie White Children's Playwriting Contest	*116*
1	New Christian Plays Award	*128*
1	New Professional Theatre Festival	*128*
1	New Works for a New World	*174*
1	NewGate Theatre New Play Development (festival)	*174*
1	Playwrights' Project membership	*264*
1	Ragdale Foundation residencies (2nd deadline)	*233*
1	SETC New Play Project	*135*
1	Women's Work	*186*
5	Headlands Center for the Arts	*229*
15	Meet the Composer/Arts Endowment Commissioning Music/USA	*204*
15	Meet the Composer Residencies (application)	*204*
15	Urban Stages Award	*139*
30	National Children's Theatre Festival	*126*
30	Next Stage (stage two)	*175*
30	Siena College Competition	*134*
30	West Coast Ensemble Musical Stairs	*141*

Contact for exact deadline during this month:
U.S./Japan Creative Artists' Fellowships   *205*

July 1998

1	Altos de Chavon residencies	*224*
1	Henrico Theatre Company One-Act Competition	*115*
1	Many Voices Multicultural Collaboration Grants	*208*
1	Many Voices Playwriting Residency Awards	*208*
1	Maxim Mazumdar Competition	*123*
1	Plays-in-Progress May Festival	*177*
1	TADA! Spring Staged Reading Series/New Play Project	*136*
1	TADA! Staged Reading Series	*84*
1	Theodore Ward Prize for African-American Playwrights	*138*
15	James H. Wilson Award	*109*

15 Paul T. Nolan Award   *109*
21 Inner City Cultural Center Competition   *115*

Contact for exact deadline during this month:
Douglass Center Workshops (4th deadline)   *166*

August 1998

1   BMI Musical Theatre Workshop (composers, lyricists)   *163*
1   Fulbright Scholar Awards   *200*
1   Lehman Engel Musical Theatre Workshop   *169*
1   New Tuners Workshop   *60*
1   Yaddo residencies (2nd deadline)   *236*
31 Broadway Tomorrow   *163*
31 Festival of Firsts Competition   *112*
31 Marvin Taylor Award   *123*
31 Ten-Minute Musicals Project   *183*

Special Interests

Here is a guide to entries which indicate a particular or exclusive interest in certain types of material, or which contain an element of special interest to writers in certain categories. Under Young Audiences, Media and Solo Performance, we list every entry of interest to writers in these fields. In the case of adaptations, musicals, one-acts and translations, there are numerous theatres willing to consider these types of material; we list here only those theatres and other organizations that give major focus to them. The Multicultural category is for those organizations expressing general interest in multicultural/multiracial works. Under African-American, Asian-American, Hispanic/Latin-American and Native American Theatre, we have included only those organizations specifically seeking work by or about people from these ethnic groups. The Student/College Submissions category refers to college writing students or students in an affiliated writing program. Young Playwrights is a special interest category only for playwrights 18 or under.

Adaptation

American Conservatory Theater *10*
Arden Theatre Company *13*
Asolo Theatre Company *16*
Bailiwick Repertory *17*
California Theatre Center *21*
Children's Theatre Company, The *24*
Classic Stage Company (CSC) *26*
Cornerstone Theater Company *28*
Coterie Theatre, The *28*
Court Theatre *28*
Dallas Children's Theater *29*

292 / SPECIAL INTERESTS

El Teatro Campesino   33
Fountain Theatre, The   37
Germinal Stage Denver   39
Guthrie Theater, The   41
Honolulu Theatre for Youth   42
Huntington Theatre Company   43
Indiana Repertory Theatre   44
INTAR Hispanic American Arts Center   45
Jomandi Productions   47
L. A. Theatre Works   47
New Jersey Shakespeare Festival   59
Northlight Theatre   62
Oregon Shakespeare Festival   64
Shakespeare & Company   77
Shakespeare Theatre, The   78
Ten-Minute Musicals Project, The   183
Theater Emory   86
Theatreworks/USA   91
Wilma Theater, The   98

African-American Theatre

Alabama Shakespeare Festival   9
Black Theatre Network   244
Blacksmyths   170
Callaloo   148
Cornerstone Dramaturgy and Development Project   164
Crossroads Theatre Company   29
Dallas Theater Center   30
Ensemble Theatre, The   34
Ford's Theatre   37
Freedom Theatre   37
George Hawkins Playwriting Contest   112
Hatch-Billops Collection   250
Jomandi Productions   47
L. A. Black Playwrights   169
Lorraine Hansberry Playwriting Award, The   119
New Professional Theatre Writers Festival   128
New Voices Play Development Program   173
Penumbra Theatre Company, The   66
St. Louis Black Repertory Company   81
Theodore Ward Prize for African-American Playwrights   138

Asian-American Theatre

Asian American Arts Alliance   241
Asian American Theater Company   15
Asian American Theater Company New Plays & Playwrights Development Program   162
Asian Cultural Council   197
Asian Pacific American Friends of Center Theatre Group (APAF) Reading Series   170
Asian Pacific American Journal   146
AT&T/East West Players New Voices Playwriting Competition   105
East West Players   33
Honolulu Theatre for Youth   42
Japan Foundation, The   201
Lamia Ink!   152
Pacific/Rim Prize   120
Pan Asian Repertory Theatre   64
United States/Japan Creative Artists' Fellowships   205

Disabilities: Theatre for, by and about People with Disabilities

Arena Stage   13
Jane Chambers Playwriting Award   116
Milwaukee Public Theatre   55
National Theatre of the Deaf   57
National Theatre Workshop of the Handicapped   259
Non-Traditional Casting Project   261
Other Voices Project   171

SPECIAL INTERESTS / 293

Perseverance Theatre   67
Playwrights Theatre of New
  Jersey   264
Sam Edwards Deaf Playwrights
  Competition   133
Theater by the Blind   86
Very Special Arts Playwright
  Discovery Program   140

Experimental Theatre

Actors' Gang Theater   8
American Music Theater
  Festival   11
American Place Theatre, The   11
American Writing: A
  Magazine   145
Bailiwick Repertory   17
Bristol Riverside Theatre   20
Changing Scene, The   23
Cleveland Public Theatre   26
Collages & Bricolages   148
Crossroads Theatre Company   29
Jane Chambers Playwriting
  Award   116
La MaMa Experimental Theater
  Club   48
Lamia Ink!   152
Live Bait Theatrical Company   49
Living Theatre, The   50
Magic Theatre   51
Maxim Mazumdar New Play
  Competition   123
McKnight Interdisciplinary
  Fellowship Grant, The   203
Music-Theatre Group   57
Northlight Theatre   62
Odyssey Theatre Ensemble   62
PlayLabs   176
Reva Shiner Full-Length Play
  Contest   132
Richard Rodgers Awards, The   180
Round House Theatre   74
Scripts and Scribbles   156
7 Stages   77
Stages   81
Stet Magazine   157

Theater   158
Theater for the New City   87
United Arts   159
Vineyard Theatre   94
Wooster Group, The   98

Gay and Lesbian Theatre

Actors & Playwrights' Initiative   7
Actor's Express, The   7
Bailiwick Repertory   17
Cleveland Public Theatre   26
Glines, The   39
Jane Chambers Playwriting
  Award   116
la telaraña   253
LIPP (Lesbian-Identified
  Performance Project)   255
Loft Production Company,
  The   50
Love Creek Annual Short Play
  Festival   122
MRTW Script Contest   126
Perseverance Theatre   67
Purple Circuit, The   266
Sinister Wisdom   157
Theatre Rhinoceros   89
WOW Cafe, The   271

Hispanic/Latin-American Theatre

Altos de Chavon   224
Arte Público Press   146
Association of Hispanic Arts,
  The   243
Bilingual Foundation of the
  Arts   19
Chicano/Latino Literary
  Contest   107
Cintas   196
Dallas Theater Center   30
GALA Hispanic Theatre   38
Gregory Kolovakos Award,
  The   114
Hispanic Organization of Latin
  Actors (HOLA)   251

Hispanic Playwrights Project *168*
INTAR Hispanic American Arts
 Center *45*
Isidora Aguirre Playwrighting Lab,
 The *168*
la telaraña *253*
Latin American Theater
 Artists *253*
Latino Theatre Initiative
 (LTI) *170*
National Hispanic Playwriting
 Contest *127*
OLLANTAY Center for the
 Arts *262*
PlayWorks Festival *177*
Plaza de la Raza *265*
Puerto Rican Traveling Theatre
 Playwrights' Workshop *180*
Repertorio Español *72*
San Diego Repertory Theatre *75*
Stages *81*
Thalia Spanish Theatre *85*
U.S.-Mexico Fund for Culture *211*

Jewish Theatre

American Jewish Theatre *11*
Dorothy Silver Playwriting
 Competition *110*
Jewish Ensemble Theatre *46*
Jewish Repertory Theatre *46*
National Foundation for Jewish
 Culture, The *258*
New Play Commissions in Jewish
 Theatre *207*

Media (Film, Radio and Television)

Adamant Program, The *223*
Alcazar Scripts in Progress *161*
Alden B. Dow Creativity
 Center *224*
Altos de Chavon *224*
American Film Institute, The *239*
Artist Trust *195*
Association of Independent Video
 and Filmmakers *244*
Brody Arts Fund *198*
Bush Artist Fellowships *198*
Byrdcliffe Art Colony *225*
Centrum Artist-in-Residency
 Program *226*
Chesterfield Film
 Company/Writer's Film Project,
 The *164*
Columbus Screenplay Discovery
 Awards *108*
Corporation for Public
 Broadcasting *247*
Djerassi Resident Artists
 Program *227*
Don and Gee Nicholl Fellowships
 in Screenwriting, The *199*
Electronic Arts Grant
 Program *199*
First Stage *166*
42nd Street Workshop, The *166*
Frederick Douglass Creative Arts
 Center Writing
 Workshops *166*
Gell Writers Center, The *228*
Harold Prince Musical Theatre
 Program *167*
Headlands Center for the
 Arts *229*
Helene Wurlitzer Foundation of
 New Mexico *229*
Hip Pocket Theatre *42*
Independent Feature Project *251*
Japan Foundation, The *201*
La MaMa Experimental Theater
 Club *48*
Leighton Studios for Independent
 Residencies *230*
Live Bait Theatrical Company *49*
Luminous Visions *255*
MacDowell Colony, The *231*
Manhattan Playwrights Unit *170*
Many Voices Multicultural
 Collaboration Grants *208*

SPECIAL INTERESTS / 295

Meet the Composer/Arts Endowment Commissioning Music/USA 204
Midwest Radio Theatre Workshop 171, 256
Millay Colony for the Arts, The 231
MRTW Script Contest 126
Music-Theatre Group 57
National Endowment for the Humanities Public Programs 206
National Playwrights Conference 172
National Public Radio 259
New Harmony Project Laboratory, The 173
New Playwrights Foundation 260
New York Foundation for the Arts Artists' Fellowships 207
New York Foundation for the Arts Sponsorship Program 174
New York Mills Arts Retreat 232
Norcroft 233
Old Pueblo Playwrights 175
PEN Center USA West Literary Awards 130
PEN Fund for Writers & Editors with AIDS 214
PEN Writers Fund 214
Pew Fellowships in the Arts 207
Players Press 154
Playwrights Forum 178
Public Broadcasting Service 266
Red Eye 72
San Diego Repertory Theatre 75
Scholastic Writing Awards 133
Scripteasers, The 181
Scriptwriters Network, The 266
Shenandoah International Playwrights Retreat 181
STUDIO for Creative Inquiry 233
Sundance Institute Feature Film Program 182
Tyrone Guthrie Centre, The 234
U.S.-Mexico Fund for Culture 211
Villa Montalvo Artist Residency Program 234
Virginia Center for the Creative Arts 235
Walt Disney Studios Fellowship Program, The 212
William Flanagan Memorial Creative Persons Center 235
Wilma Theater, The 98
Writer's Digest Writing Competition 142
Writers Guild of America, East (WGAE) 271
Writers Guild of America, West (WGAW) 272
Yaddo 236

Multicultural Theatre

A Contemporary Theatre 5
Actor's Express, The 7
Alabama Shakespeare Festival 9
Alliance Theatre Company 9
AMAS Musical Theatre, Inc. 10
American Place Theatre, The 11
Arena Stage 13
Borderlands Theater 20
Brody Arts Fund 198
Castillo Theatre 22
Centre Stage–South Carolina! 23
Cleveland Public Theatre 26
Collages & Bricolages 148
Connections 108
Coterie Theatre, The 28
Crossroads Theatre Company 29
Dixon Place 31
Dobama Theatre 32
El Teatro Campesino 33
Emerging Playwright Award 111
Frank Silvera Writers' Workshop, The 166
Free Street Programs 37
Frontera @ Hyde Park Theatre 38
George Houston Bass Play-Rites Festival and Memorial Award 112

296 / SPECIAL INTERESTS

Group: Seattle's Multicultural Theatre, The 41
Guthrie Theater, The 41
Harbor Theatre Lab, The 250
Indiana Repertory Theatre 44
Inroads 197
International Creative Collaboration 203
Jane Chambers Playwriting Award 116
La MaMa Experimental Theater Club 48
Lee Korf Playwriting Awards, The 121
Luminous Visions 255
Manhattan Theatre Club Playwriting Fellowships 202
Many Voices Multicultural Collaboration Grants 208
Many Voices Playwriting Residency Awards 208
Merrimack Repertory Theatre 53
Midwest Radio Theatre Workshop 171
Mill Mountain Theatre 54
MRTW Script Contest 126
National Children's Theatre Festival 126
National Endowment for the Arts International Program 205
National Theatre of the Deaf 57
Nebraska Repertory Theatre 58
New Federal Theatre 59
New Repertory Theatre 59
New Works for a New World 174
New York Theatre Workshop 61
Non-Traditional Casting Project 261
Odyssey Theatre Ensemble 62
Omaha Theater Company for Young People 63
Open Eye Theater, The 64
Oregon Shakespeare Festival 64
Perseverance Theatre 67
PlayQuest 176
Plays on Tape 154

Puerto Rican Traveling Theatre Playwrights' Workshop 180
San Diego Repertory Theatre 75
Second Stage Theatre 77
St. Louis Black Repertory Company 81
Studio Arena Theatre 83
Studio Theatre, The 83
Theatre Gael 87
Theatre Outlet, The 88
TheatreWorks 91
Urban Stages Award 139
Utah Shakespearean Festival 93
Van Lier Playwriting Fellowship 211
Victory Gardens Theater 94
Vineyard Playhouse, The 94
Voice & Vision 95
We Don't Need No Stinkin' Dramas 141
Westbeth Playwright Program 185
Women's Work 186
Young Playwrights Festival National Playwriting Contest 143

Musical Theatre

Alliance Theatre Company 9
AMAS Musical Theatre, Inc. 10
American Cabaret Theatre 10
American Music Center 240
American Music Theater Festival 11
Arts at St. Ann's 15
ASCAP (American Society of Composers, Authors and Publishers) 241
ASCAP Musical Theatre Workshop 161
BMI (Broadcast Music Incorporated) 245
BMI–Lehman Engel Musical Theatre Workshop 163
Bristol Riverside Theatre 20
Broadway on Sunset 245
Broadway Tomorrow 163
Centre Stage–South Carolina! 23

SPECIAL INTERESTS / 297

Coconut Grove Playhouse 27
Coterie Theatre, The 28
Ford's Theatre 37
Freelance Press 151
Genesius Guild Programs for the Development of New Plays & Musicals, The 167
Gilman and Gonzalez-Falla Theatre Foundation Musical Theatre Award 113
Goodspeed Opera House 40
Gretna Theatre 40
Group: Seattle's Multicultural Theatre, The 41
Harold Prince Musical Theatre Program 167
KC/ACTF Musical Theater Award, The 118
Kleban Award, The 202
Lehman Engel Musical Theatre Workshop, The 169
Meet The Composer 256
Meet The Composer Grant Programs 203
Music-Theatre Group 57
Musical Theatre Works 172
National Academy of Songwriters 257
National Alliance for Musical Theatre 257
National Music Theater Conference 172
National Music Theater Network 172
Nautilus Music-Theater 57
New Line Theatre Musical Theatre Competition 128
New Tuners Theatre 60
OPERA America 262
Primary Stages Company 71
Richard Rodgers Awards, The 180
San Diego Repertory Theatre 75
San Jose Repertory Theatre 75
Seacoast Repertory Theatre 76
Seaside Music Theater 76
Society Hill Playhouse 79

Songwriters Guild of America, The 267
Ten-Minute Musicals Project, The 183
Tennessee Repertory Theatre 85
Theater at Lime Kiln Regional Playwriting Contest 137
Theatre Three, Inc. 89
Theatreworks/USA Commissioning Program 184
Totem Pole Playhouse 91
University of Louisville Grawemeyer Award for Music Composition 139
Vineyard Theatre 94
Walnut Street Theatre Company, The 95
West Coast Ensemble 96
West Coast Ensemble Musical Stairs 141
Willows Theatre Company 97
York Theatre Company, The 99

Native American Theatre

Alaska Native Plays Contest 103
American Indian Community House 239
Lamia Ink! 152
Montana Repertory Theatre, The 56
PlayWorks Festival 177

One-Acts and Short Plays

Academy Theatre 5
Actors Theater, The 8
Alabama Literary Review 145
Amelia Magazine 145
American Shorts Contest 103
Asian Pacific American Journal 146
Attic Theatre Ensemble's One-Act Marathon 105
Bellingham Review, The 147
Callaloo 148
Collages & Bricolages 148

298 / SPECIAL INTERESTS

Confrontation 148
CrazyQuilt Quarterly 149
Deep South Writers Conference Paul T. Nolan Award 109
Dramarama Short Play Contest 110
Drury College One-Act Play Competition 111
Dubuque Fine Arts Players National One-Act Playwriting Contest 111
Field, The 248
George Hawkins Contest 112
George Houston Bass Play-Rites Festival and Memorial Award 112
George R. Kernodle Playwriting Contest 113
Goshen College Peace Playwriting Contest 114
Henrico Theatre Company One-Act Playwriting Competition 115
Horizon Theatre Company 43
Kalliope, A Journal of Women's Art 152
Kenyon Review, The 152
Lamia Ink! 152
Lamia Ink! International One-Page Play Competition 120
Little Theatre of Alexandria National One-Act Playwriting Competition, The 121
Loft Fest '98—Festival of Shorts, The 169
Love Creek Annual Short Play Festival 122
Mill Mountain Theatre 54
Moving Arts Premiere One-Act Competition 125
MRTW Script Contest 126
Nantucket Short Play Festival and Competition 126
National Ten-Minute Play Contest 127
New Line Theatre Musical Theatre Competition 128

Off-Off Broadway Original Short Play Festival 175
One Acts in Performance 176
Pacific Northwest Writers Conference Literary Contest 129
Pacific Review 153
Paul T. Nolan One-Act Award 109
Performing Arts Journal 153
Perishable Theatre Women's Playwriting Festival 130
Plays, The Drama Magazine for Young People 154
Poems & Plays 155
Prism International 155
Provincetown Arts/Provincetown Arts Press 155
Rag Mag 155
Resource Publications, Inc. 156
Rockford Review 156
Short Play Awards Program, The 119
Sinister Wisdom 157
S.T.A.G.E. (Society for Theatrical Artists' Guidance and Enhancement) 267
Stet Magazine 157
TADA! Spring Staged Reading Series/New Play Project 136
Tennessee Williams/New Orleans Literary Festival One-Act Play Competition 137
Theatre-Studio Inc., The 90
This Month ON STAGE 158
Tomorrow Magazine 158
Turnip Theatre Company 92
Urban Stages Award 139
West Coast Ensemble 96

Performance Art/Multimedia
(see also Experimental Theatre)

American Place Theatre, The 11
American Writing: A Magazine 145
Audrey Skirball-Kenis Play Collection 147

Coney Island, USA 27
Descant 149
Djerassi Resident Artists
  Program 227
Jane Chambers Playwriting
  Award 116
La MaMa Experimental Theater
  Club 48
Lamia Ink! 152
Live Bait Theatrical Company 49
Provincetown Arts/Provincetown
  Arts Press 155
Red Eye 72
Scripts and Scribbles 156
7 Stages 77
Stet Magazine 157
Tomorrow Magazine 158
United Arts 159
Voice & Vision 95
Wilma Theater, The 98

Religious/Spiritual Theatre

A. D. Players 5
Alliance Theatre Company 9
Cunningham Prize for Playwriting,
  The 108
Eldridge Publishing
  Company 150
Encore Performance
  Publishing 151
Lillenas Drama Resources 152
Love Creek Annual Short Play
  Festival 122
New Christian Plays Award 128
Pioneer Drama Service 153
7 Stages 77

Social-Political Theatre

A Contemporary Theatre 5
Academy Theatre 5
Actors & Playwrights' Initiative 7
Actor's Express, The 7
Actors' Gang Theater 8
Actors Theater, The 8
Alternate ROOTS 238

Bailiwick Repertory 17
Barter Theatre 18
Blue Mountain Center 225
BoarsHead: Michigan Public
  Theater 20
Borderlands Theater 20
Castillo Theatre 22
Cleveland Public Theatre 26
Collages & Bricolages 148
Coterie Theatre, The 28
Dallas Children's Theater 29
Dell'Arte Players Company 30
Detroit Repertory Theatre 31
Dobama Theatre 32
El Teatro Campesino 33
Ensemble Theatre of
  Cincinnati 35
Eureka Theatre Company 35
Festival of Emerging American
  Theatre (FEAT) Competition,
  The 111
Fourth Freedom Forum Playwriting
  Award, The 118
Free Street Programs 37
Freelance Press 151
GALA Hispanic Theatre 38
George Street Playhouse 38
Goodman Theatre 40
Goshen College Peace Playwriting
  Contest 114
Great American History
  Theatre 40
Group: Seattle's Multicultural
  Theatre, The 41
Honolulu Theatre for Youth 42
Horizon Theatre Company 43
Human Race Theatre Company,
  The 43
InterAct Theatre Company 45
Invisible Theatre 45
Irondale Ensemble Project 46
La Jolla Playhouse 48
Living Theatre, The 50
Long Wharf Theatre 50
Love Creek Annual Short Play
  Festival 122
Mabou Mines 51

Magic Theatre   *51*
Milwaukee Public Theatre   *55*
MRTW Script Contest   *126*
National AIDS Fund Award for Playwriting, The   *119*
National Children's Theatre Festival   *126*
New Federal Theatre   *59*
New Line Theatre Musical Theatre Competition   *128*
New York Theatre Workshop   *61*
Northlight Theatre   *62*
Odyssey Theatre Ensemble   *62*
Philadelphia Theatre Company   *67*
Pilgrim Project   *207*
Pope Theatre Company   *70*
Repertory Theatre of St. Louis, The   *72*
Round House Theatre   *74*
Sacramento Theatre Company   *74*
San Diego Repertory Theatre   *75*
Second Stage Theatre   *77*
7 Stages   *77*
Signature Theatre   *78*
Stage One: The Louisville Children's Theatre   *81*
Stage West   *81*
Stamford Theatre Works   *82*
Theater for the New City   *87*
Theater of the First Amendment   *88*
Theatre Outlet, The   *88*
Theatre Three, Inc.   *89*
Theatreworks/USA   *91*
Unicorn Theatre   *93*
Unicorn Theatre National Playwrights' Award   *139*
Vineyard Playhouse, The   *94*
Virginia Stage Company   *94*
Walnut Street Theatre Company, The   *95*
We Don't Need No Stinkin' Dramas   *141*
Weissberger Theater Group   *96*
White Bird Annual Playwriting Contest   *141*

Wilma Theater, The   *98*

Solo Performance

A Contemporary Theatre   *5*
Academy Theatre   *5*
Actors & Playwrights' Initiative   *7*
Actors Theater, The   *8*
Actors Theatre of Louisville   *8*
Alabama Literary Review   *145*
Alcazar Scripts in Progress   *161*
Amelia Magazine   *145*
American Music Theater Festival   *11*
American Shorts Contest   *103*
American Writing: A Magazine   *145*
Annual Blank Theatre Company Young Playwrights Festival, The   *104*
Apostle Islands National Lakeshore   *224*
Aran Press   *146*
Arkansas Repertory Theatre   *14*
ART Station   *14*
Asian Theatre Workshop (ATW)   *170*
A.S.K. Theater Projects   *162*
Asolo Theatre Company   *16*
Attic Theatre Centre   *16*
Audrey Skirball-Kenis Play Collection   *147*
Bailiwick Repertory   *17*
Barksdale Theatre   *17*
Bay Street Theatre   *18*
Bellingham Review, The   *147*
Berkshire Theatre Festival   *19*
Beverly Hills Theatre Guild–Julie Harris Playwright Award   *105*
Blacksmyths   *170*
Blue Mountain Center   *225*
Bristol Riverside Theatre   *20*
Brody Arts Fund   *198*
Byrdcliffe Art Colony   *225*
California Young Playwrights Contest   *106*

SPECIAL INTERESTS / 301

Carmel Performing Arts Festival 21
Carnegie Mellon Drama's Showcase of New Plays 163
Center Stage 22
Center Theater Ensemble 22
Center Theater International Playwrighting Contest 106
Centrum Artist-in-Residency Program 226
City Theatre Company 25
Cleveland Public Theatre 26
Coterie Theatre, The 28
CrazyQuilt Quarterly 149
Cunningham Prize for Playwriting, The 108
Dale Wasserman Drama Award 108
Dallas Theater Center 30
Dayton Playhouse FutureFest 109
Dell'Arte Players Company 30
Djerassi Resident Artists Program 227
Do Gooder Productions, Inc. 31
Dobama Theatre 32
Dramarama Long Play Contest 110
Dramarama Short Play Contest 110
Dramatics Magazine 150
Dudley Riggs Instant Theatre Company 32
Earth's Daughters 150
El Teatro Campesino 33
Emelin Theatre for the Performing Arts, The 33
Empty Space Theatre, The 34
En Garde Arts 34
Encore Performance Publishing 151
Ensemble Theatre, The 34
Eureka Theatre Company 35
Festival of Emerging American Theatre (FEAT) Competition, The 111
First Stage 166
Florida Studio Theatre 36

Foothill Theatre Company, The 36
Frontera @ Hyde Park Theatre 38
Fund for U.S. Artists at International Festivals and Exhibitions 196, 205
GALA Hispanic Theatre 38
Gell Writers Center, The 228
Genesius Guild Programs for the Development of New Plays & Musicals, The 167
George Houston Bass Play-Rites Festival and Memorial Award 112
Gilmore Creek Playwriting Competition 113
Goodman Theatre 40
Great American History Theatre 40
Group: Seattle's Multicultural Theatre, The 41
Hedgebrook 229
Henrico Theatre Company One-Act Playwriting Competition 115
Hip Pocket Theatre 42
HRC's Annual Playwriting Contest 115
Illusion Theater 44
Indiana Repertory Theatre 44
Inner City Cultural Center Competition 115
INTAR Hispanic American Arts Center 45
Invisible Theatre 45
Isle Royale National Park Artist-in-Residence 229
James H. Wilson Full-Length Play Award 109
Jane Chambers Playwriting Award 116
Jerome Playwright-in-Residence Fellowships 208
Jewel Box Theatre Playwrighting Award 117
John Drew Theater 47
Jomandi Productions 47

302 / SPECIAL INTERESTS

Kalliope, A Journal of Women's Art *152*
Kenyon Review, The *152*
Key West Theatre Festival *169*
La MaMa Experimental Theater Club *48*
Lamb's Players Theatre *49*
Latino Theatre Initiative (LTI) *170*
Live Bait Theatrical Company *49*
Live Oak Theatre *49*
Live Oak Theatre's Harvest Festival of New American Plays *121*
Loft Fest '98—Festival of Shorts, The *169*
Los Angeles Designers' Theatre Commissions *122*
Magic Theatre *51*
Many Voices Multicultural Collaboration Grants *208*
Many Voices Playwriting Residency Awards *208*
Mark Taper Forum *52*
Marvin Taylor Playwriting Award *123*
McKnight Advancement Grants *208*
McKnight Fellowships *209*
McLaren Memorial Comedy Playwriting Competition *124*
Midwest Theatre Network Original Play Competition/ Rochester Playwright Festival *124*
Mildred and Albert Panowski Playwriting Award *125*
Mill Mountain Theatre *54*
Mill Mountain Theatre New Play Competition: The Norfolk Southern Festival of New Works *125*
NEA ArtsLink Collaborative Projects *205*
New Christian Plays Award *128*
New Jersey Shakespeare Festival *59*
New Stage Theatre *60*
New Voices Play Development Program *173*
New Work Festival *171*
New Works for a New World *174*
New York Foundation for the Arts Sponsorship Program *174*
New York Mills Arts Retreat *232*
New York Theatre Workshop *61*
NewGate Theatre New Play Development *174*
Northlight Theatre *62*
Novel Stages *62*
Olney Theatre Center for the Arts *63*
Other Voices Project *171*
Pacific Review *153*
PAJ Books *153*
Paul Green Playwrights Prize *130*
Paul T. Nolan One-Act Play Award *109*
Pegasus Players *65*
Performing Arts Journal *153*
Perseverance Theatre *67*
Philadelphia Theatre Company *67*
Pilgrim Project *207*
Pirate Playhouse—Island Theatre *68*
Players Press *154*
PlayLabs *176*
PlayMakers Repertory Company *69*
PlayWorks Festival *177*
Playwrights' Center Grant Programs *208*
Playwrights' Theater of Denton Playwriting Competition *131*
Playwrights Week *179*
Poems & Plays *155*
Primary Stages Company *71, 179*
Prism International *155*
Provincetown Arts/Provincetown Arts Press *155*
Public Theater/New York Shakespeare Festival, The *71*
Puerto Rican Traveling Theatre Playwrights' Workshop *180*

SPECIAL INTERESTS / 303

Rag Mag *155*
Red Eye *72*
Remembrance Through the Performing Arts New Play Development *180*
Riverside Theatre (IA) *73*
Robert J. Pickering Award for Playwriting Excellence *132*
Rockford Review *156*
Samuel French *156*
San Jose Repertory Theatre *75*
Scripts and Scribbles *156*
Seattle Children's Theatre *76*
Seattle Repertory Theatre *77*
Smith and Kraus *157*
Soho Repertory Theatre *79*
Source Theatre Company *80*
Source Theatre Company 1997 Literary Prize *134*
South Carolina Playwrights' Festival *135*
Southern Playwrights Competition *135*
Stage West *81*
StageWest *82*
Stet Magazine *157*
STUDIO for Creative Inquiry *233*
Studio Theatre, The *83*
Sundance Theatre Laboratory, The *183*
Ten-Minute Musicals Project, The *183*
Tennessee Repertory Theatre *85*
Theater *158*
Theatre Gael *87*
Theater of the First Amendment *88*
Theatre Outlet, The *88*
Theatre Rhinoceros *89*
Theatre X *90*
TheatreForum *158*
Theatre-Studio Inc., The *90*
Theatre-Studio Playtime Series, The *184*
TheaterWorks *90*
Theatrical Outfit *91*

Theodore Ward Prize for African-American Playwrights *138*
This Month ON STAGE *158*
Tomorrow Magazine *158*
Trinity Repertory Company *92*
United Arts *159*
University of Alabama New Playwrights' Program *184*
Vineyard Playhouse, The *94*
Virginia Center for the Creative Arts *235*
Watertower Theatre, Inc. *95*
Westbeth Playwright Program *185*
Westbeth Theatre Center *96*
Williamstown Theatre Festival *97*
Wilma Theater, The *98*
Women's Project & Productions *98*
Woolly Mammoth Theatre Company *98*
Yale Repertory Theatre *99*

Student/College Submissions

Associated Writing Programs, The *243*
Clauder Competition for Excellence in Playwriting *107*
Jane Chambers Playwriting Award *116*
Kennedy Center American College Theater Festival: Michael Kanin Playwriting Awards Program *118*
Live Oak Theatre's Harvest Festival of New American Plays *121*
Marc A. Klein Playwriting Award, The *123*
PlayWorks Festival *177*
TADA! Spring Staged Reading Series/New Play Project *136*
Wichita State University Playwriting Contest *142*

304 / SPECIAL INTERESTS

Translation

American Translators Association (ATA) 240
American Translators Association Awards 103
ASF Translation Prize 104
Bailiwick Repertory 17
Bloomsburg Theatre Ensemble 19
Bristol Riverside Theatre 20
Classic Stage Company (CSC) 26
Court Theatre 28
Gregory Kolovakos Award, The 114
Guthrie Theater, The 41
Harold Morton Landon Translation Award 115
Institute for Contemporary East European and Slavic Drama and Theatre 251
INTAR Hispanic American Arts Center 45
National Endowment for the Arts Literature Program 206
National Endowment for the Humanities Research and Education Programs 206
New Jersey Shakespeare Festival 59
Northlight Theatre 62
Oregon Shakespeare Festival 64
PAJ Books 153
PEN–Book-of-the-Month Club Translation Prize 130
Performing Arts Journal 153
Renato Poggioli Award 132
Round House Theatre 74
Shakespeare Theatre, The 78
Stages 81
Studio Theatre, The 83
Theater Emory 86
Ubu Repertory Theater 93, 270
Wilma Theater, The 98
Yale Repertory Theatre 99

Women's Theatre

Arena Stage 13
Bailiwick Repertory 17
Bunting Fellowship Program 198
Cleveland Public Theatre 26
Collages & Bricolages 148
Dixon Place 31
Earth's Daughters 150
Falstaff Presents 35
Francesca Primus Prize, The 112
Hedgebrook 229
Horizon Theatre Company 43
International Center for Women Playwrights 252
International Women's Writing Guild, The 253
Invisible Theatre 45
Jane Chambers Playwriting Award 116
Kalliope, A Journal of Women's Art 152
League of Professional Theatre Women/New York 254
LIPP (Lesbian-Identified Performance Project) 255
Loft Production Company, The 50
Love Creek Annual Short Play Festival 122
Mature Women Scholarship Award 203
Midwest Radio Theatre Workshop 171
MRTW Script Contest 126
National League of American Pen Women, Inc., The 258
New Georges 260
New Professional Theatre Writers Festival 128
New Women Playwright's Contest 129
Norcroft 233
Oregon Shakespeare Festival 64
Perishable Theatre Women's Playwriting Festival 130
Perseverance Theatre 67

Plays on Tape *154*
San Diego Repertory Theatre *75*
Second Stage Theatre *77*
Shubert Fendrich Memorial Playwriting Contest *134*
Sinister Wisdom *157*
Susan Smith Blackburn Prize, The *136*
Victory Gardens Theater *94*
Voice & Vision *95*
Women at the Door Staged Reading Series *165*
Women Playwrights Project *185*
Women's Project & Productions *98*
Women's Repertory Project *182*
Women's Theatre Alliance *271*
Women's Work *186*
WOW Cafe, The *271*

Young Audiences

A. D. Players *5*
Actors Alley *6*
Actors Alliance Theatre Company *6*
Actors & Playwrights' Initiative *7*
Actors' Gang Theater *8*
Alabama Shakespeare Festival *9*
Alaska Native Plays Contest *103*
American Alliance for Theatre & Education (AATE), The *238*
American Stage *12*
American Theatre *145*
Anchorage Press *146*
Anchorage Press Theater for Youth Playwriting Award *118*
Anna Zornio Memorial Children's Theatre Playwriting Award *104*
Annual Blank Theatre Company Young Playwrights Festival, The *104*
Apple Tree Theatre *13*
Art Craft Publishing Company *146*
Arte Público Press *146*
ArtReach Touring Theatre *15*

Asian American Theater Company *15*
ASSITEJ/USA (International Association of Theatre for Children and Young People) *242*
AT&T/East West Players New Voices Playwriting Competition *105*
Audrey Skirball-Kenis Play Collection *147*
Baker's Plays *147*
Baker's Plays High School Playwriting Contest *105*
Barksdale Theatre *17*
Barter Theatre *18*
Bilingual Foundation of the Arts *19*
Birmingham Children's Theatre *19*
Blizzard Publishing *147*
BoarsHead: Michigan Public Theater *20*
California Theatre Center *21*
Carmel Performing Arts Festival *21*
Centre Stage–South Carolina! *23*
Children's Theatre Company, The *24*
Childsplay *24*
Coe College New Works for the Stage Competition *107*
Contemporary Drama Service *149*
Coterie Theatre, The *28*
Cumberland County Playhouse *29*
Cunningham Prize for Playwriting, The *108*
Dale Wasserman Drama Award *108*
Dallas Children's Theater *29*
Dell'Arte Players Company *30*
Dramafest 2000 *110*
Dramatic Publishing Company, The *149*
Dramatics Magazine *150*
Dramatists Play Service *150*
Earth's Daughters *150*

306 / SPECIAL INTERESTS

East West Players 33
El Teatro Campesino 33
Encore Performance Publishing 151
Ensemble Theatre, The 34
Ensemble Theatre of Cincinnati 35
First Stage Milwaukee 35
Foothill Theatre Company, The 36
Free Street Programs 37
George Hawkins Playwriting Contest 112
George Street Playhouse 38
Gilmore Creek Playwriting Competition 113
Great Plains Play Contest 114
Great Platte River Playwrights' Festival 114
Group: Seattle's Multicultural Theatre, The 41
Hedgerow Theatre 41
Heuer Publishing Company 151
Hip Pocket Theatre 42
Honolulu Theatre for Youth 42
Horizon Theatre Company 43
Human Race Theatre Company, The 43
I. E. Clark Publications 151
Indiana Repertory Theatre 44
Inner City Cultural Center Competition 115
Jackie White Memorial National Children's Playwriting Contest 116
James D. Phelan Award in Literature 116
Jewish Ensemble Theatre 46
Jomandi Productions 47
Laguna Playhouse 48
Lamb's Players Theatre 49
Los Angeles Designers' Theatre Commissions 122
Margaret Bartle Playwriting Award 123
Marin Theatre Company 52
Mark Taper Forum 52
McLaren Memorial Comedy Playwriting Competition 124
Meadow Brook Theatre 53
Merrimack Repertory Theatre 53
Merry-Go-Round Playhouse 54
Metro Theater Company 54
Midwest Theatre Network Original Play Competition/ Rochester Playwright Festival 124
Milwaukee Public Theatre 55
National Children's Theatre Festival 126
National Theatre of the Deaf 57
Nebraska Theatre Caravan 58
New Christian Plays Award 128
New Plays 153
New Visions/New Voices 173
Novel Stages 62
Omaha Theater Company for Young People 63
Pendragon Theatre 65
Penobscot Theatre Company 66
Penumbra Theatre Company, The 66
Phoenix Theatre 67
Pioneer Drama Service 153
Pirate Playhouse—Island Theatre 68
Players Press 154
Plays, The Drama Magazine for Young People 154
Pope Theatre Company 70
Repertorio Español 72
Resource Publications, Inc. 156
Riverside Theatre (FL) 72
Road Company, The
Robert J. Pickering Award for Playwriting Excellence 132
Round House Theatre 74
Samuel French 156
Santa Monica Playhouse 75
Seacoast Repertory Theatre 76
Seaside Music Theater 76
Seattle Children's Theatre 76
Shakespeare Santa Cruz 78
Shubert Fendrich Memorial Playwriting Contest 134

Smith and Kraus *157*
St. Louis Black Repertory Company *81*
Stage One: The Louisville Children's Theatre *81*
Sundance Theatre Laboratory, The *183*
TADA! *84*
TADA! Spring Staged Reading Series/New Play Project *136*
Theater at Monmouth, The *85*
Theatre IV *87*
Theatre Gael *87*
Theater of the First Amendment *88*
Theatre West *89*
Theatre-Studio Inc., The *90*
Theatreworks/USA *91*
Vineyard Playhouse, The *94*
Voice & Vision *95*
Waldo M. and Grace C. Bonderman IUPUI Playwriting Competition for Young Audiences *140*
Watertower Theatre, Inc. *95*
Western Stage, The *96*
Zachary Scott Theatre Center (ZACH) *100*

Young Playwright Programs

Annual Blank Theatre Company Young Playwrights Festival, The *104*
Baker's Plays *147*
Baker's Plays High School Playwriting Contest *105*
California Young Playwrights Contest *106*
Dobama Theatre *32*
Florida Studio Theatre *36*
New York City High School Playwriting Contest *129*
Pegasus Players *65*
Playwrights Theatre of New Jersey *264*
Playwrights' Center, The *263*

Scholastic Writing Awards *133*
Stage One: The Louisville Children's Theatre *81*
TheatreVirginia *90*
Vermont Stage Company *93*
Very Special Arts Playwright Discovery Program *140*
Young Playwrights Festival National Playwriting Contest *143*
Young Playwrights Inc. *272*

Index

Remember the two alphabetizing principles used throughout the book: First, entries beginning with a person's name are alphabetized by the first name rather than the surname. However, you can find these entries indexed by both names. Hence you will find the Robert Bone Memorial Playwriting Award under R and B, the Alden B. Dow Creativity Center under A and D and the Helene Wurlitzer Foundation of New Mexico under H and W. Second, regardless of which way "theatre" is spelled in an organization's title, it is alphabetized as if it were spelled "re," not "er."

A

A Contemporary Theatre 5
A. D. Players 5
AATE Unpublished Play Reading Project 239
Abe Newborn Associates 190
Abingdon Theatre Company 161
Academy Theatre 5
Academy Theatre New Play Development Program 161
ACC Residency Program in Asia 197
Acting Company, The 6
Actors Alley 6
Actors Alliance Theatre Company 6
Actors & Playwrights' Initiative 7
Actor's Company of Pennsylvania 7
Actor's Express, The 7
Actors' Gang Theater 8
Actors Theater, The 8
Actors Theatre of Louisville 8, 127
Adamant Program, The 223
Adams Ltd., Bret 191
Adobe Theatre Company 9
AFI Television Writers Summer Workshop 239
Agency, The 190
Agency for the Performing Arts 190
Aguirre Playwrighting Lab, The Isidora 168
Alabama Literary Review 145
Alabama Shakespeare Festival 9
Alabama State Council on the Arts 216
Alan Brodie Representation Ltd. 190
Alaska Native Plays Contest 103
Alaska State Council on the Arts 216
Alcazar Scripts in Progress 161
Alden B. Dow Creativity Center 224

INDEX / 309

Alfred Hodder Fellowship, The *195*
Alley Theatre *9*
Alliance of Los Angeles Playwrights, The *237*
Alliance of Resident Theatres/New York, The *238*
Alliance Theatre Company *9*
Alternate ROOTS *238*
Altos de Chavon *224*
AMAS Musical Theatre, Inc. *10*
Amelia Magazine *145*
American Alliance for Theatre & Education (AATE), The *238*
American Cabaret Theatre *10*
American Conservatory Theater *10*
American Film Institute, The *239*
American Humorist Series *11*
American Indian Community House *239*
American Jewish Theatre *11*
American Music Center *240*
American Music Theater Festival *11*
American Place Theatre, The *11*
American Renaissance Theatre of Dramatic Arts *167*
American Renegade Theatre Company *11*
American Repertory Theatre *12*
American Samoa Council on Culture, Arts and Humanities *216*
American Shorts Contest *103*
American Stage *12*
American Stage Company *12*
American Stage Festival *12*
American Theatre *145, 269, 275*
American Theater and Literature Program Contest *157*
American Theatre of Actors, Inc. *13*
American Translators Association (ATA) *103, 240*
American Translators Association Awards *103*
American Voices Reading Series *39*
American Voices Winter Festival of New Works *39*
American Writing: A Magazine *145*
American-Scandinavian Foundation, The *104, 195*
Anchorage Press *146*
Anchorage Press Theater for Youth Playwriting Award *118*
Anderson Center for the Arts, Mary *231, 256*
Anderson Playwrights Series, The Maxwell *171*
Ann Elmo Agency *190*

Anna Zornio Memorial Children's Theatre Playwriting Award *104*
Annual Blank Theatre Company Young Playwrights Festival, The *104*
Apostle Islands National Lakeshore *224*
Apple Tree Theatre *13*
Aran Press *146*
Arden Theatre Company *13*
Arena Stage *13, 176*
Arizona Commission on the Arts *216*
Arizona Theatre Company *14, 127*
Arkansas Arts Council *216*
Arkansas Repertory Theatre *14*
Arrow Rock Lyceum Theatre *14*
Art Craft Publishing Company *146*
A.R.T./New York *238*
ART Station *14*
Arte Público Press *146*
Artist Development Workshops *94*
Artist Files/Artist Files Online *261*
Artist Trust *195*
Artists Project *197*
Artists Repertory Theatre *15*
Artists-in-Berlin Programme *196*
ArtReach Touring Theatre *15*
Arts at St. Ann's *15*
Arts International *196, 205*
Artsboard *266*
ArtSEARCH *269*
ArtsLink Collaborative Projects *205*
ASCAP (American Society of Composers, Authors and Publishers) *161, 241*
ASCAP Musical Theatre Workshop *161*
ASF Translation Prize *104*
Ashland New Plays Festival *162*
Asian American Arts Alliance *241*
Asian American Arts Calendar *241*
Asian American Arts Organizations in New York & New Jersey *241*
Asian American Arts Resources and Opportunities *241*
Asian American Theater Company *15*
Asian American Theater Company New Plays & Playwrights Development Program *162*
Asian Cultural Council *197*
Asian Pacific American Friends of Center Theatre Group (APAF) Reading Series *170*
Asian Pacific American Journal *146*
Asian Theatre Workshop *170*
A.S.K. Theater Projects *162, 242*
A.S.K. Unpublished Plays Project *242*
Asolo Theatre Company *16*

ASSITEJ/USA (International Association of Theatre for Children 242
Associated Writing Programs, The 243
Association for Theatre in Higher Education 116, 243
Association of Authors' Representatives, The 189
Association of Hispanic Arts, The 243
Association of Independent Video and Filmmakers 244
ATA Chronicle 241
AT&T/East West Players New Voices Playwriting Competition 105
ATHENEWS 243
Atkinson Exchange/Clara Rotter Fellowship, Brooks 260
Atkinson Exchange/Max Weitzenhoffer Fellowship, Brooks 260
Atlanta Bureau of Cultural Affairs 197
Atlantic Center for the Arts 225
Atlantic Theater Company 16
Attic Theatre Centre 16
Attic Theatre Ensemble's One-Act Marathon 105
Audrey Skirball-Kenis Play Collection 147
Audrey Skirball-Kenis Theatre, The 162, 242
Australian Playwrights Exchange 255
Authors League Fund, The 213
AWP Chronicle 243
AWP Official Guide to Writing Programs, The 243

B

B Street Theatre, The 16
Back Stage 276
Bailiwick Repertory 17
Baker's Plays 105, 147
Baker's Plays High School Playwriting Contest 105
Baltimore Theatre Project, Inc. 244
Barbara Hogenson Agency, Inc., The 190
Barksdale Theatre 17
Barrow Group, The 17
Barter Theatre 18
Bartle Playwriting Award, Margaret 123
Bass Play-Rites Festival and Memorial, George Houston 112
Bay Area Playwrights Festival 162
Bay Street Theatre 18
Bellingham Review, The 147
Bennett Fellowship, George 201
Berkeley Repertory Theatre 18

Berkshire Theatre Festival 19
Berman, Boals & Flynn 190
Bernice Cohen Musical Theatre Fund Award 161
Bertha Klausner International Literary Agency 190
Bethel Agency, The 190
Beverly Hills Theatre Guild-Julie Harris Playwright Award 105
Beyond Boundaries National Resource Book 241
Bianchi Kids' Playwriting Festival, Marilyn 32
Biennial Promising Playwright Award 106
Bilingual Foundation of the Arts 19
Billy Rose Theatre Collection, The 261
Birmingham Children's Theatre 19
Black Theatre Connections 244
Black Theatre Directory 244
Black Theatre Network 244
Black Voices 244
Blackburn Prize, The Susan Smith 136
Blacksmyths 170
Blizzard Publishing 147
Bloomsburg Theatre Ensemble 19
Blue Mountain Center 225
BMI (Broadcast Music Incorporated) 163, 245
BMI-Lehman Engel Musical Theatre Workshop 163
BoarsHead: Michigan Public Theater 20
Bonderman IUPUI Playwriting Competition for Young Audiences, Waldo M. and Grace C. 140
Bone Memorial Playwriting Award, Robert 132
Borderlands Theater 20
Brave New Works 86
Brave New Workshop & Instant Theatre Company 32
Bret Adams Ltd. 191
Bristol Riverside Theatre 20
British American Arts Association 245
Broadway on Sunset 245
Broadway Play Publishing, Inc. 148
Broadway Tomorrow 163
Brodie Representation Ltd., Alan 190
Brody Arts Fund 198
Brooks Atkinson Exchange/Clara Rotter Fellowship 260
Brooks Atkinson Exchange/Max Weitzenhoffer Fellowship 260
Brown Theatre Company, Clarence 25
BTN News 244
Buchwald & Associates, Don 191

Bunting Fellowship Program *198*
Bush Artist Fellowships *198*
Byrdcliffe Art Colony *225*

C

CAC Playwright's Unit *163*
California Arts Council *216*
California Playwrights Competition *106*
California Repertory Company *21*
California Theatre Center *21*
California Young Playwrights Contest *106*
Callaloo *148*
Callboard *268*
Camargo Foundation *226*
Capital Repertory Company *21*
Carmel Performing Arts Festival *21*
Carnegie Fund for Authors *214*
Carnegie Mellon Drama's Showcase of New Plays *163*
Carolina Playwrights Center *246*
Cast Theatre, The *22*
Castillo Theatre *22*
Centenary Stage Company *185*
Center for Advanced Study in Theatre Arts (CASTA) *251*
Center Stage *22*
Centre Stage–South Carolina! *23*
Center Theater *106*
Center Theater Ensemble *22*
Center Theater International Playwrighting Contest *106*
Centerpieces *55*
CENTERSTAGE *267*
Centrum Artist-in-Residency Program *226*
Chambers Playwriting Award, Jane *116*
Changing Scene, The *23*
Chapbook *109*
Charlotte Festival/New Plays in America *164*
Charlotte Repertory Theatre *23, 164*
Chateau de Lesvault *226*
Cheltenham Center for the Arts *24*
Chesterfield Film Company/Writer's Film Project, The *164*
Chicago Alliance for Playwrights (CAP) *246*
Chicago Dramatists Workshop *246*
Chicago Young Playwrights Festival *65*
Chicano/Latino Literary Contest *107*
Chilcote Award, Katherine and Lee *117*
Children's Theatre Company, The *24*
Childsplay *24*
Christian Drama Magazine *128*

Cincinnati Playhouse in the Park *25, 122*
Cintas *196*
Circle in the Square *25*
City Theatre Company *25*
Clarence Brown Theatre Company *25*
Clark Publications, I. E. *151*
Classic Stage Company (CSC) *26*
Clauder Competition for Excellence in Playwriting *107*
Cleveland Play House, The *26, 175*
Cleveland Public Theatre *26, 117*
Coconut Grove Playhouse *27*
Coe College New Works for the Stage Competition *107*
Cohen Musical Theatre Fund Award, Bernice *161*
COLAB (Collaboration Laboratory) New Play Program *80*
Collages & Bricolages *148*
Colony Studio Theatre, The *27*
Colorado Council on the Arts *216*
Colorado Dramatists *247*
Colorado Theatre Guide, The *247*
Columbus Screenplay Discovery Awards *108*
Commissioning Music/USA *256*
Commonweal Theatre Company *27*
Commonwealth Council for Arts and Culture (Northern Marianas Islands) *220*
Composer/Choreographer Project *256*
Composer/Librettist Studio *58*
Coney Island, USA *27*
Confrontation *148*
Connecticut Commission on the Arts *217*
Connections *108*
Contemporary American Theater Festival *28*
Contemporary Arts Center *163*
Contemporary Drama Service *149*
Contemporary Theatre, A *5*
Cornerstone Dramaturgy and Development Project *164*
Cornerstone Theater Company *28*
Corporation for Public Broadcasting *247*
Coterie Theatre, The *28*
Council for International Exchange of Scholars (CIES) *200*
Council of Literary Magazines and Presses *144*
Court Theatre *28*
CrazyQuilt Quarterly *149*
Cross Cultural Institute of Theater Art Studies *48*
Crossroads Theatre Company *29*

312 / INDEX

Cumberland County Playhouse 29
Cunningham Prize for Playwriting, The 108

D

Dale Wasserman Drama Award 108
Dallas Children's Theater 29
Dallas Theater Center 30
David James Ellis Memorial Award 109
Dayton Playhouse FutureFest 109
Deep South Writers Conference 109
Delaware Division of the Arts 217
Delaware Theatre Company 30, 108
Dell'Arte Players Company 30
Denver Center Theatre Company 30, 112, 165
Denver Center Theatre Company U S WEST Theatre Fest 165
Descant 149
Detroit Repertory Theatre 31
Diamond Head Theatre Originals 165
Directors Company, The 167
Directory of Hispanic Talent 251
Directory of Literary Magazines 144
Directory of Los Angeles Playwright Groups 242
Discovery Series 35
Disney Studios Fellowship Program, The Walt 212
Dissertations Concerning Black Theatre: 1900–1994 244
District of Columbia (DC) Commission on the Arts and Humanities 217
Dixon Place 31
Djerassi Resident Artists Program 227
Do Gooder Productions, Inc. 31
Dobama Theatre 32
Dobie-Paisano Fellowship 199
Don and Gee Nicholl Fellowships in Screenwriting, The 199
Don Buchwald & Associates 191
Dorland Mountain Arts Colony 227
Dorothy Silver Playwriting Competition 110
Dorset Colony for Writers 227
Dorset Theatre Festival 32
Douglass Creative Arts Center Writing Workshops, Frederick 166
Dow Creativity Center, Alden B. 224
Drama League New Directors–New Works Series 165
Drama League of New York, The 165
Drama School Summerstages 76

Dramafest 2000 110
Dramarama 110
Dramarama Long Play Contest 110
Dramarama Short Play Contest 110
Dramatic Action 95
Dramatic Publishing Company, The 149, 191
Dramatics Magazine 150
Dramatists Guild, The 247
Dramatists Guild Fund, The 214
Dramatists Guild Newsletter, The 248
Dramatists Guild Quarterly, The 248
Dramatists Guild Resource Directory, The 248
Dramatists Play Service 150
Drew Theater, John 47
Drury College One-Act Play Competition 111
Dubuque Fine Arts Players National One-Act Playwriting Contest 111
Dudley Riggs Instant Theatre Company 32
Dyke Drama Award 255

E

Earth's Daughters 150
East West Players 33, 105
Edwards Deaf Playwrights Competition, Sam 133
El Teatro Campesino 33
el telarañazo 253
Eldridge Publishing Company 150
Electronic Arts Grant Program 199
Elisabeth Marton Agency 191
Elliott Exchange, Sumner Locke 260
Ellis Memorial Award, David James 109
Elmo Agency, Ann 190
Emelin Theatre for the Performing Arts, The 33
Emerging Playwright Award 111
Empty Space Theatre, The 34
En Garde Arts 34
Encore Performance Publishing 128, 151
Engel Musical Theatre Workshop, The Lehman 169
Ensemble Studio Theatre 34
Ensemble Theatre, The 34
Ensemble Theatre of Cincinnati 35
Epstein Playwriting Award, Lawrence S. 121
Essentials of a Theatre Curriculum 268
Eudora Welty New Play Series 60
Eureka Theatre Company 35
Extended Collaboration Grants 209

F

Falstaff Presents 35
Famous Door Theatre Company 165
FastForward 16
Feedback Theatrebooks 278
Fendrich Memorial Playwriting Contest, Shubert 134
Festival of Emerging American Theatre (FEAT) Competition, The 111
Festival of Firsts Playwriting Competition 112
Festival of New American Plays 24
Field, The 248
Fielday 248
Fieldwork 248
Fifi Oscard Associates 191
5th Annual Women at the Door Staged Reading Series 165
Filmmaker 251
First Floor Theatre 11
First Stage 54, 166, 249
First Stage Milwaukee 35
First Stage Newsletter 249
Fishbein Ltd., Freida 191
Flanagan Memorial Creative Persons Center, William 235
Fleetwood Stage 36
Flora Roberts 191
Florida Division of Cultural Affairs 217
Florida Playwrights Festival 36
Florida Studio Theatre 36, 103
Flying Solo and Friends Festival 8
Foothill Theatre Company, The 36
Ford's Theatre 37
42nd Street Workshop, The 166
Foundation Center, The 249
Foundation Directory, The 249
Foundation for Independent Video and Film (FIVF) 244
Foundation Grants Index, The 249
Foundation Grants to Individuals 249
Fountain Theatre, The 37
Fourth Freedom Forum Playwriting Award, The 118
Francesca Primus Prize, The 112
Frank McClure One-Act Play Award 145
Frank Silvera Writers' Workshop, The 166
Frederick Douglass Creative Arts Center Writing Workshops 166
Free Play Reading Series and Playwright Development Workshop 167
Free Street Programs 37
Freedman Dramatic Agency, Robert A. 192
Freedom Fest 38
Freedom Repertory Theatre 37
Freedom Theatre 37
Freedom-to-Write 263
Freelance Press 151
Freida Fishbein, Ltd. 191
French, Samuel 156, 192
Fresh Ink Series 44
Frontera @ Hyde Park Theatre 38
Fulbright Scholar Awards 200
Fulton Theatre Company 7
Fund for New American Plays 200
Fund for U.S. Artists at International Festivals and Exhibitions 196
Funding Guide for Independent Artists 248

G

GALA Hispanic Theatre 38
Galantiere Literary Translation Prize, Lewis 103
GAP (Grants for Artist Projects) 195
Gassner Memorial Playwriting Award, John 117
Geer Theatricum Botanicum, Will 97
Gell Writers Center, The 228
Genesis Festival: A Celebration of New Voices in African American Theatre 29
Genesius Guild Programs for the Development of New Plays & Musicals, The 167
George Bennett Fellowship 201
George Hawkins Playwriting Contest 112
George Houston Bass Play-Rites Festival and Memorial Award 112
George R. Kernodle Playwriting Contest 113
George Street Playhouse 38
Georgia Council for the Arts 217
Georgia Repertory Theatre 39
German Academic Exchange Service (DAAD) 196
German Literary Translation Prize 103
Germinal Stage Denver 39
Gersh Agency, The 191
GeVa Theatre 39
Gilman and Gonzalez-Falla Theatre Foundation Musical Theatre Award 113
Gilmore Creek Playwriting Competition 113
Glines, The 39
Gone With The Field Guide 249
Goodman Theatre 40

Goodspeed Opera House 40
Goshen College Peace Playwriting
   Contest 114
Graham Agency 191
Grants and Awards Available to American
   Writers 263
Great American History Theatre 40
Great Plains Play Contest 114
Great Platte River Playwrights' Festival 114
Green Playwrights Prize, Paul 130
Greensboro Playwrights' Forum 250
Gregory Kolovakos Award, The 114
Gretna Theatre 40
Group: Seattle's Multicultural Theatre,
   The 41
Guam Council on the Arts & Humanities
   Agency 217
Guber Playwrights' Lab, Lee 46
Guggenheim Memorial Foundation, John
   Simon 201
Gurman Agency, The Susan 193
Guthrie Centre, The Tyrone 234
Guthrie Theater, The 41

H

Hambidge Center for Creative Arts and
   Sciences, The 228
Handbook for Literary Translators, A 276
Hansberry Playwriting Award, The
   Lorraine 119
Harbor Theatre Lab, The 250
Harden-Curtis Associates 191
Harold Morton Landon Translation
   Award 115
Harold Prince Musical Theatre
   Program 167
Harris Agency 191
Hartford Stage Company 41
Hatch-Billops Collection 250
Hawkins Playwriting Contest, George 112
Hawthornden Castle International Retreat
   for Writers 228
Headlands Center for the Arts 229
Healing Guide 249
Hedgebrook 229
Hedgerow Horizons 168
Hedgerow Theatre 41
Heideman Award 127
Helen Merrill 192
Helene Wurlitzer Foundation of New
   Mexico 229
Henrico Theatre Company One-Act
   Playwriting Competition 115

Heuer Publishing Company 151
Hip Pocket Theatre 42
Hippodrome State Theatre, The 42
Hispanic Arts News 243
Hispanic Organization of Latin Actors
   (HOLA) 251
Hispanic Playwrights Project 168
Hodder Fellowship, The Alfred 195
Hogenson Agency, Inc., The Barbara 190
Hollywood Scriptwriter 276
Honolulu Theatre for Youth 42
Horizon Theatre Company 43
Horse Cave Theatre 43
Hot Seats 238
HRC's Annual Playwriting Contest 115
Human Race Theatre Company, The 43
Humor Hatchery, The 11
Huntington Theatre Company 43

I

I. E. Clark Publications 151
I.T.C. Playwrights Project 15
Idaho Commission on the Arts 217
Illinois Arts Council 217
Illinois Theatre Center 44
Illusion Theater 44
impact! 265
In Their Own Words: Contemporary
   American Playwrights 275
Independent, The 244
Independent Feature Project 251
Independent Film & Video Monthly,
   The 244
Indiana Arts Commission 218
Indiana Repertory Theatre 44
Individual's Guide to Grants, The 276
Inner City Cultural Center
   Competition 115
Inroads 197
Institute for Contemporary East European
   and Slavic Drama and Theatre 251
Institute of International Education 201
Institute of Outdoor Drama 252
Institute of Puerto Rican Culture 220
INTAR Hispanic American Arts Center 45
InterAct Theatre Company 45
International Center for Women
   Playwrights 252
International Creative Collaboration 203
International Creative Collaborations 256
International Creative Management 192
International Directory of Little Magazines
   and Small Presses 144

INDEX / 315

International Theatre Institute of the United States (ITI/US) 252
International Women Playwrights Conference 252
International Women's Writing Guild, The 253
Intiman Theatre 45
Into Print: Guides to the Writing Life 277
Inventing the Future 242
Invisible Theatre 45
Iowa Arts Council 218
Irondale Ensemble Project 46
Isidora Aguirre Playwrighting Lab, The 168
Isle Royale National Park Artist-in-Residence 229
Isolated Acts 72
ITI International Theatre Collection 253
ITI/US 252

J

Jackie White Memorial National Children's Playwriting Contest 116
James D. Phelan Award in Literature 116
James H. Wilson Full-Length Play Award 109
James Thurber Writer-in-Residence, The 230
Jane Chambers Playwriting Award 116
Japan Foundation, The 201
Japan-United States Arts Program 197
Jerome Playwright-in-Residence Fellowships 208
Jewel Box Theatre Playwrighting Award 117
Jewish Ensemble Theatre 46
Jewish Repertory Theatre 46
John Drew Theater 47
John Gassner Memorial Playwriting Award 117
John Simon Guggenheim Memorial Foundation 201
John Steinbeck Writer's Room, The 230
Johnson Richards Exchange, Mary Lea 260
Jomandi Productions 47
Jory Copying Assistance Program, The 240
Journal, The 272
Joyce Ketay Agency, The 192
Jungle Theater 47

K

Kalliope, A Journal of Women's Art 152
Kansas Arts Commission 218
Katherine and Lee Chilcote Award 117
KC/ACTF Musical Theater Award, The 118
Kelly Adopt-a-Playwright Program, Owen 32
Kennedy Center American College Theater Festival: Michael Kanin Playwriting Awards Program 118
Kennedy Center–Youth and Family Programs, The 173
Kentucky Arts Council 218
Kenyon Review, The 152
Kernodle Playwriting Contest, George R. 113
Ketay Agency, The Joyce 192
Key West Theatre Festival 169
Klausner International Literary Agency, Bertha 190
Kleban Award, The 202
Klein Playwriting Award, The Marc A. 123
Kolovakos Award, The Gregory 114
Kopaloff Company, The 192
Korf Playwriting Awards, The Lee 121
Kumu Kahua Playwriting Contest 120

L

L. A. Theatre Works 47
L. Arnold Weissberger Playwriting Competition 120
L.A. Black Playwrights 169
La Jolla Playhouse 48
La MaMa Experimental Theater Club 48
La Nueva Ola 251
la telaraña 253
Lab Program, The 94
Laguna Playhouse 48
Lamb's Players Theatre 49
Lamia Ink! 120, 152
Lamia Ink! International One-Page Play Competition 120
Landon Translation Award, Harold Morton 115
Lantz Agency 192
Latin American Theater Artists 253
Latino Theatre Initiative 170
Lawrence S. Epstein Playwriting Award 121
League of Chicago Theatres/League of Chicago Theatres Foundation 254

League of Professional Theatre Women/New York 254
Lee Guber Playwrights' Lab 46
Lee Korf Playwriting Awards, The 121
Lee Reynolds Award 254
Lehman Engel Musical Theatre Workshop, The 169
Leighton Studios for Independent Residencies 230
Lewis Galantiere Literary Translation Prize 103
Lillenas Drama Resources 152
Lincoln Center Theater 49
LIPP (Lesbian-Identified Performance Project) 255
Literary Agents: A Writer's Guide 277
Literary Managers and Dramaturgs of the Americas 255
Literary Market Place 277
Little Theatre of Alexandria National One-Act Playwriting Competition, The 121
Live Bait Theatrical Company 49
Live Oak Theatre 49, 121
Live Oak Theatre's Harvest Festival of New American Plays 121
Living Theatre, The 50
LMDA Review 255
LMDA Script Exchange 255
Loft Fest '98—Festival of Shorts, The 169
Loft Production Company, The 50
Lois and Richard Rosenthal New Play Prize 122
Long Wharf Theatre 50, 170
Long Wharf Theatre Stage II Workshops 170
Lorraine Hansberry Playwriting Award, The 119
Los Angeles Designers' Theatre Commissions 122
Louisiana Division of the Arts 218
Love Creek Annual Short Play Festival 122
Love Creek Productions 122
Luminous Visions 255

M

Mabou Mines 51
MacDowell Colony, The 231
Mad River Theater Works 51
Madison Repertory Theatre 51
Magic Theatre 51, 163
Maine Arts Commission 218
Management Memo 268

Manhattan Playwrights Unit 170
Manhattan Theatre Club 52, 202
Manhattan Theatre Club Playwriting Fellowships 202
Many Voices Multicultural Collaboration Grants 208
Many Voices Playwriting Residency Awards 208
Marc A. Klein Playwriting Award, The 123
Margaret Bartle Playwriting Award 123
Marilyn Bianchi Kids' Playwriting Festival 32
Marin Theatre Company 52
Mark Taper Forum 52, 170
Mark Taper Forum Developmental Programs 170
Market Insight...for Playwrights 277
Marton Agency, Elisabeth 191
Marvin Taylor Playwriting Award 123
Mary Anderson Center for the Arts 231, 256
Mary Lea Johnson Richards Exchange 260
Mary Roberts Rinehart Awards, The 202
Maryland State Arts Council 218
Massachusetts Cultural Council 218
Mature Women Scholarship Award 203
Maxim Mazumdar New Play Competition 123
Maxwell Anderson Playwrights Series, The 171
Mayor's Fellowships in the Arts 197
Mazumdar New Play Competition, Maxim 123
MCC Theater 53
McCarter Theatre Center for the Performing Arts 53
McClure One-Act Play Award, Frank 145
McKnight Advancement Grants 208
McKnight Fellowships 209
McKnight Interdisciplinary Fellowship Grant, The 203
McLaren Memorial Comedy Playwriting Competition 124
Meadow Brook Theatre 53
Meet The Composer 256
Meet The Composer Grant Programs 203
  Arts Endowment Commissioning Music/USA 204
  International Creative Collaboration 203
  New Residencies 204
Member Directory 238
Men's Stories Short Play Festival 8
Merrill, Helen 192
Merrimack Repertory Theatre 53

Merry-Go-Round Playhouse 54
Metro Theater Company 54
MetroStage 54
Michigan Council for the Arts & Cultural Affairs 218
Midwest Radio Theatre Workshop 126, 171, 256
Midwest Theatre Network Original Play Competition/Rochester Playwright Festival 124
Midwestern Playwrights Festival 124
Mildred and Albert Panowski Playwriting Award 125
Mill Mountain Theatre 54, 125
Mill Mountain Theatre New Play Competition: The Norfolk Southern Festival of New Works 125
Millay Colony for the Arts, The 231
Milwaukee Chamber Theatre 55
Milwaukee Public Theatre 55
Milwaukee Repertory Theater 55
Minnesota Fellowship 203
Minnesota State Arts Board 219
Mint Theater Company 56
Mississippi Arts Commission 219
Missouri Arts Council 219
Missouri Association of Playwrights 257
Missouri Repertory Theatre 56
Mixed Blood Theatre Company 56, 141
Mixed Blood Versus America 141
Model Contracts for Independent Contractors: Sample Provisions 270
Mondays at Three 61
Montana Arts Council 219
Montana Repertory Theatre, The 56
Morris Agency, William 193
Morton R. Sarett National Playwriting Competition 125
Moving Arts 57
Moving Arts Premiere One-Act Competition 125
MRTW Script Contest 126
Music, Dance & Theater Scholarships 277
Music-Theatre Group 57
Musical Theatre Works 172

N

Nantucket Playwrights Retreat 232
Nantucket Short Play Festival and Competition 126
National Academy of Songwriters 257
National AIDS Fund Award for Playwriting, The 119
National Alliance for Musical Theatre 257
National Center for Film and Video Preservation 239
National Children's Theatre Festival 126
National Endowment for the Arts
    International Program 205
    Literature Program 206
National Endowment for the Humanities
    Public Programs: Humanities Projects in Media 206
    Research and Education Programs: Collaborative Research 206
National Foundation for Jewish Culture, The 258
National Hispanic Playwriting Contest 127
National League of American Pen Women 203
National League of American Pen Women, Inc., The 258
National McKnight Interdisciplinary Fellow in Residence 203
National Music Theater Conference 172
National Music Theater Network 172
National Play Award 127
National Playwrights Conference 172
National Playwrights Directory, The 278
National Playwrights Festival 36
National Public Radio 259
National Student Playwriting Award, The 119
National Ten-Minute Play Contest 127
National Theatre Artist Residency Program 210
National Theatre of the Deaf 57
National Theatre Workshop of the Handicapped 259
Native Americans in the Arts 240
Nautilus Music-Theater 57
Nebraska Arts Council 219
Nebraska Repertory Theatre 58
Nebraska Theatre Caravan 58
NETC News 260
Network 253
Nevada State Council on the Arts 219
New American Comedy (NAC) Festival 127
New American Theater 58
New Century Voices 73
New Christian Plays Award 128
New Dramatists 120, 259
New Dramaturgs 255
New England Theatre Conference 260
New England Theatre Journal 260
New Federal Theatre 59
New Georges 260

318 / INDEX

New Group, The 59
New Hampshire State Council on the Arts 219
New Harmony Project Laboratory, The 173
New Jersey Shakespeare Festival 59
New Jersey State Council on the Arts 219
New Jersey Young Playwrights Program 265
New Line Theatre Musical Theatre Competition 128
New Mexico Arts Division 219
New Music for Schools 256
New Music-Theater Ensemble 57
New Play Catalog 250
New Play Commissions in Jewish Theatre 207
New Play Staged Readings Series 97
New Play Works 64
New Plays 153
New Plays in Process Project 77
New Playwrights Foundation 260
New Professional Theatre Writers Festival 128
New Repertory Theatre 59
New Stage Theatre 60
NEW THEATRE 58
New Tuners Theatre 60
New Visions/New Voices 173
New Voices at Intiman 45
New Voices for the Theatre 90
New Voices/New Plays 48
New Voices Play Development Program 173
New Women Playwright's Contest 129
New Work Festival 171
New Works at the Vineyard 94
New Works for a New World 174
New York City High School Playwriting Contest 129
New York Foundation for the Arts 174, 207, 215
New York Foundation for the Arts Artists' Fellowships 207
New York Foundation for the Arts—Artists in Residence Program 232
New York Foundation for the Arts Sponsorship Program 174
New York Mills Arts Retreat 232
New York Public Library for the Performing Arts, The 261
New York Stage and Film 60
New York State Council on the Arts 215, 220
New York State Theatre Institute 60
New York Theatre Workshop 61
New Zealand Theatrescripts 263
Newborn Associates, Abe 190
NewGate Theatre New Play Development 174
Next Stage, The 175, 262
Next Theatre Company 61
Nicholl Fellowships in Screenwriting, The Don and Gee 199
Nolan One-Act Play Award, Paul T. 109
Non-Traditional Casting Project 261
None of the Above Theatre Company 61
Noon Preview 267
Norcroft 233
North Carolina Arts Council 220
North Carolina New Play Project Contest 250
North Dakota Council on the Arts 220
Northlight Theatre 62
Northwest Playwrights Guild 261
Novel Stages 62
NPR Playhouse 259
Nueva Ola, La 251
Nuevo L.A. Chicano TheatreWorks 265
NYC Composers AIDS Fund 256
NYSCA 215

O

Odyssey Theatre Ensemble 62
Off-Off Broadway Original Short Play Festival 175
Oglebay Institute Towngate Theatre Playwriting Contest 129
Ohio Arts Council 220
Oklahoma Arts Council 220
Old Globe Theatre 62
Old Pueblo Playwrights 175
Oldcastle Theatre Company 63
OLLANTAY Center for the Arts 262
OLLANTAY Theater Magazine 262
Olney Theatre Center for the Arts 63
Omaha Theater Company for Young People 63
On the Edge Series 78
On the Purple Circuit 266
On Writing 271
One Acts in Performance 176
One Night Stand Series 48
One World Premiere 32
O'Neill Theater Center 172, 278
Ontological-Hysteric Theater 63
Open Eye Theater, The 64
Opening Night Calendar 269

INDEX / 319

OPERA America 262
Opportunities in New Music 240
Oral History Project 254
Oregon Arts Commission 220
Oregon Shakespeare Festival 64
Organic Theater Company 64
Organic Touchstone Company 64
Oscard Associates, Fifi 191
Other Voices Project 171
Owen Kelly Adopt-a-Playwright Program 32

P

Pacific Northwest Writers Conference Literary Contest 129
Pacific Review 153
Pacific-Asia Exchange Program 242
PAJ Books 153
Pan Asian Repertory Theatre 64
Panowski Playwriting Award, Mildred and Albert 125
Parabasis 242
Paramuse Artists Associates 192
Parness Agency, The 192
Pasadena Playhouse, The 65
Paul Green Playwrights Prize 130
Paul T. Nolan One-Act Play Award 109
PBS Packaging & Technical Guidelines 266
Pegasus Players 65
Pegasus Theatre 65
PEN American Center 114, 130, 132, 214, 263, 276
PEN Center USA West Literary Awards 130
PEN Fund for Writers & Editors with AIDS 214
PEN Prison Writing Information Bulletin, The 263
Pen Woman, The 258
PEN Writers Fund 214
PEN–Book-of-the-Month Club Translation Prize 130
Pendragon Theatre 65
Penguin Repertory Company 66
Pennsylvania Council on the Arts 220
Pennsylvania Shakespeare Festival 66
Penobscot Theatre Company 66
Penumbra Theatre Company, The 66, 164
People's Light and Theatre Company, The 67
Peregrine Whittlesey Agency 192
Performance Zone Festival 248
Performing Arts Journal 153

Performing for Los Angeles Youth 52
Perishable Theatre Women's Playwriting Festival 130
Perseverance Theatre 67
Pevner, Inc., Stephen 193
Pew Fellowships in the Arts 207
Phelan Award in Literature, James D. 116
Philadelphia Theatre Company 67
Phoenix Theatre 67
Phoenix Theatre, The 68, 111
Pickering Award for Playwriting, Robert J. 132
Pilgrim Project 207
Ping Chong & Company 68
Pioneer Drama Service 134, 153
Pioneer Theatre Company 68
Pirate Playhouse—Island Theatre 68
Pittsburgh Public Theater 69
Play with Your Food 95
Players Press 154
Playformers 176
Playhouse America! 278
Playhouse on the Square 69, 131
Playhouse on the Square New Play Competition 131
PlayLabs 176
PlayMakers Repertory Company 69
Playmarket 263
Playmarket Directory of New Zealand Plays and Playwrights, The 263
PlayQuest 176
Plays for Consideration 242
Plays on Tape 154
Plays, The Drama Magazine for Young People 154
Plays-in-Progress Festivals of New Works 177
Playtime Series 90
PlayWorks Festival 177
Playwrights' Center, The 176, 208, 263
Playwrights' Center Grant Programs, The 208
Playwrights' Center of San Francisco, The 110
Playwrights' Center of San Francisco Staged Readings 177
Playwright's Companion, The 278
Playwrights First Award 131
Playwrights Forum 178
Playwrights Foundation, The 162, 264
Playwrights Harbor 250
Playwrights Horizons 69
Playwrights' Kitchen Ensemble 178
Playwrights' Platform 178
Playwrights' Preview Productions 111, 179

Playwrights' Project, The *132, 264*
Playwrights' Stage *56*
Playwrights' Theater of Denton Playwriting Competition *131*
Playwrights Theatre of New Jersey *264*
Playwrights Theatre of New Jersey New Play Development Program *179*
Playwrights Unit *59, 71*
Playwrights Week *179*
Playwriting Center of Theater Emory, The *86*
Plaza de la Raza *265*
Plowshares Theatre Company *173*
Poems & Plays *155*
Poets & Writers *277, 278, 280*
Poets & Writers Magazine *278*
Poggioli Award, Renato *132*
Polish Plays in Translation *251*
Pope Theatre Company *70*
Portland Center Stage *70*
Portland Repertory Theatre *70*
Portland Stage Company *70*
Primary Stages Company *71, 179*
Primus Prize, The Francesca *112*
Prince Musical Theatre Program, Harold *167*
Princess Grace Awards: Playwright Fellowship *209*
Prism International *155*
Production Diaries *255*
Production Notebooks: Theatre in Process, Volume One, The *275*
Professional Association of Canadian Theatres/PACT Communications Centre *265*
Professional Playscript Format Guidelines and Sample *278*
Provincetown Arts/Provincetown Arts Press *155*
Public Broadcasting Service *266*
Public Theater/New York Shakespeare Festival, The *71*
Puerto Rican Traveling Theatre Playwrights' Workshop *180*
Purple Circuit, The *266*
Purple Circuit Directory, The *266*
Purple Rose Theatre Company, The *71*

Q

QRL Poetry Series Awards *131*

R

Radio Theatre Series for New Plays *47*
Rag Mag *155*
Ragdale Foundation *233*
Readers Theater *94*
Red Eye *72*
Rehearsal and Performance Space Guide *238*
Remembrance Through the Performing Arts New Play Development *180*
Renato Poggioli Award *132*
Repertorio Español *72*
Repertory Theatre of St. Louis, The *72*
Resource Guides on Actors with Disabilities *261*
Resource Publications, Inc. *156*
Reva Shiner Full-Length Play Contest *132*
Reynolds Award, Lee *254*
Rhode Island State Council on the Arts *221*
Richard Rodgers Awards, The *180*
Richards Exchange, Mary Lea Johnson *260*
Riggs Instant Theatre Company, Dudley *32*
Rinehart Awards, The Mary Robert *202*
Riverside Theatre (FL) *72*
Riverside Theatre (IA) *73*
Road Company, The *73*
Roadside Theater *73*
Roadworks Productions *73*
Robert A. Freedman Dramatic Agency *192*
Robert Bone Memorial Playwriting Award *132*
Robert J. Pickering Award for Playwriting Excellence *132*
Roberts Award, Summerfield G. *136*
Roberts Company, The *192*
Roberts, Flora *191*
Rockford Review *156*
Rodgers Awards, The Richard *180*
Rose Theatre Collection, The Billy *261*
Rosenstone/Wender *192*
Rosenthal New Play Prize, Lois and Richard *122*
Round House Theatre *74*

S

Sacramento Theatre Company *74*
Salt Lake Acting Company, The *74*
Sam Edwards Deaf Playwrights Competition *133*
Samuel French *156, 192*

INDEX / 321

San Diego Repertory Theatre 75
San Jose Repertory Theatre 75
Santa Fe Stages 75
Santa Monica Playhouse 75
Sarasota Festival of New Plays 36
Sarett National Playwriting Competition, Morton R. 125
Scandinavian Review 104
Scholastic Writing Awards 133
Schoolhouse, The 180
Schulman Literary Agency, Susan 193
Script 262
Scripteasers, The 181
Scripts and Scribbles 156
ScriptShare 259
Scriptwriters Network, The 266
Seacoast Repertory Theatre 76
Seaside Music Theater 76
Seattle Children's Theatre 76
Seattle Repertory Theatre 77
Second Stage Theatre 77
Self-Production Guide 248
Senior Citizens Ensemble 43
7 Stages 77
Shakespeare & Company 77
Shakespeare Santa Cruz 78
Shakespeare Theatre, The 78
Shenandoah International Playwrights Retreat 181
Shiner Full-Length Play Contest, Reva 132
Short Grain Contest 133
Short Play Awards Program, The 119
Shubert Fendrich Memorial Playwriting Contest 134
Shukat Company, Ltd. 193
Siena College International Playwrights Competition 134
Signature Theatre 78
Signature Theatre Company, Inc. 79
Silver Playwriting Competition, Dorothy 110
Silvera Writers' Workshop, The Frank 166
singular productions 79
Sinister Wisdom 157
Skirball-Kenis Play Collection, Audrey 147
Skirball-Kenis Theatre, The Audrey 162, 242
Slavic and East European Performance: Drama, Theatre, Film 251
Smith and Kraus 157
Snug Harbor Cultural Center 233
Society Hill Playhouse 79
Soho Repertory Theatre 79
SongBank 257
Songwriter's Market 279
Songwriters Guild of America, The 267
Songwriters Musepaper 257
Source Theatre Company 80, 134
Source Theatre Company 1997 Literary Prize 134
Sources of Funding 268
Sources of Publicity 268
South Carolina Arts Commission 221
South Carolina Playwrights' Festival 135
South Coast Repertory 80, 168
South Dakota Arts Council 221
South Florida Writers Contest 135
Southeastern Theatre Conference New Play Project 135
Southern Appalachian Playwrights' Conference 181
Southern Playwrights Competition 135
Southern Writers' Project 9
Soviet Plays in Translation 251
Space Chase Guide to New and Lesser Known Performance Opportunities 248
Spokane Interplayers Ensemble 80
St. Louis Black Repertory Company 81
S.T.A.G.E. (Society for Theatrical Artists' Guidance and Enhancement) 267
Stage Directions Magazine 279
STAGE of the Art 239
Stage One: The Louisville Children's Theatre 81
Stage West (TX) 81
Stage Writers Handbook: A Complete Business Guide for Playwrights, Composers, Lyricists and Librettists 269, 279
STAGES 67, 78, 81
Stages Festival of New Plays 267
Stages Repertory Theatre 182
StageWest (MA) 82
Stamford Theatre Works 82
State Foundation on Culture and the Arts (Hawaii) 217
Steinbeck Writer's Room, The John 230
Stephen Pevner, Inc. 193
Steppenwolf Theatre Company 82
Stet Magazine 157
Strawdog Theatre Company 83
Studio Arena Theatre 83
STUDIO for Creative Inquiry 233
Studio Theatre, The 83
Summerfield G. Roberts Award 136
SummerNITE, New Play Studio 182
Sumner Locke Elliott Exchange 260
Sun & Moon Press 157
Sundance Institute Feature Film Program, The 182

Sundance Theatre Laboratory, The *183*
Susan Gurman Agency, The *193*
Susan Schulman Literary Agency *193*
Susan Smith Blackburn Prize, The *136*
Swine Palace Productions *83*
SWTA Annual New Play Contest *136*
Syracuse Stage *84*

T

Tacoma Actors Guild *84*
TADA! *84*
TADA! Spring Staged Reading Series/New Play Project *136*
TAKE A GROWNUP TO THE THEATER! *272*
Tantleff Office, The *193*
Taper Forum Developmental Programs, Mark *170*
Taper Forum, Mark *52, 170*
TAPLINE *268*
Taylor Playwriting Award, Marvin *123*
TCG *145, 209, 268, 275, 279, 280*
TCG Grant Programs *209*
TEACHING ON YOUR FEET! *272*
Teatro Campesino, El *33*
Technical Assistance and Regrant Initiative (TARI) *241*
Teen Ensemble *43*
telaraña, la *253*
Television Writers Summer Workshop *239*
Ten-Minute Musicals Project, The *183*
Ten-Minute Play Festival *71*
Tennessee Arts Commission *221*
Tennessee Chapbook Prize *155*
Tennessee Repertory Theatre *85*
Tennessee Williams/New Orleans Literary Festival One-Act Competition *137*
Texas Commission on the Arts *221*
Texas Playwrights Festival *182*
Thalia Spanish Theatre *85*
Theater *158*
Theatre Artists Workshop of Westport *183*
Theatre Association of Pennsylvania (TAP) *267*
Theater at Lime Kiln *85, 137*
Theater at Lime Kiln Regional Playwriting Contest *137*
Theater at Monmouth, The *85*
Theatre Bay Area *268*
Theater by the Blind *86*
Theatre Communications Group *145, 209, 268, 275, 280*

Theatre Conspiracy Annual New Play Contest *137*
Theatre de la Jeune Lune *86*
Theatre Directory *269, 279*
Theatre Directory of the Bay Area *268*
Theater Emory *86*
Theatre for a New Audience *86*
Theater for the New City *87*
Theatre for Young Audiences Today *242*
Theatre IV *87*
Theatre Gael *87*
Theatre in the Square *88*
Theatre Journal *243*
Theatre LA *269*
Theatre LA News *269*
Theatre Listing, The *266*
Theatre Memphis New Play Competition *138*
Theatre Museum, The *269*
Theater of the First Amendment *88*
Theatre on Film and Tape (TOFT), The *261*
Theatre on the Square *88*
Theatre Outlet, The *88*
Theatre Profiles *269, 280*
Theatre Project Newsletter *244*
Theatre Rhinoceros *89*
Theatre Southwest *136*
Theatre Three *89*
Theatre Three, Inc. *89*
Theatre Topics *243*
Theatre West *89*
Theatre X *90*
TheatreForum *158*
Theatre-Studio Inc., The *90*
Theatre-Studio Playtime Series, The *184*
TheatreVirginia *90*
TheaterWorks *90*
TheatreWorks *91*
Theatreworks/USA *91, 184*
Theatreworks/USA Commissioning Program *184*
Theatrical Outfit *91*
Theodore Ward Prize for African-American Playwrights *138*
This Month ON STAGE *158*
Threshold Theater Metaphysical Play Contest *138*
Thurber Writer-in-Residence, The James *230*
TIX Bay Area *268*
TIX By Mail *268*
Tomorrow Magazine *158*
Tomorrow's Playwrights *81*
Totem Pole Playhouse *91*

Touchstone Theatre 92
Towngate Theatre Playwriting Contest 138
Towson State University Prize for Literature 139
Translation Services Directory 241
Travel and Study Grant Program 211
Trinity Repertory Company 92
Trustus Theatre 135
Tuesday Group, The 184
Turnip Theatre Company 92
Tyrone Guthrie Centre, The 234

U

Ubu Repertory Theater 93, 270
Ucross Foundation Residency Program 234
Unicorn Theatre 93
Unicorn Theatre National Playwrights' Award 139
United Arts 159
United States/Japan Creative Artists' Fellowships 205
University of Alabama New Playwrights' Program 184
University of Louisville Grawemeyer Award for Music Composition 139
Urban Playwriting Retreat 272
Urban Stages Award 139
U.S. Copyright Office publications 280
U.S.-Mexico Fund for Culture 211
Utah Arts Council 221
Utah Shakespearean Festival 93

V

Van Lier Playwriting Fellowship 211
Vanguard Festival 36
Ventana Productions/Publications 159
Ventana Publications Play Award 159
Vermont Arts Council 221
Vermont Playwrights Award 140
Vermont Stage Company 93
Vermont Young Playwrights Project 93
Very Special Arts Playwright Discovery Program 140
Very Special Arts Young Playwrights Program 140
Victory Gardens Theater 94
Villa Montalvo Artist Residency Program 234
Vineyard Playhouse, The 94
Vineyard Theatre 94

Virgin Islands Council on the Arts 221
Virginia Center for the Creative Arts 235
Virginia Commission for the Arts 221
Virginia Stage Company 94
VLA Guide to Copyright for Visual Artists 270
Voice & Vision 95
Volunteer Lawyers for the Arts 270

W

Waldo M. and Grace C. Bonderman IUPUI Playwriting Competition for Young Audiences 140
Walnut Street Theatre Company, The 95
Walt Disney Studios Fellowship Program, The 212
Ward Prize for African-American Playwrights, Theodore 138
Washington State Arts Commission 222
Washington Theatre Festival 80, 134
Wasserman Drama Award, Dale 108
Watertower Theatre, Inc. 95
We Don't Need No Stinkin' Dramas 141
Weissberger Playwriting Competition, L. Arnold 120
Weissberger Theater Group 96
Welty New Play Series, Eudora 60
West Coast Ensemble 96
West Coast Ensemble Contests 141
West Coast Ensemble Full-Length Play Competition 141
West Coast Ensemble Musical Stairs 141
West Virginia Commission on the Arts 222
Westbeth Playwright Program 185
Westbeth Theatre Center 96
Western Stage, The 96
White Bird Annual Playwriting Contest 141
White Memorial National Children's Playwriting Contest Jackie 116
Whittlesey Agency, Peregrine 192
Wichita State University Playwriting Contest 142
Will Geer Theatricum Botanicum 97
William Flanagan Memorial Creative Persons Center 235
William Morris Agency 193
Williams/New Orleans Literary Festival One-Act Play Competition, Tennessee 137
Williamstown Theatre Festival 97, 185
Willows Theatre Company 97
Wilma Theater, The 98

Wilson Full-Length Play Award, James H. *109*
Windows on the Work *82*
Wisconsin Arts Board *222*
Women Playwrights Project *185*
Women's Project & Productions *98*
Women's Repertory Project *182*
Women's Theatre Alliance *271*
Women's Work *186*
Woolly Mammoth Theatre Company *98*
Wooster Group, The *98*
Worcester Foothills Theatre Company *99*
Worldsong Children's Theatre *87*
WOW Cafe, The *271*
Writer, The *280*
Writers & Artists Agency *193*
Writers Dialogue *48*
Writer's Digest *142*
Writer's Digest Books *279, 280*
Writer's Digest Writing Competition *142*
Writer's Guide to Copyright, A *280*
Writers Guild of America, East (WGAE) *271*
Writers Guild of America, West (WGAW) *272*
Writer's Market *142, 280*
Writers Room, The *235*
Writers' Studio, The *236*
Writing Awards for Prisoners *263*
WRITING ON YOUR FEET! *272*
Wurlitzer Foundation of New Mexico, Helene *229*
Wyoming Arts Council *222*

Y

Yaddo *236*
Yale Repertory Theatre *99*
Year-End-Series (Y.E.S.) New Play Festival *142*
York Theatre Company, The *99*
Young Playwrights Festival National Playwriting Contest *143*
Young Playwrights Inc. *129, 143, 272*
Young Playwrights School Tour *272*
Young Playwrights Spring Conference *272*
Young Playwrights Summer Conference *264*
Youth Theatre Journal *239*

Z

Zachary Scott Theatre Center (ZACH) *100*
Zornio Memorial Children's Theatre Playwriting Award, Anna *104*

About Theatre Communications Group

Theatre Communications Group is the national organization for the American theatre. Since its founding in 1961, TCG has provided a national forum and communications network for a field that is as aesthetically diverse as it is geographically widespread, developing a unique and comprehensive support system that addresses the concerns of the theatre companies and individual artists that collectively represent our "national theatre."

TCG's mission is to celebrate and inspire excellence in the artistry of theatre in America. To carry out this mission, TCG serves theatre artists and not-for-profit professional theatre organizations by: recognizing and encouraging artistic diversity; providing a forum for the open and critical examination of issues, standards and values; fostering interaction among theatre professionals; collecting, analyzing and disseminating information within the profession and to others interested in, and influential to, the health of the field; and serving as the principal advocate for America's not-for-profit professional theatre.

TCG's centralized services facilitate the work of thousands of actors, artistic and managing directors, playwrights, literary managers, directors, designers, trustees and administrative personnel, as well as a constituency of more than 300 theatre institutions across the country that present performances to a combined annual attendance of more than 17 million people.

THEATRE COMMUNICATIONS GROUP

John Sullivan, *Executive Director and Publisher*

1997–98 Board of Directors

Ricardo Khan, *President*
Ruth Mayleas, *Vice President*
Kent Thompson, *Vice President*
Victoria Nolan, *Treasurer*
Benny Sato Ambush, *Secretary*
Bill Rauch, *Member at Large*

Libby Appel	Zelda Fichandler	Michael Maso
Loy Arcenas	Marian Godfrey	Robert J. Orchard
Judson Bemis, Jr.	Linda Hartzell	José Rivera
Dudley Cocke	David Hawkanson	Judith O. Rubin
Gordon Davidson	David Henry Hwang	Roche Schulfer
Peter Donnelly	Kenny Leon	Jack Viertel
Clay S. Felker	Roberta Levitow	George C. Wolfe

Related TCG Publications
Catalogue available upon request

American Theatre
The national, 10-issue-per-year theatre magazine containing news, features and opinion; includes complete texts of 5 plays a year.

Theatre Profiles
The biennial illustrated reference guide to America's nonprofit professional theatres.

Theatre Directory
The annual pocket-sized contact resource of theatres and related organizations.

A Fair Country; The Substance of Fire and Other Plays; Three Hotels: Plays and Monologues *by Jon Robin Baitz*

The Essential Bogosian: Talk Radio, Drinking in America, FunHouse and Men Inside; Pounding Nails in the Floor with My Forehead; Sex, Drugs, Rock & Roll; subUrbia *by Eric Bogosian*

The Gospel at Colonus; Sister Suzie Cinema: Collected Poems and Performances 1976–1986 *by Lee Breuer*

The Open Door; The Shifting Point *by Peter Brook*

Stories I Ain't Told Nobody Yet *by Jo Carson*

Three Sisters *by Anton Chekhov, translated by Paul Schmidt*

Cloud Nine; Light Shining in Buckinghamshire; Mad Forest; The Skriker *by Caryl Churchill*

Tales of the Lost Formicans and Other Plays *by Constance Congdon*

The Illusion *by Pierre Corneille, freely adapted by Tony Kushner*

Drinks Before Dinner *by E. L. Doctorow*

Love & Science: Selected Music-Theatre Texts; Unbalancing Acts *by Richard Foreman*

A Lesson from Aloes; Blood Knot and Other Plays; Cousins; My Children! My Africa!; Playland and A Place with the Pigs; The Road to Mecca; Valley Song *by Athol Fugard*

Statements: Three Plays *by Athol Fugard with John Kani and Winston Ntshona*

Ballad of Yachiyo *by Philip Kan Gotanda*

Swimming to Cambodia *by Spalding Gray*

Approaching Zanzibar and Other Plays; Coastal Disturbances: Four Plays *by Tina Howe*

Peer Gynt *by Henrik Ibsen, translated by Gerry Bamman and Irene B. Berman*

People Who Led to My Plays; Sleep Deprivation Chamber *by Adrienne Kennedy*

Self Torture and Strenuous Exercise: Selected Plays *by Harry Kondoleon*

Through the Leaves and Other Plays *by Franz Xaver Kroetz, translated by Roger Downey*

Angels in America, Part One: Millenium Approaches; Angels in America, Part Two: Perestroika; A Bright Room Called Day; Thinking About the Longstanding Problems of Virtue and Happiness: Essays, a Play (Slavs!), Two Poems and a Prayer *by Tony Kushner*

The Illusion (by Pierre Corneille) *freely adapted by Tony Kushner*

Six Plays *by Romulus Linney*

Blood Wedding and Yerma *by Federico García Lorca, translations by Langston Hughes and W. S. Merwin*

Reckless and Blue Window: Two Plays *by Craig Lucas*

The Floating Island Plays *by Eduardo Machado*

Testimonies: Four Plays (Annulla, Still Life, Execution of Justice, Greensboro) *by Emily Mann*

Sight Unseen and Other Plays *by Donald Margulies*

Fantasio and Other Plays *by Alfred de Musset*
Translations by Michael Feingold, Richard Howard, Nagle Jackson and Paul Schmidt

Four Plays; The Secret Garden *by Marsha Norman*

Shimmer & Other Texts *by John O'Keefe*

The America Play and Other Works; Venus *by Suzan-Lori Parks*

Full Moon and Other Plays; New Music: A Trilogy *by Reynolds Price*

The Rug Merchants of Chaos and Other Plays *by Ronald Ribman*

Marisol and Other Plays (Each Day Dies with Sleep, Cloud Tectonics) *by José Rivera*

Etiquette and Vitriol (The Food Chain and Other Plays); Raised in Captivity *by Nicky Silver*

Stage Writers Handbook: A Complete Business Guide for Playwrights, Composers, Lyricists, and Librettists *by Dana Singer*

Company; Getting Away with Murder *by Stephen Sondheim and George Furth*

Gypsy *by Stephen Sondheim and Arthur Laurents*

Into the Woods; Passion *by Stephen Sondheim and James Lapine*

Pacific Overtures *by Stephen Sondheim and John Weidman*

Driving Miss Daisy *by Alfred Uhry*

The Baltimore Waltz and Other Plays *by Paula Vogel*

The Collected Short Plays of Thornton Wilder, Volume I *by Thornton Wilder*

Jelly's Last Jam, *book by George C. Wolfe, lyrics by Susan Birkenhead*

Spunk: Three Tales by Zora Neale Hurston *adapted by George C. Wolfe*

Between Worlds: Contemporary Asian-American Plays
Editor Misha Berson; includes works by Ping Chong, Philip Kan Gotanda, Jessica Hagedorn, David Henry Hwang, Wakako Yamauchi, Laurence Yep.

Coming to Terms: American Plays & the Vietnam War
Includes works by David Rabe, Terrence McNally, Amlin Gray, Tom Cole, Michael Weller, Emily Mann and Stephen Metcalfe. Introduction by James Reston, Jr.

In Their Own Words: Contemporary American Playwrights *interviews by David Savran*

Moon Marked and Touched by Sun: Plays by African-American Women
Editor Sydné Mahone; includes works by Laurie Carlos, Kia Corthron, Thulani Davis, Judith Alexa Jackson, Adrienne Kennedy, Robbie McCauley, Suzan-Lori Parks, Aishah Rahman, Ntozake Shange, Anna Deavere Smith, Danitra Vance.

On New Ground: Contemporary Hispanic-American Plays
Editor M. Elizabeth Osborn; includes works by Lynne Alvarez, Maria Irene Fornes, John Jesurun, Eduardo Machado, José Rivera, Milcha Sanchez-Scott.

Out from Under: Texts by Women Performance Artists
Editor Lenora Champagne; includes works by Laurie Anderson, Laurie Carlos, Lenora Champagne, Karen Finley, Jessica Hagedorn, Holly Hughes, Robbie McCauley, Rachel Rosenthal, Beatrice Roth, Leeny Sack, Fiona Templeton.

Plays of the Holocaust: An International Anthology
Editor Elinor Fuchs; includes works by Nelly Sachs, Peter Barnes, Liliane Atlan, Joshua Sobol, James Schevill, Józef Szajna.

The Production Notebooks: Theatre in Process, Volume One
Editor Mark Bly; dramaturgical casebooks of Shelby Jiggets (*The Love Space Demands* at Crossroads Theatre Company), Christopher Baker (*Danton's Death* at Alley Theatre), Jim Lewis ("The Clytemnestra Project" at the The Guthrie Theater), Paul Walsh (*Children of Paradise: Shooting a Dream* at Theatre de la Jeune Lune).

The Way We Live Now: American Plays and the AIDS Crisis
Editor M. Elizabeth Osborn; includes works by William M. Hoffman, Harry Kondoleon, Harvey Fierstein, Susan Sontag, Terrence McNally, Lanford Wilson, David Greenspan, Tony Kushner, Christopher Durang, Paula Vogel. Introduction by Michael Feingold.

TCG Individual Membership

As a *Sourcebook* user, you're invited to become an Individual Member of **Theatre Communications Group**—the national organization for the American theatre and the publisher of **American Theatre** magazine.

As an Individual Member of TCG, you'll get inside information about theatre performances around the country, as well as substantial discounts on tickets to performances and publications about the theatre. Plus, as the primary advocate for not-for-profit professional theatre in America, TCG will ensure that your voice is heard in Washington. We invite you to join us today and receive all of TCG's benefits!

Members Receive These Special Benefits

- A FREE subscription to *American Theatre* magazine—10 issues...5 complete playscripts... artist profiles...in-depth coverage of contemporary, classical and avant-garde performances...3 special issues—including *Season Preview* (October), *Theatre Training* (January) and *Summer Festival Preview* (May).
- Discounts on tickets to performances at more than 230 participating theatres nationwide.
- 15% discount on resource materials including *Theatre Profiles, Theatre Directory, ArtSEARCH* and *Dramatists Sourcebook*—all musts for the theatre professional or the serious theatregoer.
- A FREE catalogue of publications.
- 10% discount on all books from TCG and other select theatre publishers.
- Your personalized Individual Membership card.
- Opportunity to apply for a customized TCG Credit Card.
- Special discount for Budget Rent-A-Car and Airborne Express.
- Up to 60% off regular hotel rates from Hotel Reservations Network.

TCG Individual Membership

As a Member, You Get a FREE Subscription to *American Theatre* ...

... That's a $49.50 Savings on What You Would Pay at the Newsstand ...

American Theatre magazine, available 10 times per year, provides up-to-the-minute coverage of the trends, artists and topics shaping American theatre today. In addition to all the articles, you'll also receive five full-length plays—the newest works by prominent playwrights like Tony Kushner, Wendy Wasserstein, Suzan-Lori Parks, David Rabe and Sam Shepard. Plus three special issues including "Season Preview" in October, listing the complete performance schedules for more than 200 theatres across the U.S.; "Summer Festival Preview" in May, listing theatre festivals worldwide; and "Theatre Training" in January, reporting on the opinions, evolution and theory of theatre education in America.

Join Now and Save

Receive 15% Savings Off TCG Resources ...

- *Theatre Profiles* provides a historical record of the national theatre movement. Contains comprehensive information on more than 200 theatres nationwide, including production histories.
- *ArtSEARCH,* TCG's twice-monthly national employment bulletin, with more than 6,000 listings of available jobs for the entire spectrum of the arts each year.
- *Dramatists Sourcebook*, the essential annual guide for playwrights, translators, composers, lyricists and librettists, listing hundreds of fellowships, grants and awards, and submission requirements for more than 350 theatres.
- *Theatre Directory*, a handy pocket-sized annual directory providing contact information for more than 300 not-for-profit professional theatres and dozens of related organizations.

... and 10% Off Other Publications

- Save 10% on all TCG publications as well as theatre books published by Nick Hern, Absolute Classics, Playwrights Canada Press and Ubu Repertory Theater.

Take Advantage Now and Save!
Become a TCG Individual Member and Receive Extraordinary Benefits!

☐ **YES**, I would like a one-year Individual Membership to TCG, which includes a subscription to *American Theatre,* among other extraordinary benefits.

☐ Individual Membership $35.00 $30.00.

☐ Student Membership (enclose copy of ID) $20.

☐ I prefer a two-year membership.

☐ Individual Membership $70.00 $55.00.

Not only would I like to become a member, but I would like to take advantage of my discounts right now!
(Discount prices are only good if you are a member. If you are not a member, please use the full price for your order.)

☐ Please begin my one-year subscription to *ArtSEARCH.*

<u>Individual</u>   ☐ with E-mail $64.00 $54.40   ☐ without E-mail $54.00 $45.90

<u>Institutional</u>   ☐ with E-mail $90.00 $76.50   ☐ without E-mail $75.00 $63.75

I would like the following resource materials:

☐ *Theatre Profiles 12* $22.95 $19.50

☐ *Theatre Directory* $5.95 $5.00
(For the first book purchase, add $3.00 for postage and handling. For every book thereafter, add $1.00.)

☐ **TOTAL ORDER** _____

To order, you may: Send this form to TCG Order Dept., 355 Lexington Ave, NY, NY 10017-0217; or Call (212) 697-5230, ext. 260; or Fax (212) 983-4847; or send E-mail to: orders@tcg.org.

☐ Check is enclosed. ☐ Please charge my credit card. ☐ VISA ☐ MC ☐ AMEX

NAME		
ADDRESS		
CITY	STATE	ZIP
*PHONE/FAX/E-MAIL		
CARD #		EXP. DATE:
SIGNATURE		
OCCUPATION/TITLE		

* **all orders must have telephone number**

For Individual Memberships outside the U.S., please add $12 per year (U.S. currency only, drawn from U.S. Bank). Allow 6-8 weeks from receipt of order.

[Mkt. code: DDSB98]